A foggy night in Lon(

Mick stood back and admir swirling fog parted just a bit, and he caught a glimpse of the full moon, barely poking its head over the roofs of the nearby deserted warehouses. It was a beautiful night for a mugging.

"What in Christ?!" Pete blurted.

And suddenly, he was flying through the air, as if he'd been hit by a bus. He slammed into a warehouse wall and slumped to the ground.

"Jeezus!" Alex gasped, backing away from the man they'd been kicking.

Amazingly, despite the savage beating he'd endured, their victim was rising to his feet.

"Stay down, you blighter!" Georgie commanded. He rammed his fist into the bloke's gut—but the guy kept getting up!

Georgie screamed. Not the loud, angry scream he gave when his blood was running hot, but a high, girlish scream. He backed away the same way Alex had. And then Mick saw why...

Blood was pouring out of Georgie's belly, like he was a split-open pig. And now his guts were spilling out, too, and splattering onto the wooden planking of the wharf. Steam rose from the entrails, and the air smelled of raw meat and loosed bowels.

Georgie's scream gasped to a sudden stop as he collapsed to his knees, his eyes wide, his mouth gaping. Then he fell onto his flabby face, dead.

The man in the coat turned, but he wasn't a *man* anymore. He was some kind of beast with a hairy face and hands, and fangs in his mouth, and claws dripping with blood. He was a *wolf!*

The wolf-man growled and leapt.

...Especially if you pick the wrong mark!

ALSO BY STEPHEN D. SULLIVAN

From Walkabout Publishing
*Manos: The Hands of Fate**
Frost Harrow 1-6 (2020-21)
Canoe Cops vs. the Mummy
Tournament of Death 1-4 (fantasy action)
Tales of the Blue Kingdoms 1 & 2 (2020)
Daikaiju Attack (giant monsters)
White Zombie (film novelization)
Manos: Talons of Fate (horror film adaptation)
The Crimson Collection
Martian Knights & Other Tales
Luck o' the Irish
Zombies, Werewolves, & Unicorns
*Winner 2016 *Scribe Award*: Best Novel Adaptation

Dragonlance
The Dragon Isles & The Dying Kingdom
Warrior's Heart – Warrior's Blood – Warrior's Bones

Legend of the Five Rings
The Scorpion – The Phoenix – The Lion

Blockbuster Movie Novelizations
Iron Man – Thunderbirds – Racing Stripes

Plus dozens more!
www.StephenDSullivan.com

DR. CUSHING'S CHAMBER OF HORRORS

STEPHEN D. SULLIVAN

WALKABOUT PUBLISHING • 2020

Synopsis: A vampire and a mummy battle to the death over an unusual family business that just happens to employ a werewolf in… *Dr. Cushing's Chamber of Horrors*!

Walkabout Publishing
S.D.Studios
P.O.Box 151
Kansasville, WI 53139
www.walkaboutpublishing.com

™ & © 2020 Stephen D. Sullivan.

ISBN: 979-8-6688-9654-7

Library of Congress Control Number: 2020914395

All rights reserved, including the right of reproduction in whole or in part in any form. No part of this publication may be reproduced or transmitted in any form or by any means, electronic or mechanical, including photocopy, recording, scanning, or any information storage and retrieval system, without written permission of the author.

Cover art by Mark Maddox © 2020

Cover design & logo © 2020 Stephen D. Sullivan.

Acknowledgements

Thanks as always to Kifflie H. Scott, and also to Steve, Vicki, Doris, Christine, and the rest of the Kenosha Writers, and to my Patreon patrons. Special thanks to Steve Rouse for extra proofing and to Christine, Derek, and Rod for the blurbs. And super-special thanks to my buddy Mark Maddox for doing the cover. It looks amazing!

Extra-special thanks to these wonderful patrons at Credit Creature level and above:
Shawn P. Conlin
David Lars Chamberlain
Kris Herzog
Rich Chamberlain
Amy Frushour Kelly
Steve Rouse
Tim Cahoon
Heath Farnden
John Appel
Adam Thornton
John Kilgallon
Patrick Clark
Jeremy L.
Sam Hawken

…And all the rest of you, too! Keep sharing the sdsullivan.com story links!

*For Mary, the Queen of the B-Movie Cast,
and to the memory of her loving husband,
podcasting legend and the King of the Monster Kids,
Vince Rotolo.*

CONTENTS

Prologue	1
1. Dr. Cushing's Chamber of Horrors	11
2. Victoria Duprix	21
3. Paul S. Longmire	30
4. The Mummies Arrive	40
5. The Ice Man	50
6. Vincent's Secret	57
7. Werewolf in London	63
8. The Mummies' Debut	74
9. Police on the Scene	86
10. Paul Visits the Chamber of Horrors	91
11. New Arrivals	103
12. Victoria's Suspicions	112
13. Monsters, Real & Imagined	122
14. Cold Relationships	133
15. Artists & Models	143
16. Changes & Portents	153
17. Erzsebet's Apprentice	163
18. Paul's Chance	175
19. Caught!	184
20. Changes in the Chamber	196
21. The Hunters & the Huntress	213
22. Dr. Jekyll in Hyde Park	222
23. Vincent's Grand Schemes	233
24. The Mummy Walks	241
25. Separated by Circumstance	253
26. Lifeblood	267
27. Paul's Dilemma	276
28. Dalliances & Deadly Decisions	289
29. Waiting for the Moon	296
30. Driving, Dreams, & Dreads	304
31. The Breaks	320

32. Victoria's Fury	331
33. Prepared for Sacrifice	338
34. Alone in the Darkness	341
35. Ritual of Blood	347
36. Wolf Trap	352
37. The Vampire	358
38. All Monsters Attack!	367
39. In the Mummy's Hands	374
40. A Blaze of Glory	380
41. Fiery Choices	389
42. Doomed	395
43. Final Horrors	399
44. Morning	405
45. Aftermath	410
Epilogue	415
About The Story	421
About the Author	427
Walkabout Publishing	429

PROLOGUE

IN THE TIME BETWEEN THE TWO GREAT WARS

Nina Ashton – Lancashire, England
The Night of the Full Moon

Nina Ashton ran for her life.

She ran as if all the hounds of hell were baying at her heels because, for all she knew, that was *literally* true.

The familiar forest around her became a blur—no longer the sheltering woodland of childhood walks with her family, but a fear-filled nightmare of tripping roots and scraping branches.

Claws!

She tried not to think of the thing's claws—gleaming in the light of the full moon—or its pointed teeth, bared and dripping with hot saliva, or its eyes... like twin torches, blazing in the darkness. Those feral eyes *wanted* Nina...

They wanted her *dead*.

The creature chasing her was no ordinary animal. It leered at her like a *man*—and it ran *upright*, too. Yet, it was covered with shaggy dark fur. How was that *possible*?

Nina's family hunted. She'd known how to work a gun since

the time she was seven, but she had never seen—or even heard of—any type of beast that ran upright.

Oh, yes, a bear might blunder around on its hind legs for a time, as might a chimp or a gorilla. But bears had long ago been vanquished from the wilds of England, even here in the outer reaches of Lancashire. The only places that you found bears nowadays were in zoos or traveling shows. The same went for the great apes.

Could one of those creatures have escaped from a local circus?

No!

The fear twisting in her gut told Nina that this brute was something worse than any natural beast—something far more *terrible*, some abomination, part animal, part man.

Owooooooooooo!

The thing's piercing howl filled the chilly spring air.

The cry echoed through the forest, assaulting Nina from all sides at once.

She was weaponless; she hadn't even thought to bring a pocket knife. Why would she, taking a midnight walk in the family woods she knew so well?

Without any defense, all she could do was *run*, run from the beast that was *not* a beast—run to preserve both her life and her sanity.

Never in all her nineteen years had Nina felt so terrified. Her heart pounded in her chest; her skin tingled as if on fire. The odor of her own fear assaulted her, as rivers of sweat ran down her smooth, pale face and drenched her supple body.

Please, God... Please! she pleaded silently, though it had been ages since she'd set foot in church.

If she died un-confessed, would she go to heaven, or...?

She didn't *want* to die. Not here. Not *now*.

All the sins of her short life rushed back to Nina in an instant.

She regretted every one.

Bless me, Father, for I have sinned…

Why had she chosen to sneak out *tonight*? Why hadn't she at least told *someone* where she was going?

In her mind, Nina imagined her family and their servants, all snug in their beds, dreaming pleasant dreams, while she was being pursued by this living nightmare.

How long would it take them to find her—to find her *body*—if…?

No! She wouldn't think about that.

Nina crushed her fears into the darkest recesses of her mind and concentrated on running.

Her limbs ached, and her head throbbed. Her skin dripped with sweat.

The smell of dry leaves and soft earth wafted up around her. But beneath that wholesome redolence lay something else… something *bestial*.

How long had she been running? It seemed like hours, though it couldn't have been more than a few minutes.

The gatehouse *must* be nearby now.

You can make it.

The howl again. That unearthly baying/

Owoooooooooo!

Terror shot down Nina's spine like ice water.

Just keep running.

Despite herself, she glanced back.

As she did, she tripped over the hem of her fur-lined cloak and pitched face-first toward the forest floor.

She stuck out her hands, trying to stop the fall.

It didn't work. The rocks and grit of the game trail scraped the pale skin off of her palms.

Nina gasped, "Jesus…" and gazed at her ruined hands, covered in blood. "Sweet Jesus, *help* me!"

Pain shot through her as she pushed herself to her knees.

She looked up.

The beast loomed over her.

It grinned down at Nina, fangs dripping, clouds of hot breath billowing white in the moonlight. Its eyes blazed bright red.

Nina felt the heat of the thing's body burning into her; its reek—like decaying meat—made her retch.

She wanted to get to her feet, wanted to run, but fear held her tight in its grip. She gazed up at the monster, paralyzed.

A low growl—like the purr of a hungry cat—emanated from the creature's massive throat.

To Nina, the werewolf almost seemed to be smiling.

She screamed.

Opal Cushing – London, England
That Same Night

Opal Selene Cushing sat bolt upright in bed, screaming.

Her eyes shot wide; her heart pounded in terror; sweat poured down her eighteen-year-old body. She looked around, frantic.

Her sister, who shared the same bed, appeared beside her in an instant. "What is it?" Topaz asked. "Opal, what's wrong?"

"He killed me!" Opal wailed. "He *killed* me! I'm *dead*!"

"No, darling, no," Topaz said softly, putting her arms around her twin. "Everything's all right."

"I was walking through the forest," Opal blubbered, "and he chased me down. I tried to escape but…"

"It was just a *dream*," Topaz assured her. "You're safe at home, in our own bed. And I'm here. There's nothing to be afraid of when we're together. I promise."

Her sister's calm voice pierced the veil of panic that had descended over Opal. The forest surrounding her melted away, and she saw the papered walls of their third-story bedroom.

The soothing odor of worn sheets and down pillows filled her nostrils, along with the familiar aroma of her sister. The pale light of the full moon filtered in through the open window next to their rickety four-poster bed. A cool breeze tugged at the window's flimsy curtains.

Everything seemed so… normal.

"Oh, thank God," Opal muttered, crumpling into her twin's arms. "Thank God…!"

"It's all right now," Topaz said, running her fingers over her sister's dark hair. "Everything's all right."

The pair hugged each other tight.

Suddenly, the door to the bedroom burst inward, and a slender, middle-aged man barged inside.

"What's going on? I heard a scream. Is everything all right?"

Both girls jumped slightly, but it was only their father, Leigh Cushing—*Doctor* Cushing, as he often styled himself.

Father looked almost comical in his paisley nightgown, bare feet padding across the worn wooden floor, skinny arms and legs flailing, his glasses perched crookedly on his hawkish nose, and his nightcap half falling off his greying head. He brandished an umbrella as though it were a sword.

Topaz actually giggled, and Opal couldn't help but smile.

Our knight in satin armor.

Such a dashing figure he tried to be. But even in his nightclothes, their father smelled of fine tobacco and well-worn tweed. Opal found the scent comforting.

"It's all right, Father," Topaz assured him.

"I just had a nightmare," Opal added. "That's all."

"Oh," said their father, letting the umbrella droop in his hand. "I was afraid it might be a tad more serious—a prowler, or something of that nature." He patted his chest and then mopped his forehead with his nightcap. "Well, thank heaven it wasn't!"

"What is all the commotion up here?" demanded a deep, feminine voice.

"Is everyone all right?" asked a similar, but more nasal, masculine voice.

It was their landlords—Victoria and Vincent Duprix—who lived on the floor below. The couple stood framed in the doorway, adorned in matching dressing gowns: burgundy with white trim and collars. Improbably, Vincent was carrying a lit candelabra.

Opal suppressed a giggle. The Duprixes always looked so dapper. Even in the middle of the night, it appeared as though they'd just left some posh dinner party—or maybe a romantic rendezvous. Perhaps that was why Vincent had brought the candles, when switching on the electric lights would have worked much better.

"The girls just had a bad dream," Dr. Cushing explained.

Opal's temper spiked a tiny bit. She didn't like it when people—even their father—lumped her and her twin together.

"*Both* of them?" Vincent asked wryly, studying the sisters carefully with his bright blue eyes.

If he hadn't been an artist, Opal might have found his scrutiny unsettling. But since he was—in fact—a very fine sculptor and owner of the Duprix Waxworks, Opal found his gaze... *flattering*.

Her sister blushed and adjusted her nightgown where it had slipped a bit low on her bosom. Topaz was definitely the more modest twin.

"It was Opal who had the nightmare," Topaz informed their landlord. "Not me."

"Young girls often have trouble sleeping—or so I'm told," their father added.

"Especially when around young *men*," suggested Victoria Duprix, her hazel eyes betraying just a glimmer of a smile.

Opal tried not to frown. There was something about Victoria that she found creepy. Mrs. Duprix was still good looking for her age, with very little grey showing in her deep brown hair, and she behaved like a Grande Damme. But every time the two met, Opal sensed a feeling of *envy* radiating from the older woman.

"Young men?" Dr. Cushing asked. "Have there been young men in the exhibit lately? I hadn't noticed."

Vincent's handsome face broke into a sly smile. "I have remarked one or two fetching young fellows lurking around your Chamber of Horrors, Dr. Cushing—when your daughters are working, of course."

Opal's father looked slightly surprised.

Again, Topaz blushed. "I'm sure Mr. Duprix just means Barry and Francis. We met them sledding in the park over Winter Holiday. We told you all about them, Father. Remember?"

"And we *are* eighteen now," Opal added. Though they'd celebrated their birthdays just last month, boys had been hanging around the twins for *at least* the past three years. How like their father not to have noticed.

Now it was Dr. Cushing's turn to blush. "Well, yes… Of course," he said. "I suppose we must have a talk about that sometime soon."

Victoria mimicked her husband's sly grin. "Perhaps we had better retire," she said to him.

"Yes. Perhaps we'd better. Glad it turned out only to be bad dreams. Goodnight, all." He and his wife turned and swept down the hall leading to the second-floor stairway.

Dr. Cushing closed the door behind them.

"Now, about those boys…" he began.

"Oh, Father, it's nothing to worry about," Opal said, slipping off the bed and putting an arm around his shoulder. "Topaz and I know all about the birds and bees."

"Well, yes, my dear," he replied, "but *knowing* is one thing… Putting it into practice, though, can be entirely…"

"Father, it's nothing *serious*, I swear—*we* swear," Topaz said.

She slipped off the bed as well, and flanked their father on the other side.

The girls called this ganging up against a common opponent "twinning"—and it was a tactic they'd frequently used over the years on their beleaguered remaining parent.

"If it *becomes* serious, you'll be the first to know." Opal assured him.

"Well," he said, looking from one girl to the other, "I certainly hope so. I mean, this may be the 'Jazz Era' and all, but we Cushings still have standards to uphold, you know."

"We know, Father," both girls chimed.

"Good," he said. "Because I still have a lot to do to get ready for my trip tomorrow."

"Must you go, Father?" Topaz asked.

Opal couldn't be sure if her sister was kidding or not. (Topaz had always been the more clingy of the two.)

"Of course, I must," Dr. Cushing replied. "I don't want this lead on the fabled Arctic Ice Man to grow cold. Er… You know what I mean."

Both twins laughed. "Yes, Father."

"In any case, you have nothing to worry about while I'm gone," their father continued. "Everything in the Chamber of Horrors is well in order… Though you *do* remember that I'm expecting that shipment of mummies from my Egyptian expedition while I'm gone, don't you?"

Opal rolled her eyes. "Yes, Father."

"How could we forget," Topaz added—though Opal sensed that her sister *had* forgotten. And, truth to tell, so had Opal.

If the twins shared an uncanny ability to read each other's thoughts at times—and they did—they also seemed to share an ability to have things completely drift out of their minds.

Must be the boys, Opal thought. Though she'd be damned if she'd give up spending time with young men just to improve her memory.

Dr. Cushing looked from one to the other, from blonde Topaz to brunette Opal, seeming to sense the truth, as he often did.

"I'm sure you'll be able to handle it," he said.

"I'm sure we will," Opal replied.

"*If* we get some rest," Topaz added, guiding their father toward the door.

"Yes," he said. "You two get back to sleep. Let's have no more nightmares tonight, shall we?"

"No, Father," both replied.

Though Opal couldn't help but worry. Sometimes the dreams the twins had *weren't* exactly *dreams*. Sometimes they seemed more like portents of things to come—premonitions.

But, if that were true, had Opal just experienced something that *had* happened, or something that was *about* to happen?

Somewhere in England, was a girl really lying in the forest, horribly wounded, her lifeblood bleeding away?

Gazing out the bedroom window at the full moon, Opal couldn't be sure. The nightmare had certainly *felt* real. She hugged herself to ward off a shiver.

She and Topaz could talk about it once their father had gone. The twins had grown apart—each asserting her independence—in the past few years, but only slightly. Aside from a few physical differences—like hair color—and subtle choices of temperament, they remained as alike as any two people could be.

Fraternal twins were still *twins*, after all.

Opal watched the back of her sister's blond head as Topaz escorted their father to the door.

He paused at the threshold.

"Don't worry, my dears," he said. "Mr. and Mrs. Duprix will help you look after the business while I'm gone. But don't forget to unpack those mummies and get them properly displayed, when they arrive."

"Yes, Father."

"And please look after each other."

"We will, Father."

Dr. Cushing straightened his nightgown. "Very good," he said. "Thank you, my dears. I hope you have a jolly good time while I'm tramping around the frozen tundra. Don't you worry about me. I'll be back in a week or two. A month at most."

1

DR. CUSHING'S CHAMBER OF HORRORS

Topaz Cushing – 1951 Fisher St., London
The Day of the New Moon

Six weeks had passed since Dr. Leigh Cushing went on his Arctic expedition, leaving his teenage daughters in charge of his Chamber of Horrors.

Topaz Artemis Cushing and her twin weren't worried about his tardiness; their father wasn't known for his punctuality. Often, he would lose all track of time when engaged in a project, whether setting up a fresh exhibit or searching the world for a new attraction.

And they'd had a letter from him, from Norway, two weeks back—or was it three now?—hot on the trail of his so-called "Ice Man." He'd been filling the girls' heads with tales of this mythical creature for years: It had been seen frozen in the ice by a lone half-starved hiker, who could *not* lead his rescuers back to it. Then it was spotted at the edge of a glacier in Finland, and later drifting on an iceberg in the Arctic Sea... For someone who was supposedly frozen in a block of ice, the Ice Man sure did seem to get around!

So there were a lot of places left for Dr. Cushing to explore and many leads to follow up, which was why the sisters weren't concerned about their father—or at least *Topaz* wasn't.

She had a feeling that Father was all right. Not the kind of feeling that most people get, but a deep-down assuredness that had never failed her in the past.

The twins didn't like to use the word "psychic," but there was no denying that each of them seemed connected to the world in a way that eluded most people. Not only were they bonded to each other—frequently feeling one another's emotions, and even sharing dreams—but they often received other insights as well.

Sometimes, their dreams came true. Usually in small ways—a messenger arriving at the door, a friend falling ill, or a portent of a sudden turn of luck—but the confirmation of what they dreamt happened frequently enough that the girls had learned *not* to ignore such premonitions.

In fact, the twins had spent a great deal of time honing this eerie sixth sense.

The result was that Topaz proved particularly keen at intuiting the feelings of people and animals—almost to the level of reading their minds—and her sister had an uncanny ability to tell the future with cards.

Which was exactly what Opal was doing now: sitting on the hardwood floor of their chambers on the top story of the Duprix manse and turning the tarot.

With her left hand, Opal deftly laid down one card… two… three… four… and five.

Topaz frowned. "You know, five-card readings aren't very accurate."

Opal pursed her lips, her blue-green eyes flashing up at her sister. "I don't have time for a longer reading."

Eye color was one of the things the twins shared. They were fraternal, and—to Topaz's mind—as un-like each other in as many ways as they were similar: she blonde, Opal brunette, she thoughtful and shy, Opal impulsive and forthright. Both had attractive figures, but Topaz's form was more sleek and slender, Opal's more muscular and busty. Their body types seemed to reflect their personalities. Topaz liked to think and plan; her sister was always ready for action.

Which was probably why Opal had jumped right into a short, less-reliable card reading rather than opting for a longer and more detailed one.

"What question are you asking the cards?" Topaz inquired, though she had a feeling she already knew the answer. That was part of the trouble with being a twin: you knew, but you had to ask anyway.

"I'm not casting for myself. I'm doing it for Father."

Ah. As expected.

"You *know* you're only supposed to cast tarot for yourself or a legitimate querent," Topaz reminded her sister, "not for other people—not even Father."

"Just because *you're* no good at casting for other people…" Opal replied. "Besides, who made you arbiter of the rules? *I'm* the older sister."

Topaz sighed. "By thirteen minutes."

Opal shrugged. "Still older. And that means I'm in charge, unless Father says otherwise—which he didn't."

Topaz sat down beside her twin. She knew it was pointless to argue. Both girls had spent so much time fending for themselves that self-reliance seemed almost like an inherited trait, rather than a learned behavior.

The sign in front of the building read "Dr. Cushing's Chamber of Horrors," but it more accurately could have read "*Daughters* Cushing & *Father's* Chamber of Horrors" since the twins ran the exhibition most of the time, while their sole parent was traveling, seeking the latest attractions for his macabre museum.

The chamber was a walk-down storefront in the basement of an aging Victorian manse on the outskirts of London, at 1951 Fisher St., next to the wooded end of Olde Kennington Park. It shared the building with the *Duprix Waxworks*, run by Vincent and Victoria Duprix, the landlords who lived in the grand quarters on the second floor. The Cushings rented the basement for their attraction, and the third floor—with its eccentric nooks and crannies and gabled ceilings—for their residence.

The waxworks occupied most of the mansion's first floor, though the building was strangely shaped, so that the waxworks and the Chamber of Horrors abutted each other in the middle, with only a short flight of stairs, a pair of frosted glass doors, and, (when those doors were open for ventilation), a red velvet rope separating the two attractions. Most of the time, customers did *not* pass from one exhibit to the other, though, with a little work on the part of the Cushings and Duprixes, that *would* have been possible.

But, Victoria—Madame Duprix—spent most of her time running the waxworks or taking tea with her friends, while Vincent labored endlessly in his second-floor studio loft, which vaulted up into the space that otherwise would have been occupied by the third story. (He was a sculptor—and quite a good one.) The house also contained servant's quarters with a separate entrance in the back of the building, near the seldom-used kitchens.

Perhaps the Duprixes had once employed domestics, but Topaz and Opal had never seen any staff since they and their father had moved in. And if there had been any servants there recently, the twins would have noticed some indication. The girls—often alone for the last ten years—had plenty of time to look around and discover all of the old house's secrets.

But the secrets of other human beings and the world outside…! Those remained largely a mystery to both girls. Though lately, there *had* been a boy or two…

"All right," Topaz said to her sister, "if you're so good at absent readings... What do the cards say?"

Opal flipped up the first card on the right. "The distant past... I'd rather skip this and just look for the future..." she said.

"But that's *not* the way it works," Topaz agreed. "Assuming you can get it to work at all."

Opal stuck out her tongue at her twin.

The picture on the pasteboard showed a woman in an elaborate robe wearing a crown topped by an orb.

"*The High Priestess*," Topaz noted.

"Our father's past, surrounded by mysteries and hidden influences," Opal read.

"Which only makes sense, since he's been collecting occult artifacts all of our lives."

"And *before* we were born as well," Opal noted. She flipped the second card; it showed a trio of swords piercing a stylized heart. "*Three of Swords*, inverted."

"Father's more recent past," Topaz said. "The loss of something dear to you—I mean, to Father. I'm guessing that would be Mother."

Opal grinned at her sister. "Who *said* you weren't any good at this?"

Topaz tried, unsuccessfully, to fight down a blush. Her sister was *so* good at nettling her! But then, Opal undoubtedly felt the same way about Topaz.

Opal turned the next card—the one in the center of the reading. "The present..."

Topaz nodded. "The *key* card."

The illustration showed the face of a bright moon beaming down upon two animals, a dog on the left and a wolf upon the right. The beasts were flanked by two solid-looking watch towers.

"*The Moon*," Opal intoned, "a time of loved ones in peril and tricky choices. Choose your companions well, or they may betray you."

"*Father*, you mean," Topaz said, fighting down a nervous flutter. She felt certain that Father was all right, that nothing bad had happened—or was *about to* happen to him—and yet… "Do you think that he chose the right people to go on the expedition with him?"

"Father is always careful about such things," Opal replied, but Topaz sensed the worry in her. "Let's see about the future…" She flipped the next card.

It showed eight wooden staffs laid diagonally across a rural landscape.

Opal smiled. "Soon: The *Eight of Wands*. A journey leads to your—I mean *Father's*—desired goal."

Topaz couldn't help but grin as well. "He'll find the Ice Man, then? Oh, good. He's wanted to for so long." She felt better now. Whatever present troubles Opal had foreseen, clearly, they would soon pass.

"And one thing more…" Opal said, obviously feeling better now, too. "What comes after that…"

She turned the final card, the one all the way on the left.

Topaz gasped. "*The Tower*! Disaster!"

Opal put her hand on her sister's arm and gave it a reassuring squeeze. "But it's inverted, a warning that we need—I mean *Father* needs—courage and to be watchful for danger."

Opal was right; the card did *not* mean the querent's fate was hopeless, just that she—or *he*—needed to be on guard against dire circumstances. They would have to be wary, for both their father and themselves.

"But what danger could there be?" Topaz asked. "We haven't had so much as a bad dream since that night six weeks ago. And I'm sure that I would *feel* it if Father were in trouble."

"It's the *future*, remember?" Opal said. "And probably a long way off. Whatever's coming, we still have plenty of time to avoid it."

Topaz took a deep breath. "I hope so."

"It *must* be a long way off," Opal said. "If *you* don't feel it, and *I* don't feel it…"

Just then, a bell rang—long and hard—throughout their chambers.

"Someone at the front door," Opal announced, quickly rising and straightening her skirt.

"It could be Father," Topaz said, rising as well. "Or something *from* Father."

Quick as a flash, the twins bolted out of their bedroom and down the two flights of stairs leading to the house's main door.

They pulled both sides of the huge portal open.

On the top step of the front stairs stood a gruff-looking, burly man wearing a poor-boy cap and chewing on the stub of a cigar. In one thick hand, he clutched a well-worn clipboard, and a pencil was tucked behind his right ear. Behind him, several other burly men were unloading some large crates from a lorry and setting them onto the curb.

"This the Cushing residence?" the burly man asked.

Both girls nodded.

"I got some boxes for Mr. Cushing," he said.

"*Doctor* Cushing," Topaz corrected.

The man looked at a sheet of paper on his clipboard.

"Yeah… Doctor," he said. "I got that. Anyway, I need him to sign for these. Come all the way from Egypt, it looks like."

"He's away right now—" Topaz began.

"—But we're his daughters," Opal finished. "We can sign for them."

The man looked from one girl to the other. By silent agreement, both twins flashed their winningest smiles.

The burly man rubbed his head. "Yeah, I guess," he said. "Address is right, anyway: 1951-B Fisher St."

"That's here," Opal said enthusiastically.

"The 'B' is for the basement—where our business is," Topaz added. Her heart was pounding with excitement, now, and she could tell Opal's was, too. The *mummies* were finally here!

The man looked up, seeming to notice the business sign for the first time.

"Chamber of Horrors…" he said, and then frowned. "Doesn't seem right for a couple of pretty girls like you." He grinned, showing several missing teeth.

"It's our father's business," Opal replied, returning his smile with a far better one.

"And he'll be back very soon," Topaz put in.

Opal batted her eyes at the man. "Won't you please help us get the boxes inside, before he returns."

"Yeah. Alright," the burly man replied. He summoned his companions, and the three of them began moving the crates inside and down the stairs, into the lobby of Dr. Cushing's Chamber of Horrors.

It took the men the better part of an hour to wrestle the five large crates inside, and when they were done, Opal tipped them each a shilling and sent them on their way.

"Three shillings?" Topaz moaned after the delivery men had left.

"Stop worrying," her sister told her, shutting the door to the Chamber of Horrors behind them. "Six admissions, and we'll have made it up."

"But we won't be able to open *at all* today, with these huge boxes sitting here—and maybe not for a couple of days after that!"

"Unpacking won't take that long. I'm sure we'll be able to find some young, strong bodies to help out, like those two that seem to be chasing after you… What are their names? Francis and… Bernie? What those two young swells see in a shy girl like you, I'll never know."

"It's *Barry*," Topaz replied, a bit miffed. Her sister was teasing her now. She knew the boys' names just as well as Topaz did—even if they hadn't seen the pair in a while. "And you *know* that Frank is more interested in *you* than in me, anyway."

Opal grinned. "That'd be nice… if it were true."

"It *is* true, and you know it," Topaz said. "Frank hasn't paid me any attention for nearly a month now." She took a deep breath. "But you *still* shouldn't have tipped so much. A sixpence each would have been more than enough."

Opal shrugged. "It's only money. And besides we don't want to appear stingy like old lady Duprix, do we?"

Topaz laughed. "I guess not. Sometimes I think she was *born* middle-aged. How old do you think she *is*, anyway?"

"Ancient," Opal replied. "At *least* thirty-five. Older than her husband, at any rate—judging by the way he looks at *you*."

"Looks at *us* you mean. And what about it? He *is* a sculptor, after all—as you've reminded me every time he gawks at *you*," Topaz said. She primped her blond hair. "As you've said, it's his *job* to look at beautiful young ladies." She giggled, despite herself.

"I'm not sure his wife feels the same way about his wandering eye," Opal replied.

"Then maybe *she* should spend more time in the studio with him, rather than frumping around their waxworks," Topaz said. "You know, I think they could make twice as much money if they'd just hire someone more… *engaging* to tend the admissions."

"Someone more *attractive, you mean*," Opal said thoughtfully. "Though I'm sure she was quite the dish in her day."

"Oh!" Topaz gasped, anticipating the knock on the business' door a moment before it happened.

Knock! Knock!

Opal shook her head and chuckled. "I may be better with

cards," she said, "but you always know when something's coming."

"Not *always*," Topaz replied. "I don't know who's on the other side of the door, for instance."

"Well, open it and find out!"

Topaz did.

On the other side of the threshold stood a middle-aged woman in a posh burgundy dress. Her stern hazel eyes looked from one twin to the other.

"Madame Duprix," Topaz blurted. She almost added *"We were just talking about you,"* but then thought better of it. So, instead, she said, "How nice to see you," and gave a slight curtsy.

Victoria Duprix swept into the room with the authority of someone who owned it, which, in point of fact, she did.

"My dear young ladies," she said in her proper English tones, "I have something vitally important to say to you…

"The time has come… to pay your *rent!*"

2

VICTORIA DUPRIX

Victoria Duprix – Dr. Cushing's Chamber of Horrors
That Same Day

Both girls gaped at Victoria, as if they were codfish or as though the word "rent" were entirely foreign to them.

"But our father..." the brunette one, Victoria thought she was called *Opal*, began.

"—Is away," Victoria said, cutting the teenager off, "as I well know. Gone some six weeks now, though I had been under the impression that he would be back within a month."

"That happens sometimes, when an expedition gets busy," the blonde—*Topaz*? Yes. That was it—said.

"He's in Norway," the brunette added, as if that made any difference.

"Yes, Norway, or some other far-off place, I'm sure," Victoria continued. "Always gallivanting around the globe, your father. Always some excuse. Because do you know what he *forgot* to do before leaving?"

Victoria waited a moment, though she didn't really expect the twins to answer. Impertinent little vagabonds they were!

Before either girl could reply, she answered her own question: "Your father neglected to *pay the rent*. That means you're nearly two months in arrears, now. Two more months of my husband and I carrying your shabby little enterprise on our backs."

"It's *not* shabby!" Opal barked.

"The museum is Father's life's work!" Topaz added.

"*'Museum…'* Ha! You call this collection of dusty junk a museum? I've never understood why my husband allowed you people to rent the basement of our home in the first place."

"Because you've been squandering your husband's wealth and needed the mon—" Opal began, but Topaz clapped her hand over her sister's mouth.

Victoria glared at the two of them. Impertinent little snips! How *dare* they…?!

"We don't have much cash," Topaz, the blonde, admitted quickly, "because visits have been down, and our new exhibit hasn't opened yet."

Victoria arched one carefully plucked eyebrow. "New exhibit?"

"Yes," Opal continued. "A display of Egyptian artifacts—"

"You mean to tell me that your father has been squandering his money on *more* junk instead of paying the rent?"

"—including several mummies," Opal finished.

"I'm sure that once we've got the display set up, it will bring in more customers," Topaz added. "Then we'll be able to pay the rent."

"Including the back rent we owe you," Opal concluded.

"With the income from some *mummies?*" Victoria scoffed. Clearly, both these girls were half-wits. Either that or they'd completely bought into their father's belief in all this supernatural nonsense. "My dears, mummies were old hat when *I* was a girl."

"That long ago?" Opal, the brunette, shot back.

Victoria tried not to let it show, but the barb stung.

Lately, she'd been fighting regular skirmishes against Father Time. Grey hairs seemed to crop up daily, and parts of Victoria had begun to sag that had no *right* to. And were those crow's-feet furrowing at the edges of her hazel eyes? Why, she was barely even forty. And here these pert, young nothings thought they could jest about her age!

Despite her best efforts at self-control, Victoria's eyes narrowed, and she felt sure that—if these little moppets were paying attention—they would have spotted the angry fire burning in the center of her skull.

The blonde must have sensed Victoria's displeasure, because she shot her twin a withering look.

"We're sorry we haven't kept up with the rent," Topaz said.

"We're trying so hard," her sister put in.

"Maybe if you understood our business better, Madame Duprix, you could give us some tips," Topaz suggested. "After all, you run a successful waxwork, and have a lot more experience in business and such."

"Topaz is right," Opal agreed. "With your help, I'm sure our new exhibit would be *much* more successful—and we could get up to date on the rent in no time."

Victoria knew that the twins were trying to change the subject, to distract her from her rent-collecting mission…

Yet, the flattery felt *good*. And what harm could it do to have these scruffy moppets dote on her—if only for a little while—before she lowered the boom on them?

"Very well," Victoria said. "How should we begin?"

"We could show you around the chamber," Topaz suggested.

"We've never given you the full tour before," Opal added.

Victoria crinkled her nose; the very idea of plodding about their sordid attraction was distasteful, but…

"Yes. Please, show me around your so-called *business*," she told the pair.

Both girls bowed slightly and parted so that Victoria could precede them into the exhibit.

Dr. Cushing's Chamber of Horrors was a dark and dismal place (thought what did she expect?) with occasional glimmering pinpricks of light. In those spotlights, Victoria could make out a collection of strange objects, some familiar—a skull, a shaggy rug framed and hanging on a wall, some weapons—while others remained elusive and unrecognizable.

"Before we begin," Topaz said, pausing on the top step of the exhibit's entryway, "it is important to note that *all* the items that you are about to see are genuine paranormal artifacts, collected at great expense by Dr. Leigh Cushing himself, during his world-spanning expeditions."

Victoria huffed at *"great expense." Great expense at slacking on the rent*, she thought. But clearly this was part of the girls' patter—just as she had a script to greet people entering the waxworks. For now, at least, she would indulge them.

"Some of the supernatural items in Dr. Cushing's collection are, in fact, *dangerous*," Topaz continued. "So please be sure to observe the 'Do Not Touch' signs and other warnings. They are there for *your* safety, as well as the safety of the group."

"We'll start with the End of the World," Opal announced, picking up the tour from her sister. She indicated a fist-sized black stone, spotlighted atop a pedestal. "This is the fabled Meteor of Tunguska, the explosion of which flattened nearly a thousand square miles of Russian forest on the morning of June 30th, 1908."

"That tiny rock?" Victoria said skeptically.

"Of course, this is only a *fragment* of the original," Opal explained. "Most of it was vaporized in the explosion. If it had exploded over London, rather than in the wastes of Siberia, the city would have been destroyed—killing millions."

Victoria stifled a yawn, though she could see that the girl was impressed by her own story.

The sisters looked at each other nervously.

"Over here, we have the Siamese Mermaid," Topaz said, pointing to a wizened, three-foot-long oddity inside a glass case. It appeared to be a shriveled monkey with two heads and the tail of a carp. Its skin, what there was of it, looked like leather.

"Like its more famous cousin, now traveling the United States, this creature was collected in the South Seas. Not in Fiji, though. This particular mermaid came from the islands of the Philippines—as did the next item in our tour: the scales of an actual Filipino Fish-Wife. These seductive creatures are rumored to be beautiful women by day, only to turn into fish-like monsters by night."

Victoria looked at the scales, which rested in a yellowing glass jar near the so-called mermaid. The scales were the size of a shilling coin and greenish blue in color. *Probably from a larger carp*, Victoria thought, her patience already wearing thin.

No wonder these addle-pated waifs couldn't pay the rent.

"Yes, yes, yes," she said, "I'm sure that's all very nice. But I've seen the likes of these things in every sideshow from here to Aberdeen. I hope you have better attractions for paying customers than *this* lot."

The girls exchanged worried glances.

"The pelt of the Beast of *Gevaudan*," Opal said, pointing to a huge, shaggy reddish-black wolf skin framed and hanging on the wall. "In eighteenth-century France, this monster attacked over two-hundred people—and killed more than one hundred! It's said that no normal weapon could pierce its hide, and that only a bullet blessed by the Pope himself finally brought the beast down."

"It looks more like a mangy bear rug than a wolf skin," Victoria observed. "Another fabrication, like the 'mermaid,' I assume."

Opal's face reddened. "No! This is the genuine artifact. I assure you. Our father says so."

"Don't let the size of the pelt fool you into thinking it's a bear," Topaz put in. "Look at the long tail. Have you ever seen a wolf that size? It's Herculean! Bigger than even the largest full-grown man."

"And that's why I *know* it to be a fake," Victoria said, "stitched together from smaller skins, the way your 'mermaid' is stitched together from dead monkeys and desiccated fish. Really, girls, if you want the public to take notice, you'll have to do better."

In Victoria's opinion, the girls would earn more selling their services on the streets than trying to peddle this rubbish to gawkers. Certainly, they were attractive enough to make good money as showgirls or escorts or models…

The thought of models brought Victoria back to the days of her youth. She'd been an artists' model when she met Vincent. He'd been so handsome back then—and rich, too—and she'd been *so* beautiful…

Yes, eligible men were easy to catch before the days of greying hair and sagging breasts and wrinkles. Now she had to rely on her wits, or her perceived station, to get what she wanted.

Never let them know how old you are or how little money you've got, she reminded herself.

But the girls, clearly panicked, were just babbling now.

"We have so many other interesting attractions…" Topaz said.

"The footprint of a living dinosaur… the iron maiden of Baron von Latos… the knife of Jack the Ripper…" Opal offered.

"The guillotine that beheaded Marie Antoinette… The noose that hanged Burke, the body snatcher…" added Topaz.

Victoria rolled her eyes. "What's *this* then?" she said, pointing to what looked like a bathroom set in the middle of the exhibit space. "The bath where poor Marat was killed by Charlotte

Corday? Alas, *pauvre* Marat!" She meandered toward the gilded bath tub and matching mirror, just more chintzy flummery pretending to be extraordinary.

"No!" Opal cried. "That's one of our best pieces!"

"That mirror belonged to Elizabeth Bathory, the Bloody Countess," Topaz explained.

"She believed that she could restore her fading youth by bathing in the blood of virgins," Opal put in.

"Really?" Victoria asked drolly, arching an eyebrow. She glanced in the mirror.

And the most extraordinary thing happened.

For a moment, what she saw reflected in the mirror was *not* herself—not the drab surroundings of the Cushing displays—but utter blackness and an elegant dark-haired woman wearing an elaborate dress and flashing jewelry. The woman smiled at Victoria.

And then she was gone.

Victoria gasped and blinked her eyes.

"What is it?" Topaz asked.

"Are you all right?" Opal chimed.

"I'm fine," Victoria said, though her heart was pounding. She blinked and looked in the mirror again.

But all she saw now was herself—her plain, middle-aged self—and the dingy surroundings of the Chamber of Horrors, and the twins, standing nearby, gawking.

"I nearly tripped on one of these dratted floorboards," Victoria elaborated. She stubbed the toe of her shoe against the floor, to make her point. "That's all. You should have them fixed."

"Yes, ma'am," the twins replied in unison.

That sent a chill down Victoria's spine to join the fright she'd just had with the mirror. When the girls spoke at the same time, it was almost like they were one person—a single soul—though they were obviously *two*, very different looking young women.

Victoria wondered, for just a moment, whether they were virgins.

Then her common courtesy and hard-won breeding reasserted itself.

Seeming to sense their impending doom, Topaz put herself forward again. "And over here, you'll find the genuine skull of the Marquis de Sade—possibly the most wicked man who ever lived." She pointed to a bleached and grinning skull, under glass, on a pedestal.

"*All* men are wicked," Victoria observed, "as both of you will no doubt discover, in due time. But I'm afraid this is not *enough*, girls. There is nothing here that makes me think that the two of you—or your wastrel father—will ever be able to keep this business afloat and repay what you owe me… and my husband."

"B-but…" Topaz began, tears budding at the edges of her stunning blue-green eyes.

"We can trade you something for the rent," Opal interjected.

"Yes," Topaz agreed. "There must be *something* you want."

Victoria looked both girls up and down. Aside from their youth—which they obviously couldn't give her—she couldn't imagine what they had to trade.

"We could give you the pelt of the beast," Opal offered. "You said it looked like a bearskin. It would make a fine rug. Think how good it would look in front of the fireplace in your living room…"

"It would look shabby," Victoria replied.

"What about a mummy?" Topaz said, going to the boxes that occupied most of the chamber's main landing. "We have three. You could take one, and we'd exhibit the rest. I'm sure we can keep up with the rent once the mummy exhibit opens—even with just *two* mummies."

Victoria frowned. "*Tosh!* What would *I* do with a mummy?"

Both girls looked crestfallen.

"Although…" Victoria's eyes roamed around the exhibit until settling on the thing she wanted. "I *could* use a new mirror."

"Bathory's mirror?" Topaz asked.

"But that's one of our best exhibits!" Opal objected.

"Take it, or leave it," Victoria replied. "And if you leave it, I assure you that I will have the constable visiting forthwith to either collect the rent owed or turn you urchins—and your flea-bitten exhibit—out onto the street."

Anger burned behind Opal's blue-green eyes, and it looked as though she might say something nasty.

Then Topaz stepped in: "We'll take it."

"Good," Victoria said—but, really, what other choice did the girls have. "Perhaps my husband can help you with the unpacking of your mummies later, *if* he ever deigns to poke his head out of his studio. Until then…"

And here she smiled sweetly at the twins.

"You two can help me take my new mirror up to my bed chamber."

Victoria ran her hand over the gold filigree surrounding the dark pane of glass.

The woman in the mirror smiled back.

3

PAUL S. LONGMIRE

The Werewolf – Transylvania
The Night of the Full Moon

The man moved through the moonlit forest at what for him probably seemed a quick and silent pace.

But, to the beast, his every footstep and rustle of clothing echoed like thunder. The man was slow, too, and he reeked of body odor and something the werewolf's animal nature could barely identify—*cologne*, a terrible, unnatural stench.

Involuntarily, the wolf's black lips curled away from its sharp teeth, and it nearly growled. But then it remembered itself. This was no ordinary man; this was its *foe*—the being it had been created to kill. And the beast knew instinctively that the man sought to destroy it, as well.

The werewolf feared nothing. The full moon beamed all her occult fury into its hairy frame. The preternatural animal could sense its own power, its own near invulnerability. All the world was its prey, and its talons and teeth were sharp enough to rend the flesh of any mortal.

And, yet, somehow, the monster knew that this man had the means to destroy it: weapons of silver—proof against even the supernatural power of the beast—and a gun loaded with silver bullets.

Reflexively, the wolf-thing clutched at its shoulder; blood still trickled there.

The creature's memory was brief and blurry, but it remembered the man wounding it, not long after moonrise. They'd skirmished briefly, before the shot had rung out and the fire of silver tore through the monster's shoulder.

The wolf had fled then, seeking the safety of the deeper woods, leaving the battered hunter amid the corpses of his hounds, which would track the beast no longer.

But the man had recovered, and it seemed *he* could track, too, though not as effectively as his dogs.

Nor as effectively as the wolf, for the monster had recovered, as well.

The silver-inflicted wound still stung it, but the bullet had passed cleanly through.

And the creature was strong—even when wounded—far stronger than any man.

The hunter moved quickly and nearly silently past the tree where the wolf lay waiting. The beast had hidden in the upper canopy, leaping from tree to tree, to avoid leaving a blood trail on the ground.

The wolf-thing was clever—*more* clever than the man, as well as stronger.

The time had come to prove it!

The monster sprang.

The hunter turned, as if sensing his peril at the last instant.

He raised his gun toward the werewolf's slavering jaws.

BANG!

Paul Longmire - Llanwelly, Wales
More Than a Year Later

Paul Shaw Longmire woke with a start on a sweat-drenched bed.

He staggered to his feet and gazed out the window at the rising moon, fear clutching at his heart.

The pale orb haunted Paul, a nightly reminder of his own personal hell.

His entire body felt cold, but perspiration beaded on his skin. The hair on his arms and the nape of his neck prickled.

How long had it been? How long since the last full moon?

Paul couldn't remember. He could *never* remember.

Was that part of the curse?

He thought it must be. Otherwise, no sane man would ever venture outside of an iron-barred cell during the three days of the full moon.

Am I insane?

Paul thought it likely—at least a little. But who *wouldn't* be insane with what he had to go through month after month…?

The moon is rising!

He braced himself, leaning against the sill of the bedside window in the modest little inn.

Where were his *chains*? Could he get to them in time? Would they help?

They hadn't helped the night he'd found that girl—that *poor* girl—in the forest. He'd killed her… he *thought*. Or rather he *assumed* he'd killed, because the beast's memories were never very clear once he woke. They were more like dreams… dreams of blood and carnage… his own living nightmares.

Paul looked around the tiny room…

Where were those manacles? Why hadn't he left them out, where they were needed? Why had he fallen asleep during the late afternoon in the first place?

The curse…!

He needed to search… look everywhere… find those chains…

Under the bed. They *must* be under the bed, in his suitcase.

He got down on all fours… reached for it…

Too late!

The moon had cleared the tops of the surrounding trees now. The silver orb beamed its cold, relentless illumination into Paul's tiny bedroom.

Fear clutched at his heart.

No!

He clawed his way to his knees and turned to face his nemesis.

Her light shone pale upon his trembling body.

Every muscle tense, every nerve tingling, Paul returned the gaze of his pale mistress.

"It's not full…" he gasped.

Relief hit him like a shotgun blast to the belly, and he crumpled to the floor.

"It's *not* full."

Thank God.

A pale sliver of moon shone in the late-spring sky.

Tears of relief streamed down Paul's ill-shaven face. It *wasn't* the full moon, just another ordinary night—a night under the mounting threat of the new moon's waxing crescent.

"I have two more weeks," he muttered to himself, "or close to it." He knew he must keep better track, somehow. He'd had a notebook once, jotting down each day, each phase of the moon…

But he couldn't find that notebook any longer; the *curse* had taken it—or rather, made him lose or destroy it. He had to come up with a better system… somehow.

"Two more weeks to end this curse forever," he mumbled.

If he could find the key, the way out, the thing he'd been searching for so long…

With the fear of the moon lifting, Paul's memories came flooding back… He'd come to England seeking a treatment, the cure he'd traveled the world over trying to find ever since that awful night in the Carpathians…

He tried not to think about what had happened, but memories of the incident still haunted his nightmares. How could it *not*?

"Concentrate," he told himself. "Concentrate on your goal."

If it was *this* hard for him to hold himself together now, how hard would it be during the next full moon?

It's only fear, he told himself. *The full moon is still two weeks away.*

"Get a grip. You came here for a reason—to talk with those gypsies. If anyone can help you, *they* can."

That's what he *hoped*, anyway. And if they failed him—as all the rest had, from Tibet to Saskatchewan—he prayed that this would not be his *last* hope.

Forcing himself to breathe deeply and calmly, Paul stripped off his sweat-soaked shirt and retrieved a clean one from his battered suitcase. As he pulled the valise out from under the bed, he tried not to look at the destination stamps plastered on the outside—tried not to think of all the places he'd been, all the failures…

This time it will work, he prayed. *This time, I'll find what I need.*

The stainless-steel chains secreted in the bottom of his luggage gave a reassuring *clink*.

They were still there—and the key with them.

They'll be ready when you need them... In three weeks.

No! Not three weeks—*two*.

He pounded his fist on the rough-painted window frame, gazing at his pale, implacable enemy arcing into the night sky.

He'd slept too long; it was time to go. The night was wasting.

"You didn't chase these gypsies across half of Europe and most of England just to lose them now," he told himself.

Shirt changed, Paul Longmire fled his rented room, pausing only long enough to lock the door behind him.

The lodgings he'd chosen weren't the best he'd stayed in, nor by any means the worst. The wood and plaster interior was worn but well-tended to. He felt grateful to make it out the door without being accosted by the affable landlady.

Hospitable locals, welcoming even to strangers, waved at Paul as he left the inn, but he ignored them. It wouldn't do for him to make friends, not even briefly. He—or rather the *wolf*—was a danger to everyone he came in contact with. So, he couldn't linger, couldn't put down even the tiniest roots.

He hurried past the stone-and-timber houses to the edge of the village, where the long-sought gypsy camp lay.

The rag-tag gypsy wagons—most of them still horse drawn, rather than pulled by automobiles, Paul noted—lay settled in a rough circle in a field at on the town's south-westernmost outskirts. Colorful tents of various sizes and shapes stood scattered amid the site, as well. The caravans varied in their states of repair, from well-worn to newly trimmed and painted, and a large bonfire burned in the middle of the cluster. The aromas of sawdust, burning wood, and simmering stews filled Paul's nose.

The sounds of music and laughter—a reminder that not everyone in the world had doom hanging over their heads—drifted to Paul as he approached. A teenage girl with black hair and a flashing smile was dancing for tips around the blaze as other gypsies played the violin, guitar, and drums.

The girl caught Paul's eye and danced over toward him as he approached, but Paul turned away.

She laughed, a light, musical sound.

"Come back to the fire, Jaelle," a gypsy man called. "We've paying customers here!"

The girl did as she was told.

Paul faded into the shadows between the ramshackle structures, trying to make himself as inconspicuous as possible. Some of the townsfolk sneaking into the fortune-telling tents nearby seemed to be embarrassed to be seen here as well. Others walked boldly through the tent flaps, laughing and joking about "gypsy superstitions."

Paul hoped that he'd find more here than just old wives' tales.

They must have the secret to the cure. They must!

He didn't know what he'd do if he'd spent all this time searching only to come up empty—again.

"Is there a woman named Maria in this camp?" he asked a gypsy man tending some horses. "Maria Alekseyevna?"

"Oh, sure," the man said, "everybody knows Maria. The caravan with the red wheels and the blue trim—nicest in the camp." He pointed. "Right over there. You can't miss it."

Paul's heart soared, feeling hope for the first time in what seemed like ages. "Thank you," he said, heading for the wagon in question.

"I'm not sure she's telling any more fortunes today, though," the man called. He frowned and walked away, scratching his head as though worried, as Paul hurried off.

Paul's stomach clenched. "She'll see me," Paul muttered to himself. "She *has* to."

Maria's caravan *was* the nicest he'd seen: freshly painted in blue, yellow, white, and red and with a big sign blazoned "Fortunes" hanging over the door in the back.

Paul's heart sank, though, as he noticed a smaller sign below: "Closed."

He went to knock on the door anyway. He *had* to try, and he *couldn't* wait until tomorrow.

But before his knuckles could rap on the wood, a mellifluous voice from inside said:

"Come in."

Paul mounted the short flight of steps at the back of the wagon, opened the door, and went inside. The smells of exotic spices, homespun wool, and burning wax brimmed in the air as he entered.

The caravan was dark, lit by only a single candle in the middle of a small table draped in calico cloth. At the far side of the table sat a woman in a silken gypsy dress with a scarf over her head.

Paul couldn't tell her age. In this light, she might be anywhere from thirty-eight to eighty, but her voice came to him strong and clear, and her dark eyes glinted in the candlelight. "Please... Take a seat."

"My name is Paul Longmire," he began, too nervous to sit.

"I know who you are," said the woman. "And I am Maria—the one you've been seeking."

"How did you—?"

"We gypsies are a clannish people, Mr. Longmire," she said. "You shouldn't be surprised, when asking from camp to camp for Maria, that she would hear about you before you eventually found her. Please... Sit."

Despite his nerves, Paul took the stool opposite her.

"I have questions—a problem—and I've been told... that is, I *hoped* you might help."

"You carry the mark of the wolf," the old gypsy said matter-of-factly. "I sensed your curse the moment you entered the camp. Others will have noticed it, too. Ask your questions, Mr.

Longmire, because now that you are here, my people will not stay in this place for even a single night more."

So many things swirled through Paul's head that he could barely think straight. The gypsies *knew* he was coming; Maria knew of his curse, but they were *leaving*... This might be his only chance to get the answers he needed.

Paul prayed that the curse *wouldn't* cloud his mind—that he'd be able to find the *right* questions...

"Is there a cure?" he asked. "Can I be free of this curse, once and for all?"

"Show me your palms," Maria said.

Paul reached across the table toward her and turned his hands palm up.

Maria's wizened hands appeared out of the folds of her silk dress, and she grasped his wrists firmly, carefully examining each of his palms. Her slender fingers felt warm—almost hot—to his touch.

"The left hand shows your past, the right hand your future," she began. "You have had a difficult life, Paul Longmire—suffering much loss—"

Images flashed through Paul's head: his parents, long gone now... his dead wife and child, and the fire that had taken them from him... And then the hunt—that *awful* hunt...! He tried to push all the nightmarish memories aside and concentrate on her words. He didn't want to miss a single thing that the gypsy witch might tell him.

"—And the road ahead of you remains thorny, Mr. Longmire... Though there is hope."

"Please," Paul said, "what is it? What must I do to break this curse?"

"The doom that courses through your veins is very ancient. It descends from the fabled *Beast of Gevaudan*. To break its scourge, you must destroy the progenitor of the line."

"The Beast of..." Paul began. He seemed to remember

hearing about such a monster during his long months of looking for the cure; he didn't like what he remembered.

"But the Beast lived hundreds of years ago," he said forlornly. "It must be long dead by now. That doesn't help me at all!" He felt as though victory had been snatched from his grasp—and just when he'd been so *close*! "How can I destroy something that's already dead? How can I break this curse? Please! You *must* tell me! In just a few days, the moon will be full again, and…"

He trailed off, unable to bring himself to say the words: *"… And I'll kill again!"*

"Calm yourself, Mr. Longmire," the gypsy witch said. "All is not as hopeless as you believe. Though the beast itself is long dead, it was no ordinary creature. It was an *enchantment*, a spell woven through dark magicks into a wolf skin. If you can destroy that pelt, your curse will be broken."

"So, that wolf skin still exists," Paul muttered, his emotions roller-coastering between hope and despair. "Where?"

"I cannot say for certain," Maria replied. "Though I do remember once hearing something during my travels…"

"What did you hear? You *must* tell me: Where should I look? Where can I start? Please! I have so little time…"

"I noticed an article in a newspaper when our caravan passed through Lyon," Maria said. "I believe it mentioned something about the pelt of the beast being exhibited… in London."

Paul's heart pounded in his chest. *London!*

"Then that's where I have to go."

4

THE MUMMIES ARRIVE

Opal Cushing – The Chamber of Horrors
The Day of the First Quarter Moon

Dr. Cushing's Chamber of Horrors was a mess, no doubt about it. The five big crates that had arrived from Egypt must have been larger on the inside than on the outside, it seemed to Opal, because how else to explain the amount of floor space the unpacking took?

And they hadn't even *finished* yet!

"We won't be able to open the museum *tomorrow*," Topaz moaned. "Or maybe even the day *after*… never mind *today*."

Opal laughed. She was far more concerned that all this unpacking and sorting might leave her no time for *fun* tonight—although, she wasn't having a *terrible* time, considering the company…

"Where should I put this?" Francis Browning asked her, his brown eyes flashing mischievously. In his long-fingered hands he held what looked to be a golden torch.

A smile tugged at the corner of Opal's lips, but she resisted saying what popped into her mind. Perhaps her sister was right, and Frank *was* more interested in Opal herself.

"Oh!" interjected her sister, before Opal's conversation with Frank could go any further. "The *Torch of Sekhmet*! Father wrote to us about this; do you remember, Opal?"

"Of course," Opal replied, though actually, she didn't. She took the artifact from Frank and examined it. It was a torch, all right, shaped in the form of a papyrus-reed bundle and made of —or at least covered in—gold. The metal felt oddly warm in her hands, and for just a moment, an image of raging fire flashed through Opal's mind.

"It was used in sacred ceremonies in the temple," Topaz explained to the well-dressed boy following her around like a puppy. (An occurrence not unusual for her sister, Opal noted. Topaz seemed to attract boys as easily as flowers attracted bees.)

Is it her demure attitude? Opal wondered. *I could be more shy...* Though, no, probably she really couldn't; Opal wasn't patient enough to be shy. When she wanted something, she went after it... usually. With Frank, she was playing a little harder-to-get, which was difficult but seemed to be paying off.

Or maybe it's her hair, Opal thought, wondering if she should bleach her wavy dark-brown locks blonde.

"The legend is," Topaz continued, "that once lit, nothing on earth can put this torch out—except, of course, for its cap, which acts as a snuffer."

"A *sacred* snuffer," Opal added jovially. She pulled the cone-shaped cap off of the torch, revealing a blackened wick—or whatever passed for a wick in ancient Egypt. It smelled vaguely of oil and sandalwood.

"Hey, that's a better guarantee than my Ronson De-Light," Frank joked. "'A flip... and it's lit.'"

"Do you think it could be *true*, about the torch I mean?" asked the teen who'd been following Topaz, his eyes wide with wonder.

His name was Barry Ripper. He was shorter than Frank and more solidly built, but Opal had to admit that he was rather cute with his mop of brown hair and his big blue eyes.

Not as cute as Frank, though.

"Let's find out," Frank suggested, producing a silver Ronson lighter from his pocket and flicking it into flame.

A long-fingered hand seemed to appear out of nowhere and snapped the lighter shut.

"I'll have to ask you not to casually brandish open flames in the building housing my waxworks," Vincent Duprix said with a (perhaps overly sincere) smile. "One little bit of fire and… POOF!" He made a gesture of everything going up in a cloud of smoke. "And if that happened, where would these delightful ladies live?"

As he asked the question, Vincent put an arm around the shoulders of both twins—though, since they were standing a bit apart, it proved something of a stretch to do so.

Topaz gave him a sincere smile. "I hope we never have to find out, Mr. Duprix," she said.

Opal grinned at their landlord as well, but her expression was only a facade.

Though she felt grateful that Mr. Duprix had come to help with the unpacking, she wasn't too thrilled with the amount of time he seemed to spend gazing at her and her sister, amid the chores.

The sculptor's glances seemed less fond and paternal than she had remembered and more… predatory.

And to think, I used to find his gaze flattering, Opal thought. *Have I just grown up, or has he changed—for the worse?*

Whatever the case, her sister didn't seem to have noticed, or at least, Topaz wasn't letting it show.

Opal decided to take the same tack. *I won't let him see that I'm uncomfortable, even if he decides to stare down my cleavage.* And perhaps there was even some way she might turn their landlord's lechery to their advantage—playing him off against his wife, Victoria (who didn't seem to much like them), for instance.

"Yes, we're *so* happy to be here," Opal said. She put the cap back on the torch and handed the artifact to her sister. "And we're so very grateful that your wife decided to give us—and our father—a break on our rent."

"She did?" both Barry and Frank blurted, and for a moment it was almost as though the girls' beaus were twins as well.

Opal suppressed a giggle, and she could see that Topaz was doing the same.

Vincent Duprix arched one dark eyebrow. "How very unlike her."

"Yes," Topaz elaborated. "We traded her a mirror from our exhibit in lieu of back payments."

"Oh, well that explains it," Vincent said, waving his hand in a dismissive flourish. "Victoria always has been a vain creature." Then he added in a stage whisper, "And, believe it or not, at one time, she had *reason* to be."

"Your wife is a very attractive woman, Mr. Duprix," Frank said politely.

"I see she has *you* on the payroll as well, Mr. Browning," Vincent replied with a grin.

"N-no…" Frank stuttered, "I…"

"Don't get all flustered, Mr. Browning. I meant nothing by it," Vincent assured him. "Girls, tell your young admirers that I'm a man of good humor and casual jests."

Frank looked at both girls, and his face reddened; Barry's did the same. Clearly, though they were both attracted to the twins, the boys were embarrassed to have it pointed out.

Opal and Topaz laughed. The sisters exchanged a glance, and then, in their best twin-speak, said:

"Mr. Duprix is a man of good humor and casual jests."

That made the entire company laugh, which (thankfully) broke the tension, and everyone went back to the unpacking.

Opal decided that maybe she'd even been too sensitive about Duprix's wandering gaze. She'd felt uneasy around him since accidentally stumbling into a nude modeling session in his second-floor studio a few weeks back.

She'd come to ask their landlord to fix a leak in the Cushings' third-floor bathroom, and had no idea, at the time, that he *wasn't* working alone. Vincent had laughed it off, as had his model (whom Opal didn't know, and whom Vincent had never introduced), but Opal had been torn between being scandalized and thrilled, ever since.

Of course, she'd admired his sculptures; she'd *known* how those lush nudes were made—in *theory*. But after the encounter, it seemed so much more... personal.

When she'd told her sister about it, Topaz had merely laughed it off. *"That's just what artists do,"* she'd said. *"You've been to the museums."* How strange that her shy sister should be more comfortable with the "facts of modeling life" than she.

Topaz hadn't *seen*, though.

And since that time, Opal couldn't help but wonder what it would be like to pose like that for an artist... What it would be like to be naked in front of *any* man. Frank, for instance...

"Hey, look at me! I'm a mummy!" Frank moaned theatrically. He was holding a carved and painted mask from one of the crates in front of his face.

"Frank, don't!" Topaz scolded.

"Why? I'm not hurting anything?"

And while that may have been *technically* true, something about the visage of her would-be-beau sporting a red-ochre face and glass eyes sent a stab of pain behind Opal's eyes. For a moment, she saw Frank wrapped in bandages, and reaching out to her from beyond the grave... Then her vision cleared again.

"Seriously, Frank," Topaz continued. "That funeral mask is three thousand years old."

"Yeah, Frank," Barry agreed. "Quit being a jerk."

"Frank, please," Opal added, not quite able to shake her uncanny vision. Had it been some kind of *actual* premonition, or had she just been unpacking too long?

"*Funeral* mask?" Frank said, his handsome face going pale. He carefully laid the painted visage back down in the excelsior-filled box from which it had come. "Okay. Sorry."

"Oh, my!" Vincent exclaimed. "*This* is really quite remarkable! I think we may have finally reached the core of your new exhibition, my dears."

Opal, her sister, and the other two teens quickly came to peer into the box he was examining—one of just two remaining unpacked. After an afternoon of un-crating chairs, jars, and other similar items, the youngsters were ready for a break.

Inside lay a beautiful casket, carved and painted in the likeness of a very lovely young woman.

Topaz checked one of the bills of lading and smiled. "This must be *Bastiti*, one of three mummies our father helped discover and acquired as compensation. Legend has it that she was a queen of Egypt, though details of her dynasty have been lost to the ages."

"A queen without a kingdom, eh?" Frank mused.

"Good looking, though," added Barry. "For a girl who's a couple of millennia old, I mean."

"Exquisite," Vincent agreed.

"Father theorized that she was married to *King Sethmosis*," Opal said, remembering some of Dr. Cushing's letters. "But the king wasn't found in the tomb with her, though several other mummies were."

"Father thinks one is the royal advisor, *Sethotep*, and the other a guard who went by the name of *Nekure*," Topaz elaborated. "Their names are carved on their coffins."

"I can read a bit of Egyptian," Vincent said. "I was quite the art history buff at school. I'll just clear away some more of this packing and—*Ouch*!"

A dark flash went off inside Opal's mind, and for a moment, she saw a mummified hand reaching for her, again.

"What is it?" Topaz asked.

"I just—" Opal began before realizing that her sister wasn't talking to her.

Vincent Dupris had withdrawn his left hand from the mound of excelsior surrounding the sarcophagus and was sucking on his middle finger. A little blood tricked out the sides of his lips.

"It's nothing," he assured the rest. "I just pricked my finger. There must be a rough edge or something on this coffin."

"I'll get some mercurochrome," Topaz offered.

"No need, no need," Vincent countered. "I'm all right. And, besides, I wouldn't want to slow down your work. I'm really anxious to see the entirety of this casket—and the sarcophagi of the other two mummies, of course."

Carefully, the four teenagers removed the rest of the shipping crate and its packing material, until the sarcophagus inside stood revealed in its full glory.

"This really is *exquisite*," Vincent said. "Notice the subtlety of the carving… the almost lifelike quality of the face…"

"That's quite a compliment coming from an artist of your caliber, Mr. Duprix," said Frank.

"Oh?" Vincent asked. "You've seen my work?"

"I've been through your wax museum a few times," Frank replied.

"Me, too," agreed Barry. "We think your Joan of Arc is quite a dish."

"Though Barry's favorite is Lady Godiva," Frank put in.

Barry blushed.

"Well, thank you, boys. Thank you very much," Vincent said. "It's always nice when young people today admire the arts." He'd bandaged his injured finger in a white handkerchief, now, though a spot of blood had managed to stain all the way through. "My humble efforts are but mere shadows of the genius of these ancient craftsmen. Why, looking at this... this queen depicted here, I almost feel as though she's still alive, standing right before us."

"It's pretty good work, that's for sure," Barry agreed.

"Why don't we open the casket and take a look at her," Topaz suggested.

Something inside her—maybe the vision of that bandaged hand—made Opal want to say *"Stop!"* But she didn't.

"Can we?" Frank asked skeptically.

"Well, it's *our* exhibit," Topaz replied.

"Our *father's*," Opal stressed, still feeling wary.

"But we have to know what we're exhibiting," Topaz reminded her. "And if the old girl's *worth* exhibiting, so..."

"Excellent," Vincent declared. "Help me loosen this lid, all of you—and do be careful with your fingers."

The other three teens stepped forward and carefully began prying at the top of the sarcophagus, alongside Vincent. But Opal hung back, unable to shake the disquieting feeling seeping through her.

For a moment, there was a groan and scrape as ancient wood and painted linen grated against each other, and then suddenly, the lid came free and Opal's sister and the rest gently set it aside.

The smell was the first thing that struck Opal, the aroma of old linens, as well as cedar, myrrh, cinnamon, and other ancient perfumes that she couldn't identify.

As she stepped closer, the form of the mummy came into view. Bastiti was shapely, or must have been in life—even the desiccation of her linen-wrapped figure couldn't hide the feminine swell of the late queen's hips and breast. Her face was covered with a painted wooden mask, resembling the visage on the casket.

Carefully, Topaz removed the mask to reveal the mummy's face.

Opal gasped. For just a moment, she thought she'd seen a *living person* beneath that painted façade. But no. It had only been an illusion. (Happily, none of the others seemed to notice her momentary surprise.)

Bastiti's face was leathery, her dark skin pulled tight over a well-formed skull with high cheekbones and gleaming white teeth. Her eyes lay closed, and black wiry hair—what little remained of it—covered her wizened head.

She must have been relatively young when she died, Opal realized.

Vincent gazed upon the mummy's shriveled face and sighed. "It's almost as if she's only sleeping."

"I wouldn't go *that* far," Frank said.

"But she is amazingly well preserved," Barry added.

"How old did you say she was?" Frank asked.

"At least three thousand years," Topaz replied. "Though Father's not really sure—yet."

"She could be much older," Opal added, feeling—somehow—as if that were true.

"Well, whatever her age, she's lovely," Vincent said. "If she got up out of her coffin right this minute, I'd ask her to model for me."

"If she gets up out of that coffin, I am *leaving*," Frank put in.

"Me, too," Barry agreed.

Vincent turned to the twins. "I don't mean to sound like my wife—who has always been overly concerned with money—but it amazes me, girls, that your father can travel the world collecting such objects and still have trouble scraping together enough money to pay the rent."

"Our father has doctorates in history, archeology, and mythology—with a specialty in occult artifacts," Topaz said. "The research, the collecting of these things—this exhibit—is his life."

"Surely you understand the pursuit of one's passion to the

exclusion of all else, Mr. Duprix," Opal added. "You are an artist, after all."

Vincent cocked his head and pursed his lips, as if letting the notion seep in. "Yes," he finally said. "Yes, I suppose I do. The pursuit—and creation—of beauty in all its forms has long been a driving force in my life." He smiled at both twins.

A shiver ran through Opal.

"And what does it matter about the rent," Vincent continued, still gazing at the mummy, "when there is beauty such as this to be found all around us?"

"Just so long as we can keep your *wife* happy," Topaz said.

"Yes," Vincent replied thoughtfully. "Yes. We'll have to keep at that. But with your assistance, girls, I'm sure we can work something out—even if your father *is* off tramping the farthest reaches of the world."

"He'll be home soon," Topaz said.

Both twins gave their landlord a smile—Vincent's heart *did* seem to be in the right place, after all—but, again Opal didn't really *feel* the face she'd put on.

She wished that she could be as confident as her sister that their father was all right and would soon return.

Opal longed to know… Was he facing peril, as the cards had predicted, even now?

Why can't these "visions" show me something useful? she wondered. *Like… Why hasn't Father come home to us yet? And where is he, right now?*

5

THE ICE MAN

Dr. Cushing – The Coast of Norway
That Same Day

The Arctic gust whipped Leigh Cushing's face, yanking back the hood of his parka. The wind was bitter for this time of year, even in Norway—it was late spring, after all—but Dr. Cushing was used to adverse conditions during his expeditions. He'd suffered sandstorms in Egypt, swarms of blood-sucking flies in Siberia, and caught a tropical fever in Southeast Asia.

The trials of this venture had been neither more nor less difficult; they had just been different. Troubles or no, it was these upcoming minutes that he lived for, the moments when, at last, his search would come to fruition.

Cushing pulled his hood snug around his face and dug the toes of his cleated boots more securely into the iceberg's slick surface.

No sense falling to my death when I'm this near to my objective, he thought with a smile.

It had taken him years of research, rumor gathering, and

fruitless pursuits to come to this point, but now, the legendary Ice Man seemed within his grasp.

Taking a deep breath, he climbed the last few steps to what passed for the top of this beached mountain of ice. The area was remote, and exactly when the berg had run ashore, nobody knew for certain—days? Weeks? Months? Perhaps even a whole year.

He'd first heard news of the iceberg, and its strange passenger, more than three years ago—from a fur trapper, who'd landed ashore on the floating berg to chase seals. The man had encountered little luck with his hunt, but he'd returned to the mainland with yet another rumor of a huge man, frozen in the ice.

Unfortunately, at that time, Cushing's attempts to track down the iceberg had proven futile—as had his previous attempts to find and recover the Ice Man.

After so many years, so many rumors...! he thought, his heart swelling as he tramped across the berg's cracked and crevassed surface.

The vast icy expanse that lay before him looked more like a glacier than something that could possibly float. Its vast blue-white bulk was longer and wider than a city block and easily as tall as Big Ben. Yet, float the iceberg had, until currents—and perhaps Providence—had grounded it here on this inhospitable Norwegian shoreline, high above the Arctic Circle, for Cushing to discover, at last.

The day was sunny and might have been warm and hospitable, except for the harrowing wind, which picked up snow from the berg and, at times, blanketed the sunshine with a blizzard of blinding white flakes.

During less gusty moments, Cushing could see the blue-grey Norwegian Sea, stretching into the endless distance, beyond the top of the floe. Far below, resting well above the high-tide mark, lay the small tent-village of men and sled dogs that Cushing had hired to help with his venture.

He tried not to think about the cost. *"Cost should never be a barrier to science,"* as he often said (especially to his creditors). Still, with any luck, his new Egyptian exhibit—and the one resulting from *this* expedition—would help him recoup his considerable expenditures.

"Dr. Cushing!" a voice called to him, and out of the current wind-blown whiteout emerged Tor Johansen, the leader of Cushing's hirelings. The two had worked together on several expeditions in the past, and Cushing was glad to have the big Norwegian along again.

Johansen stood at least six and one-half feet tall and was built like a lumberjack, which, indeed, had been his profession before he became one of the best outdoorsmen and wilderness guides in the Arctic.

"We have it, Doctor," Johansen said. "We've freed it from the ice. You're just in time!"

"Excellent," Cushing replied. He felt an extra spring in his step as he followed Johansen to the crevasse where their team had been working.

Johansen fastened a rope around Cushing's waist, and helped lower the doctor down into the enormous crack, before rappelling down himself.

Cushing took a deep breath to steady his nerves. He wasn't claustrophobic, as such, but it didn't pay to think too much about the millions of tons of sheer ice walls towering over them. The cast of the light at the bottom of the crevasse was distinctly bluish, giving the whole environment an eerie feeling, almost like being underwater.

Ahead of him lay a small cave in the ice, an opening that had been carefully hacked away and expanded by the half dozen men—and one woman—who stood before him.

"How goes it, Ingrid?" Cushing asked, addressing the sole female worker.

Ingrid Johansen smiled at him. "Well, doctor, *ja*. I think we've finally got this here bugger loose for ya."

Despite himself, Cushing blushed at the use of the word "bugger." Ingrid may have learned her English from sailors, but she was the finest sled-team leader in the area, and matched her husband in wilderness skills as well. Plus, she stood nearly as tall as Tor did.

"Capital!" Cushing declared.

"It's gonna take some heavy work with block and tackle to get this bugger out of here," she continued, "but once we get it down to the sleds, it should be easy enough to lug to port."

"Stand back, doctor, and we'll haul it out into the light, where you can get a better look at it," Tor offered.

Cushing stepped aside to make room for the rest to pull on the ropes they'd wrapped around the huge block that they'd hacked from the ice.

"All right, you sons-of-sled-dogs…" Ingrid called to the rest. "Heave!"

The Johansens and the other six—all burly wilderness men in their own right—hauled on the ropes.

The block of ice groaned and crept forward a few inches.

"Heave!"

Another few inches.

"HEAVE!"

And, as if by magic—or perhaps via melting of the ice beneath it—the block suddenly rocketed forward, toward the wall where Cushing stood waiting.

He nimbly hopped out of the way, as the block skidded to a halt.

"Ha ha," Ingrid laughed. "Nice steppin' there, doctor! Ya nearly got a quick lesson in slimmin' down."

Cushing adjusted the snugness of his parka's collar. "I think I'm quite skinny enough already, thank you."

"Any skinnier and you'd be nothin' but skin and bones," Tor observed. "You English are a puny lot!" He smiled, showing one golden incisor amid a sea of ivory.

"Nothing puny about this fellow, though," Ingrid said, patting the block of ice they'd just heaved to the edge of the crevasse. "Take a look."

With one seal-skin glove she polished off a section of the newly freed ice block.

Cushing stepped forward to get a better glimpse.

Inside the block loomed an enormous figure, like a man trapped in blue-white amber.

"Big fella, ain't he?" Ingrid noted.

"*Ja*, even for a Norwegian," Tor agreed.

"Extraordinary!" blurted Cushing.

The Ice Man made even the Johansens look tiny by comparison. Freed from the ice, he would have stood at least seven feet tall—possibly more—and he was as broad as any two normal human beings. He seemed to be pale of cast and shaggy of hair, with bony features and long, knobby fingers—thought it was hard to make out precise details through the ice.

His eyes remained open, literally frozen in a ghastly stare.

"Yes," Cushing mused, "quite an exceptional find. Thank you so much—all of you—for helping me to recover it."

"You're welcome, Doctor," Tor said.

"But there's still a long way to go to get this bugger back to your museum," Ingrid added.

"Yes, yes. Of course," Cushing said. As he did, he realized that the journey returning to civilization might prove just as difficult as getting here and discovering this find had been. He had no doubt, though, that—with the Johansens' help—he would accomplish his goal. "What a splendid exhibit he shall make. An Ice Age man brought back to…"

And then something struck him.

"What's wrong, doctor?" Ingrid asked.

"I've just realized that this fellow isn't from the Ice Age at all!"

"He's not?" Tor said.

"No. He can't be. His clothes are all wrong."

Tor pressed his face up near the ice, to get a better look. "They look pretty old to me."

"Old, yes," Cushing said. "But not old enough. They're *far* too modern. I'd say this fellow comes from the nineteenth century, eighteenth at most. That's only one- or two-hundred years gone by."

"Still seems pretty old to me, doctor," Ingrid said, her blue eyes twinkling in the gleam from the glacier and the glow from their electric lanterns.

"Are you saying he's *worthless*?" Tor asked, concern growing on his ruggedly handsome face.

"Oh, no," Cushing replied. "I'm not saying that at all. It's just that the rumors all seemed to point to the Ice Man as being some kind of relic—a throwback to a bygone era— like the rumored gill-men of the Congo, or the wild hairy giants supposed to inhabit the northwestern Canadian wilderness. This fellow looks far more modern, almost like he stepped out of a production of Dickens' *A Christmas Carol*."

"We seen that in the movies," Ingrid said.

"It was pretty good," Tor admitted. "Didn't seen no fellas that large in it, though—except maybe that Christmas Past guy. He was pretty big. You sure this fella ain't one of those giants from Viking times, doctor?"

"Positive. I can't help but speculate where he *did* come from, though. I wonder—"

"*Min Gut!*" Ingrid swore.

"What is it?" Cushing asked.

"H-he looked at me!" Ingrid blurted. "I swear, Doctor… He just looked at me with those awful, pale eyes."

"Preposterous!" Cushing insisted.

"Doctor, you don't think this fella could still be alive, frozen in there, *could* he?" Tor asked.

"Impossible," Dr. Cushing replied. "No, it must just have been a trick of the light."

"*Ja*, I guess so," Ingrid agreed. But a shiver still shook her enormous frame.

"I assure you both that there is no possible way for a man to remain alive after being frozen in ice," Cushing said. "Not for one hundred minutes, never mind one hundred years."

"I hope you're right, Doctor," Tor said. "'Cause if that big fella were to get free, *I* wouldn't want to tangle with him, I'll tell you that for sure!"

The other six men in the ice cave grumbled their agreement, and Ingrid nodded as well.

"No need to worry about that, I assure you," Cushing said, patting the ice block with one mitten-clad hand. "I intend that he remain frozen all the way from here back to London, where we'll put him on display in my museum. We wouldn't want the old boy thawing out and rotting away, like those Siberian mammoths, would we?"

"Nope," Tor said, and Ingrid shook her head in agreement.

"Capital. So, let's get this fellow out of here, onto the sleds, and shipped back to civilization, shall we?" Cushing said. "I'm sure my daughters will be delighted to see him,"

He grinned. It had been a long time coming, but this triumph—like all the others before it—tasted *sweet*.

"After that," he continued, "we can resume looking around this iceberg and searching the surrounding countryside to discover if there are any more of his kind to be found. Eh? What fun!"

6

VINCENT'S SECRET

Vincent Duprix – The Studio at 1951 Fisher St.
A Night of the Waxing Gibbous Moon

Vincent Duprix rose from the couch in his studio, feeling refreshed yet strangely disturbed. Something had changed, but he couldn't quite put his finger on it.

He walked over to the sculpture he was working on and pulled off the covering that kept the work moist and pliable. It was merely cold clay now, but one day it would be glorious wax with all the warmth and luminosity of real flesh.

That might be hard for some to imagine, here, in the semi-darkness with the chilly light of the stars beaming down through the skylights and only a single electric lamp burning nearby, but in Vincent's imagination, the finished waxworks piece loomed as clear as day.

He ran his hands over the sculpture, subtly reshaping the breasts, making them more realistic—easy to do, since he'd been handling the actual things just a few minutes before. Then he worked on the waist, slimming it, and the torso, defining every firm rib that he'd recently found beneath his fingers.

Yes, sleeping with a woman always made sculpting her *so* much easier—at least until his wife found out.

But she wouldn't. Not this time. She was at the theater tonight, and Vincent had feigned illness to avoid accompanying her. After more than twenty years, he'd had quite enough of Victoria.

Despite that, somehow, he couldn't bring himself to leave her. Was it the thought of what she might cost him in alimony?

No. Not that. Vincent had never been that concerned about money. He didn't care about it when he had been young and rich, and he didn't care about it now that he was much older and on the verge of being broke, either.

His *art*—that was the thing!

Victoria cared about the money, though, cared enough to badger those poor Cushing girls almost night and day—and this after she'd claimed that ornate, and undoubtedly valuable, mirror from them. From what Vincent knew of antiques, that piece alone should have covered the Cushings' rent for a year. Yet, Victoria wanted more.

Always more...!

At first, her insatiable appetites had been alluring. They'd done everything together... *everything* (even before they were married). They'd traveled, seen all the great art of Europe, and even been to America once. And they'd drunk, and dined, and made love to excess at every possible opportunity. It was a wonder that they hadn't become fat, alcoholic slovens within a year.

And yet, Victoria had maintained her figure, and so had he. (Perhaps it was all the energy they expended in lovemaking.) And what a pleasure she had been to sculpt...

That face... Those breasts... Those hips... That *derriere...!*

Vincent gritted his teeth, torn between the lusty memory and the unpalatable present.

His left thumb slipped, crushing the delicate cheekbone he'd been trying to re-shape. A stab of pain shot through his hand and up into his spine.

"Ouch!"

"What's wrong, darling?" his current model called from the couch. She turned over and sat up, but didn't cover herself up. (What was the point? He'd seen it all—and handled every inch of her—anyway.) "Is anything wrong?"

"No, nothing," he said, wiping off his hands and sucking on his left middle finger. "I just slipped, that's all. Nothing I can't repair later. Maybe I should stop until morning."

"What about that finger?" she said, nodding toward him. "I noticed you were favoring it earlier—or were you just holding back?"

Vincent crossed to the couch, took her in his arms, and kissed her savagely.

"I never hold back," he said. "Not with you."

She pulled away slightly, and he winced. "Oh, really?" she said.

Vincent scowled. "It's nothing. Just that finger I pricked a week ago while helping those Cushing girls unpack their mummies."

"Are you sure that's *all* you helped them unpack?"

He ignored her salacious implication. "It doesn't seem to have healed properly."

"Let me take a look," she said in a motherly tone.

He sat down beside her and laid his hand in hers.

"Oh, my!" she exclaimed. "That *does* look awful. It might be infected. Have you been keeping it clean?"

"I work with clay all day, but other than that…"

"You should see someone about it."

"I'll just pop down to the chemist's and get something for it, after you've gone."

She reclined on the couch once more, opening her arms in welcome. "I'm sure we have time for just a little bit more."

Vincent rose, shaking his head. "Victoria's due back from the theater within the hour, and you know it wouldn't do to have her find you here. She doesn't even know you're posing for me."

His model laughed. "And what would she do if she found out? Would she leave you?"

Vincent pulled on his pants. "I should be so lucky. No. I don't actually know *what* she might do—and that's what worries me, and it should worry you as well."

"I can handle your wife," the woman said. She sat up and reached for her clothing.

"You may think so, but she hasn't seemed quite herself lately." *Just as I haven't* felt *quite like myself,* he thought. He walked to the room's full-length mirror, buttoning his shirt, the festering wound on his finger making him grimace. *I'll definitely have to get something for this.* "You should get dressed."

"If you insist," his model said, rising from the couch and starting to reassemble her clothing.

Vincent glanced in the mirror, intending to gaze at her nude body one final time—for tonight.

Then he gasped.

For in the mirror, he saw not his lover dressing, but an entirely different woman—a woman with long black hair and dark-tanned skin dressed in nothing but glittering golden jewelry. And behind her, almost completely hidden in the shadows, stood a man wearing only a loincloth and a gold skull cap. Both of the strange figures looked Egyptian, but it was the woman who seemed to return the sculptor's gaze. She was stunning!

Vincent shook his head and blinked, not quite able to believe what he was seeing. And when he opened his eyes again, much to his disappointment, the strange woman and her companion were gone.

His finger throbbed.

"What's wrong?" Vincent's lover asked.

"Nothing," he replied. "Just this damn finger."

She crossed to the mirror and hugged him, then took his wounded finger and kissed it.

For a moment, the flames of lust rose up within Vincent once more. Then the finger throbbed, and the fire faded.

"Please get that looked at," she said.

"I will. I'm going right now. There's a chemist that's open late just three blocks away."

She nodded. "Good."

"Oh," he said, tying his tie, "take the back stairs, would you?"

"The *servants'* stairs?" she asked. "Is that all I am to you, Vincent?"

"Of course not," he replied. "But no one ever uses those stairs, so there's less chance you'll be seen."

"I thought you said Victoria wasn't coming home for another hour."

"We don't live *alone* in this house," he reminded her. "And besides, you never can tell with my wife. She might take it into her head to return early out of sheer paranoia."

The model put her arms around his neck and kissed him. "Do you think she suspects?"

"I wouldn't put it past her, even though we've been careful. Let's continue being careful."

"If you insist," she said with an insolent nod of her head. She turned to leave.

Vincent swatted her on the bottom. "Begone, wench! Don't darken my doorstep again until I summon you."

She laughed, flipped him the double finger "V," and then exited out the back way.

Vincent chuckled and shook his head, then realized she'd distracted him; he'd done his buttons up wrong.

He returned to the mirror and straightened them, making sure he looked presentable.

But try as he might, he couldn't catch another glimpse of the girl he'd seen in the mirror.

I'd swear I know *her from somewhere.*

He shrugged. No time to figure it out now if he was to get to the chemist and back before Victoria returned.

With a spring in his step, he left the studio by the front exit and made his way toward the chemist's shop, three blocks away.

There, he quickly secured a tube of ointment suitable to the job.

"I guarantee this will clear it up in no time," said the chemist.

Vincent thanked the man, paid, and went on his way.

He'd barely gone a block, though, when something unusual caught his eye.

Victoria?

Sure enough, his wife was getting out of a horse-drawn carriage two blocks away from their home at 1951 Fisher.

Such an extravagance! Vincent thought. *She must not want me knowing she's wasting money on hansoms rather than taking an ordinary taxicab.*

The carriage driver helped Victoria down. Then he took her in his arms and kissed her.

Victoria kissed back—passionately.

Vincent's eyes narrowed, and a stab of pain shot through his skull.

So! Victoria's up to her old tricks again, is she? Well, this time she won't get away with it.

"This time," Vincent muttered to himself, "she'll *pay!*"

7

WEREWOLF IN LONDON

"Mick" McDowell – London
The Second Night of the Full Moon

The night was young, barely past dark, really, but already Mick and his friends were out of drinking money.

This was a problem, because the pubs where they were drinking, down near the wharfs, knew the foursome well enough not to extend them credit. But it *wasn't* a problem, because none of the group had any scruples as to where they got the money for their *next* drinks. Though, naturally, none of them wanted to put out *too* much effort or do any actual *work* to line their pockets.

After all, why should a bloke spend a full day toting barges or lifting bales when there were plenty of gents in London with more largess than they *needed*?

Unfortunately, those types of swells rarely wandered through the parts of town that Mick and his gang frequented—and it was too late for a quick smash and grab followed by a run to the local pawn shop, either.

So, that left the docks, which were happily not too far away from the Black Swan, where the quartet had been drinking.

"Le's go see wot's up, then," Mick suggested; his threesome of bullyboys quickly nodded agreement.

All four ambled out of the pub and quickly made their way through the London fog to the waterfront. In the past, they'd frequently found good pigeons here, especially careless (and solo) sailors either heading for or returning from shore leave. If the sailors were drunk, so much the easier.

"Hope we fin' someone to roll soon," Georgie said. "I'm gettin' parched." And he belched, as if to make his point.

"Parched like yer head," Pete put in—as though *that* made any sense.

Mick laughed and shook his head. "Don' be impatient, lads," he told his boys. "We jus' got to find the right bird to pluck." And he laughed again, because the four of them had "plucked" a few birds in their time as well as rolled more than their share of drunks.

The others laughed at this crude joke, too.

"Mebbe we'll find a nice *rich* bird," Georgie said, practically drooling at the fantasy. "Then we can pluck her an' roll her, too." He laughed at his own "joke."

"Shhhh!" Alex suddenly hissed, and he froze warily.

Mick froze as well. "Quiet, now, lads… *Quiet!*" he whispered. He and the rest pressed themselves up next to the wall of a nearby warehouse.

Right next to the waterward side of the wharf, a figure emerged from the fog.

He was walking fast with his head down, a long woolen coat pulled tight around his frame.

He looked to be a fairly large man, but Mick and his crew were no pipsqueaks (except for Alex who stood five-foot-seven and tipped the scales at barely eight-and-a-half stone). Also, the man seemed to be muttering to himself, which was either a sign of being addle-brained or drunk. Either diagnosis was good news for Mick's gang. And besides, even if the mark had all his wits about him, there were *four* of them.

"Alex, you an' Pete get ahead of 'im." Mick whispered his commands quickly; his boys were used to the routine. "Me an' Georgie will chat 'im up from behind."

Alex and Pete nodded their assent and quickly darted off through the fog; Mick and Georgie emerged from the shelter of the warehouse and fell into step behind their quarry.

The man kept moving, not seeming to notice that he was being followed, which was fine with Mick.

Too bad he's no bird *to pluck,* Mick thought. He licked his lips, remembering Lily, back at the saloon. But she was an *expensive* bird; this target would have to be a real moneybags to have any chance with her. But, who knew? They did say that people who talked to themselves had money in the bank.

"It's not too late… I still have time…" That's what the mark was telling himself, near as Mick could make out.

Rushing to his own funeral—maybe, Mick thought, and he fingered the switchblade secreted in his pocket. Beside him, Georgie slipped a set of brass knuckles onto one oversized fist, just in case things got rough—which, with Georgie, they often did.

Still, the pair of them might as well see if this sheep would *agree* to be fleeced without any trouble.

"Hey, gov," Mick called to their mark. "Spare a few bob for some blokes down on their luck?"

The man in the coat shook his head. "I'm late," he said. "I have to get back to my room…"

"Not even time for a bit of a friendly chat?" Georgie asked, slapping his brass-knuckled hand into his other palm.

"What? No," the man replied, not even turning around. "I can't stop. I have to get back." He seemed annoyed, like he didn't have any time for the boys.

"Toss us a quid, then," Mick said, "and we'll call it even."

The man glanced back at Mick and Georgie, and Mick saw a wild glint in his eye.

A nutter, all right.

"I'm sorry," the man said, not breaking pace. "I can't help you right now. The moon's almost up. I don't have any money."

"Don' have any money?" Alex said, stepping out of the shadows in front of the man. "Wif a fine coat like that?"

"An' 'em fine shoes?" Pete added, appearing out of the fog beside Alex.

"No," the man repeated. "No, I'm sorry." He glanced at Pete and Alex and, maybe because he was larger than both of them, put his head down once more and tried to bull his way through the duo.

But Alex and Pete weren't having any of it. They grabbed the man by both arms and shoved him backwards.

The mark staggered, seemingly surprised at being accosted.

The dimwit really *didn't* have any idea what was going on.

Mick chuckled and shook his head. He almost felt sorry for the bloke. Almost.

"Look," the mark said. "If I had any money, I'd give it to you, but I left it in my room. I really didn't mean to come out at all tonight, but…"

"But he likes a nice stroll in the fog," Georgie said, and barked a deep laugh. Mick and the others laughed as well.

"You don't understand," the man insisted. "The fog doesn't matter. The *moon* will be rising soon…"

"A moon watcher, thissun," Alex said. "Some kinda 'stronamer."

"He'll be seeing *stars*, soon enough, awright," Georgie said, slapping his knuckles into his hand again.

Another round of laughs.

The man looked confused, almost frantic.

"You don't understand," the mark insisted. "The moon, you fools. The *moon*! If you don't let me go, it'll be *too late!*"

"Guv," Mick replied with a grin, "it's *already* too late." And he flicked open his switchblade. "Take 'im, boys. Let's see what 'e's got under that fine coat."

"No!" the man cried, and tried to run, but—as Mick had said—it was too late. Pete and Alex grabbed the mark by both arms before he'd taken even a single step.

The man struggled, realizing his predicament too late. He twisted like a cat caught in a net, and managed to throw Alex —*the poof!*—to the ground, but by then Georgie had got to him.

Georgie outweighed his mates by at least three stone and had paws the size of hams. Now he slammed his brass-clad fist into the man's stomach, and the bloke went down, falling to his knees on the wharf and gasping for air.

Mick smiled. They'd picked a nice, isolated spot for their ambush. Nobody was likely to trundle by and interrupt them.

"Too late!" the man kept gasping. "*Too late!*"

Georgie smiled a wicked smile. "Damn right, Guv," he said. "Shoulda forked over when you could. Now we gotta teach you a *lesson*."

And with that, he, Pete, and Alex began kicking the bloke.

Mick just stood back and admired the work of his gang. He pulled out a cigarette, lit it, and took a draw. The swirling fog parted just a bit, and he caught a glimpse of the full moon, barely poking its head over the roofs of the nearby deserted warehouses. It was a beautiful night for a mugging.

"What in Christ?!" Pete blurted.

And suddenly, he was flying through the air, as if he'd been hit by a lorry. He slammed into a warehouse wall and slumped to the ground.

"Jeezus!" Alex gasped, backing away from the man they'd been kicking.

Amazingly, despite the savage beating he'd endured, their victim was rising to his feet.

Mick flicked away his cigarette and walked toward the man, whom Georgie was still trying to kick.

"Stay down, you blighter!" Georgie commanded. As the mark rose, Georgie rammed his fist into the bloke's gut—but the guy kept getting up!

Georgie screamed. Not the loud, angry scream he gave when his blood was running hot, but a high, girlish scream. He backed away the same way Alex had. And then Mick saw why…

Blood was pouring out of Georgie's belly, like he was a split-open pig. And now his guts were spilling out, too, and splattering onto the wooden planking of the wharf. Steam rose from the entrails, and the air smelled of raw meat and loosed bowels.

Georgie's scream gasped to a sudden stop as he collapsed to his knees, his eyes wide, his mouth gaping. Then he fell onto his flabby face, dead.

The man in the coat turned, but he wasn't a *man* anymore. He was some kind of beast with a hairy face and hands, and fangs in his mouth, and claws dripping with blood. He was a *wolf!*

Mick froze, just as Alex had done, though a few paces further back.

The wolf-man growled and leapt.

Before Alex could even move, the werewolf fell upon him.

With a single snap of his gleaming white fangs, the beast ripped Alex's throat out. Alex toppled to the ground, clutching futilely at his neck, spraying a red rainbow into the night air. He tried to cry out, but only a bloody gurgle escaped his throat. His body twitched wildly as he went down, but he quickly became still.

Pete screamed, which saved Mick, at least for a moment. The werewolf wheeled, looking away from its next obvious victim

(Mick standing paralyzed, so nearby), and focused on the source of the sound.

Pete turned and tried to run, but he must have still been woozy from his fall. His legs seemed to get caught among themselves, and he stumbled.

With two great leaps, the werewolf closed the distance between them and pounced on the dazed mugger.

Pete kept screaming.

Mick turned and ran back the way he'd come. As he went, a horrible ripping sound assaulted his ears. He glanced back just enough to see the monster tearing Pete's head off.

That stopped the screaming.

The werewolf howled in triumph.

Mick's feet pounded across the rotting boards of the wharf, his blood thundering in his ears.

What in the hell was going on? This was *impossible*!

Mick didn't believe in God or Jesus or any of the saints, but he began praying to every one of them as he ran.

He promised to give up mugging people, to give up whoring, even to give up drinking. He swore that he'd find an honest job, that he'd join the Church of England and sing in the choir—become a deacon, if he had to—whatever it took to save his soul… and save his hide!

The pad of swift feet, coming up behind him, echoed to his cauliflower ears.

Mick whirled, switchblade at the ready.

"You want this?" he cried. "Come and get it, ya bast—"

Then the werewolf fell upon him. The heat of its body slamming into the mugger burned Mick like the fires of hell.

He cursed and stabbed the beast in the gut, frantically thrusting his slender switchblade into the furry torso again and again and again.

The werewolf took no notice and tore him to pieces.

Paul Longmire

Paul Longmire awoke covered in blood, not for the first time. Not nearly.

Where was he? For a moment, he had no idea.

It was still dark, but the moon had obviously set—the *damnable* moon!

He was lying on his back on a wharf, the gentle sounds of waves lapping around the pylons whispering in his ears, and the acrid stench of blood and gore assaulting his nostrils.

Paul sat up and looked around, but he saw no sign of anyone, either living or dead. Except, of course, for his blood-drenched clothing. That told him that *someone* else had been here. *Had* been.

"Not again," he whispered, clutching his hands to his head. "Please, God… Not again!"

But it had *happened*. He'd lost track of time once more. The moon had woven its siren spell around him and tempted him out into the night, when he should have been safely chained and locked away from all of humanity.

The wolf had killed someone—*he* had killed someone—*again*.

More than one person, if the amount of blood drenching Paul's clothing was any indication.

There were no bodies lying nearby, but that didn't in any way delude Paul about what he'd done while a werewolf.

But who had he killed? And where? And how?

He staggered to his feet and took a deep breath, leaning against a warehouse wall to steady himself.

He had to get back to his room above the dockside bar. He had to—!

Then the memories of the wolf, what he could decipher of them, hit him. And with them came the relentless tide of grief and remorse.

He'd been in the city, looking for clues to locate the pelt of the Beast of *Gevaudan*—searching for ways to end his curse—when he'd realized that he'd lost track of time. He hadn't *meant* to be out after dark.

But that was how the curse worked; that was how the cognizance of hours and minutes slipped through his grasp just when he needed it most. The beast would have its way! It didn't *want* to be locked up—as it had been the previous night.

Each time he succeeded in chaining the werewolf, the next moonrise proved even *more* difficult.

But Paul had to *try*. He *always* had to try.

So, he'd hurried back to the docks, hoping beyond hope that he could make it to his rented room in time, back to the imagined safety of steel manacles and a locked closet.

He *hadn't* made it. Something had stopped him.

Muggers!

He remembered the four of them now, all predatory smiles and bullying bravado. They'd tried to take his money, though he didn't have any.

He'd killed every last one of them.

They *deserved* it!

Without meaning to, Paul licked his lips.

No! Nobody deserves it. Ever!

Nobody deserved to be killed by the wolf. The beast had no sense of right or wrong; it only knew hunger… and rage.

The things he'd done…!

Paul collapsed to his knees and threw up, trying to ignore the taste of blood and raw meat as he puked his guts out into the River Thames.

For a while, the world swam in dizzy circles.

They'll find the bodies, a voice inside him finally cautioned.

Yes, even though his victims weren't *here*, lying dead beside him, there remained no doubt that the police would discover the bodies. The werewolf didn't believe in cleaning up after itself.

A momentary urge to turn himself in gripped Paul. He would go to the police station and confess to everything. They'd think he was mad, but at least they'd lock him in a cell. Then, when the moon rose, they'd see.

It would be easy...

No. I can't! Not when I'm so close. Somewhere in this city is the pelt of the Beast of Gevaudan. If I can find it, and destroy it, I'll be free of the wolf forever.

Then Paul remembered the paper—the flyer he'd found just before realizing he'd been away from his room too long. He'd stuck that scrap of broadsheet in his pocket...

Patting his gore-slick clothes, Paul quickly found the piece of crumpled poster.

But like all the rest of him, it was drenched in blood. He could only make out a few words, not the address.

"Chamber of Horrors," he read aloud in the dim pre-dawn light. He knew there'd been more last night, but his head was pounding, and he couldn't remember the rest.

He needed sleep. If he got some sleep, maybe he'd remember.

He had to get back to his room. But he couldn't go like this.

Being careful he wasn't observed, Paul found a nearby boating ladder and lowered himself into the chilly waters of the Thames.

It took him the better part of fifteen minutes to scrub all the blood and gore out of his clothes, skin, and hair.

Then he climbed out and trudged back to his dingy rented room above a tavern overlooking the docks.

"Blimey, what happened to *you*, Mr. Long?" the barmaid, who also acted as the innkeeper, asked when he entered. She was a consumptive-looking girl in her late twenties. *Billie*, Paul thought her name was.

"I got mugged," he replied. "They threw me into the river."

"*Cor*! I hope you wasn't hurt none!" Billie said with genuine concern.

Paul shook his head as he trudged up the stairs leading to his tiny room. "It's not as bad as it looks."

And that was true. It was *far worse* than it looked.

It wouldn't get better until he could break the curse for good.

But there was only *one night* of the full moon left this month.

And before the wolf could hurt anyone again, Paul swore he would find that Chamber of Horrors.

8

THE MUMMIES' DEBUT

Topaz Cushing – The Chamber of Horrors
The Third Day of the Full Moon

"Are we ready yet?" Topaz asked hopefully. "Are *you* ready yet?" She looked at her sister, who was still adjusting the fit of her rose-pink blouse, trying to make sure that enough bosom showed to be interesting without appearing sluttish.

As usual, Topaz was less concerned about her appearance. Yes, she wanted to look good—*especially* today—but she'd always felt more comfortable in her own skin than her sister seemed to. Or maybe it was just that Topaz didn't much care about impressing anyone, not even boys, not even now, in the prime of her teenage years.

But maybe that was because boys seemed attracted to her without Topaz even trying. Or was it *because* she didn't try that boys were attracted?

In any case, Opal was in full "knock their eyes out" mode, which Topaz had to admit would probably be good for today's business.

It had taken the better part of two weeks after the mummies arrived for Topaz and her sister (and their occasional helpers) to get all the boxes unpacked, inspected, sorted, and ready for display. During that time, Dr. Cushing's Chamber of Horrors remained something of a mess, and the twins had only been able to conduct very limited tours.

Naturally, their attendance (and income) had fallen off.

And, of course, neither girl had been surprised when Victoria Duprix began sniffing around the place again, dropping hints about the rent soon coming due.

"I expect she'll be the first one at the door when we open today," Topaz told her sister, as they busied themselves with straightening and dusting and other final preparations. "She'll come just to keep an eye on her 'investment.'"

"I'll be happy if that's *all* she keeps her eyes on," Opal replied.

Topaz chuckled her agreement. She, too, had noticed Madame Duprix assessing every young "helper" that ventured into the chamber over the last few weeks, a group that included not only Barry and Frank (as usual) but also tow-headed Charlie Bates ("Bonnie Prince Charlie," Opal called him) and Frank's Anglo-Indian friend, Naveen Patil, as well.

The newcomers were schoolmates of the first two, and had become intrigued with all the work being done in the Chamber by Barry and Frank. So, Naveen and Charlie stopped by to help one day, and just kept coming back.

"Pull them in with the mystery; keep them with sex appeal," Opal had joked when the new "recruits" returned for the third time—and Topaz thought there might be something to that.

Naturally, her sister flirted mercilessly with them all, though Topaz suspected she was doing it more as a pre-emptive strike than anything else. *"The best defense is a good offense,"* and all that.

Because Topaz *did* seem to attract boys more easily than her much-more-forward sister. *"Like hummingbirds to nectar,"* Opal had said—more than once.

So, it wasn't really surprising that the elder twin kept trying to be "extra sweet."

There were no boys flitting around the chamber this morning, though. Both twins felt too nervous to share today's duties with their prospective beaus.

"They'd only stumble all over each other, trying to help," Opal had noted, and Topaz had to agree with her.

The sisters had been working late last night and all morning for the chamber's early afternoon "Grand Re-Opening"—and now the hour was upon them.

"Ready," Opal announced, striding toward the chamber's locked entryway. "Finally. You?"

Topaz nodded. "As ready as I'll ever be."

Opal took a deep breath and unbolted the big double door that served as the Chamber's entrance.

Topaz half expected to find Victoria Price waiting to pounce —like a cat on twin canaries—on the other side.

But instead, she saw the beaming faces of all four of their helpers, each dressed in his Sunday best.

"We've been waiting all week for this," Barry enthused, grinning from ear to ear.

Opal gave him a bemused smile and said fondly: "You idiots! You've already seen the exhibit. You worked on it every day for the last two weeks!"

"B-but how could we miss opening d-day?" Charlie put in shyly.

"These are for you," Frank said, thrusting a bouquet of maroon and white posies into Opal's hands. Opal looked surprised.

"And these are for your very lovely sister," Naveen said. Stepping forward, he handed a bouquet of yellow and white daisies to Topaz and then bowed slightly.

"Thank you," both twins said.

"You really shouldn't have," Opal added.

"They're lovely," Topaz concluded.

The boys all kept smiling.

Opal stepped aside and gestured that they should enter.

"What about ad-m-mission?" Charlie asked.

"Yes, we can't come in without paying," Barry said.

"But you helped us…" Opal began.

"Nonsense," Frank said, digging in his pockets. "How much is it—a quid?"

"Only sixpence," Topaz said, blushing despite herself.

"Well, it's worth a quid," Frank replied. "Here's a bob, then," and he tossed the coin into their coffer. "I guess I'm paying for Barry, too." Then he proceeded into the exhibit's entryway.

"The devil you are!" Barry exclaimed, shoving his hand deep into his own pocket. Topaz had noticed that while he wasn't as rich as Frank, he would never let anyone pay his freight. He, too, tossed in a whole shilling and followed after Frank.

Charlie grinned wordlessly and did the same, though Topaz noted he had to dig slightly harder to come up with the coin. Charlie's family was well off, but not nearly so much as the other three. Probably he couldn't entirely afford it, but he wasn't about to let his friends embarrass him.

Naveen stopped and nodded a polite bow to each of the twins. "I was going to give you sixpence each," he said. "But I find myself short on small change, so a shilling each it will have to be." He tossed the coins in the admission box and joined his friends inside. The other boys laughed convivially at his extravagance.

Topaz smiled. She knew that outspending his fellows was Naveen's way of fitting in, and the others gladly tolerated it. Sometimes the rest, even Barry, would let Naveen pay for ice cream and such when they were out and about. Last week, after a hard day's work, he insisted on buying "American-style Malted Milkshakes" for everyone. (As near as Topaz could tell, the only difference from the usual malted was the higher price.)

More paying customers waited beyond the quartet of young men, though, to Topaz, none appeared likely to be as generous as the twin's prospective beaus.

There was a slender man in a bowler hat, carrying a newspaper and umbrella under his arm (though today's paper had not predicted rain). Then came a sour-faced woman—*nanny*, Topaz thought—with two boys about half Topaz's age. After that, two dapper middle-aged fellows chatting non-stop as they waited.

Art critics, said something in Topaz's mind. Though she wasn't quite sure where such thoughts came from, she had learned to trust her instincts; they seldom failed her, just as the cards seldom failed her sister.

And, last night, the cards had been propitious for today's opening, which put both girls more at ease.

The pair smiled and took a sixpence from each customer, ushering them into the foyer of the exhibit space.

As each stepped over the threshold, Opal gave them the standard greeting:

"Welcome to Dr. Cushing's Chamber of Horrors. Our first tour will begin in a few minutes. Please feel free to look around the exhibits until then."

Soon, quite a number of people were standing and admiring the exhibits, waiting for the next tour.

"Not the swarm I was hoping for," Opal whispered to her sister, "but…"

"But hopefully enough to give us a leg up on the rent," Topaz whispered back. She flashed her dark-haired twin a smile.

Opal returned it, her blue-green eyes flashing playfully. "At least our 'willing victims' have given us a head start on that."

Both girls laughed quietly for a moment. Then Topaz asked: "Who's conducting the first tour, you or me?"

"You go ahead. I'll stay here and enjoy the jingling of cash in our coffers." Opal gave the till a little shake. "Ah! Music to my ears."

"And biscuits in our bellies," Topaz added. "Be back soon."

With that, she joined the small crowd in the foyer.

"Welcome to Dr. Cushing's World-Famous Chamber of Horrors," she began. "We're so glad that you could join us on this very special occasion. Today, we're opening a brand-new exhibit: The Accursed Mummies from a Forgotten Dynasty!

"These three mummies were acquired at great expense—and considerable peril—by our father, Dr. Leigh Cushing, during his most recent trip to Egypt. Three members of his expedition perished during the recovery, and Dr. Cushing himself only barely escaped a hair-raising death."

This last was only partly true. The worst that had happened to their father was a bout of tropical fever, which *had* been life-threatening, if not actually hair-raising. But a porter and a guide had been slain by devilish traps secreted within the tombs, and (later) a young Egyptologist had perished under mysterious circumstances. Though this death was likely caused, like their father's fever, by an unknown malady, the locals had said it was the curse of the forgotten queen buried in the tomb.

"So, before you enter the exhibit," Topaz continued, "be warned: Not all who have looked upon the faces of these mummies have survived." She pointed ominously toward an unlit space in the exhibit hall where the new display rested.

"To ward off any bad omens or evil spirits still attached to these mummies, I will now light the Everburning Torch of Sekhmet, the lion-headed warrior goddess who was daughter to the sun god Ra. The torch was discovered in the tomb of Sethotep—master tomb builder, and the first mummy I'll be showing you today."

Normally, Topaz and her sister would have saved the mummies for the end of the tour, but today they had decided to do the new attraction first, to reduce crowding and increase traffic flow.

Topaz picked up a lit candle that they'd placed on a small table by the torch's wall sconce for just this moment, so they wouldn't have to fiddle with temperamental lighters and ruin the exhibit's atmosphere.

She took down the torch and held it near to the flame.

"It is said," she intoned gravely, "that once lit, the flame from this sacred torch is unquenchable. It will burn forever unless snuffed by its golden cap, seen here connected to the base of the torch by a gilded chain. Behold!"

And with that, she lit the torch.

It flared up immediately, producing a brilliant almost-white flame.

The small crowd gasped appreciatively.

Topaz was impressed, too, every time she lit it. And, so far as she knew, the claim she'd made was true. She and Opal had not managed to extinguish the torch by any means other than using its special snuffer, though they'd tried water and smothering with a wet rag (which caught fire) and several other non-destructive means.

"What craft of the ancients may have constructed this amazing artifact remains unknown, but neither Dr. Cushing nor we, his daughters, have been able to extinguish its light other than by the prescribed means. And now, with the light of Sekhmet protecting us… Let's visit the mummies!"

Topaz carried the torch into the unlit space while, at the same time, Opal flipped the switch and the lights came up in that tiny section of the room, revealing the three mummy cases, one unadorned (the guard), one carved with elaborate hieroglyphic curses (the tomb builder/architect), and one painted in fabulous colors (the queen).

The first tour went well, and though the exhibit space was small and somewhat cramped, those visiting did seem to appreciate the artifacts, especially with Topaz spinning (mostly true) tales of the ancient past and the perils braved to recover the items in the display.

The four young men seemed suitably impressed (though they'd seen all the pieces during the unpacking), as did the nanny's youthful charges. The art critics buzzed appreciatively, and lingered with the mummies while the tour moved on through the rest of the museum.

The suitors continued wandering around the chamber as further tours commenced—even though they probably knew the Chamber of Horrors like the backs of their own hands at this point.

That made a happy glow spring up in Topaz's chest. *They really are quite wonderful fellows... all four of them.*

The second tour, which Opal conducted while Topaz tended the till, also went well, as did the next, which Topaz took, again.

Topaz was just finishing up with that third tour group when a commanding figure appeared at the chamber's entryway.

There stood Victoria Price, dressed very stylishly (and fashionably late, as usual). She flashed a bright smile, which Topaz took as insincere, and said, "Good afternoon, ladies. Let's see what all the racket you've been making for the past weeks has been about."

"There's sixpence admission," Opal told her flatly.

Topaz swooped up the short steps to the entryway quickly. "But for you, Madame Duprix, admission is *always* free." She curtsied and tried to put more genuine warmth into her smile than Victoria (or Opal) had managed.

Opal stepped back and theatrically bowed their landlady into the entryway, "Welcome to Dr. Cushing's Chamber of Horrors. Our next tour will begin in a few minutes. Please feel free to look around the exhibits until then."

"What's all this mummy frippery you've been fussing about

since those dreadful boxes arrived?" Victoria asked. "Such a clamor! Do you really think it will bring more customers?"

"See for yourself," Opal replied through gritted teeth.

"Yes, they're here *now*, darling," Victoria said, "but will they return, day after day, week after week?" Her eyes glinted darkly as she glanced around the newly rearranged chamber. Then those hazel orbs lit upon something they liked…

"Still," Madame Duprix said, "there may be *some* things here worth looking at." And with that, she wandered over toward the handsome young suitors.

"It's gonna be hard to ogle our boyfriends with two black eyes," Opal muttered, rolling up the sleeves of her blouse and girding the belt of her maroon skirt.

"Don't let her bother you," Topaz whispered. "The boys won't be interested in her. She's just an old bag of bones."

"It's what she wants to *do* with those bones that worries me," Topaz shot back. Her face reddened as Victoria took Charlie's arm. "Bonnie Prince Charlie" seemed more than willing to show the older woman around.

"Easy, girl," Topaz said as Opal growled under her breath.

"Sorry to be so late," said a pleasant voice. "Have I missed anything?"

Both twins turned to find Vincent Duprix at the entryway. The sculptor beamed at them.

"Sixpence, isn't it?" he asked, and dropped his coin in the box before waiting for a reply.

Topaz noticed that his left hand was bandaged, and for a moment, it reminded her of the mummies they were displaying. She shuddered.

"I see you've already got the party started," the sculptor said. The gaze from his bright blue eyes wandered around the chamber before settling on his wife, now hip-to-hip with Charlie and clutching the boy's arm tight. Vincent's eyes narrowed. "Well," he said, "at least *some* of us are having a good time." He gave the twins a slight bow. "Pardon me, ladies, I think I'll go have a look at a mummy."

"I wonder if he means his wife," Opal whispered as he left.

Topaz giggled. "He can look at her any old time."

"But I don't think he cares to."

Indeed, Vincent barely spared a glance at Victoria and instead went directly to the new mummy exhibit. Victoria flashed him her insincere smile as he passed.

"I have a bad feeling about those two," Topaz said. "We don't want them quarreling in the exhibit. Do you want to keep an eye on them, or should I?"

"You," Opal replied. "I don't think I could without punching her."

So, Topaz wandered the exhibit answering questions and conducted the next tour as well. And it was a good thing she was out and about, as it didn't take long for the Duprixes to "bump into" each other. When they did, the sparks began to fly, and Charlie quickly (and wisely) beat a hasty retreat.

"I won't have you hanging around, bothering these girls and pooh-poohing their new exhibit," Vincent was saying as Topaz came within earshot.

"But I'm not bothering them, dearest," Victoria replied. "I was just talking to one of their friends."

"More than *talking*, it looked like to me."

"Can I help it if young men find me charming?" Victoria asked.

"With a little *encouragement* from you," Vincent said.

"Just as *you've* encouraged a model or two in the past—and perhaps even now. Who is your current model, dear husband? Is it one of the twins? Is that why you haven't pressed them about their rent?"

"Don't be absurd! Why should we continually nag our tenants over a few shillings?"

"Because we *need* the money, dear Vincent. Your waxworks makes even less income than the twins' pathetic displays."

Vincent stepped closer to his wife, blue eyes blazing. "Perhaps if you took better care of our finances and fewer trips to the theater…"

Just when Topaz thought she was going to have to step in, up swept a blonde woman in a fashionable green ensemble. She smiled at both of the Duprixes.

"Victoria, darling! Your new exhibit is ghoulishly delightful," the woman said, seeming actually delighted. Topaz now recognized the newcomer as Lily Carlson, one of Victoria's best friends. She visited the waxworks frequently, and often had dinner with the Duprixes.

"It's not *mine*, darling," Victoria replied. "It belongs to our charming tenants."

"Close enough," Lily said. "They do pay rent to you, after all. *Their* success is your success."

Victoria frowned. "Vincent and I were just discussing that."

"Were you?" Lily asked drolly.

"Lily," Vincent said, giving her a slight bow to acknowledge her arrival.

"Vincent," she said, bobbing her blonde head in return. She held out her hand, and he kissed it.

A wave of relief washed over Topaz. With their friend here, there was no way the Duprixes would make a scene. She could go back to conducting tours and answering questions.

As she slipped back into the crowd, though, a man brushed past her.

"Excuse me," he said and continued walking, with his head down, until he'd swept past Opal and out the exit.

Topaz gasped, and a chill shot through her entire body.

She felt dizzy for a moment—though not long enough for anyone, even the suitors, to notice. When she recovered, she hurried to her sister, still tending the door.

"That man who just left…" Topaz said. "Do you know who he was? Did you get a good look at him?"

"No," Opal said. "Why?"

"He bumped into me, and—"

Her sister's eyes blazed angrily. "Are you saying that creep groped you?!"

Topaz shook her head. "No, no. Nothing like that. He was just trying to get to the door. But when he brushed past me, I got the most awful feeling, like he'd been involved in some terrible crime… murder, or—"

"I usually don't doubt your intuitions, sister dear, but he just seemed like a normal person to me."

Topaz shuddered. "Opal, I'm *certain* of it. There's something dreadful hanging over that man's soul. Either he's committed a terrible crime recently… or he's going to very soon. Maybe even *tonight!*"

9

POLICE ON THE SCENE

*Inspector Harry Dennis – The Docks of London
That Same Day*

Inspector Harry Dennis shook his head, exhausted. It had been a long day already, and this visit to the docks made it clear that his tour of duty wasn't going to end any time soon.

What lay before him was a *terrible* crime.

Most of his juniors were busy losing their lunches, either around the corners of the nearby dilapidated warehouses or off the side of the wharf into the Thames. (Damn considerate of them to try not to spoil the crime scene.)

And what a horrific scene it was!

With all the mess, it was a wonder someone hadn't run across the murders sooner—not that a situation like this would have been easier to stomach after *breakfast* rather than after lunch.

Dennis didn't blame the junior officers and patrolmen for getting sick, but he'd been in the Great War and had seen more than a few appalling things out on the front lines. Few as horrendous as this, though:

A wide swath of blood and guts carpeted the aging riverside boardwalk, and body parts lay strewn all around. It was an awful thing to have to see, and the carnage made it hard to tell how many people might have been slaughtered.

Dennis had a hunch he knew the number of victims, though: *four*. And he probably knew who all of them were, too—"Mick" McDowell and his gang. (Dennis had recognized one of the severed heads.)

"S'pose I'll have to give the wife a ring, if we can find a phone anywhere around here," he mused aloud. "Tell her I'll be late for dinner."

"I think I spotted a call box a few blocks back when we were drivin' in," Sergeant Bruce Hoey observed. He was the only other member of the team who wasn't busy vomiting. (He'd fought against the Germans as well.) "I'm sure the operator back at the station wouldn't mind patchin' you through to home."

"Thanks, Sergeant. I may just do that, once we get this mess a bit more… tidied up."

"Tidied up is right, sir. I haven't seen anythin' like this in all me born days, not even during the war. Nor do I hope to ever see its like again!"

"I agree with you there, Sergeant."

"Although…"

And the sergeant paused, as if waiting for permission to continue.

Dennis furrowed his brow. Sometimes, Hoey could be a bit obtuse and over-deferential where authority was concerned, even though the two of them had been working together for close to five years. "Although *what*, Sergeant?"

"It does put me to mind of somethin' I heard from me old dad recently…"

Hoey's father, Nigel Hoey, was Chief of Police in Longford, a small town in Derbyshire, about a half day's travel from London. "Well? Out with it, man."

"About a month back, me old man ran across a similar grizzly scene."

"Murder?"

"Well, that's the thing of it, sir. It was hard to say for sure. The victim was near ripped to pieces, just like these blokes. He was a stone-cutter by trade, worked in one of the local quarries. He was something of a rapscallion, as you might say—bit of a drunkard who liked to get into fights. Also did a bit of poachin', to hear me dad tell it.

"The thing is, even for all that, nobody in town seemed to hold enough of a grudge against the man to want to kill him—not like *that*, anyway. Found what was left of him in the woods, they did, practically torn limb from limb."

"Maybe he ran into another poacher and got into some kind of dispute."

"Me dad checked into that, sir, but it didn't pan out. All the locals are pretty upstandin' citizens, as you'd understand in a place as small as Longford. It's not a good spot to be tryin' to keep secrets—not more than the usual ones, anyway—and there hadn't been no itinerants drifting through the area lately, either."

"Well, if your father didn't think it was murder, Sergeant, what was it?"

"*Wolves*, sir."

"Wolves, Sergeant? Don't be absurd! There haven't been any wolves in England since the seventeenth century—not even in Derbyshire."

"They said there was one up in Scotland back around the turn of the century, sir."

"But Scotland is *not* Derbyshire—and it's certainly not London. You're not suggesting that a wolf did *this*, are you Sergeant? I'm sure we'd have had reports if any had escaped from a zoo. And it would take a whole pack of wolves—rabid ones, at that, I'd say—to overpower four grown men like this. 'Mick' McDowell and his bully boys were *not* known for their delicate and retiring ways."

"Be that as it may, sir. I'm just tellin' you what happened with me old dad, up north. A wolf was what the coroner figured done it, though me dad figured it was more likely some kind of large dog or hound. They never did turn one up, though, despite searchin' the farms and kennels from Derby to Stoke-on-Trent. Checked the circuses and travelin' shows, too, and even the local gypsies. Didn't find neither a hair nor a tooth of the beast what done it."

Inspector Dennis rubbed his temples, futilely trying to ward off the headache building behind his eyes.

"I'm not sure what help all that is here, Sergeant," he finally said. "Unless you're suggesting that some kind of dog might have done this." He tried to make plain with his tone that he didn't think it likely.

"Maybe a *trained* dog, sir," Hoey suggested.

"Trained dog…!" Dennis scoffed. "Although…"

"Although what, sir?"

"A dog trained by a rival gang, and then used to cover up their crimes… That *might* explain it."

"It might indeed, sir."

Dennis frowned. "That doesn't seem very likely, though. Why go to all that trouble?"

"McDowell was not much liked, sir."

"But it's not like he and his mates were a *real* gang, either," Dennis noted. "They were just ruffians who liked to beat up strangers for drinking money. Certainly, there were a few more serious crimes on their rap sheets, but nothing that might have put them in the way of the tongs or the IRA or any *true* gangsters."

"Maybe they decided to branch out into new territories, and bit off more than they could chew, as it were."

"Maybe," Dennis said. He doubted it, though. "I almost wish it *were* a gang, Sergeant."

"Why is that, sir?"

"Because, Sergeant, if it's *not* a gang, then that means we've got a *real* problem on our hands. Lack of a gangland connection means there's a maniac loose on the streets of London, and we have no idea who he is or where he might strike next."

10

PAUL VISITS THE CHAMBER OF HORRORS

Paul Longmire – London
The Next Day

Paul Longmire stood in the shadows, watching the entrance of Dr. Cushing's Chamber of Horrors very carefully, waiting for it to open. He kept himself hidden in the alleyway across the street, between a bakery (already closed until late afternoon, following the morning rush), and an antique store that didn't look like it was ever really open.

He could have perched himself on a bench beneath the trees in Olde Kennington Park, just down the street, but he would have been much easier to spot there, and after the incident two nights ago, he wasn't sure whether the police might be looking for him or not.

Thank God he hadn't killed anyone last night. But even chained, the beast had still made a shambles of his room above the tavern. Luckily, Billie the barkeep hadn't been brave enough to see what all the commotion was about. Nor had she called the police during the incident, probably because many of her tenants were engaged in other activities even less savory than

Paul—in werewolf form—bursting out of the closet and tearing up the place.

Paul had cleared out of the inn as soon as he'd recovered his senses. He'd even left most of his money to pay for the damages, though he knew it wouldn't be nearly enough.

Had Billie called the police by now? Certainly, she *should* have. And if she had, and if drink and tuberculosis hadn't clouded her mind, she should have been able to give the authorities a pretty clear description of "Paul Long," the bloke who had committed the mayhem.

Are they hunting for me even now? Paul wondered as he stood in the shadows, waiting.

Would they catch him *right this moment,* just when he seemed so close to the end of his quest?

I can't let them take me, he thought frantically, every nerve in his body jangling. All his senses seemed magnified, especially hearing and smell, a phenomenon he'd noticed before, especially during the days after he'd turned into the wolf.

But at least the third night of the full moon had passed. He had survived, and he hadn't killed anyone else. It would be a whole month before the curse took him again, and by then—God willing—he would have found his cure.

Please let this be it, he prayed.

After more than a week of fruitlessly searching every museum in the city, he'd found his only clue in an ancient poster pasted on a battered street kiosk. The flyer had been largely plastered over with other announcements, but just enough of it had remained to catch Paul's attention.

He'd quickly torn off the obscuring posters and found himself staring at a flyer for Dr. Cushing's Chamber of Horrors and its list of attractions. There, among the other tawdry entries, lay the phrase he'd been hoping to find, the thing he'd been looking for ever since meeting the gypsy witch Maria:

The pelt of the Beast of Gevaudan!

The words seemed to leap off of the ratty broadside and sear themselves directly into his brain.

That had been two days ago, just before he'd tried to return to his room by the docks. Just before those men had tried to mug him, and...

He couldn't bear to think of it.

Though he'd stuffed the flyer into his jacket pocket, the paper had been badly damaged in the fight. He could no longer read the name of the exhibit, nor where it was located. It had taken Paul most of the day yesterday to track down the chamber's address—Dr. Cushing's Chamber of Horrors wasn't a very well known, or advertised, attraction.

I was lucky to find it at all.

But he had found it, and once inside, he *thought* he'd caught a glimpse of the thing he most desired—the wolf skin he needed to destroy.

The exhibit had been crowded, though, far too crowded to try anything rash, or even to be *certain* that the object of his quest was indeed hanging there, in a picture frame on the wall.

Please let it be true. Please let it be the one.

He wanted to linger and make sure, but then—thank heaven—he'd had a moment of clarity:

It was getting late! The sun would set soon, and then the moon would rise, and after that, Paul wouldn't be responsible for his actions—after that, he'd kill again.

So he had fled the tiny museum as quickly as he could and returned to his rented room. There, he'd chained himself up and locked himself in the closet.

And those restraints had been enough—*barely*—but they'd been enough.

He had *not* killed again.

For *once* he'd beaten the curse!

And if he could just destroy that pelt, he'd defeat it for good.

But I have to be sure...

So, now he waited in the alley for the museum to open, and shortly before noon, it finally did.

An attractive brunette girl—eighteen perhaps—stepped through the big double doors that led to the exhibit and put out a placard that read: *Open for Business.*

That's what Paul had been waiting for. As the girl retreated into the building, he checked left and right, looking for police, one last time. He didn't see any, so he stepped out of the shadows and walked briskly across the nearly deserted street and up the short flight of steps to the entrance.

He opened the door and quickly slipped inside the eight-by-ten-foot entryway. A small chime affixed to the top of the door sounded as he came in.

To Paul's left stood short flight of stairs up leading to a glass-paned doorway marked "Duprix Waxworks" with a sign hanging on it that said "Closed." Ahead lay a solid oak door that, he assumed, must lead to a stairway and the living chambers he'd noticed above the street-level shops. To his right a pair of grand double-doors opened up onto a landing atop the stairs that led down into the Chamber of Horrors, which lay partially below street level.

A sign on the landing read: *Admission – Sixpence.*

Paul fished into his pockets. He thought he had just enough to pay his way inside and then perhaps get a meal and a cheap room later. If he was lucky, he might stretch what he had a few days longer. He would have to act quickly though, before his money ran out.

I'll come back tonight, after they close, and steal it, he mused.

At least, that was the plan *if* the place really did contain the beast's pelt. *If* fate wasn't playing another terrible joke on him.

Paul closed his eyes and tipped his face up toward the ceiling.

Please...!

"May I help you?" asked a pleasant voice.

Paul opened his eyes and tried to relax, but every fiber of his being remained tense.

Before him stood the brunette girl he'd seen opening the shop a few minutes before.

"I'd like to take the tour," he said, thrusting his hands into the pockets of his trench coat, so that she wouldn't see him trembling.

The girl's blue-green eyes sparkled, and she held out a smooth-skinned hand. "You're our first customer of the day," she said. "Sixpence, please."

She was very beautiful—so young and full of life—but Paul hadn't come here to flirt with pretty girls. He forced his hand to stop shaking and gave her the money. She dropped it in the admission box resting on a stand at the top of the stairway. The coin made an empty *thunk* when it hit the bottom of the box.

"Do you want me to run the tour, Opal?" someone called from deeper inside the little museum. Paul caught a glimpse of blonde hair flashing between the exhibits.

"That's all right, Topaz," the brunette—Opal, Paul deduced—said. "I'll take this one. You can tend the gate." She looped her slender arm around his. "Right this way, sir. Mind the step."

"I'll be there after I dust the Marquis' skull," the other girl, Topaz, now hidden around a corner, called back.

"Opal and Topaz, eh?" Paul said, interested despite himself. "Quite a pair of precious stones. Are you sisters?"

"Twins, actually," Opal said as they walked down the stairs to the exhibit floor. "I'm the older one."

"Only by thirteen minutes," Topaz called from the hidden nook where she was working.

"And you're Opal?"

"Yes."

"I'm Paul. Are you related to the doctor—Dr. Cushing, I mean?"

"We're his daughters," Opal explained. "We run the place while he's off on expeditions—which is most of the time."

She smiled at him, and for a moment Paul's troubles seemed to slip away. In that instant, he was just a young man talking to a pretty girl in the heart of a thriving city.

"Does your mother work here, too?" he asked.

The girl's face darkened. "She's dead."

"Oh. I'm sorry."

"Don't be. It happened a long time ago." She sighed away the sadness and smiled at him again. "But listen to *me*, Paul, talking about family when I'm supposed to be giving you a tour." She took a deep breath, her eyes flashing playfully again.

"Welcome to Dr. Cushing's World-Famous Chamber of Horrors," she said, "home to an exciting new exhibit: The Accursed Mummies from a Forgotten Dynasty. We'll get to the mummies near the end of our tour, but I have a lot to show you before then. For our first stop, we come to the End of the World. This is the fabled Meteor of Tunguska, the explosion of which flattened nearly a thousand square miles of Russian forest on the morning of June 30th, 1908…"

The girl, Opal, was charming, and Paul supposed that the information she was relaying to him about the museum's exhibits must have been very interesting, but he couldn't concentrate on any of it. Meteors and sea monsters and iron maidens and mummies… none of it mattered to him.

There was only one display that he really needed to know about, but he didn't want to arouse suspicion by asking her to skip all the rest and go there directly. After all, if the pelt went missing after he demanded to see it above all the other items in the Chamber of Horrors, who would the police come looking for?

And the police were the *last* thing Paul needed—even if by then he *had* broken the curse.

Please, let this be the one…

Just when his anticipation had built to nearly the breaking point, they came to it:

"And this," Opal said, "Is the pelt of the *Beast of Gevaudan*."

The words shot like fire through Paul's nervous system.

It was true! It was *here*! He'd found it!

"In eighteenth-century France," the girl continued, "this monster attacked over two-hundred people—and killed more than a hundred! Legend has it that no normal weapon could pierce its hide, and that only a bullet blessed by the Pope himself finally brought the beast down." She smiled at him, pleased with her presentation. "Quite a beauty, isn't it?"

The reddish-black scruffy pelt hung on the wall, framed in rustic wood and pinned behind a thick sheet of glass. It was at least nine feet long and half that wide.

"Are you sure that's a wolf?" Paul asked, his mouth dry. He could hardly believe that his quest for a cure might be coming to its end. "It looks more the size of a bear."

"Don't let the size fool you. Note the point of the snout and the long tail—both clearly indicating that this pelt belongs to a wolf.

Paul could barely breathe. "Not an ordinary wolf."

"No, sir," Opal said. "This monster terrorized the French countryside for three years before a lucky hunter felled it."

"Yes," Paul mused. "You'd have to be lucky to kill such a beast."

"Are you a hunter, sir?" the girl asked.

Painful memories of being both hunter and prey flashed through Paul's mind. "Yes," he replied. "Yes, I was. Once. A long time ago."

"Then you can imagine what it must have taken to bring down such a brute—a lucky shot, and a silver bullet, blessed by no less than Pope Clement XIII."

"*...A silver bullet...*"—the one sure way to bring down a werewolf. But, if the beast had been properly killed, why had the werewolf line continued? Had the gypsy been wrong, or…? What *exactly* was it that she'd told him…?

Paul felt a black cloud descending over his brain, and knew that the curse was fighting him again, confusing his mind, trying to keep him from the cure. He squeezed his eyes shut and tried to concentrate.

"Are you all right, Paul?" Opal asked.

"What's going on? Is something wrong?" asked a new voice.

No! He couldn't let anyone see anything was wrong. He had to appear normal.

Paul opened his eyes and saw Topaz, her bright blond hair seeming to glimmer in the dim light of the exhibit hall. She stared at him with her gem-like blue-green eyes.

Something about those liquid eyes seemed to peer right into the blackness at the center of Paul's soul. He felt as though his heart were being squeezed by an invisible fist.

"No, I…" he began. "I don't feel well, all of a sudden. I need to get some air."

And with that he dashed to the nearest stairway and through the door at the top of it, out of the exhibit hall.

"Wait!" Opal cried after him. "That's not—!"

But by then he was through the door and had it closed tight behind him.

"Oh!" gasped an unexpected female voice.

And then… *CRASH!* Something large clattered to the floor.

Paul looked around, the cloud of panic clearing from his brain. He wasn't outside at all; he was in another exhibit space, one filled with strangely costumed people.

It took him a moment to realize that only *one* of the people was moving, a handsome middle-aged woman with slightly greying hair. As Paul gaped at her, she stooped and tried to pick up the display cabinet she'd apparently knocked over when he arrived.

"I'm terribly sorry," he said, going to help her. "Here. Let me get that…"

The woman looked at him, sternly at first, but then her expression softened. "It's quite all right," she said. "I'm sure you didn't mean to."

"No, I didn't," Paul replied. "I just got somewhat dizzy down in the Chamber of Horrors. I needed a little air, but I guess I stumbled out the wrong door."

"Well, I can't say I blame you," the woman said, putting her hand on his shoulder as he stooped to pick up the cabinet, "all those *dreadful* things they've got down there."

Her fingers felt warm, even through his shirt.

Behind them, the door he'd come through swung open, and Opal appeared at the threshold. "Paul," she said, "are you all right?"

The older women's eyes grew cold once more. "Everything's fine, silly girl," she said. "We had a bit of an accident, but it's all better now. Isn't it?"

"Yes," Paul replied. "Yes, I guess it is."

Opal didn't look convinced, but the older woman glared at her until she closed the door anyway.

"Those Cushing girls…!" the woman said with a *tsk*. "Never far behind when something goes wrong."

"I don't think that's very fair," Paul replied. With a mighty heave, he righted the cabinet. Fortunately, the items inside it—books, mostly—seemed neither breakable nor damaged. "She was only trying to help."

"Well, Paul…" the older woman began. "Paul… That *was* your name, wasn't it? Or had that Cushing girl got it wrong?"

"Yes. It's Paul. Paul… Shaw."

"Well, Mr. Shaw, I'm sure you're probably right, and the girl didn't mean any harm. But it's such a trial living with teenagers underfoot!"

"Oh, do you live here as well? I thought Opal had said her mother was dead."

"I'm not her mother, *per se*—though sometimes I certainly feel like it, despite the fact that I'm obviously not old enough to be."

"Obviously."

She extended her hand, and Paul shook it. "I'm Victoria Duprix. My husband and I own this building, including the space we rent to the Cushings, as well as this waxworks that you're standing in currently."

Now that his heart had started beating regularly again, Paul took a better look around. The room they stood in was very large and filled with tableaus of wax figures: Joan of Arc, Richard III, Helen of Troy, Napoleon, Lady Godiva on her horse, and numerous others that he didn't recognize immediately, as well as more than a few classical-looking nudes. The figures seemed to be expertly sculpted, though the displays were somewhat bland compared to the lurid exhibits in the Chamber of Horrors.

"It's very nice, Mrs. Duprix," he said. "I'm sure you and your husband must be very proud."

"Oh yes," she said, "but do call me 'Victoria.'"

"Very well, Victoria."

"My husband is a sculptor, as you might guess. He spends most of his time working in his studio, while I run the business."

"That must be a lot of work."

"It is," she replied. "More work than one person can handle, at times. And Vincent… Well, you know, his head's in the clouds most days; he's not much for cleaning up and rearranging the displays. I shouldn't even have been trying to move that cabinet by myself, but…" She shrugged.

"Well, it's lucky I stumbled in, then."

"Yes. Lucky," she said, and a gleam came to her pretty hazel eyes. "You know, Mr. Shaw…"

"Call me Paul. Please."

"You know, Paul, you seem like a strong, vital fellow. You wouldn't by chance be looking for work, would you?"

With the current state of the economy that was almost a silly question—many, many people were looking for work, not just in London but worldwide, nowadays—but her query still caught Paul somewhat by surprise.

Was he looking for work?

Yes, he was nearly out of money, but could he even *think* about such things with this curse hanging over his head?

When he hesitated, she smiled and batted her eyes at him. "Of course, I couldn't pay much, but it would be steady employment..."

"Working here? With you?" he asked, more to buy time to think than anything else.

"Yes, with me and my husband," she replied, "here in the waxworks—cleaning and fixing and moving things and such."

Here, in the waxworks... Right next to the Chamber of Horrors that held the key to his salvation.

Yes! Why not? It was almost as though, after daunting him for years, God was finally giving Paul the opportunity he needed—the opportunity to be *free*.

He would work in the waxworks and find out everything he could about the operations of it and the chamber. Then, when the time was right, he'd steal the wolf skin and destroy it. That's what the gypsy had said—he remembered it now—he had to *destroy* the pelt.

"How soon can I start?" he asked.

"You can begin tomorrow, bright and early, and I'll pay you every Friday, after closing. Will four shillings a day be enough? It will be hard work, but it won't be full-time. You'll have plenty of moments to relax."

She smiled winningly at him.

The money wasn't much, but Friday was only three days

away. He could stretch his pocket change to last until then—if he was careful.

"Yes. Yes, that would be fine."

And maybe by then he'd have figured out when and how to destroy the pelt.

And once he did that, he'd be free.

Finally, free!

11

NEW ARRIVALS

*Opal Cushing – 1951 Fisher St.
Several Days Later*

Paul Shaw's sudden appearance as a new employee at the waxworks had taken both twins by surprise, though only Opal seemed to be thrilled with this new development:

"Having a handsome young man around the place every day?" she'd remarked the day after he started. "How can that be bad? Besides, he's only working for the old witch part time. Maybe he can help *us* in his free time." She grinned in anticipation, and not just about moving boxes and rearranging displays.

"It depends on what kind of 'help' you want, I guess," Topaz had replied, as usual seeming to sense her sister's inner thoughts. "Besides, he's not *that* young. I bet he's at least five or six years older than you and me."

"Young enough," Opal had said with a wink. "Besides, I'm a little tired of *boys*, and it'll nice to have a *man* on hand if you need one."

"You? Tired of boys?" her sister had countered. "Not bloody likely!'

And maybe—Opal had to grudgingly admit—her sister had been right.

For while she'd found numerous occasions to test Paul's handiness in the days that followed, she'd certainly never turned away Frank Browning when he showed up, either. And Frank seemed to be dropping by more and more frequently "Just to check in."

Sometimes he came with the others—who still seemed determined to win her sister's favor (though Topaz remained largely aloof)—and other times he came by himself. Often, he brought flowers, and once even a small box of chocolates. (Though he brought one for Topaz as well, seeming not to want to incite any sibling jealousy.)

Opal wondered if, perhaps, this surge in teenage attentiveness was due to Paul's presence. Were the young wolves responding to an older one encroaching on "their territory"?

She grinned. If so, so much the better for her!

Paul, for his part, almost seemed eager to spend time in the Chamber of Horrors with the twins. He helped them with various minor tasks, which basically consisted of any small thing that Opal could devise for him to do. Occasionally, Topaz would (reluctantly) make a request as well.

Despite his helpfulness with the chamber, Paul still spent far more time working for Victoria—which was only right, as she was paying him (if only a pittance).

It did seem to Opal, though, that Madame Duprix's chores were largely make-work, as well.

Did she just hire him to have a handsome man around the waxworks? Opal wondered. It certainly seemed possible. She and Topaz had both noticed the older woman's eyes wandering over "their" young men—and pretty much any handsome hunk of manhood that ambled in or around 1951 Fisher.

Topaz remained more cautious, so it didn't surprise Opal when, while tidying up the chamber for opening on the Sunday after Paul started working for Victoria, her twin said:

"I'm still not sure about Mr. Shaw." Topaz's blue-green eyes, mirrors to Opal's own, narrowed. "There's something I don't trust about him—something he's not telling us."

"I'm sure there's a *lot* he's not telling us," Opal replied. "We've only known him a little while, and Victoria monopolizes most of his time. She's even got him working *today*—and this is supposed to be his day off."

"I'm certain he needs the money," Topaz noted. "She's not paying him very well. *We* could almost pay him that much."

For a moment, the thought of paying Paul, at having him at her beck and call all the time, glittered in Opal's thoughts like a brass ring dangling just out of reach—so tantalizing. Then she sighed, the fantasy vanishing.

"We *could*, if we weren't behind on the rent," she said, "*and* all our other bills."

"Again," Topaz moped, plopping down on a mid-exhibit settee and resting her chin on her hands.

The sensation of the new mummy display hadn't carried over for very long. Probably because of the depression, now, less than a week later, the chamber's attractions had barely more paid attendances than they'd had before the arrival of the trio of bandage-wrapped Egyptians. The opening day surge had only caught the bills up a bit.

Opal found it frustrating, and she knew that her sister did, too. Their father could travel the world and discover amazing artifacts that no one had even known about before, but what did it matter if no one came to see them?

We'd probably make more money if we went into fortune telling, Opal thought. Her mind went to the nightstand upstairs that held her tarot deck. Except for the sisters' brief forecast before the exhibit opened, Opal hadn't consulted the cards in ages, not since asking about their father. Most of that day's predictions seemed to have come true, save for the last. But how long were they to be wary against impending danger?

For some reason, that train of thought brought her back to Paul.

"You don't still think he's the 'doomed man' that brushed by on opening day, do you?" Opal asked her sister.

Topaz shrugged and shook her head. "Maybe. I don't know. There was so much that happening that day, and it all went by so fast… There's a deep melancholy in him, though, even if he hides it well."

Opal nodded. She'd sensed it, too, though her sister's insights about such things were usually clearer and more reliable.

"Paul may not be perfect," Opal agreed, "but at least he's not as creepy as Victoria. What's with her lately?"

"Jealous?" Topaz offered.

That certainly seemed possible. Madame Duprix's hazel eyes had always been on the greenish side when looking at the twins, and they seemed even greener when Paul spent time with the girls.

Opal was used to her envious gaze by now, though, and Paul's friendly, flirting presence more than made up for any chill in Cushing-Duprix relations.

"Jealous, sure," Opal said. "But I feel like there's something more…"

"Me, too," Topaz agreed. "Something's changed. There's something almost… *sinister* about her nowadays."

"Maybe she's *sex* starved," Opal whispered as she sat down next to her sister.

Topaz laughed. "Aren't we all?"

The bell on the front door chimed, and a heavy knock sounded on the chamber's front door.

Opal rolled her eyes; she'd *just* sat down. "We're closed!" she called.

"We'll be open in an hour," Topaz added. "Please come back then."

"Delivery!" a deep voice bellowed.

Both girls looked at each other, puzzled.

"On *Sunday?*" Topaz called.

"Won't wait!" the voice called. "'Less you want it to melt!"

"Melt?!" the twins blurted in unison. Both were on their feet and flying to the door in an instant.

"What is it?" Opal asked breathlessly as she flung open the door.

"Is it from Father?" Topaz inquired.

The bull-like man at the entryway shrugged. "Beats me. 'S from Norwegia, or someplace cold like 'at." He held out a clipboard. "Sign 'ere."

Opal took it and signed, reading the paper as she did so. "It *is* from Father!"

Behind the man, on the sidewalk, stood a huge crate, at least ten feet tall and five feet wide and deep, covered in insulating blankets. Topaz pushed past him and ran to the box, pressing her face up against the side.

"Do you think…?" she asked, her breath coming out as a cloud of steam. "Could it be…?" Her face beamed with delight and anticipation.

"We won't know until we open it," Opal said, and then, to the man, added: "Help us get it inside."

The bull-like man shook his head. "Sorry," he said. "It's me day off. Boss said I 'ad to deliver it, but 'e didn't say nothin' about luggin' and 'aulin'. I got it off the lorry. Now it's your problem."

"We could pa—" Opal began, but then she saw her sister vigorously shaking her head.

Topaz was right; they couldn't afford to pay the man, not

with Victoria breathing down their necks and other bill collectors starting to sniff around.

"All right, thank you," Opal said. "Have a nice Sunday."

The man tipped his cap, got back into his lorry, and drove away.

Topaz snapped her fingers. "I know! We'll call the boys."

"But it's Sunday morning, they're probably still in services," Opal countered. Which was true; all of their suitors' families were devout churchgoers. "And by the time they get out, we get word to them, and they come to help, it may melt!"

"Do you have a better idea?" Topaz asked.

Opal grinned. As a matter of fact, she did.

In less than two minutes, Victoria Duprix was looking down her long nose at Paul Shaw, scowling. Opal and Topaz stood nearby, hopeful.

"That's *not* what I'm paying you for," Madame Duprix said. "You work for *me* and the waxworks, remember? *Not* these… tenants."

"This is my day off, remember?" Paul replied amiably. "And I've pretty much finished everything you asked me to do. And I won't need to do any cleaning until after you've closed tonight. Besides, if I don't help the girls *now*, whatever is in that box will melt."

"Please, Madame Duprix," Topaz pleaded, "won't you let him help us?"

"Yes, *please?*" Opal added, playing more for Paul's sympathy than Victoria's.

The older woman's eyes narrowed. "They can't *pay* you, you know. They can't even pay their own rent."

"I'll just put it on account then," Paul said with a smile.

"And we will pay you just as soon as we can," Topaz put in.

"This new exhibit might even help," Opal suggested.

Victoria pursed her lips, fuming. "It didn't help much with those accursed mummies," she muttered. "Very well. Waste your time, for all I care, Mr. Shaw. But if you end up dog tired, don't ask me for a day off tomorrow."

"Don't worry," he replied. "I won't." Then smiling, he turned to the twins. "Come on, girls, let's see about this problem you've got…"

It took the better part of an hour for the three of them, using ropes and two dollies borrowed from the Vincent's studio, to wrestle the box up the entry stairs and down into the chamber. (Naturally, Vincent wasn't on hand to assist, and Victoria refused to.)

Frank showed up near the end of the process (flowers in hand) and got in the way as much as he helped, but Opal appreciated him trying.

"Well, that was quite a chore," Frank declared, wiping the sweat from his brow when they'd finished.

"You're lucky there was that disused walk-in freezer down here," Paul said. "And lucky the box fits inside."

"I'm sure Father took that into account when renting the place, way back when," Topaz said. "And when he was shipping this… artifact."

"He *does* like to think ahead," Opal noted.

"Too bad the freezer's not working," Paul continued, "but I can get you some blocks of ice, and that ought to keep things chilly enough in there for a while."

"I can help get the ice," Frank offered, and Opal noticed he flexed his muscles just a bit, showing off. She managed not to giggle.

"Sure, that'd be great," Paul said. "We could do that now."

"Before we see what's in the box?" Frank blurted.

All the others laughed.

"Of course, *not* before we open our 'present,' Frank," Opal teased.

"But maybe right after," Paul added. "Once the box is open, whatever is inside will start to melt more quickly."

It only took them a few minutes to remove the insulating blankets. When they did, they found a note attached to the front of the crate.

Topaz read it, her blue-green eyes going wide as she did. "It's from Father," she said. "And… Oh! Opal! It is! It *is*!"

Opal knew just what she meant. Her heart pounded at the thrill of it—though both girls refused to elaborate what was inside for the boys.

"Wait and see," Opal told them, beaming.

Working under the spell of the girls' enthusiasm, and using a couple of crowbars, the men quickly pried off the front of the crate.

A great billow of chilly mist filled the freezer room as the big wooden panel fell away. An icy, vaguely salty smell—an odor coming directly from the arctic wastes—filled the room. It took a few moments before any of them could see anything through the fog.

Then slowly, a blue-white slab of ice emerged from the mist, and frozen inside that ice… the figure of a man.

He was huge, far larger than even Paul (who was quite tall), and looked somewhat ghastly in appearance, with long limbs and pale, distorted features.

"Behold the newest exhibit in Dr. Cushing's museum," Opal said quietly, "the fabled Ice Man."

Frank loosened his collar. "Rather creepy, if you ask me," he said. "Those murderous eyes… It's almost like he's alive… like he's staring right at us."

Topaz reached out and laid her hand on the surface of the ice. "He seems almost… *sad* to me."

Paul laughed. "Well, sad or creepy, he sure should bring in the rubes—customers, I mean. This might be a turning point for you girls—"

"Let's hope!" Opal put in.

"—assuming he doesn't *melt* first," Paul finished.

"We should get that ice," Frank said, still sweaty and looking a bit nervous.

"Yes. Let's," agreed Paul.

"I'll go with you," Opal offered.

"That's fine," said Topaz. "I want to stay here and… study this chap for a while. Then I'll open up the exhibits."

"Great," Opal said. "We'll be back before you know it."

But as she looked at her sister staring intently at the frozen man, she couldn't help but think:

All of the boys in the world to choose from, and my sister wants to hang around with one frozen in a block of ice!

12

VICTORIA'S SUSPICIONS

*Victoria Duprix – 1951 Fisher St.
The Night of a Waning Gibbous Moon*

Naturally, Victoria didn't knock before entering Vincent's studio. "Darling," she said, "we need to have a little chat…"

"Don't bother me now," he snapped, not looking up from his work. "Can't you see I'm busy?"

Indeed, her husband *was* busy, running his hands over the slender torso of a naked woman, reshaping the clay to his liking. Victoria wondered if it was difficult for him to sculpt with his left hand bandaged and covered in a latex glove. Unusually, he seemed to be working without benefit of either sketch drawings or a live model.

Victoria pursed her lips, caught between relief at not finding a nude girl lounging around the studio and a continuing ache of abandonment from when *she* had been the only model he needed.

And the bust torso he was working on wasn't his *only* new subject, either. Another, life-size nude lounged nearby, reclining like one of Titian's mythological odalisques. Both sculptures were different women, and both looked vaguely familiar to Victoria—though she couldn't place them.

"Busy or not," she said, tamping down her suspicions, "this is a discussion that needs to be had."

"Very well, talk if you must," Vincent said. "But I hope you don't mind if I continue working."

She did, but there was no point in arguing about it. "Vincent my dear, it's about our money—"

He sighed. "That old sop, again?"

She continued, ignoring his jibe. "—or, rather, lack of it. As you've probably failed to notice, attendance at the waxworks has fallen off. The economy is bad, and even the chance to leer at a suffering martyr or a nude Venus isn't luring the populace in the way it used to."

"You know these things run in cycles, Victoria. What's 'out' today may be back 'in' tomorrow—and I'll have some new work ready soon, that's usually good for a spike in customers."

"In the past, it may have been, my dear, when your sculptures were the toast of London. And if you rendered your final pieces in stone, or bronze—"

"My dear," he said acidly, "you know that wax is my preferred medium. A wax rendering has a glow to the skin, a lifelike transparency, that can't be achieved with bronze or marble."

"But there is no market for *wax* figures, save perhaps to other museums—and you refuse to sell to them."

"They're our *competitors*. Why should I sell them my best work?"

"Because, to put it bluntly, my dear: We're broke."

"Nonsense, I have plenty of money in my trust."

"No. You *used* to have plenty of money in your trust. Now, there's almost literally nothing left."

"That's absurd. When my parents died—"

"—They left us a considerable sum, that's true." She stared at the back of his head, as if she might bore into his skull with her graze, but he continued working. "For more than a decade now, you've lavished our wealth on your penny-ante waxworks and this decaying Victorian manse."

He turned suddenly and rose, towering above her and glaring. "Ours is the *best* waxworks in London!"

They spent so little time together, now, Victoria had almost forgotten how tall her husband was. She took a step back. "Your figures may be the best, yes," she admitted, "but what does it matter if no one comes to *see* them?"

He waved his right hand dismissively and began to stalk around the studio. "Is our lack of publicity *my* fault, when I'm so busy sculpting?" he asked rhetorically. "Besides, if our financial situation is so dire, why aren't *you* doing anything about it? I don't see you cutting back on your trips to the *theater*."

He said the last word with a sneer. Did he suspect the theater was just an excuse? Did he suspect her dalliances (as she suspected his)? Surely, he had no proof…

"And what about that handyman?" he continued. "If money is so tight, why did you hire him, eh?"

The wicked gleam in his eye told Victoria that her husband had gleaned her true motive, but in no way would she admit it to him.

"There's *work* to be done, Vincent," she replied, her voice growing louder. "Work around the waxworks—and around this house. *Someone* has to do it, with you locked in your studio all hours of the day and night…!

"We can't afford *not* to have someone fixing the place up. If you think attendance is bad now, imagine how it will be when a customer trips over a loose floorboard, or when a piece of the celling falls on his head.

"And it's not like we can count on those Cushing brats to

help out," Victoria fumed. "They seem to have plenty of money for new exhibits, but they're behind in their rent—again."

Weirdly, her fury seemed to have a calming effect on her husband. He stopped pacing, returned to his stool, and resumed fiddling with the clay torso. "I thought you'd settled the rent issue with those girls," he said. "I thought they'd given you that gaudy mirror—which you seem to delight in—that's in your bed chamber."

"They used that mirror to settle the amount in *arrears*," Victoria replied (more haughtily than she intended), "but their obligation for living and doing business under our roof is ongoing."

"Yes… I suppose it is," her husband said. "But they're pleasant enough tenants, and their Chamber of Horrors seems a good compliment to the waxworks…"

"You'd *think*," Victoria noted icily, "but it doesn't seem to be attracting any more customers for either them *or* us."

"Hmm…" Vincent stroked his chin, though Victoria couldn't guess what gears might be turning in his mind.

Artists! So unpredictable—and just when you want them not *to be.*

"You know," he finally said, "maybe you had something earlier."

"What? When?" she asked, puzzled.

"Perhaps the girls could pay their rent by modeling for me, as you suggested the other day. They're pretty enough."

Victoria felt her face go red. When she'd said it, it had been an *accusation*, not a suggestion. How like her husband to twist things that way.

"But they're only seventeen!" she protested.

"*Eighteen*, since three months ago," he corrected. "That seems old enough, nowadays. This is the Jazz Era, after all—emancipation and free love, and all that. Besides you were only *seventeen* when you first posed for me."

He grinned at her in a way that, at one point, Victoria would have found alluring. Now she found it infuriating.

"There was a time when you didn't *need* other models," she fumed, turning away so that he wouldn't see the tears welling at the corners of her eyes. "There was a time when *I* was enough!"

"Well," he began (she sensed, rather than saw his shrug), "that was a long while ago, my dear. And I'm afraid that time and gravity are often unkind to the female figure."

She wheeled on him, furious. Part of her wanted to strip off her clothing right then and there, to thrust her body against him and *dare* him to deny her attractiveness; another part wanted to pick up one of his sculpting knives and stab him through the heart.

"If you shared my bed more often, maybe you'd find out that you're mistaken," she countered.

"Perhaps that's why I avoid it in the first place," he replied.

Again, she imagined plunging a clay-covered blade into his chest.

She turned away, trying to master her anger, to act casually. "Are you telling me that I *wasn't* one of the fairest in London, when we met?"

"You undoubtedly were."

"Are you saying that the others since—all those lovely anonymous bodies—could ever match up to what you had when we met?"

"Perhaps not," he admitted. "But that was then. Today is something else."

"How many have there been?"

He was back working again, running his right hand over a smooth collar bone. "A few. More than a few. I've lost track."

"That's your age showing, Vincent," she jibed. Though she was seething inside, she kept her tone light, almost playful. "*'I've lost track...!'* So many dalliances and so little memory. Have you lost track of their names as well?"

"Of course not," he replied, annoyed.

"Well...?"

"Well, there was Gwendolyn... and Eve... and Piper... and Angela..."

"Piper... She was a whore, wasn't she?"

Vincent laughed. "What of it? Lautrec painted whores; Degas, too. It's not every girl who will take off her clothes for a handful of tuppence, you know."

"But you've found more than a few, haven't you, my love?"

"Victoria... Is there a *point* to all this?"

"You don't have the money to pay for even tuppenny whores now, my love. I know; I've been watching the accounts."

"Is *that* what this is about?" Vincent said, exasperated. "Jealously?"

"You haven't been paying for models, my dear, so whom *are* you working from? Who is *this*?" she pointed to the torso he'd been lovingly fondling, and then to the reclining odalisque. "And *this*?"

Again, he laughed, almost triumphantly. "I have years of practice looking at beautiful women, my dear—you included, once upon a time."

"Answer my question!"

He stood, and put his hands on her shoulders, patronizingly, looking directly into her eyes.

His touch both thrilled and reviled her.

"Sadly, my dear," he said, "nowadays I work entirely from my own imagination ... and my memories—past *pleasant* memories."

She turned away, not believing a word of it. "Ha!" she scoffed.

"Believe me or not, as you like," he said. "But, in either case... Leave. I have work to finish, and if we're to have any chance of making money with the waxworks, I need to complete it." He began working his hands on the figure's sides, tenderly defining one rib at a time.

Victoria stood, paralyzed by anger, wanting to kill him and yet not daring to. He would *never* have talked like this to her when she was younger—would never have taken to working from other models.

"Old age kills a woman one grey hair at a time," she remembered her mother saying a very long time ago. She hadn't understood it then, but now…

"Unless, of course, you'd like to find a job yourself," Vincent continued nonchalantly as he worked. "Though I doubt that servicing busboys or coachmen would pay the kind of salary you'd like to be accustomed to. Still… Perhaps there'd be *someone* willing to pay the freight for what you have to offer." He glanced at her with a snide smile.

Coachmen… Could it be possible he knew?

She glanced at the knife lying on the table next to him. But, as if reading her thoughts, without even a glance, he picked it up and began to work the clay with it.

Damn you to hell, Vincent Duprix! she thought.

Unable to think of a snappy reply, she turned and stormed out of the room, slamming the door behind her.

As she walked down the hall, she heard the soft sound of Vincent, chuckling inside his studio.

The nerve of that man—all but accusing her of an affair, even as he sculpted a likeness of his own lover.

The face topping that slender torso was *so* familiar to Victoria. It *must* be one of his past models—someone he'd taken as a lover once more. But who?

Victoria kept walking, not wanting to even be on the same floor of the building with her husband.

She turned on the stairway, intending to go down to the waxworks—perhaps smash a few things before starting the day.

It would serve him right if I destroyed some of his precious sculptures.

Suddenly, she ran into something solid. "Oh!"

"Oh, yourself," said a pleasant masculine voice. "Are you all right?"

She'd been so wrapped up in her own thoughts that she'd run right smack dab into Paul Shaw, coming up the stairs as she descended.

For a moment, the two of them stood there, almost pinned against each other. His young, strong body felt warm against hers.

"I'm sorry... I... You..." she began. She stomped her foot. "You should watch were you're going."

"I'm sorry," Paul replied. "But you should, too. I was just coming up to ask if you needed me to do anything else in the waxworks today. I'll go home, otherwise."

"Well," she said, leaning into him, "there's *something* you could do for me..."

She opened her lips slightly, started to put her arms around his neck...

But he intercepted her embrace and turned it gently aside with his strong hands. "Mrs. Duprix..." he began.

She shook herself, as if suddenly waking from a (not-unpleasant) dream. "I'm sorry, Mr. Shaw. Perhaps you misunderstood me. I have nothing else for you today. You may leave, if you wish."

Paul nodded gratefully. "Thank you, ma'am. I'll see you in the morning, then."

"Yes," she said tersely. "Bright and early."

"Bright and early." He pivoted and headed toward the front door.

A man like that... Victoria thought *...he'd never have turned me down when I was younger!*

Anger rose within her again, replacing her embarrassment at being spurned.

She wheeled, went back upstairs and into her bedroom, and locked the door.

She looked into her golden-framed mirror, assessing herself for a moment.

No. No, she didn't look bad.

"For an old woman," said a voice in her head.

"I'm *not* old!" she insisted. And just to prove it to herself, she stripped off her clothes.

She stood there a long moment, looking at her herself. In the reflection, she could still see the body that had seduced a proud young artist, but... Yes, her breasts had begun to sag a bit... and her belly, too. And her thighs and upper arms were thicker than they used to be—thicker than she liked.

And was that *another* grey hair?

"Damn it all," she whispered. Where did those grey streaks *come* from? How could she *stop* this horrible march of time?

"Blo-o-o-od!" whispered the voice in her head.

And suddenly, her reflection grew young again, all the damage of years and gravity fading in an instant. Victoria stood there, young and proud and beautiful once more.

It was a miracle!

"Thisss can be yoursss," said the voice in her head.

And at that moment, a beautiful, dark-haired woman in a fine dress and expensive jewelry stepped up beside her refection.

Victoria whirled. How had someone gotten into her room?

But there was no one there. She stood alone in her bedchamber.

She turned back to the mirror; the woman was there—as was Victoria's young and vital reflection.

"I almost thought I *imagined* you," Victoria muttered.

The other woman laughed softly and shook her head.

"Who are you?"

"Erzsebet."

"Can you really make me young again?"

"No," the reflection of Erzsebet replied. *"But I can teach you. Do what I sssay, and you will become as lovely asss you were in the flower of your youth—as young and beautiful asss I."*

Victoria stepped closer to the mirror, reaching out, trying to touch her new ally. But her fingers encountered only cold black glass.

"What must I do?" Victoria asked.

"The sssecret... isss blood. The taking of life... young life... will ressstore you!"

I wicked smile spread across Victoria's face.

"I know just the person!"

13

MONSTERS, REAL & IMAGINED

Paul Longmire – The Philippines
The Dark of the Moon

The bright orange glow of the burning house lit up the darkness, and the smell of smoke—sweet, like burning hay, and yet horrible in its implications—filled the humid night air.

For a moment, Paul stood staring at the blaze, caught between shocked bewilderment and fear. Then he ran, screaming, straight into the heart of the fire.

As he plunged through the door, the flames shot up around him, hissing their deadly intent, roaring their anger. Heat scorched Paul's skin, and smoke choked his lungs and stung his eyes. He found it almost impossible to see; everything around him was a blur of orange and yellow with sudden bursts of blinding white and smothering red.

He staggered, his body reflexively trying to turn back the way he'd come.

But he *had* to continue… He had to find…

"Caliso!" he cried. "Judith!"

He hadn't seen them outside; they *had* to be here in this inferno, somewhere.

Wreathed in flame and smoke, the living room was unrecognizable, but their house wasn't that big—barely larger than most native huts—and Paul knew it well; he could find his way through all of it in the darkest night without so much as a candle to guide him.

He stumbled toward where he knew the bedroom must lie—and beyond it, the nursery.

"Caliso…! Where are you?"

The bamboo and thatch construction made the whole place like a tinderbox; nearly every inch of it was burning now.

"Judith…!"

The only sound that came in reply was the crackling laughter of the conflagration.

Hands blistering, he seized the bedroom door and wrenched it open.

WHOOSH!

A gout of flame and heat burst through the doorway, a huge fireball. The impact of it knocked him backward, and for a moment, the whole world became keening, white nothingness.

When Paul's eyes cleared, he was outside—somehow—and strong hands were dragging him away from the burning structure.

"No!" he cried. "You don't understand. They're *inside*. My wife and daughter are inside!"

But the hands kept pulling, and he couldn't find the strength to resist.

Filipino faces, grim and determined, stared down at him.

Paul tried to talk again, but all that came out was a croaking cough. He tried to take a deep breath, but found he couldn't. It was as though someone had taken a Brillo pad to the inside of his lungs.

"P-please…!" he finally managed.

The natives stopped dragging Paul. They stood in a circle, staring down at him, exchanging worried glances.

"Please!" Paul gasped again, and then coughed out: "You have to h-help me!" And he pointed back toward his blazing house.

"*Isda*," one older man said, shaking his head.

"*Isda-asawa!*" agreed another.

They were speaking Tagalog, and though Paul had a working knowledge of the language, he couldn't make sense of what they were saying.

"My wife and child are in there!" Paul said, still gasping for breath.

All the Filipinos, there were six men as well as three of the local women, gazed fearfully toward the burning house.

"*Isda-asawa*," the eldest man insisted.

"*Oo. Isda-asawa*," the women whispered to each other, in agreement.

"*Isda-asawa. Isada-anak*," muttered another of the men.

Paul had seen some of these people in the time he'd lived here, but he did not know them personally; his wife, a native Filipino, handled most of the family's interactions with the locals.

After another coughing fit, Paul tried again. "You don't understand: Caliso, my wife, is in there. And our daughter, Judith. You have to help me save them!"

Mustering every ounce of strength he had remaining, he staggered to his feet.

The Filipinos blocked his way.

"*Hindi!*" said the eldest man. "No!"

"*Isda*-asawa," added a younger woman. "*Mapanganib!* Dangerous!"

"*Isda-asawa. Isada-anak*," the rest echoed.

What were they trying to tell him? That his wife and daughter were some kind of monsters? Paul remembered now that the locals had always been suspicious of his wife, something to do with her family...

"No!" he cried. "You superstitious fools! They're *not* monsters! Why can't you understand? They're my *family*! You must help me!"

He started lumbering back toward the blazing building.

Then something hit him on the back of his head, and the world swam and faded toward black, and for a moment, Paul thought he imagined the wail and clang of a fire engine coming... Coming to help...!

And he woke up.

The fire engine, at least, was real—here and now—screaming down the narrow street outside of his London flop. Its emergency lights painted the crumbling plaster walls a flickering red.

Red... like that long-ago fire, Paul thought, though he would have much preferred to forget.

But how could he?

That was the moment when his whole life went to hell—and, since then, it had only gotten worse.

In the flophouse hallway, the pay phone rang, echoing the headache ringing in his head. The walls were paper thin in this place, but it was all he could afford—ironic considering he had grown up heir to a vast fortune.

But then came the Philippines, and the fire... And later, the wolf.

Paul checked his watch:

Three A.M.

He doubted he'd get back to sleep tonight.

1951 Fisher St., London
The Day of the Last Quarter Moon

"Paul! We're so glad to see you!" Opal enthused as Paul came through the main entrance of 1951 Fisher. The brunette hopped up the steps from the Chamber of Horrors and gave him a quick hug.

"Hi, Paul," Topaz called from the bottom of the short flight of stairs leading to the chamber.

"Well, I'm glad to see you, too," Paul said. "Both of you." He'd grown fond of the twins—especially Opal—in the short time he'd worked here, though he also suspected that a greeting *this* enthusiastic probably came with a price tag.

Still, the brief press of the teenager's body against his had been a nice sensation. If only he weren't six years her senior… He smiled, deciding to play along with the girls. "What, no hug from you?" he asked Topaz.

"Nope. Hands full," she explained, holding one of the exhibits—a large glass jar—in her hands as she mounted the stairs. "You can have a kiss, though." And she pecked him on the cheek.

Now Paul *knew* the pair of them were up to something.

But before he could ask, the label on Topaz's jar caught his eye.

Paul's body went stiff, and his heart skipped a beat. The label read:

Scales of the isda-asawa.

He grabbed Topaz's wrist. "Where did you get these?" he demanded.

"Paul, you're hurting me!" Topaz gasped, fear clouding her blue-green eyes.

Paul let go. "I'm sorry, it's just that… That word, *isda-asawa*… I've heard it before."

Opal looked concerned. "Probably when we took you on the tour."

"No. I didn't see it on the tour. I would have remembered."

The twins stood side-by-side, eyeing him warily, their flirting abruptly ceased. Topaz clutched the jar with both arms.

"What does it mean?" Paul asked. "Please. It's important. I mean... It *might* be. It might explain something."

"Um," Opal began, "these are the scales of an actual Filipino fish-wife..."

"The fish-wife is a near-legendary, siren-like creature," Topaz continued. "By day, she appears to be a beautiful woman, but by night she becomes a hideous man-eating monster."

Paul collapsed onto the bench atop the stairs, next to the admission stand. He shook his head. "Well, I guess that explains it—as much as it can ever be explained."

"Explains what?" the twins asked simultaneously.

"I used to live in the Philippines, years ago," Paul said. "I had a... I knew someone who was killed. When she died, the natives kept saying that word: *isda-asawa*. I guess they though she was..."—he choked up for a moment—"...some kind of monster. But they were *wrong*. She was..." He trailed off, unable to say anymore.

His life was filled with terrible irony. The natives had thought his wife and child were monsters, while *he* was the actual monster—at least, *now* he was, anyway. Would his suffering never end?

Into Paul's mind came the image of a silver bullet, the final way that he might end his misery.

The coward's way out.

But was it *really*? Was it cowardly to kill yourself so that others—your future victims—could go on living?

The curse won't let me kill myself, he thought, suddenly sure of that fact. If he couldn't even keep track of the full moon, what chance did he have of ending his own life?

I just have to go on killing until someone kills me.

He bowed his head and clutched his temples, momentarily unable to bear the terrible burden.

Topaz set down her jar, and both twins knelt beside him. All traces of fear had left the girls; they looked... sympathetic.

Paul could hardly stand it.

"We're so sorry," Opal said, running one smooth, warm hand down Paul's cheek.

"I can put the exhibit away for a while, so you don't have to see it," Topaz offered.

Paul forced himself to smile at both girls. He couldn't give up now. Not when he seemed so close. He stood, taking a deep breath and glanced at the wolf skin, barely visible, hanging on the far wall of the exhibit. "No. That's all right," he said. "It was a long time ago now. I should be getting to work."

The twins stood as well, exchanging a glance that said that maybe they didn't believe him—as well as exchanging some other like-minded communication that Paul couldn't quite figure out.

"About that work…" Opal said.

Ah! That was it; their ulterior motive.

"We're worried about the Ice Man," Topaz began. "We can't afford to keep having ice brought in every day, so he doesn't melt—and besides, we need to be able to *display* him, to help attract more customers."

"We're hoping that maybe you might be able to *fix* the freezer, and also maybe cut an opening and put a window into it —so people can see the exhibit," Opal continued. "Like you said you would."

"Did *I* say that?" Paul asked, some of his playful spirit returning. It was hard to stay morose around the twins. They were so full of life! Perhaps that was why he liked being with them so much.

"Please, Mr. Shaw," Topaz said. "A more permanent display of the Ice Man could be a real help to our business."

"And, yes," Opal added, "you *did* say that you would."

Paul shrugged theatrically. "Well, if that's how I said I'd help… I guess today is the day."

He grinned at both girls, and they came and hugged him.

That was plenty of reward for Paul. For a moment, it made him feel almost... human.

※

"You're not *really* going to help those girls with their ridiculous exhibit, are you?" Victoria asked Paul. She tried to make it sound playful, but Paul detected notes of bitterness and envy in her pleasant, contralto voice.

"I thought you wanted them to be able to pay your rent," Paul replied. "They need help getting the display set up, so they can make more money."

Victoria paced the waxworks like a hungry cat. "Of *course*, they need to be able to pay the rent," she said, "but I'm not at all amused by the time and effort you're expending. These little 'tasks' for them seem to be taking you away from your job here, in the museum."

"I'm getting my work done. The repairs I'm doing, fixing up that old freezer for them, won't have any effect on what I do here at the waxworks."

"You say that *now*, of course," she noted, "but I mean... As I told you before, they can't afford to *pay* you." And she gave him a disapproving glance that said: *"..At least not with* money."

"I mean," Victoria continued, "work on their wretched display if you feel you must, but you're not going to do it for *free*, certainly."

Even though it was a long while until the full moon—three weeks if he remembered right—Paul felt his blood rising.

The jealousy flowing from Mrs. Duprix was almost palpable. She hated the twins. Was it because they were younger and prettier than she? Paul had seen the sculptures in the waxworks that she'd posed for—she'd taken great pleasure in showing them off—and she'd been a real beauty in her day. Even now, she remained a handsome woman... or she *would* have been if not for the green-eyed monster riding on her back.

"What I do on my own time is my own business," he told her, keeping his temper under tight control.

"But *I'm* the one that's paying you," Victoria said, "not those little… *girls*." She actually stamped her foot—not dramatically, but audibly. She'd only raised her heel an inch or so, but when she brought it down it almost sounded like a gunshot when it hit the oak floorboards.

She looked chagrinned, clearly not intending to have made such a display.

Paul smiled at her as disarmingly as he could. "Yes, you're paying me," he replied, "but not very much."

Victoria looked flustered and turned away. She paced over to the Joan of Arc display, and then turned.

"Well," she said, far more calmly, "you know that we… *I* can't pay you more than I am until business gets better…"

Paul knew it. The depression made business tough all over right now, with not much chance it would improve anytime soon. Of course, he wasn't *actually* working here for the *pay*…

"But perhaps I could make our little arrangement more worth your while," she mused.

"How do you mean?" For a moment, Paul thought she might be propositioning him.

"You know we have a servants' quarters in the rear of the house on the second floor?" she asked. "It's not being used, because we have no servants right now."

He'd noticed the disused rooms when helping her move some furniture, so he said: "Yes."

She continued pacing, but more calmly now, as though she was thinking, making this up as she went. She didn't look at him as she spoke.

"Well, I can't offer you more *pay*, Mr. Shaw, but if it would help, I could let you stay in one of those rooms—as part of your compensation, so to speak."

The suggestion took Paul by surprise.

"The rooms available aren't much, I'll admit," she continued, "but you can pick the one that seems best to you and fix it up to your liking. Use the leftover materials from your work here in the waxworks, if that will help."

It was a generous offer—too generous, in a way. Paul wondered what kind of strings might come attached to it. He couldn't very well ask about those, though.

"Thank you, Mrs. Duprix," he said.

"*Victoria*," she insisted, looking at him with her hazel eyes.

Those eyes were really lovely, now that Paul noticed.

"Thank you, Victoria. I'll think it over."

Her eyes sparkled at him, and then she turned away once more. "You do that, Mr. Shaw."

"*Paul*," he said. "If I'm to call you Victoria, you must call me Paul."

She smiled, now—genuinely—and Paul thought that, indeed, she must have been very beautiful in her prime.

"Very well, Paul," she said. "Please consider it while you go about your work. No rush, but the offer won't stay open forever." And again, she smiled.

He nodded. "Thanks."

He picked up his hammer again, to resume work on repairing a display cabinet, and she whisked out of the room, leaving him alone with his thoughts.

Should he take her offer?

He certainly needed a place to stay, and even in its present state, the room here *must* be better than the flophouse where he was crashing currently.

No sense paying rent when you can live somewhere for free...

But he wasn't really *here* to live, or to make a living; he'd come here to steal the pelt of the beast and break his curse, once and for all.

The next full moon was three weeks away; he *had* to destroy the thing by them.

As yet, though—even while becoming fairly chummy with the twins—he hadn't found the chance.

Living here would give me more opportunity...

That was certainly true.

At least, it *seemed* to be. Though with the curse holding so much sway over his life, it was hard to tell when he was thinking completely rationally.

Would living in this house—under the same roof with the girls and the pelt and Victoria—*really* help?

Or would it just bring more danger and destruction into his life and the lives of everyone closest to him?

14

COLD RELATIONSHIPS

Piper – Soho, London
That Same Night

The girl smiled when she opened the door of her shabby third-floor walkup, happy to see her unexpected visitor.

"Well, look who's 'ere!" she exclaimed. "I 'aven't seen you in a dog's age." She giggled and covered her mouth with her hand, hiding sloppily applied makeup. "Oh! Sorry, didn't mean anything by the 'dog' remark—just an expression, if you know what I mean. What's it been—two years? Three? Come in, come in and make yourself at 'ome."

The girl was short and very skinny with mousy brown hair and glassy brown eyes. She wore a faded blue flower-print dress, several years out of date, probably because she couldn't afford anything newer. (Tuppenny whores weren't known for their fashion sense.) Dog-eared calendar prints and crepe paper flowers decorated her cheap, backroom flat on the third floor. The girl's smile was genuine enough, though.

"Do you want something to drink? Brandy's what you like

best isn't it—or was it red wine? Sorry I don't recollect. It's been so long, you know?" The girl grinned again.

She smiled too much, probably because she was drunk or stoned, which was likely a regular habit with her. Her body had been magnificent once, but now—like the rest of her—it seemed to be rapidly fading.

She'll do, though. She'll do.

"Don't matter much nohow," the girl continued with a giggle. "Only got one thing to drink around 'ere." She fetched a half-empty liquor bottle from a nearby cluttered shelf.

She held it up to the light—a single bulb, suspended from the ceiling—and examined it. The contents sloshed lazily inside the glass container.

"Not sure if it's gin or vodka," she said. "Could be something else, I suppose. Not much difference, is there? It's the effect what counts." Then, something occurred to her. "Ooh! You ain't brought your own, 'ave you?"

She looked hopefully at her visitor, and then her face fell. "No. Didn't expect you 'ad. Never mind, love. Piper 'll do right by you."

That was her name… *Piper*. How odd not to remember until now; it was almost like living someone else's life.

Piper poured two fingers of the clear liquid into each of a pair of dirt-smudged glasses. She handed one to the visitor and then quickly drained hers.

"I've always done right by you an' yours, 'aven't I?" Piper said. And, again, she smiled her sloppy smile.

"So, what brings a swell like you out on a night like this, and it raining cats and dogs, too? Decided you need Pretty Piper's services again, 'ave you? Now, you know it don't make no difference to me, but 's this time for *you*, or for your…"

"For me," the visitor insisted in an unfamiliar voice.

"Now ain't that a twist in the air!" Piper laughed drunkenly. "'Aven't taken up art yourself, 'ave you?"

"No," the visitor replied. "There's just something I need."

"Something Pretty Piper can supply, eh?"

"Yes."

"Well, you know that whatever it might be, Pretty Piper is ready, willing, and able! You got something special in mind?"

"Yes, I have something special planned... something *very* special."

Again, Piper's sloppy, expectant smile.

The knife flashed silver in a quick, straight line.

Piper gasped and clutched at her throat where a second, red-rimmed smile had opened up.

Blood squirted out between the whore's pale fingers.

She gasped, but her breath had gone, and her life was quickly following—a delicious crimson fountain.

Filled with glee and anticipation, the visitor whispered:

"Not what you expected—was it?"

Topaz – 1951 Fisher St.

Topaz sat bolt upright, clutching her neck, gasping.

She wanted to scream, but she couldn't even find her breath.

She groped to her left, fingers scrabbling spiderlike across the bedclothes, trying to find her sister. Opal would help her... Opal would stanch the wound before Topaz could bleed to death.

Her questing hand found nothing; her twin's side of the bed lay empty, her usual spot on the mattress cold.

I'm going to die alone! Topaz thought.

Then—after what seemed like an eternity—her breath returned.

She gulped in great lungfuls of air, sobbing, still clutching her throat.

My fingers aren't wet... There's no blood... It was only a dream!

"Only a dream…" she repeated out loud, just to reassure herself.

The sound of her own voice *did* reassure Topaz, but she still longed for the warmth of her twin, sleeping beside her.

Where was Opal?

Had she been in the dream? Had she been the one who was ki—?

No. That was someone else. Her twin was fine; Topaz could sense it. But where *was* she?

"Opal?" Topaz called into the still darkness.

No reply came.

Oh… That's right.

She'd gone out with Frank and wasn't expected home until late. Topaz had gotten so caught up in the nightmare that she'd forgotten. What time was it, anyway?

The light of the last quarter moon shone through her window, giving just enough illumination to make out the face of the clock on the dressing table.

Quarter to midnight.

Late, but not *that* late. Opal might not be home for a while yet.

A long while, if Frank has anything to say about it.

Topaz wondered what her twin might be up to right now. Sometimes, she got clear images of what Opal was doing and feeling, but—though she knew her twin was safe—this was *not* one of those moments.

Topaz felt very alone. The big Victorian house loomed nearly empty and silent around her.

She sat on the bed quietly, taking deep breaths and willing her heartrate to calm.

She thought that perhaps, by relaxing, she might pick up some kind of sensation from her twin.

But did she really *want* to know what Opal was doing? What

if Opal were in some type of... romantic clench? Did Topaz want to "look in" on that?

She sighed. Though it was the jazz age, she and her sister remained virgins. Not that they were afraid of boys or sex—far from it. Nor were they so old-fashioned as to believe that sensual pleasures should wait for marriage...

They just hadn't found the right person yet—not either of them.

It would figure *if she found someone first.*

Though males in general seemed more attracted to Topaz, there was no doubt that Opal was more comfortable around *actual* boys. Maybe it was because her sister didn't seem to *feel* things as acutely as Topaz, not about other people, anyway.

Sometimes, Topaz seemed to know what other people were going to do or say before they did it—like she could read their minds.

That was proving difficult to take with young men—even well-mannered ones, like their current suitors. Boys at this age seemed to be all nerves and anticipation and lusty energy. Not that Topaz didn't feel all of those things as well, but...

She tried to keep her emotions under control, though being around randy males made it more difficult.

Topaz wished, sometimes, that she lacked this "gift." She wished that she were more like her sister, who—though she could more reliably obtain glimpses of the future in her cards—got to at least live day-to-day without knowing what was twisting through other people's minds.

Except maybe for her sister's.

Topaz calmed her thoughts and reached out for her twin once more, embarrassing circumstances be damned.

Then she heard something.

"Opal?" she asked aloud.

But no. It was someone else... someone calling to her...

"Someone in the house...?"

Rising, she threw on her pale blue dressing gown and cinched it at the waist.

"Hello?" she called softly as she left the bedroom.

Could it be the Duprixes that she'd heard?

But she'd sworn the voice had called her name. Why would her landlords to that?

She crept to the door atop the landing and opened it.

"Father?"

Perhaps he had returned home without any warning. Father often did that.

Topaz padded barefoot down the stairs past the Duprixes apartments on the second floor, and to the mid-floor landing where she could peer at the door leading to the first floor.

She saw no one.

She went down and opened the door. "Father?"

No one stood on the front landing.

But the call came again—her name, she felt sure of it, though she could hardly make out the word.

It was coming from the basement... from the Chamber of Horrors.

Topaz was turning the latch of the chamber entrance before she remembered that she'd left her keys upstairs, on the dressing table.

But the doorknob turned. Dr. Cushing's Chamber of Horrors was unlocked!

Summoning her courage, Topaz opened the door and stepped inside. The chamber remained dark, with only a little bit of light leaking in from the small high windows at street level.

Topaz saw no one.

"Hello?" she called, a little bit louder now.

Who could be in the chamber at this time of night? Could her sister be using it for an assignation?

"Opal?"

Nothing.

"Father?"

A sound then—not a call but a clatter—something bumped or kicked or overturned.

"Who's there? Come out!"

Fear and anger mingled within Topaz. She groped for the light switch by the door, but her hand shook, and she couldn't find it.

A single light came on, further in the chamber.

"I'm sorry," said a familiar voice. "It's only me."

"Mr. Shaw?"

Paul Shaw stepped out into the light. "It's only me, Paul." In one hand he held an adjustable spanner. He smiled sheepishly.

"What are you doing here?"

"I remembered something I'd forgotten to do," he said. "Something I didn't fix right in the freezer. I didn't want you to come down in the morning and find your Ice Man melted, so I came back. I let myself in from the waxworks. Victoria… I mean, Mrs. Duprix gave me a key. I hope you don't mind."

Topaz felt greatly relieved, though Paul did seem more than a little nervous. Was he telling the truth?

Topaz concentrated on him, but her telepathic powers—if that's truly what they were—couldn't seem to focus on the handyman.

She frowned. "Paul, did you call me? I thought I heard someone calling."

"No," Paul replied. "I didn't call you. I didn't want to disturb anyone. I thought probably everyone was asleep."

Topaz narrowed her eyes and peered around the dimly lit chamber. "Is there anyone else here?" Though *Opal* wasn't having an assignation in the chamber, perhaps Paul was. Perhaps that's why he seemed nervous.

"Nope. Only me. Unless you count our friend in that block of ice." He shrugged.

She pulled her robe tighter around her, suddenly aware of how little she was wearing in the hired man's presence. She liked Paul, but…

"I guess you better finish fixing the freezer, then," she said. "It's late."

"That's okay," he replied. "I've finished. I was just about to leave."

"Oh. All right." No matter how she concentrated, she couldn't get a reading on him. Maybe she was just tired. "You can use the front door." She stepped out of the way so that he could exit.

"Thanks." Paul hopped up the steps jauntily and came to a stop beside her. "Is everything all right?" His concern seemed genuine.

"I'm fine. I just thought I heard voices. That's all."

Paul smiled warmly at her, not seeming at all nervous now. "Maybe I was talking to myself. I've been told I do that sometimes."

She returned his smile. "Maybe that was it."

"Well, good night then, Topaz. See you in the morning."

"Good night, Paul."

He nodded goodbye to her and then left by the front door, vanishing quickly into the foggy London night.

Topaz made sure the door was locked behind him.

Then she went down into the chamber, turning on lights as she went, and checked the other doors as well: all locked.

Had Paul *really* come in through the adjoining door to the waxworks? And if he hadn't, how *had* he come in and what was he doing here?

Topaz pondered that for a while, but couldn't reach any conclusion. So, she went to check on the Ice Man.

Everything seemed to be in order there, too. Paul had done a wonderful job of modifying the freezer to display her father's latest prize. The big slab of blue-green ice rested right next to the large pane of glass the handyman had installed. Once she and her sister had finished dressing out the exhibit, customers would have a fine view of the entombed figure.

Like a fly caught in amber, she thought.

But at the same time, so much more terrible. This was a *human being*, after all—a real person who had, through design, chance, or misfortune, come to such an awful fate.

Once he had been a living man with thoughts and emotions and desires just like anyone else.

A wellspring of pity formed within Topaz's breast, and she placed her hand against the cold glass.

"I'm so sorry," she said. "So sorry you came to this."

"Sorry..." a voice echoed in her mind.

Topaz blinked. Had she imagined it, or was she just tired?

Peering through the ice at the frozen giant, she almost felt as though he were peering back at her—but of course, that was impossible.

Her gaze wandered over his body—huge, gangly, and pale, and dressed in ragged colonial-period clothing—before settling on his face. The features were bony and rough-chiseled with an almost cruel cast to them. The rough-cut long black hair didn't do that face any favors, either. With those features and that size, surely the folk of this man's time must have seen him as a monster.

"No matter who you were," Topaz said, her hand still pressed against the glass, "you and I are going to be *friends*. My name is Topaz... Topaz Cushing. I don't know how other people treated you in life, or how you came to be frozen like this, but—even though you're going to be on display in our museum, and even though you're dead—I will treat you with the same respect I would give any other human being."

She smiled, and she felt—for a moment—as though the Ice Man understood.

But of course, that was impossible.

Tearing her eyes away from him, she said, "Well, after all this excitement, I can't sleep, and I bet you can't, either. If you don't mind, I think I'll read for a while, to settle down."

A stack of her father's old books stood on a disused butcher block nearby—all things they'd have to find new storage space for, now that the freezer area would be joining the chamber's exhibits.

Topaz picked up the nearest volume and blew the dust off the cover.

Paradise Lost, by John Milton.

A notion seized her.

"You know, I bet it's been a long time since anyone read to you," she said to the Ice Man.

Smiling, she plopped down next to the freezer window, opened the book and began reading.

"Book One: Of Man's First Disobedience, and the Fruit of that Forbidden Tree, whose mortal taste brought Death into the World, and all our woe…"

And as she read, despite the strangeness of the evening and the horror of the nightmare and the absence of her sister and the grim poetry scrolling down the book's pages—despite all that and all of life's other uncertainties—for the first time in ages, in Topaz Artemis Cushing felt content being alone.

"Topaz…!"

15

ARTISTS & MODELS

Vincent Duprix – The Studio at 1951 Fisher
A Night of the Waning Quarter Moon

"So, Vincent," Victoria said as she prowled through the artist's studio like a hungry cat, "which of your current harlots is *this* waif?"

Anger rose up within Vincent; he'd had quite enough of his wife's needling—*more* than enough, actually. And now, with his left hand nearly healed, he was making great progress in his work. Couldn't she *see* that?

"Jealousy is unbecoming of you, my dear," he replied, keeping his temper in careful check. Part of him longed to take one of his sculpture knives and plunge it straight through his wife's black heart. Instead, he decided to try a more subtle form of cutting. "These little fits exaggerate the lines around your mouth and eyes, which completely offsets any youthful benefits to your appearance that you might have gained since starting to dye your hair."

"I *haven't* dyed my hair," Victoria said coldly. "I've *never* dyed my hair."

Vincent shrugged, secretly pleased that his dig had worked. "If you insist. You needn't worry, though; I wasn't going to *tell* anyone."

"Who would *you* have to tell?" she countered.

"Oh! Splendid! Nice riposte!" he said, beaming. "If I had a heart, you might have pierced me to its very center."

"*If* you had a heart, I might have cut it out already."

"*Touché!* But, since you insist on prying… This figure I'm working on is neither waif nor harlot." He ran his hands lovingly over the sculpture, now nearly finished, and so much better than the torso he'd been working on previously. "This lady is royalty of the highest order—a *queen* in her own time, and, if you must know, the current ruler of my dreams." He grinned and theatrically clenched his hands over the center of his breast.

Victoria's hazel eyes narrowed. "But who *is* she?"

"That, my dear, is for *me* to know and you to wonder endlessly about." He walked past Victoria on his way to fetch more clay, pausing only long enough to give her a peck on the cheek as he passed. He knew the brief kiss would further infuriate his wife, and felt pleased when the buss had its intended effect.

"Vincent…!" she hissed, smoldering.

He waved off her rebuke as well as her lingering question. "All in good time, my dear. All in good time." He returned to his sculpture with the new clay and began filling out her buttocks; those delicate cheeks needed to be rounder…

Victoria, apparently flustered by his cavalier attitude, merely stood there, steaming.

"You know my dear," he told her has he worked, "I was thinking about what you said—about changing the exhibits to bring in a larger segment of the public… Perhaps my Wax Museum…"

"*Our* wax museum," she corrected.

"Yes," he replied drolly, "*our* museum... I was thinking that perhaps it *should* focus on more lurid themes as well as on beauty. Life is not all mimosa and roses, after all." This, too, was a dig at his wife, tweaking at her favorite beverage and flower.

Her eyes remained narrow. "Nor is it brandy and trollops."

"More's the pity." He gave the newly-rounded butt cheek of his sculpture a little slap; Victoria flinched, whether from the sudden action or some form of artistic sympathy, Vincent couldn't tell.

"In any case, I was thinking that I might solve *two* problems with one fell swoop."

"Two *birds* with a single stone, as it were," she said, her voice low and deadly.

Vincent understood the birds pun, but chose to breeze right by it.

"Yes. And why not?" he said. "It occurred to me that if we were to combine exhibits with those of the Cushings, open the doors connecting the two display floors, and use some of my sculptures alongside their artifacts—in an expanded Egyptian motif, for instance—then perhaps that might increase the customer flow for both businesses."

"You want to marry our museum to the tawdry exhibits of those... girls?" she asked contemptuously.

"Well, not to the girls specifically," Vincent replied, "but to their father's collection, yes. We could each show off our wares to the others' customers, that way and maybe even have a 'special combined admission' price for both attractions. Of course, I don't know for sure, but I suspect such a joint venture might prove very popular."

"Or it might be like hitching their dead horse to our already struggling team," his wife replied.

"Oh, really, Victoria... Don't be so melodramatic. What harm could it do?"

She turned away from him, as if not wanting to face his gaze, and paced to the broad bank of greenhouse-like windows occupying the studio's north side. "Better to ask yourself what *good* it could do. And the answer, I fear, would be '*none*.'"

"But aren't *you* the one who suggested that we try something different to perk up business?" he asked. Despite his best efforts to needle her, and not the other way around, her blasé attitude was beginning to get to him.

Victoria didn't look at her husband, but instead gazed out the studio windows toward the street below. She seemed to be looking for something—or perhaps *someone*.

"Really, Vincent," she said, "if you can't tell the difference between a *sensible* idea and another of your wild flights of fancy…" Now his wife turned haughtily and settled her cold, hazel eyes—they looked almost blue in this light—upon him. "…Well, then I don't see any point in discussing it any further."

She strode toward the studio door and paused at the threshold. "I'm sure you'll do what you want, anyway. You *always* do."

"Where are you going?" he snapped.

"Out," she shot back, slamming the door as she left.

Vincent fumed.

His wife was off to see her coachman lover, no doubt, or some other new peasant that she'd lured, black-widow-like, into her embrace.

Vincent clenched his fists, realizing only after he'd done it that he'd crushed the lumps of clay he'd been holding in his hands. Their wet mass oozed out between his fingers, like cold grey entrails.

He shook his head and chuckled.

"We really are quite a couple, aren't we?" he said to the statue he'd been working on. "Well, if my wife wants to expand her stable of lovers… Two can play at that game."

His mind flashed to the lovely girls working downstairs. *So close at hand…*

The middle finger on his left hand, injured more than two

weeks ago, throbbed. He'd taken the bandage off, and it was nearly healed, but it still looked a little purplish and withered. It wasn't hampering his sculpting anymore, though. In fact, he was doing some of the best work of his life.

Maybe he *would* ask the twins to model for him, just to vex his wife. The pair were teenagers... impressionable... they shouldn't be hard to lure into his studio—and out of their clothes.

Yes, it would serve Victoria right, if he did that. He would even *pay* the girls, which would annoy his wife further.

And if one thing led to another—as it had many times in the past—well... So much the better.

Twins posing for a twin conquest.

Vincent grinned at the thought.

Then the early morning sunlight reflecting in through the big studio windows caught the face of his new sculpture, and he noticed something he'd missed before—something he didn't like.

"Heavens!" he exclaimed. "I am *so* sorry, my dear. I haven't gotten your cheekbone quite right, have I?"

He leaned toward the clay visage and examined it closely. "Yes, I've definitely missed the loveliness of your left zygomatic arch," he told the sculpture. "I do apologize."

Vincent stepped back and rubbed his chin, heedless of the fact that he was smearing himself with clay. "It's not right... but what exactly am I *missing*?"

He stared at the sculpture for a good ten minutes, but just couldn't figure it out.

"Well," he finally said, wiping his hands on his work smock, "I guess I'll just have to go and check."

He paused briefly at the sink and washed the clay off his hands, arms, and face before removing the smock and laying it aside. Then he hurried downstairs into the waxworks and opened the door adjoining the Chamber of Horrors.

It was early in the day, well before opening, so he didn't expect to find either Opal or Topaz in the exhibit, and even if he did, he *was* their landlord, after all, it was his right to inspect the place from time to time (especially considering all the changes they'd been making lately).

Maybe I'll be inspecting them *as well, soon,* he thought, leering. Who would he start with first: Topaz, the willowy blonde, or the well-rounded Opal? Whom should he first persuade out of her clothes to sit for a bit of sculpting? *Hmm...*

Vincent wondered which one would annoy his wife more. She'd always seemed more jealous of blondes; though it was *redheads* who really set her off. Such a pity Victoria had lost her shape—and developed such an annoying personality.

"Duprix...!"

The sound of the voice in his head gave Vincent a start, instantly shattering his reverie.

He'd grown used to hearing the voice since injuring his hand, but not so accustomed to hearing it out of the blue. Usually, it crept into his mind while he was working, purring to him softly like a cat, or hissing secrets like a serpent in his ear.

And, of course, it wasn't the voice he *really* wanted to hear; it was the man's voice, not *hers*.

"What is it?" Vincent whispered back, though he didn't really expect an answer. The voice was good at telling him things, and not nearly so forthcoming with responses.

Then he realized he wasn't alone. *Someone* was in the Chamber of Horrors with him.

Vincent froze. The basement chamber lay dark, dappled only by spots of sunlight leaking in from the narrow street-level windows. There was more than enough light to see by, but still plenty of shadows to hide in.

And standing at the edge of the gloom on the far side of the museum lurked a figure, facing away from Vincent.

It's a man, Vincent realized, though not the familiar lanky figure of Dr. Leigh Cushing. Francis, or one of the girls' other suitors, perhaps? The sculptor peered into the dark shadows, but couldn't quite recognize the intruder. *What's he looking at?*

The trespasser seemed to be staring at that huge reddish-black rug that the girls had framed and mounted on one wall.

Then, as if sensing Vincent's presence, the man suddenly wheeled. In his hand he clutched a large spanner, holding the wrench as if it were a weapon.

"Who's there?" he barked.

"Shaw?" Vincent said, stepping from the shadows.

Paul Shaw peered at him from the darkness. "Oh, it's only you, Mr. Duprix. Yes, it's me, Paul." He stepped into the light and smiled.

"What are you doing here at this hour, Mr. Shaw?"

The handyman looked a bit sheepish. "I came to check the work I've done on the freezer for the new exhibit," he said. "I know your wife gets mad at me if I come down here to help out the girls when I'm on break, so I thought I'd do it now, before the waxworks opens."

"It's very sensible of you to avoid Victoria's wrath," Vincent said. "That's something I try to do myself. I suppose you'd better get back to your work, then."

"Oh, I've finished," Paul said. "I was just about to head upstairs."

"When you stopped to admire that pelt," Vincent observed.

"Yes, I guess so. Opal says it's a wolf, but it looks more like a bear to me."

Vincent crinkled his brow. "I haven't given it much thought before, Mr. Shaw, but I suppose you could be right."

Paul shrugged. "I'll be getting to work, then. By the way... Why are *you* down here, Mr. Duprix?"

"I've had a notion for a new sculpture—an Egyptian sculpture," Vincent explained, "and I thought I'd drop down for a little inspiration before business hours."

"That's a good thought," Paul said. "If you had an Egyptian display, it might help draw customers from one attraction to the other."

"That's just what I was telling my wife," Vincent said, "though she didn't seem to think very much of the idea."

"Speaking of your wife," the handyman began, "I assume you know that she's invited me to take a room in the old servants' quarters of the house, as partial compensation for the work I'm doing." He smiled again—something he seemed to do almost as readily as Vincent. "Easier than giving me a raise, I guess."

"Yes," Vincent mused, stroking his chin, "far easier, at the moment." Though looking at Shaw, from broad shoulders to narrow hips, Vincent suspected that his wife might have other motives as well.

"So, you're okay with that?" Paul asked eagerly.

"Yes, yes. It's fine. I heartily approve," Vincent said, though a headache was forming just behind his eyes. He rubbed his wounded finger, which had begun throbbing again, too.

"I suppose I should get to work then," Paul said. He nodded and headed for the short stairway joining the two exhibits.

"And I as well," Vincent said as the handyman passed him. When Paul reached the stairs, Vincent asked: "Oh, are the girls around this morning?"

"No. They're not here right now."

"Funny, you working here without them."

"They went out to fetch some items to dress up the new exhibit," Paul told him. "I'm sure they'll be back shortly. I'll see you later, Mr. Duprix. Enjoy the mummies."

"Yes," Vincent replied. "Yes, I will."

Paul went into the waxworks and closed the door behind him.

As soon as the meddler had left, Vincent strode quickly to the mummy exhibit.

He sighed as he stood before the queen's mummy case,

enraptured. He gazed at the carved face, so vital and lovely that she might almost be alive. He drank in the delicate cheekbones (that he couldn't quite capture—yet), luxuriated in the warm ochre skin, and gazed at the gleaming onyx eyes.

It was almost as though the queen were here with him…

"Oh, Bastiti, my love, how will I ever do you justice?" he asked. "I've attempted to sculpt you faithfully, just as I saw you in the studio mirror that day—but try as I might, it's no use. I may never be able to capture your true loveliness. Why won't you appear to me again, that I might complete your sculpture and recreate your beauty for all to see?"

"Why try to recreate my queen's beauty, when you might revive *it?"* said the voice in Vincent's mind, a voice that—over the past week—he had come to realize belonged to *Sethotep*, one of the other mummies in the exhibit. Sethotep was the man Vincent had seen standing in the shadows of the mirror, behind the queen, that night.

During her rule, Sethotep had been Bastiti's confidant, high priest, and chief architect. It was he who had constructed her fabulous tomb as well as the lost crypt of her husband, Sethmosis.

Or so Vincent gathered from his mental conversations with the ancient builder.

While Vincent had glimpsed Bastiti that one time, it was Sethotep who whispered to Vincent in quiet moments, telling him about the glories of the queen's all-but-forgotten dynasty. The high priest-cum-architect also revealed secrets from the *Book of Thoth*, a tome that he claimed could resurrect the dead.

But were such things actually possible?

"Yes," Sethotep hissed, replying to Vincent's innermost thoughts. *"All things are possible,* if *one is willing to pay the price."*

Vincent looked from the mummy case of his beloved to that of the priest; Sethotep's obsidian eyes, carved into the casket lid, stared back at the sculptor.

"What must I do?" Vincent asked. He needed to see that astounding woman again—that slender, dark-skinned Venus—and he was willing to pay any price… to do *whatever* it took.

He crossed his arms over his chest, bowed his head, and knelt before the ornate coffins of his queen and her honey-tongued advisor.

"I'll do *anything*."

In the shadowed light of early morning, it almost seemed as if the carved face of Sethotep's sarcophagus smiled.

"To revive my queen," the high-priest purred in Vincent's mind, *"a* sacrifice *must be made… A* human *sacrifice."*

16

CHANGES & PORTENTS

*Opal Cushing – 1951 Fisher St.
A Day Later*

"Is it true, Paul? Are you really moving into the old servant's quarters?" Opal asked.

Paul Shaw, standing on the landing just inside 1951 Fisher's front door, smiled at her. "It's true. Though, really, I don't have much to move."

Topaz poked her head out of the Chamber of Horrors entrance. "Oh?" she asked skeptically.

Paul looked uncomfortable, which made Opal prickle. Why did her sister always have to be looking gift horses in the mouth?

"I've been traveling a lot," Paul explained. "You can't accumulate a lot of stuff when you're traveling; it holds you back."

Topaz glanced at her sister before ducking back inside to tend the exhibits. *"Holds you back..."* the look seemed to say—a reminder that maybe a man like Paul didn't want to be tied down by *anything*.

Which Opal was to assume included *romantic* entanglements, as well.

So subtle, sister dear.

She was tempted to stick out her tongue at her twin, but resisted.

"I'll bring all my stuff over at lunch time," Paul continued, apparently unaware of the sisters' byplay. "Even Mrs. Duprix can't complain if I move in during lunch hour."

"Well, even if she *does* complain, I think it's great," Opal said. Spontaneously, she threw her arms around his neck, leaned up, and kissed him on the lips.

Paul looked startled. "What was *that* for?"

"For all the help you've given us," Opal replied, though really, she'd just wanted to kiss him.

"Oh," he said. "I thought you were sort of… spoken for."

A prick of guilt wheedled at Opal's brain. Was it wicked of her to be kissing another man while dating Frank? She didn't think so. Not *very* wicked, anyway. It wasn't like she and Frank had exchanged promises or anything.

"What's a little kiss between friends?" she said coyly.

"What indeed?" he asked. And he took her in his strong arms and kissed her again.

Opal put her arms around his waist and kissed back, luxuriating in the muscular warmth of his body. As their lips met, a tingling sensation started down at the tips of her toes and spread all the way to the top of her head.

The kiss didn't last long, but the glow lingered even as Paul disentangled himself.

"I should be getting to work," he said, seemingly embarrassed by the sudden passion of their embrace.

"Me, too," she replied, noticing that her face had reddened as well.

And with that, he ducked through the door to the waxworks, and Opal stepped into the Chamber of Horrors.

She expected to find her sister waiting for her just inside the doorway, but Topaz wasn't there. Instead, she was puttering around the exhibit floor, dusting the Iron Maiden of Baron Latos.

"Bathory's tub could use a good rubdown," Topaz noted, without looking away from her task.

"Somebody been filling it with blood again?" Opal asked.

Topaz laughed—a light, musical sound—though Opal knew it wasn't entirely spontaneous; her blonde sister had other things on her mind.

"Nope," Topaz replied. "Nor bathtub gin, either."

"More's the pity."

"It's just collecting a lot of dust," Topaz continued, "like everything else since Mr. Shaw began working on modifying the freezer."

"I think he's done now."

"Yes," Topaz said. "He told me the other night."

A cold chill ran down Opal's spine. Was Paul making time with her sister, too? "The other night?"

"Yes, I found him working late, after I woke from my nightmare."

"Working late?"

"Yes."

"In the chamber… just you and him… alone."

"Yes. Well, I wasn't working. I just came down because I thought I heard something."

Opal tried hard not to frown, though her stomach was twisting in jealous knots. It wasn't like her sister to withhold information. "You told me about the nightmare, but you didn't tell me about Paul."

"Didn't I? It must have slipped my mind. Sorry." Topaz stopped dusting. "Look, Opal, you don't have anything to worry about on my account. I'm not interested in Mr. Shaw. Really, I think both of us should be careful around him—you especially."

Opal's pangs of jealousy quickly turned to annoyance. "What do you mean?" she asked, her eyes narrowing.

"Well, he's too old for us, really."

"You said that before. And I'm not sure that *you* get to determine who's too old for *me* in any case."

"And there's something *odd* about him. Something sad… almost tragic. Can't you feel it?"

"I feel something tragic all right," Opal replied. "It's tragic, you mooning over that block of ice in the other room."

Topaz blushed. "Stop trying to change the subject."

"I'm serious," Opal continued. "Why do you come down here at all hours of the day and night and just *sit* there, reading to that thing as if it were alive?"

"It… *He* was alive… once."

"But he's dead *now*. He's been frozen in that block of ice for at least one hundred years."

"But he's not like our other exhibits," Topaz countered. "He's a *human being*—at least, he was, when he was alive. And when I'm near the exhibit, I… I can't help it; I feel *sad*. He seems so lonely. Haven't you felt it, when you look at him?"

Opal shook her head. "He feels creepy to me. There's something about him that doesn't seem *human*. It's not just his size, either. Something about the Ice Man just feels… *off*."

"Like Mr. Shaw feels *off*?"

"Don't drag Paul into this."

"You *know* that's not his real name—Mr. Shaw, I mean," Topaz said.

"What?" Opal blurted, genuinely surprised.

"He's not who or what he's pretending to be," her sister continued. "I feel it every time I'm around him. I mean, he *seems* nice enough, but a lot of things about him just don't add up. I mean, he's an American. You can tell by his accent, right?"

"Right…"

"But he lived in the Philippines, and some things he's said

make it obvious he's done a lot of traveling, but at the same time, he doesn't have any money."

"Father does a lot of traveling," Opal countered, "and *we* don't have a lot of money."

"But Father's money is all wrapped up in our exhibits," Topaz said. "How does Paul have enough wherewithal to travel from America to the Philippines to London, and yet he has so few things that he can move into the servants' quarters over lunchtime?"

"Maybe he works odd jobs—pays his way as he goes."

"Have you looked at his hands, Opal?"

"What about them?"

"They're too smooth for a seaman or day laborer."

Opal didn't want to admit it, but her sister was right. Paul's hands *were* very smooth. There was no way he'd been working at manual labor all his life. "Maybe he *had* money, but he's lost it."

"That's what I think," Topaz agreed. "But how—and *why*?"

Opal threw her hands in the air angrily. "Well, how should I —?" Then an idea hit her. "I know; we'll use the cards."

"You want to do a Tarot reading for Paul?"

"Why not?" Opal replied. "It worked when we tried it for Dad, didn't it? How much time do we have before opening?"

"About half an hour."

"That's plenty of time," Opal said. "Stay here; I'll get the cards." And, without waiting for Topaz to reply, she dashed out of the chamber and upstairs to their bedroom.

It took her only a few minutes to dig the tarot cards out of their nightstand and return to her sister.

"Do you really think this is a good idea?" Topaz asked.

Opal opened the case containing the deck.

A sudden rapping sound echoed through the Chamber of Horrors. "Excuse me, ladies," said a familiar voice.

It was Vincent Duprix, poking his head through the door connecting the chamber to his waxworks.

"Could I have a few moments of your time before you open for the day?" he asked.

"Sure," both twins agreed.

Opal was annoyed, though; she'd already gotten in the frame of mind to do a reading, and she didn't want to break concentration. Doubly annoying, she suspected that her sister was actually *relieved* by the interruption.

Vincent strolled down the steps, looking (as always) very dapper, and walked up right next to the sisters—almost uncomfortably close. He smiled his showman's smile (the one he seldom used around his wife).

The hairs on the nape of Opal's neck stood up, just a bit.

"I have a proposition for you," Vincent began. "No, wait... That's the wrong word... A *proposal?*"

Opal doubted that he'd misspoken. Usually, it was her twin who got stronger sensations of people's motives and thoughts, but Vincent seemed far less subtle than usual. The smile he was sporting this morning barely hid the lascivious leer lurking behind it.

"What kind of proposal?" Topaz asked. Opal felt sure that her sister was picking up their landlord's less-than-savory signals, too, but her twin didn't show it. (She was always better at hiding her feelings—at least in social situations.)

"It's about the rent..." Vincent said.

"I know we're behind again," Opal blurted, "but we—"

"Oh, I'm not here to badger you about it," Vincent said, cutting her off. He turned away from the girls and began looking around the exhibits, casually running his fingers over many of the intervening surfaces.

Opal noticed that his middle finger, which he'd hurt during the mummy unpacking, was no longer bandaged. The digit still looked a little purplish, though, and something about the color made Opal shudder.

"I thought that we might be able to work out something to… ease your burden," Vincent finished.

A series of unpleasant carnal options flashed through Opal's mind, but she kept her lips buttoned. No need to verbally pounce on the old lecher… yet.

"What do you have in mind, Mr. Duprix?" Topaz asked innocently.

"It was my wife's notion, really," Vincent said, now casually running his fingers over Bastiti's mummy case.

"Mr. Duprix, please," Opal said, with a glance to the sarcophagus.

Duprix withdrew his hand and looked chastened. "Oh, I'm sorry! I wasn't thinking. Such lovely, sensual things, they almost beg to be touched, don't they?"

Like some other *lovely things in this chamber, I bet,* thought Opal.

"As I was saying, as you know, I am in continual need of models for my work, but—as you certainly have noticed, the economy could be better in terms of sales and attendance at our attractions. My dear wife recently mentioned the perhaps-fortuitous coincidence that while I am short on funds to hire models, the two of you are short on funds to pay the rent…"

Here it comes…

"So, it occurred to me… to us, I mean… that perhaps we could help each other out. The two of you could model for me, and in return, I could ease the burden of your rent." He smiled at the twins, like the cat ready to eat the canaries.

Opal was about to tell him where to stick his offer, when Topaz said:

"That's very generous of you, Mr. Duprix. It certainly would seem to be an arrangement advantageous to all concerned."

"We'll have to think about it," Opal put in, afraid that her sister might—for the sake of the business—accept the offer out of hand.

"Could you give us a few days?" Topaz said, picking up her sister's hint.

Vincent looked at his wristwatch. "Of course. Take as long as you need. I'll try to keep my wife from… pestering you until you can make a decision."

"Thanks," said Opal.

"We appreciate that," Topaz added.

With a wave of his fingers and a final, predatory smile, Vincent swept across the room and mounted the stairs, pausing only briefly once he'd reached the top. "Good luck with today's business," he said, and with a bow of his head, he existed and shut the door.

"I bet he hopes business is bust, so we have to model for him," Opal said, fuming. "You weren't really going to take up his offer, were you?"

"No, of course, not," Topaz replied. "Not unless we *really* have to."

"You don't mean to say you'd actually consider taking off your clothes for that old lech, do you?"

Topaz shrugged. "The human body is a beautiful thing, certainly nothing to be ashamed of—"

"I know. I've seen yours ever since we were born."

"—but I have a feeling that things *might* not stop with just sketching and sculpting," her sister finished. "And I have no desire to give up my virtue to Monsieur Duprix."

"Nor do I," said Opal. Truth to tell, she had several more attractive possible candidates for that honor at the moment. "I wonder what our landlord's *really* up to—besides the obvious."

"If you're curious, turn the tarot for him and find out."

"Maybe I will. *After* we find out a little bit more about the mysterious Mr. Shaw." She uncased the tarot and began to shuffle.

"Or whatever his *real* name is," Topaz said. She pulled a seat for herself and another for her sister around a small round table in the exhibit room.

In her mind, Opal formed the question she wanted the tarot to answer—*"Who is Paul Shaw?"*—and then dealt the five cards, face down, onto the table.

She flipped up the first card, Paul's deep background and origins.

"Ten of Pentacles," Topaz announced.

Opal grinned. "So, he *was* rich, but he lost his fortune."

"But how? And when?"

"Maybe the next card will tell." She turned it up: Paul's more recent past. "The World, inverted."

"Someone in power had it out for him—and maybe still does," Topaz interpreted.

"Whoever it was, it shook up his life," Opal agreed. "Let's see what the present holds." She flipped over the card.

Topaz gasped. "Death!"

CRASH!

Both girls sprang to their feet. Opal's hand caught on the edge of the tabletop as she leapt up, overturning the table and spilling the entire deck of cards to the floor.

She cursed. "What was that?"

"Something fell," Topaz replied. "The pelt of the Beast of Gevaudan—its frame came off the wall." She moved quickly through the displays to where the fallen artifact lay, its frame face-down on the floor.

Opal frowned. "What could have caused *that*?" she asked. "Is the display all right?"

"The glass isn't broken," Topaz told her, tipping up the heavy frame. "I guess the rest of it is all right, too."

Indeed, despite the fall, the artifact seemed undamaged. "Hard to hurt an old wolf skin, I guess," Opal observed. "Odd that the glass didn't break—but thank heaven it didn't!"

"You bet," Topaz agreed. "We don't have any extra money to spend on repairs, right now."

She and Opal examined the wall where the frame had hung; the hangers seemed to be in place; nothing looked broken or amiss.

"I don't understand it," Topaz mused. "There's no reason it should have fallen off the wall."

Opal shook her head, and chill of worry ran through her heart. "It's almost like someone—or some*thing*—didn't want us to finish reading Paul's fortune."

17

ERZSEBET'S APPRENTICE

Victoria Duprix – Soho, London
The Night of a Waning Crescent Moon

Victoria peered through the London fog at the woman in high heels clicking down the Soho back streets—the woman she'd been following all evening.

The model appeared as Victoria remembered her: tallish and slender but well-rounded in the hips and bosom, a fact not quite disguised by the woman's fashionable straight-contour evening dress. The dress was turquois, made of some silk-like fabric, rayon probably, as only a high-end model could afford actual silk. Vincent's model was not high end, not yet, anyway. If she'd been doing *well*, she wouldn't be entering her third club of the night, unaccompanied.

Surprising how long it takes a girl to sleep her way to the top, nowadays, Victoria mused. Unless the girl didn't like men, of course…

Though she seemed to like my husband well enough…

A girl could change teams, Victoria supposed, but *somebody* (aside from herself) was sleeping with her husband, and this shapely twenty-something seemed a likely suspect. She had strawberry blonde hair, for one thing; Vincent had always liked redheads.

And this woman certainly looked more like the sculpture in Vincent's studio than the whore Victoria had killed last week. Clearly it *hadn't* been that girl, as she was now dead, but Vincent's modeling continued at an even more frenzied pace.

Victoria rubbed the back of her black-gloved hand, the place Piper's hot blood had spilled on her. The skin there had looked younger once Victoria rubbed the blood off, no doubt about it. And hadn't her hair gotten a bit less grey? She thought so. Vincent seemed to have noticed it, too. He'd remarked about her dying her hair... *Ha!*

If only he knew...

How much blood would it take for Victoria to be truly *young* once more?

She didn't know, and her advisor in the mirror—*Erzsebet*—had remained maddeningly elusive, never appearing when Victoria wanted. (Victoria had even tried the old "mirror, mirror..." incantation from the fairy tales, to no avail.) And when Erzsebet *did* appear, she tended to reveal what *she* felt like sharing, rather than answering Victoria's questions.

"Blood..." the spectral figure insisted. *"Blood isss the key..."*

But *how much* blood?

That's what Victoria wanted to know. And exactly what was she to *do* with it? Drink it? Paint the walls with it? Sacrifice it to the gods? Drench herself in it? What?

"The taking of life—young life—will ressstore you!"

Victoria kept rubbing the back of her hand, unconsciously. Certainly, slaying Piper seemed to have had some beneficial effect—and Victoria had enjoyed doing the deed, as well. She'd never guessed how satisfying it would feel to kill a romantic rival.

If I'd known, I would have tried it long ago, she thought with a wicked smile.

Her shadowy mentor had seemed pleased when Victoria had returned home, fresh blood on her hands.

"What must I do next?" Victoria had asked.

Erzsebet had merely grinned back at her and said, *"More!"*

So, Victoria had chosen her next victim, still aiming to track down and slaughter her husband's current paramour.

This fashionable little slut, Angela by name, had intended to be an actress but settled for being paid for taking her clothes off. Victoria understood that. Modeling, whether on stage or for artists, could be a very pleasant and profitable way to earn a living.

But *not* if it included sleeping with her husband. She might have put up with that kind of nonsense once, but no longer. If Vincent wouldn't take Victoria to bed anymore, she'd decided that he'd take no one else, either.

Or if he did, she would make sure that those paramours would *pay*.

Angela laughed tipsily as she tripped over her own heels at the entrance to the Enfield Arms, a run-down public house hidden in a dismal alleyway. The sound of jazz, clumsily played, drifted out from inside the tavern. Angela propped herself up against the doorway, and then stumbled gaily inside.

Victoria took a deep breath and dropped the veil, which was attached to her fashionable black hat, over her face. The veil matched her ensemble—conservative ebony dress and knee-length overcoat—and in a bohemian neighborhood like this, the veil wouldn't be much remarked, she hoped. It would, however, effectively conceal her identity.

She tucked her prop—a sketchbook she'd borrowed from Vincent's studio—securely under her arm and walked casually into the pub.

Looking around the smoke-filled room, she soon spotted Angela standing at the bar, peering through the gloom, sizing up prospects. It was late, though, and most of the people in the pub were already in their cups. Few looked even marginally attractive to Victoria, and none seemed to have noticed, yet, that the young model had entered.

Victoria walked up and took the stool next to Angela, laying the sketchbook on the bar. When the barkeep approached, Victoria pointed to the glass of pale brown liquid, over ice, in front of Angela and said:

"I'll have what she's having."

The barman grunted and went to fetch the drink.

"I wouldn't," Angela cautioned. Then she whispered, "The whiskey's not very good here."

"Then why are you drinking it?" Victoria asked.

The girl shrugged, using an exaggerated motion which set her considerable bosom to jiggling. "Beggars can't be choosers."

"Are you begging tonight?"

Another shrug. "Work's been slim, but not *that* slim. Why? You looking?"

The barman brought Victoria's drink.

"She'll have another," she said, indicating Angela's glass. The bartender refilled the girl's whiskey.

"Thanks," Angela said. "Here's mud in your eye!"

"Cheers!"

They clinked glasses and drank.

The girl was right; the whiskey tasted terrible. Victoria fought hard not to wince as she kept smiling and ordered them both another. The barkeep complied, and Victoria paid him.

"Let's take a table," she suggested, picking up the sketch book and moving toward a shadowed corner of the room, far away from the dismal jazz band.

"Do I *know* you?" Angela asked as they sat down.

Victoria sipped her drink and peered out at the girl from beneath her veil. "That would be telling."

"Because you seem familiar-like to me. Maybe if you lifted

your veil...?"

"Here? In a place like this? No, my dear; that would be indiscreet."

"Oh, a real Lady, are you? Out slumming a bit?"

"Something like that."

"Are you suggesting we go somewhere else?" Angela asked.

"That would be up to you," Victoria purred.

"Because if we did," Angela continued, "you should know up front that I'm not into girls."

"I assure you, I'm no girl."

Angela crinkled her smooth, pale brow, slightly confused. "Nor into *ladies*, neither, ma'am—if you catch my meaning. Well, there was this *one* time with this fashion magazine publisher and his wife, but..." She reddened. "But the blighter never put me in his magazine, anyway!"

"*Tsk tsk!*" Victoria shook her head in sympathy. "Of all the nerve."

"I know, eh? A right wanker, that one."

"Or *should* have been, anyway," Victoria added in a conspiratorial whisper.

Angela giggled drunkenly. "Yeah. His witchy wife coulda helped." She tossed back the rest of her drink. "Anyway, I don't do that kind of stuff. Not no more. I learned my lesson. So, if it's that kind of girl what you're looking for..."

Victoria reached across the table and patted the girl's hand.

The touch felt warm, even through the black silk of Victoria's glove. "I assure you, my dear, that I have only one use for girls." She moved her hand from Angela to the sketchbook lying on the table and patted the well-worn cover.

"Oh..." Angela said. "You're an artist. So, you're looking for a model? At this time of night?"

"I couldn't sleep."

Angela adjusted her evening dress, which had begun to slip off her shoulders, showing quite an expanse of pale flesh and décolletage below her collar bones. "Well, I ain't got nothing better to do. Where's your studio?"

Vitoria noticed that the drunker Angela got, the more her cockney dialect showed.

"Just across the river."

Angela shook her head; Victoria was slightly surprised it didn't rattle.

"That's too far," the model said. "My place is closer, if you don't mind—assuming you have the money…"

"I paid for the drinks, didn't I?"

The drunk model grinned. "I s'pose you did at that." She stood, nearly toppling over as she did so. "Well… Let's get going, then."

Victoria knew where Angela lived—she'd acquired that knowledge before following her—but she let the girl lead her through the foggy Soho alleys to an even less fashionable district than they'd met in.

Together they mounted the rickety outside steps leading to the second-floor apartment that Angela called home. Several times along the way, she'd had to caution the girl to remain relatively quiet. "To avoid any chance of scandal," Victoria had told her.

For the most part, Angela complied, though she couldn't seem to suppress the occasional giggle.

Inside, the flat proved better fitted out and maintained than Piper's had been; the furniture was all relatively new and clean, and the space kept orderly, aside from the clothes, which were strewn carelessly about, hanging over furniture and the backs of doors and such.

Funny that a model who sometimes worked in fashion should be so cavalier about her outfits. Or perhaps that was *why* she was: too many bits of clothing to care about, and by the time you got around to wearing one again, it had gone out of style.

Victoria closed the door behind them and hung her overcoat

on a peg by the entrance.

"Sorry about the mess," Angela said. "I'd have tidied up if I'd known anyone would be stopping up."

"It doesn't matter," Victoria replied.

The girl smiled—a stupid, drunken smile. "So, you want me to put something nice on, or you want me in the altogether?"

"Altogether."

"Right, then. Get your pencils ready darling." With that, she began stripping off her dress.

Victoria made a pretense of getting ready to draw.

"Standing… sitting… or reclining?" the nude model asked.

"Sitting would be fine."

"You want a chair f' yourself, too?"

"Yes. Please."

Angela drew several wooden chairs up near to each other, in the center of the living room. (She had to move aside several rumpled outfits to do so.)

She sat down in one, facing backwards, her legs straddling the seat, and rested her arms and chin atop the chair back.

"That's fine," Victoria said, pulling her chair up close and sitting down. She opened the book and pretended to draw. She'd had some lessons in school, but never much practiced.

The model stared at her as Victoria worked.

"You *sure* I don't know you?" Angela asked.

"Perhaps," Victoria said, and lifted her veil. She did it casually, as she continued sketching, as if she were merely trying to get a better view.

For a few moments, the girl stared at her—puzzled… thinking.

Then her eyes widened. "Wait… Aren't you…?"

"Yes," Victoria said, her voice low and dangerous. "I'm Victoria… Victoria Duprix, Vincent's wife."

At first, the model appeared concerned, but then she apparently decided Victoria couldn't possibly know about the affair with Vincent, and therefore Angela should be pleased at this little "reunion." Drunkenness was dulling what few wits the model possessed, but she forced a smile for Victoria, anyway.

"I remember you now," the nude girl declared pleasantly.

"Yes, you… *modeled* for my husband, for a time."

"I always liked working for Mr. Vincent… Mr. Duprix, I mean. A right regular gent he was." Once more, the drunken grin.

Of course the little slut liked modeling for Victoria's husband! She liked it far *too* much.

"You've been modeling for him again recently, haven't you?" Victoria asked, glancing up while pretending to work.

Angela almost stood, then decided against it and settled down again. "Oh, no, miss… I mean, ma'am. I ain't… I mean, I haven't seen Vincent… Mr. Duprix in years."

The girl seemed on the verge of panicking, but Victoria couldn't be sure whether it was because of the current affair, or the old one.

Well… No sense taking chances…

"Oh, dear, you've moved," Victoria admonished.

"Did I?" Angela replied, biting her lower lip.

"Yes," Victoria said, rising from her chair. "I'll just help you fix it—recapture the pose."

The girl looked distressed, caught between worry about past —and present—misdeeds and the possible loss of tonight's modeling fee. Her naked body trembled slightly as Victoria approached, sketch pad in hand.

"Your left elbow was like this, you see?" Victoria told her. She stood behind Angela and gently eased girl's arm back into place with her left hand.

With the other black-gloved hand, Victoria silently drew the long, slender blade she'd secreted in the loose binding of the sketchbook.

"Y-yes, I see…" Angela said.

As she pulled the blade loose, Victoria let the book fall; it hit the wooden floor of the apartment with a loud *SLAP!*

Angela turned, startled by the noise.

When she did, Victoria quickly drew her blade across the girl's throat.

A spray of bright crimson filled the air.

Angela gasped, but Victoria quickly clamped her gloved hand over the model's mouth, smothering any attempt she might make to scream.

"No one can have my husband but *me*," Victoria whispered in the girl's ear.

The model's blue eyes went wide with terror as she realized what was happening, but Victoria leaned into her, pinning the girl's naked body against the wooden chair.

Angela struggled, but it was no use. Victoria dropped the knife and held tight, feeling the life quickly drain out of her victim. The cut had been deft and deep; it did its job well.

The spray of blood splashing onto Victoria's face and clothes soon petered off to merely a trickle. And when it stopped running entirely, she let the model's nude corpse slump gently over the chair once more.

It was almost a pity; the girl had been quite beautiful.

But she'd never again dally with another woman's husband.

Victoria rose, smearing the gore off of her face with the back of her glove-clad arm.

She licked her lips; the blood tasted *good*.

But she couldn't linger. She'd been careful, and the apartment was isolated, but someone still might have heard.

Victoria used Angela's bathroom mirror to make sure she'd wiped any visible blood from her face. Then she quickly gathered her things and threw her knee-length coat over her bloodstained dress and hurried down the stairs into the fogbound street.

So far as Victoria could tell, nobody saw her, but it took her a long time to walk back home. She didn't dare hail a cab, on the chance that she might be discovered or some trace of her crime noticed. (Funny to think of her righteous vengeance that way, as a crime.)

It was well after two A.M. by the time the mistress of 1951 Fisher crept through the servant's door and up the back stairs toward her third-floor bedroom.

Sounds on from the second floor made her pause on the way up, though.

Who would be messing about in the servant's quarters at this time of night? Her husband and yet another lover? Could it be she'd killed an innocent girl *again*?

Not innocent. Never innocent. Neither of them. They'd deserved what they got—for past transgressions if nothing else.

Then Victoria remembered… *Paul*. He lived on the second floor now…

She'd gotten so wrapped up in her scheme that she'd almost forgotten. And she certainly hadn't expected to find him still awake at *this* time of night.

Victoria listened, but she couldn't make out the words. There were definitely two people in Paul's room though—and one of them was a woman. Who…?

A flash of fiery jealousy shot through Victoria as she realized: *The Twins.*

Or one of them anyway. Which one?

The brunette. Listening intently, Victoria felt almost certain of it.

She'd never paid much attention to the girls over the years they'd lived in 1951 Fisher, barely learned to tell them apart, really—and she certainly couldn't distinguish them by just their voices.

But she'd observed the way Opal made doe eyes at Victoria's handsome employee. She couldn't help but notice; the girl was *so* obvious!

Part of Victoria wanted to rush into Paul's room, to catch the two of them flagrante, and stab them both to death.

The more sensible part of her knew that was a foolish idea, though, a sure way to get caught. She needed to finish her current mission. Dealing with the twins, and any other complications, would have to wait until later.

Silently, Victoria mounted the rest of the stairs, unlocked the servant's entrance to the third floor, and passed inside. She re-locked the door behind her and then slipped, unseen, into her bedroom.

Only when she'd locked that door as well did she breathe a sigh of relief.

She'd *done* it! Again!

Unable to resist grinning, she hung her cloak in the wardrobe. She hid the sketchbook there as well; she'd have to sneak it back into Vincent's studio later. Happily, it hadn't gotten any blood on it.

In the past, Victoria had often regretted the decision to take a different bedroom from her husband's. She'd done it as "punishment" for one of his dalliances, but, at the time, she hadn't realized it would be as much a punishment for *her* as for him—perhaps more for her, as Vincent just continued his philandering ways undeterred, and Victoria's sex life had fallen to almost nothing. (Until she started taking paramours of her own.)

Tonight though, she relished having the room to herself. She wouldn't have been able to exact her revenge—or her rejuvenation—with her husband looking over her shoulder.

Her every nerve tingling, Victoria strode to her mirror. What was it those bobble-headed girls had called it "Bathory's Mirror?" Is that who her shadowy advisor Erzsebet was? This Bathory person? Funny that Victoria hadn't considered that before.

Perhaps, some night, she would ask. Tonight, though,

Victoria had more important things on her mind.

She stood before the glass and gazed at her reflection. The bloodstain on her black dress seemed more like a mark of honor than evidence of a crime.

She moved closer... Could it be?

It was hard to tell in this dim light, especially with the soiled dress distracting her...

Victoria stripped off her clothing and then switched on every lamp in the room.

She stood before the mirror clad only in a few splashes of blood that had leaked through her clothing.

She looked *glorious*.

Her skin was smoother, the wrinkles around her eyes vanishing; the grey streaks in her hair had gone.

Yes, she wasn't perfect yet—still sagging in places she didn't like—but she definitely looked *younger*. She *couldn't* be imagining it.

"Thisss isss my gift to you," a sibilant voice whispered in her head.

Erzsebet Bathory emerged from the shadows in the mirror. Somehow, though the bedroom was brightly lit, the area just beyond the surface of the glass remained nearly pitch black. Perhaps Victoria's perpetually young mentor didn't like the light.

"Thank you," Victoria said. "But it's not enough. I want *more*."

A cunning smile spread across Erzsebet's lovely face. *"I knew you would."*

"What must I do?"

"We need more girlsss... More blood."

Victoria grinned. Whether she'd finally slain Vincent's current paramour or not, there were plenty of her husband's whores who still needed to be paid back. How delicious!

"But how...?"

"Bring the nexxxt one to me, and I will ssshow you."

18

PAUL'S CHANCE

*Paul Shaw (Longmire) – 1951 Fisher St.
That Same Night*

Paul pressed his lips against Opal's, enjoying the taste of her mouth and the warmth of her body next to his.

How long had they been locked in this embrace, whispering sweet words to one another? He wasn't sure; a long time, probably, he thought.

It had started as an "innocent" late night visit "to see your new room" she'd said. But it quickly turned into conversation and then into... What?

Was this an actual romance?

Paul didn't intend it to be; he didn't *want* it to be. But it had been so long since he'd let anyone get close—since his wife's death, really.

Sure, there had been a few women during his travels, but never anything *serious*... or even anything that Paul had *imagined* might become serious. That had been deliberate.

After Caliso and Judith had perished, he'd had no desire to let anyone get close to him ever again. But the body had needs, and sometimes Paul had taken comfort where he could, though he wasn't particularly proud of it.

He knew that the Roaring Twenties had brought in the current, modern age—and an ethos of "free love" with it—but, even in his rich playboy days, he'd never been entirely comfortable with casual sex.

To Paul, something as deeply emotional as lovemaking seemed to require some kind of meaningful commitment.

Of course, the chance for *any* kind of commitment for Paul had vanished with that awful hunt and the advent of The Curse.

Yet, here he was, with his arms wrapped around a girl more than five years his junior… And somehow it felt *so* right.

But Paul knew it *wasn't*. Opal was young, despite her grown-up appearance, and neither she nor her sister seemed very experienced in the ways of the world.

He didn't want to take advantage of the girl, though she seemed willing—*more* than willing, actually.

This isn't what you're here for, a rational voice inside his head reminded him. But Paul only had ears for the whispers of Opal Cushing.

The two were standing near his bedside in his newly painted servants' quarters room, still fully clothed. Paul guessed that neither the standing nor the fully clothed situations was likely to last much longer.

"Oh, Paul," Opal gasped in between kisses. She leaned down and rested her head against his chest.

Paul held one arm tight around her waist and, with his other hand, stroked her wavy, dark-brown hair. Her body… her hair… they both felt so wonderful…

Despite himself, an image of another woman with soft dark hair flashed through Paul's mind: Caliso, his dead wife.

Paul's stomach twisted, and he started to pull away, but she held him tight.

"We can't…" he breathed.

"We *can*," Opal insisted. "It's all right. I *want* to." She stepped back just enough to pull the bottom of his shirt out from beneath his belt. Then she began unbuttoning his shirt, from the top down.

He took her hands, stopping her.

"It's too fast," he said. "We hardly know each other."

She shrugged. "Since when does that matter nowadays? We both want to. So, what's stopping us?"

"What about that boyfriend of yours—Frank?"

That brought her up short. She stepped back, the spell of kisses and warm bodies pressed against each other broken, at least a bit.

"He's not my boyfriend," Opal said. "Not really. It's not like we've made promises or anything." Then, something seemed to occur to her. "Is there… Do you have someone else?"

Paul shook his head. "No," he replied. "No. Not now. There was someone once. But she died." And in his mind, he saw the smiling faces of his murdered wife and their infant daughter. He would never understand why they'd been killed—and he wasn't even sure he wanted to.

Knowing why won't bring them back. Nothing will.

"Oh," Opal said, clearly surprised. "I'm sorry."

"Yeah," Paul said ruefully, "me, too."

"Were you… was she…?"

Paul wasn't sure what Opal was about to say, and maybe she wasn't, either, but he decided to cut off this line of questioning, before it went any further.

"Look, we don't have time to discuss it right now," he said, turning away. He couldn't bear to look at her. He thought that if he did, he might not have the strength to make her leave. "I have to work tomorrow, early in the morning. So, I need to get some sleep. It has to be past one already."

"Past two, actually," Opal said, her voice sad and quiet.

"Even worse. It's hard enough dealing with Victoria when I'm well rested and on my game…"

"And do you?" she asked, a flash jealousy sparking in her blue-green eyes.

"Do I what?"

"*Deal* with her… with Victoria?"

"You know what I mean," he snapped. "She's hard to work for in the best of circumstances."

"Like a cat, always on the prowl."

"Yes. I suppose. Anyway, I need my rest."

Opal nodded, but he could see moisture welling at the corners of her eyes. "I understand. Paul… I'm sorry."

Despite himself, he grabbed her and held her tight.

"Me, too," he said. "I… Maybe we can talk about all this some other time."

"Yes."

"Maybe tomorrow."

"A-all right."

"But not tonight."

"No," she said, sniffing back a tear. "Not tonight."

He kissed her on the forehead. "Good night, Opal."

"Good night, Paul."

She left without looking at him; he closed the door behind her.

Liar! accused his conscience.

"Shut up!" Paul whispered, clutching the hair at his temples. "What else could I say?"

He couldn't tell her the truth, certainly—that he might be *gone* tomorrow, that she might never see him again.

Though if his plan succeeded, maybe she *could*. Maybe they…

But no. It was crazy to think that way. Either his plan would succeed, his curse would be lifted, and she'd despise him for what he'd done, or his plan would fail, and the doom of the wolf would still be hanging over him, and he'd kill again during the next full moon.

Maybe even kill her!

Paul couldn't bear the thought. True, he hadn't seen the mark of the pentagram on her hand or face, as he'd seen in his first few victims, but that didn't necessarily mean Opal was safe. With the wolf, *nobody* was safe.

And even if he didn't kill Opal, he might kill her sister, or her boyfriend, or one of the Duprixes.

Won't this torture ever end?

He needed to stick to the plan. That was his only chance.

He hadn't come here, hadn't agreed to room in this house above the Chamber of Horrors just to get closer to Opal—or to anyone else for that matter. He'd come here for a specific purpose.

And tonight was the night he'd carry out that objective, whatever the outcome might be.

Paul turned off all the lights in his room, in case Opal hadn't gone, in case she might be lingering, watching quietly outside his door.

He didn't want to take any chances, so he waited half an hour longer before opening the door and peeking into the hall connected to the stairway beyond. He neither saw nor heard anyone.

Good.

The servants' stairway stretched through all three stories of the 1951 Fisher, and down into the basement as well. The doors adjoining the second and third floors—where the Duprixes and Cushings lived—were kept locked, as there were no actual servants to wait on the tenants' needs. (Though Paul suspected that Opal might have left the third floor unlocked, in case he changed his mind and came to visit her tonight.)

The servants' door exiting into the basement was blocked by packing boxes, luggage, books, and other things that didn't fit in with the Cushings' exhibits. There was an outside bulkhead door into the basement as well, though that was padlocked, and Paul didn't have a key.

That left Paul only two avenues of approach: the main entrance to the chamber and the door that joined the chamber to the waxworks. The main door would surely be locked from the inside. He could use that doorway to make his escape, later, but first he needed to reach his objective.

Paul ducked back into his room, closed the door, and made certain he had everything he needed. He couldn't chance coming back to the second floor, once he'd obtained his prize. He'd have to leave directly after stealing it.

His heart pounded, though he wasn't sure whether it was the prospect of stealing from people he liked or the anticipation of finally being free of the wolf that caused his palpitations.

Everything seemed to be ready. He needed to take action *now* or chance being discovered—or risk losing his nerve.

Taking a final deep breath, Paul stepped out of his room and into the hallway.

He stopped and listened, every fiber of him alive, every sense keener than those of a normal man, though not yet (thankfully) *wolf* keen.

Almost three weeks left, he thought. *Three weeks...* Was that true, or was it shorter—tomorrow, maybe? He couldn't be positive. Either way, he needed this to end tonight.

Silently he descended the stairs and entered the waxworks on the first floor. He crept through the frozen tableaus, making for the adjoining door that was his only way to enter the Chamber of Horrors.

Chamber of Horrors... Ha! A metaphor for my life.

But he couldn't think about that now. He had to concentrate on his task...

He swiftly crossed to the door, opened it without a sound, and descended the short flight of steps into the chamber.

Paul paused and willed his heart to stop pounding; his pulse calmed, but only slightly. He needed to keep his head, to stay alert, get the deed done and then escape before anyone found out. He *couldn't* make any mistakes, couldn't do anything that might rouse the Cushings or the Duprixes.

He would steal the pelt of the Beast of Gevaudan, flee the house, and destroy the cursed thing.

He wasn't sure exactly *how* he'd manage that destruction, or *where* he'd do it, but first things first…

Get the damned thing off the wall; then destroy it.

Burning seemed the most likely method; that's what he'd try first. He'd tucked a lighter and a can of extra fuel in his shirt pocket, and if that failed, he'd brought his Bowie knife as well. That long blade had been with him through all his travels, back even to when he'd been a teenage big game hunter, and it hadn't failed him yet. If somehow it *did* fail, if somehow the accursed hide couldn't be burned or cut, he still had a whole month to figure out some other method.

No. Not a month. That was the curse, clouding his mind.

Two weeks, he reminded himself. *Three at most.*

He'd find those gypsies again, if he had to. They would know how to destroy it. Surely Maria would help him once more, if he asked—though finding her might prove tricky.

I have time. There's still time.

But first, he had to steal the wolf skin…

Concentrate!

Paul had grown familiar with the layout of the exhibits during the time he'd worked with the girls, so he moved through the darkness quickly and efficiently. His curse-enhanced eyes were keen at night, and the wan illumination leaking in through the narrow street-level basement windows provided more than enough light to see by.

He stopped, brought up short by something he'd noticed:

those damned fish scales. They glistened wetly in their jar, in the dark.

Scales of the isda-asawa, he remembered, *the Filipino fish-wife.*

Why had the villagers been calling that phrase—*isda-asawa*—when they'd burned his house down? Did it have something to do with his wife or her family? Did the villagers think Caliso and their daughter were cursed somehow, just as Paul was cursed now?

Keep moving, he chided himself. *Finish the job.*

He reached the pelt. It hung on the wall above a plaque describing the thing's history for the tourists. "The Pelt of the Beast of Gevaudan..."

The inscription didn't say anything about Paul's curse, however—about this wicked artifact siring a line of wolf-men. But why *would* it? Nobody believed in werewolves these days.

With cars and telephones and electric lights and even airplanes, Paul couldn't blame people for their skepticism. The modern world was ruled by science, not superstition. Paul himself had never believed in such things until Count Zarkoff and his terrible "game"...

But he couldn't think about that now. That way lay distraction... and madness.

Paul grabbed the rustic wooden frame containing the wolf skin and lifted it off its hooks.

The damned thing was cumbersome, heavier than he expected, but Paul was strong and in good shape; he lowered the frame to the floor with little trouble.

Now he had a decision to make. He doubted that just plunging his knife into the reddish-black fur piece would break his curse, so there was no point in even trying that here.

If he took the wolf skin out of the building *in* its frame, it would be easy for anybody—the police, for instance—to spot him; the frame was ten feet long and almost as wide as Paul was tall. So, he needed to get the pelt out of the frame.

Smashing the glass would be quicker, but someone might hear him. Cutting it out from the back of the frame would be quieter, but take longer.

You have the time. Just don't make any mistakes.

Paul got out his knife and flipped the frame around to cut away the paper backing. There would be some kind of mounting board behind that—maybe Masonite or plywood—but his knife should make short work of those obstructions. He'd either pry out the staples holding the board or, if he had to, cut straight through it. (Though doing *that* would take even *more* time.)

He drew back his knife to start cutting.

Suddenly, everything went white.

Paul gasped and blinked, momentarily blinded.

When his eyes cleared again, he found himself crouching in the beam of a very bright flashlight.

Just beyond the edge of that beam, light filtering through the basement window glinted off of a gun barrel.

"Don't move!" commanded a voice from the darkness. "I have a revolver aimed precisely at your heart."

19

CAUGHT!

Paul Shaw (Longmire) – The Chamber of Horrors
Moments Later

"Kindly lay down your knife and stand up very slowly. And please, do me the favor of not taking any sudden actions," the voice told Paul. The tones were high and reedy, but clearly those of a man—a very well-spoken man.

"I am not a violent person," the voice continued, "and I'd hate to shoot you if I didn't actually *need* to. Nevertheless, provoke me, and I will most assuredly fire." The speaker remained hidden in the dark shadows on the far side of the exhibition room, but the man's flashlight lit Paul up as bright as day.

Despite being at a terrible disadvantage, for a moment Paul considered leaping at his opponent. The gunman didn't sound very formidable, and—despite the dire warnings—Paul thought he stood a good chance of taking his would-be captor by surprise.

And even if the man *did* shoot Paul, would it really do him any good? It took a silver bullet to kill a werewolf, after all, and

Paul doubted the man, whoever he was, had come prepared for that eventuality.

But then Paul remembered a warning he'd been given in a gypsy camp in Transylvania: *"A werewolf who is slain while a man becomes a werewolf* forever. *He will then track down and murder all those he used to love, until destroyed in wolf form."*

Could that possibly be true?

It wasn't a chance Paul could take. If this gunman, whoever he might be, got lucky and killed Paul, then Opal and Topaz wouldn't stand a chance. The whole of 1951 Fisher would become an abattoir!

Paul needed to find another way out of this fix. "Look," he said, "there's been some kind of mistake here."

"Yes, indeed, young man," replied the man in the shadows, "and *you* have made it. Despite what some in the government may think, there are laws against thievery in this country."

"But I wasn't *stealing* anything," Paul protested. "I happen to work here."

"In the middle of the night?"

"Well, no. Not usually. But I couldn't sleep. So, I came in to do some repairs, you know, to kind of work off my anxiety."

"And did working off said anxiety include removing a prized exhibit from its frame?" the gunman asked.

"No," Paul replied. "There's a *problem* with the frame. It fell off the wall the other day, and I thought I should take a look at it. I fix a lot of little things around here. I'm the Cushings' handyman."

The man with the gun moved closer. At this point, he could hardly miss if he tried.

"I don't believe you, young man," he said. "I happen to know that no handymen work here. For you see, I am the *owner* of this little exhibition you seem intent on pillaging."

Paul's heart skipped a beat, and he backed up a few steps. "You're Dr. Cushing?"

The man stepped forward again, and now a shaft of light from the street revealed his face. He was a thin, well-dressed older gentleman with an angular face, greying hair, and piercing blue-grey eyes.

"None other," Dr. Cushing said. "And I warn you that though I may not *look* very formidable, I am nevertheless a crack shot."

"But I'm Paul—Paul Shaw. I work for your daughters."

"I doubt that very much, unless our fortunes have improved considerably here."

"No, no. You don't understand," Paul said. The revelation of his captor as Opal's father had him rattled. His heart raced like mad, and sweat beaded on his skin. "Victoria... Mrs. Duprix hired me, but I help the girls out when I can. In my spare time. Look, I live in the old servant's quarters on the second floor."

"A fine arrangement for a prospective thief," Dr. Cushing noted. "Certain unscrupulous collectors would pay a pretty penny for some of these exhibits. I have spent my lifetime amassing them, you know."

"Yes, I know. But, look... I'm *not* stealing. I work around the place, fixing things."

"In the dark."

"Well..."

"With a hunting knife."

Paul knew there was nothing more he could say. Dr. Cushing had caught him red handed.

Paul shook his head. "Look... It's more complicated than that," he said. "Do you mind if I sit down?"

"Please do," Dr. Cushing replied, and he indicated a nearby antique chair by waving the barrel of his gun. "Slowly."

Paul sat; Dr. Cushing flicked on the main lights and set aside his electric torch.

"That's better," Cushing said. "Much easier to have a conversation with the lights on—the better to appraise the man who intended to steal my wolf skin."

"I…" Paul began, but then he put his head in his hands. He felt exhausted, as if all the weeks of planning and worry and deception had caught up with him. "Yes, I was going to take the pelt, but it's not what you think. I *wasn't* going to sell it."

Dr. Cushing regarded him skeptically from beneath bushy eyebrows. "Why take it, then?"

"Because I *had* to," Paul said. "Because I…" How much should he tell? Cushing collected mystical artifacts from all over the world, but did he really *believe* in the supernatural? Paul had seen some strange things during his travels—including a man-like amphibian in the Congo—but even *he* had thought werewolves a myth… until he *became* one.

He decided to go for something close to the truth, but not quite so outlandish.

"Because I have a rare disease," Paul confided.

"Indeed?"

"Yes, and I need the pelt of the Beast of Gevaudan to effect a cure."

"Who told you that?"

"Maria the gypsy," Paul said, the truth spilling out before he could come up with a better alibi; he was nearly exhausted, not thinking straight.

"A cure recommended to you by a gypsy?" Cushing scoffed. "I'm surprised you didn't try to tell me that you've been *cursed!*"

"So, you *do* believe in curses?" Paul asked, almost frantic now. If he couldn't convince Dr. Cushing—if he couldn't do what he'd come to do… "Look, whether you believe in curses or not, you have to help me. I need to destroy that pelt. It's the only way I can reclaim what's left of my life, the only way I can ever hope to be *normal* again!"

"You *do* seem quite abnormal at that," Cushing remarked. He took a seat in a nearby chair but kept the gun trained on Paul.

"Please! You *must* believe me."

"I *must* believe that you are cursed by gypsies?"

"No." How had Paul cocked this up so badly? "Not by gypsies. Just cursed."

"And you believe that to break that curse, you must destroy the wolf skin that hangs upon my wall?"

"Yes—the pelt of the Beast of Gevaudan. The gypsy Maria told me it's the root of my... problem. Destroying it will free me."

"You asked if I believe in curses, young man," Cushing said. "I have seen many strange things over the course of my travels, heard many tales even stranger, but I have *never* seen anything that would convince me that such things as witchcraft or curses exist. However, I have met many people who *believe* in supernatural powers of all kinds. And I *do* believe that *you* think that you are cursed."

Paul leaned forward in his chair. "Then you must help me. *Please!*"

Dr. Cushing shook his head and chuckled skeptically. "I wish I could, young man, but even if everything you've told me is true, I'm afraid that I have some disappointing news for you... That wolf skin you were attempting to steal is *not* the pelt of the Beast of Gevaudan."

"What...?" Paul's heart felt as if it had fallen into his shoes.

"Yes," explained Cushing, who put down his gun and started polishing his wire-rim glasses. "I'm ashamed to admit that the pelt we're exhibiting is a fake."

"What?" echoed a crestfallen feminine voice.

Opal!

"What's going on here?" asked Topaz's voice, so similar to that of her dark-haired sister.

If Paul had thought he couldn't feel any worse, he had been wrong. He turned and saw both girls, in their nightgowns, standing at the entryway to the chamber. Topaz clutched a flashlight in her hand; Opal looked as though she'd just been struck by lightning. Both of them stared at Paul.

"Oh, hello," said Dr. Cushing. He rose from where he'd been sitting, hidden from the twins' view.

"Father!" both girls blurted, and in a flash, they rushed down the stairs and threw their arms around him.

"We're so glad you're home," Topaz said.

Dr. Cushing hugged them back, smiling and chuckling approvingly to himself. "It's very good to see both of you again, too. I'm sorry I didn't write and tell you when to expect me, but you know how these things go."

But Opal had broken away from the little family reunion; she was staring at Paul. "Paul," she said warily, "what are you doing here? What's going on?"

Paul couldn't think of anything to say. His tongue felt like sandpaper.

"I caught this young man skulking about in the dark," Dr. Cushing explained. "It seems he was intent on stealing and destroying one of our artifacts."

Opal gasped. "Paul!" Her voice held a world of disappointment.

Paul plunged his head into his hands, unable to look at any of them. "I wasn't going to steal it," he moaned. "I just had to… destroy it."

"Oh, Paul," Topaz said. "How *could* you?"

"*Why*, Paul?" Opal asked. "Why?"

Paul just shook his head.

"The young man seems to believe that he is cursed," Dr. Cushing explained, "and by destroying the pelt, he will break the curse."

"But you said the pelt is a *fake*!" Paul exclaimed. "Now I'll *never* be free!"

"The curse is in your own mind," Dr. Cushing said. "Your cure must be found there as well. If you like, I can recommend a good psychiatric practice near Covent Garden. I hear they're doing wonderful things with insulin shock therapy."

"But, wait…" Topaz said, confused. "The pelt of the beast is a *fake?*" She seemed stunned by the very idea, as if her father had never done anything wrong or even told a lie before.

"Yes, I'm afraid it's true," Dr. Cushing admitted. "I'm terribly sorry for deceiving you both this whole time—but I didn't think letting you in on my little secret would do any good. You see, I've had this old wolf skin a long time; it's one of my earliest exhibits."

"I don't ever remember it *not* being in the museum," Topaz mused quietly.

"No. You wouldn't, either of you. I obtained it when you were quite small, but I was, I'm ashamed to say, 'sold a bill of goods.' By the time I discovered that the pelt was not what I believed, it had already been on display for a number of years. Admitting the mistake at the time would have caused a scandal, and probably doomed our little enterprise before it had barely begun. I feel bad about mislabeling it all this time, but it's far too late to change it now."

"But father," Topaz said, "how can you display a *fake?* The chamber is supposed to be a museum of genuine supernatural oddities and artifacts."

Dr. Cushing put one long-fingered hand on her shoulder. "But it *is* a genuine artifact, my dear. It is! It's the genuine skin of a Transylvanian dire wolf—a beast thought to have gone extinct in the Ice Age. Legends say that its hide is so tough that it is proof against blades, arrows, and even fire. And, from a few small tests I made—once I discovered the thing's true identity—those claims are actually true. So, our 'friend' here would have had a devil of a time destroying it, even if he *had* managed to steal it."

"You were going to *destroy* it?" Opal said to Paul, as if she could still barely believe his confession. She hadn't spoken at all since asking Paul *"Why?"* and tears welled in her blue-green eyes. She looked more angry than sad, though.

Paul gazed up at her, feeling pitiful. "I…" he began, and then couldn't go on. How could he have cocked up this whole situation so badly?

"*That's* why you came here, isn't it?" she accused. "That's why you went to work for Madame Duprix, and took the room upstairs, and…" Weeping, she spun away.

Paul's heart ached for her. He hadn't wanted to hurt the girl, but… "Opal, I…" he began. "That wasn't the way it was at all. What you and I had… what we *have*…"

She slapped him hard across the face. "The cards were telling me not to trust you," she said. "They were saying tragedy followed in your wake. I should have listened to them!"

Tears streaming, she dashed up the stairs and vanished from the chamber.

Paul's heart broke as she left. He hadn't felt this awful since his wife and daughter died. Right at that moment, not even the curse mattered.

"Opal, wait!" he cried, leaping from his chair.

Dr. Cushing fumbled for his gun.

"No, Father," Topaz said. "Let him go."

As Paul ran after Opal, Dr. Cushing set aside his revolver.

"Well," he said, "it seems things have gotten a bit *complicated* since I went away."

That was the last thing Paul heard as he fled the Chamber of Horrors.

He ran up the stairs to the twins' third-floor room, but found their door closed. Adrenaline coursed through his system, urging him to action. He almost put his shoulder to the door, to burst in, but then he heard Opal sobbing on the other side.

He stopped and knocked gently. "Opal…?"

"Go away!"

"Opal, I know you're hurt, but the pelt… It didn't have anything to do with you."

"I said, *go away*!"

"Opal, I love you, no matter what you think."

"I think you should go away! *Leave*, Paul! I don't ever want to see you again!"

"Opal, I…"

"GO!"

Paul hung his head and staggered down the back stairway, heading for his quarters. What else could he do? He couldn't have fouled tonight up any worse if he'd tried.

The pelt was a *fake*! After all the time and trouble he'd gone through—all the lies he'd told—so he could gain access to it…!

And worse, he'd fallen hard for Opal amid all his schemes. He hadn't meant to—and he certainly didn't *want* to—but it had happened, and over the course of just a few short days. He hadn't felt that deeply about anyone since his wife died. But despite his feelings for the girl, he'd still acted like a complete idiot.

How had he never fully considered what destroying the pelt might do to his budding love affair with Opal? Why had he ever thought that he could steal the artifact and then just come back to her and carry on as if nothing had happened? Had he gotten so used to hiding his true identity and motives that he couldn't even be honest with himself?

He stumbled into his second-floor room, closed the door, and leaned heavily against it. His head pounded. The air inside the apartment still smelled of fresh paint, but that didn't make the place feel any more like his home.

Paul realized now how good his life had been—at least until tonight—living here, having some kind of regular work, and helping the twins on the side. The combination of all those things had almost made him feel *human* again, like he could have a life outside of the curse.

And he'd actually dared hope that it might be over…

Fool!

"I suppose that's why I let my guard down," he mumbled to himself.

In a daze, he wandered over to the dresser, pulled out the middle drawer, and found the bottle he'd hidden in the back, behind his underwear.

He unstoppered it and took a long swig.

The whiskey burned like fire all the way down. It felt like both penance and redemption.

Part of him knew the liquor wouldn't help—not really—but sometimes it was the only thing that took away the pain, that allowed him to forget all the horrible things that had happened to him, and the even more terrible things that he'd done.

Though he didn't remember much from when he became the wolf, the faces of the beast's victims still haunted Paul's dreams nearly every night.

Would he see Opal's face among those people tonight?

No! He'd hurt her feelings, but he hadn't actually *harmed* her—not like what he'd done to that girl in the woods... or that poacher... or those muggers on the docks.

But despite the comparative paucity of this "crime," Opal's pretty brunette face swam before him, even now, her blue-green eyes staring at him accusingly.

Paul continued drinking.

He didn't stop until the world swirled to grey and thoughts of Opal—her touch, her smell, her kisses—were only a dim, pleasant memory in the back of his cloudy brain.

Finally, he set the bottle—now more than three quarters empty—down atop the dresser. His fingers fumbled with the slick glass as he did, and the whole thing almost toppled over. He only caught it just in time, and, with fingers feeling thick as sausages, he somehow managed to shove in the stopper.

He plopped down heavily on his bed, more of a cot, really; the metal slats beneath the thin mattress squeaked in protest.

"Shut up, you," he said, punching the pillow. The cot creaked in reply, the sound like fingernails on a blackboard to his ears.

If only his head would stop pounding…

But he knew the headache was his fault, too, and… No… Wait…

It wasn't just his head. Someone was rapping on his door, very softly.

Despite the spinning room and his throbbing head, Paul's heart leapt at the sound.

It was *Opal*. She'd come to talk… Maybe even to *forgive* him.

"Come in," he said, fumbling for the light switch, not really sure when he'd previously turned the lamp *off*.

The door opened, and a lithe figure entered and then silently shut the door behind her.

Paul finally wrangled the lamp atop the dresser into his fist and twisted the switch on. The lamp was old and the bulb dim and covered by a red, paisley patterned shade. The circle of light it shed barely reached the foot of the door.

But in that circle, Paul saw long, slender legs framed by a silken burgundy robe and a figure only slightly obscured by a purple gossamer nightgown that left little to the imagination. Paul couldn't see his lover's face in the shadows, but he could imagine her disappointment in him.

"Opal…" he began, his bleary mind groping for the right words. He didn't want to blow this chance. If only he hadn't had so much to drink…

Fool! the tiny, rational part of his brain chided.

"No," said a woman's deep voice. "Not Opal. Someone *better*."

Victoria Duprix stepped into the pale circle of light. She looked like a Greek goddess, tall and slender with her long black hair piled up atop her head. Paul did not remember her ever looking this good before.

"Trouble with your young friend?" Victoria asked, her voice almost a purr. "I'm not surprised. Teenage girls like that… They never *really* know what they want. I, on the other hand, know *exactly* what I want."

She stepped forward and let the robe drop. Even the dim light from Paul's lamp was enough to reveal *everything* beneath her flimsy nightgown.

Without meaning to, Paul licked his lips as he tried to think of what to say. He knew he should tell Victoria to go, but he sat dumbfounded on the edge of the bed.

Before he could form even a single word, she straddled him and kissed him hard on the lips.

She tasted hot and sweet.

And then their hands were roaming over each other, tugging off clothes, exploring.

Victoria's body felt so good next to his… warm and surprisingly soft for a woman of her age.

Locked in her embrace, and with the booze still sloshing in his head, for a while, at least, Paul forgot everything.

20

CHANGES IN THE CHAMBER

Topaz Cushing – 1951 Fisher
The Next Morning

The chirping of the birds just after dawn woke Topaz bright and early the next morning.

She rose and stretched, enjoying the feel of the sunshine on her face and body. For a few moments, all seemed right with the world.

Then she noticed Opal, still slumbering heavily, her brunette head thrust deep under her pillow, and Topaz remembered the events of the previous night—well, very early in the morning, actually.

Poor Opal!

Her sister had fallen hard for Paul Shaw, despite the brevity of their acquaintance, and despite the near-constant attentions of her other suitor, the charming Frank Browning.

Maybe she'll go back to thinking about boys her own age, now, Topaz thought, and then chided herself for being unkind to her twin.

Opal had cried herself to sleep after the scene in the chamber, and Topaz could hardly blame her. Imagine finding out that the guy you were in love with was only looking to steal from your family! What could be worse?

Nothing that Topaz could think of. She found herself wishing, just for a moment, that their tarot reading for Mr. Shaw hadn't been interrupted. The cards were clearly trending badly in that forecast. If they'd been able to finish, maybe they would have found some warning—maybe Opal, who was better at fortune telling than Topaz, would have seen what was coming and avoided any romantic entanglement with the man.

Still… How were they to know? The cards weren't *always* right, especially when dealing with people you were emotionally attached to.

Topaz sighed (softly so as not to wake her sister).

Then she took a change of clothes into the bathroom, showered (though the water pressure was never very good on the third floor), and readied herself for the day.

First thing she did was to go down into the Chamber of Horrors.

Everything seemed to be in order, including the barricade they'd put up in front of the door adjoining the waxworks.

We'll have to talk to the Duprixes about installing a lock, if they'll let us. Her family didn't want any more untrustworthy types sneaking in from the wax museum, after all.

Since she was there, Topaz decided to tidy up the exhibit and save her sister and father the trouble.

Father! It was so good to have him home. If not for the trouble with Opal and Paul, the joy at his return would have been overwhelming. As it was, his arrival only added to the confusion of the night. And his revelation about the pelt…!

Topaz had always considered everything their father did as above reproach. Yes, he was eccentric, to be sure, but this was the first time she ever remembered him having done something dishonest.

If Paul hadn't tried to *steal* the darn thing, would her father *ever* have revealed the truth?

She stared at the wolf skin, still hanging in its frame (no thanks to Paul) on the exhibit wall. She read the plaque describing it: *The Pelt of the Beast of Gevaudan*...

But that was a *lie*. According to Father, it was really the pelt of a Transylvanian dire wolf, but when he'd discovered the truth, he'd been reluctant to change it because the lie had gone on so long.

Topaz didn't quite understand that. Part of her wanted to take down the plaque that very moment and put up a new, more accurate one. Should she do it without consulting Father and Opal?

Her conscience said *"Yes,"* it was the right thing to do, but her loyalty to family said otherwise.

Frowning, she went and sat down on the floor next to the Ice Man display. "It's like if we were telling people you were a cave man or a Viking or something, when we know full well you're not," she confided to the frozen figure. "How would you feel about that?"

Of course, the Ice Man didn't reply; like the pelt itself, the ice-encased giant couldn't have feelings one way or the other. Both were long past worldly cares—unlike Topaz.

Was it so wrong to put a more sensational title on a display just to boost ticket sales? Certainly, the Siamese Mermaid was a bit of flummery—but everybody *knew* that, going all the way back to P.T. Barnum's similar display.

Like the wolf skin, that Far-Eastern chimera was a genuine artifact, even if it *wasn't* a genuine mermaid.

"I guess there's no harm in letting the situation stand," Topaz announced, though privately she decided that if they ever moved the museum, she would change the plaque to something more accurate, at that time.

The whole incident made her wonder, though:

Has Father lied about any of the other exhibits here? Are even more of our artifacts fakes?

She really had no reliable way of telling.

Often, Topaz had a strong intuition about things (and people), but most of the museum's collection confounded whatever preternatural ability she possessed. She could never quite nail down feelings about these objects.

The pelt felt strange—*unnatural*, somehow—but that could be said about nearly everything else in the chamber as well... except maybe for the mermaid (which was a known fake), and the meteor and the *mokele-mbembe* dinosaur tracks and the Ice Man, of course, which were merely natural objects, if unusual and interesting ones.

Topaz sighed.

The only real way to get to the bottom of this was to ask their father. Yet, if she didn't train her telepathic abilities on him, how would she know if he was telling the truth? And she *didn't* want to use those talents on family; doing so wouldn't be right.

"I guess I'm in a quandary," she told her frozen companion. "I wish you could give me some advice."

A shiver ran up her spine and lodged in the base of her brain. For a moment, she almost felt as if someone had answered her, but someone so far away that his whisper might be mistaken for the wind.

"Whoa!" she blurted, scrambling to her feet. She looked around the chamber, eyes darting quickly from one shadowed corner to the other, but she was—as she'd thought—totally alone. Except for the Ice Man...

She looked at him, her silent "friend and confidant" entombed in ice. Naturally, he didn't move. He stood frozen with his arms splayed slightly to the side, hands open and fingers stretched wide. His skin was pale and yellow, and his expression forlorn. His black-lipped mouth hung open, as if he were talking or pleading, and showed twin rows of straight white teeth. His pale, lifeless eyes stared back at Topaz.

Opal's twin could never quite determine the color of the Ice Man's eyes. They seemed to change depending on the lighting in the chamber. At times, they were almost as pale as the bloodshot whites surrounding them, a dead, cataract-like appearance. When the sun hit them right, they seemed yellowish, or even golden. And sometimes, at night, they almost seemed to glow with a pale-greenish fire. It was *odd*.

Neither Topaz nor her sister had ever seen eyes anything like those; they looked... *inhuman*. The Ice Man's size made him seem more monster than man as well. If not for his eighteenth-century clothing, he might almost have been mistaken for a Biblical giant, or some titanic relative of humankind, vanished before the coming of modern people.

There were giants in the earth in those days...

"Who *are* you ... I mean, who *were* you?" Topaz asked.

She laid her bare hand on the window of the display. She and her sister had polished the ice block to a smooth surface and, together with Paul (curse him!), they'd pressed the block right up against the glass, so that customers could have a clear view.

But the bluish ice still obscured the giant, somewhat, making him look as though he were hanging suspended underwater. The fact that he seemed to be floating, rather than standing on the ground, added to the eerie atmosphere of the exhibit. And he had proven popular, though he might have been more so if they'd been able to afford *real* advertising. (Not that she didn't appreciate having Frank and his friends circulate news of the Ice Man's arrival via word of mouth.)

Despite staring at the giant's pale eyes and concentrating as hard as she could, the only thing that Topaz felt through her hand as she touched the glass was... *cold*. Not surprisingly.

It seemed that, like most everything else in the chamber, the Ice Man defied her powers to get a clear "reading."

Maybe I should have Opal cast the tarot for him, she mused.

That could come later, though. For now, she needed to get back to work. She wanted to finish tidying up before the rest of the household roused themselves—wanted to give everyone a fresh start, following their rough night.

After cleaning the chamber and straightening as much as she thought necessary, Topaz double-checked the makeshift barricade blocking the door adjoining the waxworks.

As she did, she was surprised—stunned really—to hear several familiar voices on the other side of the portal.

The tones of Victoria Duprix were clearly audible even through the thick oak (though Topaz couldn't make out what she was saying). But it was the other voice that took Topaz by surprise:

Paul!

What was *he* doing in the waxworks with Mrs. Duprix? Didn't he even have the decency to flee the scene of the crime after trying to steal one of Dr. Cushing's treasures?

Any sensible person—a man with the least bit of honor—would have done so. Yet, here Mr. Shaw remained, apparently going about his job in the waxworks as though nothing had happened the night before.

The lout!

For a moment, Topaz was tempted to press her ear to the door, to listen in on what Paul and Victoria were saying. Was it possible that Mrs. Duprix might be involved in Paul's duplicity somehow?

No. That didn't make any sense. Victoria didn't want the pelt. The twins had offered it to her, in lieu of rent—and since they were behind in the rent again, all Victoria needed to do to obtain the wolf skin would have been to ask for it.

I'd gladly hand it over even faster, now that I know it's a fake.

So, why was Paul still here?

A new shiver ran up Topaz's spine, but this time the sensation was the kind that brought one of her telepathic insights. Victoria had never really *needed* a handyman; she'd always wanted Paul for one reason and one reason alone: his body.

They're lovers.

In the instant the idea crossed her mind, Topaz knew that fact as certainly as she knew her own name. Her telepathy made her sure of it.

How long had the two been carrying on? Had Paul been sleeping with Mrs. Duprix all the time he was courting Opal?

The cad!

But that notion didn't seem right, either. Topaz had sensed something odd about Paul from the moment Victoria hired him, but she *hadn't* sensed any previous connection between the two. Nor had she sensed any deception aimed at her sister, other than the usual type of "best face" that men and women tried to put on for each other when dating.

In fact, the feeling that seemed to emanate the most from Paul was *sorrow*. Topaz got the feeling it had something to do with that woman he mentioned being killed while he was in the Philippines. She'd sensed Paul's sorrow so acutely when he told that story, or at least the part he'd shared before he couldn't go on.

That woman was related to him somehow, Topaz realized. Funny how it hadn't been clear to her at the time; sometimes distance really did bring perspective. Now that she wasn't worried about Paul courting her sister, it all seemed so obvious.

She was his lover... or maybe even... his wife?

Yes. Either of those seemed very possible. It wouldn't be unusual for someone of Paul's age to be married. In fact, in some parts of the world, it would have been downright odd if he *weren't*.

But he's not *married now*, she thought, remembering the lack of a wedding ring, or even an impression of one, on his finger. So, the woman, whether lover or wife, had died some time ago, but the anguish still lingered.

Could her death be the curse Paul had been babbling to Father about?

Topaz backed away from the door adjoining the waxworks. The temptation to listen in on Paul's conversation with Victoria —his *new* lover—had passed.

Poor man...! she found herself thinking, and then upbraided herself for being too soft hearted.

Her realizations had made Topaz feel more sympathy for Paul, but she *still* wouldn't forgive him for his attempted theft. Nor would she let him near her sister ever again—not close enough to hurt Opal, anyway. No more than he already had.

As she locked up the chamber and went upstairs, Topaz decided *not* to tell Opal about Paul and Victoria. What would be the point? Her sister would discover soon enough that he hadn't departed 1951 Fisher, and that he was still… "assisting" Victoria. That would be plenty of heartache for Opal to handle, in and of itself.

Her mind made up, Topaz strolled to the third-floor kitchen and made breakfast for the household. Supplies were running a bit thin, but she decided to splurge and use up some of the things they'd been saving. If Father's homecoming wasn't a special occasion, Topaz didn't know what might be.

Soon, the kitchen air was redolent with the sweet smells of a modest feast: back bacon, scrambled eggs, grilled tomatoes and mushrooms, baked beans, and fried toast. Plus a good, black breakfast tea, of course. She wished she'd had some sausages to go with the rest—it didn't seem like a full English breakfast without them—but there were none in the house, and she didn't have the time to fetch any, since she hadn't noticed the lack until she started cooking. (Nor, truth be told, did they really have the money to spare.)

"This will have to do," she told herself as she laid place settings for three in the flat's small dining room and brought the food out in covered dishes.

"Are we expecting company?" her father asked as he entered the room. "It seems you've made enough food to feed a whole regiment."

Topaz wasn't surprised by her father's sudden entrance, as she'd heard him performing his morning rituals in the bathroom (which wasn't very far away; nothing *was* in this flat) while she readied the food.

"It's a celebration," she replied, "of your return."

"And a magnificent fete, too, it seems," Dr. Cushing observed. He rubbed his hands together in anticipation and then took a brief peek into every one of the covered dishes. "Ah!" he exclaimed after inspecting each. "Grand! Very grand, indeed." He seated himself and pulled into the table.

Topaz smiled. The fact that all three members of her family were together once more filled her with tingling warmth. She sat down and tucked in, too.

"Oh, I'm sorry," her father said, half standing again. "I should have done that for you. I'm afraid my time in the wilds has affected my manners once again."

"Don't worry about it, Father."

"Well," he said, placing his napkin on his lap, "at least I shall hold the chair for your sister. I assume she will be joining us?"

Topaz paused in fiddling with her napkin. Because of the cooking, she hadn't had time to check on Opal. Now she took a deep breath and emptied her mind.

"She's still sleeping," Topaz said, a moment later. "I think we'd probably better let her. The food will keep."

"I suppose," her father agreed. "Though it seems a shame not to enjoy such a repast when it's piping hot." They took turns exchanging dishes until both their plates were covered with food.

"Tea, dear?" Dr. Cushing asked, proffering the pot.

"Yes, please."

He poured, and then the two of them clinked cups.

"To happy reunions," he said.

"And successful expeditions," she added.

"Yes, indeed. I was very impressed with the display the two of you have mounted for our Ice Man. Quite a feat of engineering!"

Topaz felt her face redden. "We had some help."

"Oh? From whom?"

"Well, Frank and Barry and some of their friends."

"Ah. Those would be the young men you wrote to me about."

"Yes," Topaz said. "But mostly from… Paul."

Her father's brow furrowed. "Ah."

Uncomfortable silence hung between them for a moment as they ate.

"He seemed like a really nice guy at the time," she finally said.

"Most of them do—at the time."

They ate again for a little while, until he ventured: "So… How long had you… had your sister known this Paul fellow before becoming… *attached* to him?"

"Not long," Topaz said. "We only met him about two weeks ago, right before Mrs. Duprix hired him as a handyman."

"Quite handy in several ways, it seems," her father quipped.

Did he know, or had he guessed, Paul's current connection to Mrs. Duprix? No. That wasn't likely; he probably just meant handy in both mechanics and in breaking Opal's heart.

"At least until he *wasn't*," Dr. Cushing finished, confirming Topaz's guess.

"He's still here, you know," Topaz remarked, feeling her father should be given at least that much information, if not the scandalous details.

Her father arched his greying eyebrows in disapproval. "Oh?"

"Mrs. Duprix couldn't pay him much," Topaz explained. "So, she's letting him stay in the old servants' quarters."

Dr. Cushing frowned and put down his knife and fork. "A fox in the henhouse, it seems. Not what I would call an ideal situation."

"He only moved in a few days ago," Topaz said, determined to forge on until she'd gotten all the painful background information out in the open. "He and Opal quickly got more… serious, after that."

"I see. And do you think this gentleman—and I use the term loosely—has any genuine affection for your sister, or has he merely been using her to further his larcenous ambitions?"

Topaz shook her head. "I don't know. He seemed genuine enough… until last night."

"Yes. Well, I'm just glad I arrived home when I did. Otherwise, we'd be out one valuable exhibit."

"Even if it *is* a fake."

Her father grumbled repentantly. "Well, it is a genuine *beast*," he finally said, "just not *the* genuine beast, as it were." And he chuckled at his own jest.

"Father," she said, "are any of the others that way, too—fakes, I mean?"

"What? Why, certainly not!" he replied. "I may have made some mistakes in my youth, my dear, but I have tried not to repeat them as I've gotten older and wiser." He extended his hand across the table to her. "This I promise."

She took his hand and squeezed it; her father's grip felt warm and powerful, despite the fact that he looked to be nothing more than skin and bones.

"I'm so glad to hear it," she said, feeling confident that he was telling the truth (and very relieved for it).

"Well, that's enough business and tawdry discussion for now," he said. "No sense letting the troubles of last night entirely ruin this wonderful breakfast you've prepared. Assuming, of course, that those troubles will not continue forward?" The way he arched his eyebrows at her conveyed his worry plainly enough. He was asking:

"Is your sister pregnant?"

"No need to worry on that account, Father," she assured him. "Things never got *that* serious between the two of them, thank goodness. I think we can enjoy our breakfasts in peace for the foreseeable future."

Just then, a knock sounded on the flat's main door.

"Come in," Dr. Cushing called before Topaz could get up or try to use her gift to figure out who was on the other side.

A moment later, Vincent Duprix's smiling face appeared at the kitchen threshold. "Dr. Cushing," he said, "I heard from my wife that you'd come home—though God only knows how she knew. Ears of a bat, that one, I guess. In any case, Doctor, it's so good to see you again. And my… Something smells scrumptious!"

"Topaz has made the most marvelous breakfast," Dr. Cushing said. "We have plenty. Join us if you like. But please, Mr. Duprix, call me 'Leigh.' I insist."

"Only if you will call me 'Vincent,' Leigh," Duprix replied. He took a chair and sat down between Topaz and her father. "With you away so much of the time, Leigh, it's so easy to fall into old habits of formality."

"Indeed."

"I'll get you a place setting," Topaz said, starting to rise.

"Don't bother," her father told her. "He can use Opal's. We'll fetch her another if she decides to join us."

Duprix cocked his lead like a curious bird. "Still sleeping? Well, I suppose that's to be expected. Victoria said she'd had some kind of falling out with our handyman?"

Dr. Cushing forced a quick smile. "Something like that," he replied.

"*All* of us have," Topaz added frostily, and then thought: *Except your wife.*

She knew it best not to mention that, though. The various flings that both Duprixes had conducted over the years were nobody's business but their own. (Topaz had tumbled to their "little deceptions" as soon as she was old enough to understand "the birds and the bees.")

"Well, I'm sorry to hear that," Duprix said. "He's seemed a very useful fellow to have working on the exhibits—for both of us."

Dr. Cushing went back to eating. "So my daughter informs me."

"And, in a round-about way, that brings me to the reason I've stopped up this fine morning..." Duprix noted, stuffing a forkful of bacon into his mouth.

"Oh?" Topaz's father said.

"I can't help but notice that attendance in your Chamber of Horrors is not what, shall we say, one would like it to be..." Duprix replied.

Here it comes, Topaz thought with dread, *the part about the rent, and how far behind we are.*

"...And truth be told," Duprix continued, "the same could be said for my waxworks."

What? This was not what Topaz expected; she tried not to audibly sigh with relief.

"I'm sorry to hear that, Vincent," her father said.

"As am I. But that got me to thinking: Perhaps we've been going about this the wrong way. We both have excellent exhibits, but there's not enough crossover business between the two." Duprix grinned his cat-like grin. "Suppose, though, that we were to team up—to use both of our extraordinary talents to mount an exhibit that only a blind idiot could overlook."

The idea took Topaz by surprise, but her father appeared interested.

"What did you have in mind, Mister... I mean, Vincent?" Dr. Cushing asked.

"Well, it could be anything," Duprix said with a shrug. "We could build on something one of us already has—take your mummy display, for instance. Here you have three of the finest mummies this side of the British Museum, but after spiking attendance for a few days..."—he made a *"Poof! Up in smoke!"* gesture with his hands—"...nothing. Why do you think that is, Leigh?"

"I'm sure I don't know, Vincent."

Topaz had no idea why, either. While her family seemed to have a great ability to find and mount exhibits, apparently none of them possessed the gift of attracting attention to their work.

"No *sex appeal*," Duprix proclaimed. "And it's the same with my waxworks. Everything in our respective museums is top notch, but we both lack that sensational fire that will bring the public through the doors on a regular basis.

"So, my thought is that we mount a series of joint displays every year combining your artifacts with my sculptures. We could start with the mummies... Do a display that will be the envy of royalty, recreate the actual tomb where the mummies were found with wax figures to represent how they really looked when they were alive."

Duprix's enthusiasm was building now, and even Topaz found herself being swept up in it.

"Imagine if you will, Queen Bastiti reclining on her couch, attended by her lover, Sethotep."

"I should remind you that it is only a theory that the two were romantically linked," Dr. Cushing said.

"But it's a *sensational* theory, the kind that will bring the public streaming through our doors. Imagine the two of them together, plotting her husband King Sethmosis' death, and then carrying out their dastardly plan... It has everything people nowadays want—something even the movies can't give them: real life and death, in three life-like glorious dimensions.

"Of course, patrons would have to buy a joint-exhibit ticket to get the full story. It would start in my waxworks and then climax in your tomb display with the actual mummies themselves."

"The mummy of King Sethmosis has never been recovered," Dr. Cushing pointed out.

"That doesn't matter," Duprix said. "Who's going to know what three mummies you have on display?"

"We won't lie about our exhibits," Topaz said, flashing her father a look that admonished *"not again."*

Duprix waved away the suggestion. "Who said anything about lying? We tell our visitors that the conspirators did their jobs so well that the king's body wasn't recovered—and may *never* be. That kind of story is better than having his actual mummy there, anyway."

Dr. Cushing chuckled. "You seem to have considered all the angles, Vincent."

"Well, I confess I *have* been giving it a little thought. I've even started work on some of the wax figures. They will be my greatest work to date!" Duprix's blue eyes gleamed with the fires of inspiration, and he rubbed his hands together as if preparing to count the money flowing in.

"There is one thing you haven't taken into account, though," Topaz's father said.

"Oh?"

"Yes, you have failed to consider *who* will mount this exhibit."

"Why, *we* will—you and your family, and me and my wife."

Dr. Cushing shook his head. "I'm afraid I won't be able to assist you," he said. "For you see, I'm leaving on another expedition almost immediately."

Topaz's heart sank. "Oh, Father… Must you?"

"I'm afraid I must, my dear. I'd hoped to break the news to you and your sister later, but Vincent's most excellent plan has forced my hand. I've obtained a hot lead on *el Organo de los Huesos*, the legendary Organ of Bones, an occult musical instrument said to be able to call the dead from their graves and, once summoned, control them."

"What a gruesome thought!" Duprix exclaimed. "I can't imagine why one would want to bring some poor soul back to life. Let the dead stay buried, I say."

"Amen," agreed Topaz.

"That's as may be," Dr. Cushing said, "but this is an artifact I've sought for many years, and I can't afford to let this opportunity pass. You remember how long it took me to track down the Ice Man, Topaz."

She sighed. "Ages, Father."

"Yes, because I *once* let a good lead go cold, as it were. I will *not* squander this opportunity."

"Nor should you," Duprix said with a smile. "I would no sooner keep you from your expeditions than you could keep me from my sculpting. I'm sure that your daughters, my wife, and I can handle this on our own. And we have our workman, Paul, too. He's been very handy around the waxworks, and your exhibits as well.

"I don't see any reason that excellent arrangement should change just because of a shattered teenage crush, do you?"

Dr. Cushing pursed his lips. "I suppose not," he said. "Yes... Perhaps that's the *least* he can do. So long as he is strictly supervised and keeps his hands off of exhibits that he is not working with."

"And keeps his hands off my sister, as well," Topaz added.

"I'm sure that won't be a problem," Duprix told them.

"Additionally, I would insist that all doors leading to our exhibits be securely locked at night, and that *only* your family and mine should have keys," her father said.

"That seems a wise enough precaution," Duprix agreed.

Dr. Cushing rose and extended his hand. "Very well, then. The Cushings and Duprixes will embark on this venture together, and with luck, it will increase *both* our fortunes."

Duprix took the proffered hand and shook it. "I'm sure it will. Here's to our grand new venture!"

Both men grinned, and Topaz forced a smile as well, though something about this "grand new venture" felt wrong to her.

No… Working with both the Duprixes *and* Paul Shaw didn't feel right at *all*…

21

THE HUNTERS & THE HUNTRESS

Inspector Harry Dennis – London
The Day of the New Moon

"I don't care what the papers say," Sergeant Hoey opined, "the methods in these three sets of murders are nothin' alike. Nothin' at all."

"I certainly hope you're wrong, Sergeant," said Inspector Dennis, sitting slumped behind his desk at police headquarters. "Because if you're *not*, then we've got at least *two* raving maniacs on our hands, rather than just one—and one is plenty for me and this department, thank you very much." Harry Dennis spoke the words with brave certainty, but in his heart, he feared his sergeant could be right.

"I'll give you that the murders of these two women and the men on the docks are spectacular," Hoey continued, "but that's where the similarities end. For instance, the men's throats were torn out, and some of those blokes were literally ripped apart.

"And while I will admit that both of these unfortunate women died from neck wounds as well, in each case, those wounds were caused by a single slice of the blade. It's merely the excessive amounts of blood at the trio of scenes that makes the crimes appear at all similar. Only newspapermen—and not very good ones at that—would conflate these last two murders with the first ones.

"If you want *my* opinion, Inspector, they're more interested in sellin' papers and drummin' up panic than in helpin' to solve these crimes." Hoey bobbed his head in a quick nod, as if punctuating his theory with a definitive full-stop.

It wasn't even noon yet, and already a headache had started to build behind Dennis' eyes. "You're right about the newspapers," he said. "Every time some poor girl gets slaughtered, the tabloids declare that a new Jack the Ripper is on the loose. You'd almost think they *want* these killings to continue."

"Blood baths are good for newspaper sales, sir."

"I'm sure they are, Sergeant. Not very good for the police department, though—or our public relations. The commissioner is already breathing down my neck about all this, and the tabloids will only make it worse."

"Sorry, sir. Me and the boys are doin' the best we can."

"I know you are, Sergeant," Dennis said. "But the bloody reporters are still camped outside of every precinct house from here to the West End."

"Newspaper men!" Hoey complained. "Can't live with 'em, can't arrest the lot of 'em."

Despite his headache, Dennis chuckled. "Though God knows I often wish that we could."

He shuffled some papers around on his cluttered desktop before finding the one he was looking for. He glanced at it, then flipped it back onto the pile and rubbed his temples.

"As to your theory, Sergeant Hoey… It seems that the coroner agrees with your conclusions. This latest victim, Miss Angela Court, died of a single, clean wound to the throat—same as the previous victim—and though she was found nude, there is no indication that she was interfered with in any way."

"Aside from the throat-cuttin', you mean," Hoey put in.

"Yes, well, obviously. What do you think that might indicate, Sergeant?"

"That it's not a sex crime, sir. Nor was the other one, Miss Miller."

Dennis rifled through his papers again. "Yes... Piper Miller, a young lady of similar age, though no other apparent connection, meeting a similar tragic end."

"One was a whore and the other a model," Hoey noted. "Me missus considers the two to be very similar—both women of low morals, as it were. 'Whores, models, and actresses... they're all a bad lot,' she says. The fact that Miss Court was found slumped over a chair in a state of total undress might seem to confirm me wife's hypothesis."

"Yes, I suppose there *could* be something there. I wonder if we dug deeper into the two women's backgrounds whether we'd find some similar connection. Perhaps the Miller girl modeled at one time..."

"Or perhaps the Court girl was a whore."

"I suppose it's possible, though preliminary reports did seem to indicate that she was a respected model working her way up in the fashion world."

"Maybe working her way up a bit *too* quickly, if you catch me meaning."

"Are you suggesting that she might have been killed by a jealous rival, Sergeant?"

"Such things do happen, sir."

Dennis shook his head, which only made it ache more. "No, that doesn't make sense. If it *was* a rival—either professional or business—why would she have been nude? I don't take my clothes off for a rival."

"I certainly hope not, sir."

"Whom might I... I mean might *one*... undress for?" the detective inspector mused.

"A payin' customer, sir," Hoey suggested. Then, as if a light came on in his brain: "Or a lover!"

"Indeed. Perhaps we can connect these girls through a mutual liaison. A former lover might return into one's life without arousing suspicion. Both women appear to have been slain very quickly, as if taken by surprise—as if they trusted the person who killed them."

"And a *spurned* lover might just suddenly appear to settle an old score," Hoey elaborated. "He comes in all nice and friendly like, and then…" He slashed his index finger across his throat as though the digit were a knife.

"Yes," Dennis agreed. "The single cut on both victims tends to indicate calculation, rather than a crime of passion—as does the lack of other evidence at both scenes."

"And the fact that both killin's took place at the victims' flats indicates that they knew the killer, sir, as well as trusted him."

"Killer or *killers*, Sergeant. We still haven't ruled out that there could be separate murderers in each case."

Hoey took out a handkerchief and mopped his forehead, though it wasn't excessively warm in Dennis' office. "*Three* killers, sir? Won't the tabloids have a field day with that?!"

"Which is why we're not going to suggest it to them, Sergeant. Let them keep chasing their stories down the 'single maniac' rabbit hole. It may give the perpetrators, whether two or three, a false sense of security. With luck, that might be enough for us to trip them up."

"Let us hope, sir. We could use a good break on these cases."

A knock sounded at Dennis' door, and the police receptionist's face poked in.

"Someone to see you, Inspector," she said.

"I'm busy right now, Doris," Dennis replied.

"Says she wants to talk to someone about the murders on the dock," Doris continued.

"Get someone else to take her statement, then. The sergeant and I are trying to sort through some leads."

"But it's a Lady, sir."

Dennis' headache throbbed. "I don't give a whit about her gender, Doris…"

"No, I mean a *Lady*, sir—with a capital 'L'—Lady Kathryn Ashton, from Lancashire."

"All the way from Lancashire?" Hoey asked. "What's she doin' down here in London?"

"I couldn't say, Sergeant," Doris replied. "She said she had to talk to someone urgently—about those slayings at the docks, two weeks back."

Inspector Dennis rubbed his temples harder. God help them all if members of the peerage started taking an interest in these cases! Still, he couldn't very well turn a titled woman away; doing so might cause… repercussions.

"Show her in, Doris."

Harry Dennis wasn't exactly sure what he'd expected Lady Ashton from Lancashire to look like—a grey-haired busybody matron, probably—but the woman who stepped through his office door a few moments later didn't fit his expectations in *any* way.

She was tall and sinewy with a tanned, angular face and flashing blue eyes, which instantly seemed to take in everything in the office, including Sergeant Hoey, slouched in a chair, and the considerable clutter on Dennis' desk. The inspector estimated she was in her mid-twenties; not a doddering matron in any way.

The young Lady Ashton wore tan slacks, a white silk blouse with the sleeves rolled up, and tan driving gloves. Her dirty blond hair she kept tied in a ponytail, which draped down just past her shoulders. Her stern expression stated plainly that here was a woman who put up with very little nonsense.

Hoey stood quickly as she entered, knocking over his chair; Dennis rose with considerably more dignity.

"Lady Ashton," he said, extending his hand.

She shook it with a firm grip. "I understand that you're the man in charge of the 'Dockside Ripper Slayings,' as the papers are calling them, that your rank is Detective Inspector, and that your name is Harrison Dennis."

"You understand correctly. But most people call me 'Harry.'"

"Perhaps—as our relationship progresses, assuming it does," she replied.

"And this is my sergeant, Bruce Hoey," Dennis said.

Hoey bowed slightly. "Pleased to meet you, milady."

"And you."

"How can I help you today, Lady Ashton?" Dennis asked.

"I've read in the papers that the dockside slayings were committed by the same fiend that perpetrated two more recent killings," she said. "I can assure you that they were *not*."

"Oh?" said Dennis, suddenly interested.

"And how would you be knowing that, milady?" Hoey asked.

"Because I have been tracking this man since he slew my sister, Nina, two and a half months ago."

"I'm sorry," Dennis put in, so taken by surprise that he wasn't sure what else to say.

"I *assume* that he is a man, though I have no actual proof," Lady Ashton continued, "because it seems unlikely to me that a woman could, or would, commit an attack of such ferocity."

"I remember hearin' about that incident, sir," Hoey offered. "It even made the London papers: 'Young Lady Ashton killed in the woods by an animal.'"

"I recall that now as well, Sergeant."

"It was no animal, I assure you," Lady Ashton insisted. "I've hunted all my life—first picked up a rifle when I was four—and there are no wild beasts in England that could perpetrate this type of mauling. No, it takes a *human* animal to cause such depraved carnage. You did not see the state of my sister's body, but if what I've read in the papers of the dock massacre is even half true, it would seem to match the butchery done to my younger sibling."

"I'm... terribly sorry to hear that," Dennis replied.

Lady Ashton took a cigarillo out of her breast pocket and put it to her lips. She brought out a lighter, struck it, and then paused. "I beg your pardon," she said. "Do you mind if I smoke?"

"Go right ahead," said Dennis, still a bit nonplussed. Usually, he didn't like smoking in his office—having had a terrible time giving up the habit after the war—but this brash and forward woman was like no Lady he'd ever met before; he wasn't quite sure what to make of her.

She took a few puffs on her slender cigar. "As I was saying... Since my sister's death, I have spent considerable time and resources trying to ferret out the perpetrator of this dastardly crime. To date, I have not found him.

"I have, however, traced what I believe is his progress across Europe as well as through England itself. His murderous spree has continued for at least the last six months, and possibly extends even longer than that. I did not look any further back because I am far more concerned with the slayings he *may yet* commit, rather than those he has committed previously."

"You're telling me that this man killed not only your sister, but also those men on the docks?" Dennis asked.

"Yes, and numerous others, as well, including—ironically—a butcher in Hamburg and a stone-cutter in Derbyshire. All those and more fit this maniac's pattern. But these two recent slayings touted by the newspapers do not."

"And what pattern would that be, your ladyship?" Dennis asked.

"Ah," she said. "I suppose that since you did not know of these other cases, you haven't yet detected the connecting thread. Am I right, Inspector?"

"We may know more than we've let on," he said, "but humor us. Pretend we know nothing about any of these cases you've mentioned." At the moment, such a supposition didn't seem terribly far from the truth to Dennis. Right now, he felt like a fish out of water. Could these cases be much *deeper* than he and Hoey had supposed?

"Why, the dockside killings and the others I mentioned—including that of my sister—have taken place during the three days of the *full moon*," Lady Ashton proclaimed.

"What?" responded Dennis, shocked once again.

"I thought there was only *one* day of the full moon," Hoey interjected.

Lady Ashton blew a smoke ring. "The days before and after that single day are near enough to full for the human eye," she explained. "And apparently near enough for our killer to fulfill his fiendish lust for blood."

"So, you're telling me that you believe that this man, whoever he is, is an actual *lunatic*," Dennis said, "someone driven wild by the full moon? I hope you won't be offended if that seems a little farfetched to me, Lady Ashton."

"Farfetched or not, it does fit the pattern of the murders, which is why you need to *find* this maniac as quickly as possible. In a mere two weeks, the moon will be full, and he will kill again, mark my words. Ten weeks ago, it was my sister; a month after that, the stonecutter; two weeks ago, those men on the docks—and before those unfortunates, the butcher and who knows how many more? It's possible there could be others we don't know about, too, perhaps one victim for each of the three nights of the full moon… Though I pray to God that one slaying per cycle is enough to sate this fiend's perverse bloodlust. We can't be sure without digging much deeper, but in any case, we need to track this monster down before he can do any more harm."

"That's quite a theory, milady," Hoey said.

"Excuse me," Dennis put in, "but did you say '*we*' need to track this man down?"

"Indeed, I did, Inspector. Because if you and your force will not root out this maniac, I am determined to do so myself.

"I have brought my rifle and my other hunting equipment to London with me. I am going to find the person who killed my sister and put that gun to good use."

Dennis stood, anger coursing through his veins. How dare this woman, whatever her title, suggest such vigilantism?!

"Not in *my* city, you won't!" he barked. "The police—and the courts—take a dim view of people, even Lords and Ladies, taking the law into their own hands."

"I'm aware of that, Inspector," Lady Ashton said, looking for an ashtray to stub her cigarillo out in. Finding none, she snuffed it between two leather-gloved fingers. "That's why I have come to you first, in hopes that we might work together."

"My superintendent frowns upon collaborations with civilians," Dennis said, trying not to let his temper show any more than it already had. "We thank you for your information, though."

"And we hope that you will come to us with any further information, rather than doin' anything rash on your own," Hoey added stiffly.

Lady Ashton regarded them both, her blue eyes steely with determination. "I hope that you catch this fiend, gentlemen," she said. "But I will see justice done, one way or the other."

With that, she turned and swept out of the office without so much as a "goodbye."

Hoey shut the door behind her and let out a long sigh.

Dennis shook his aching head. "Just what we need: a titled kook thrown into the mix!"

22

DR. JEKYLL IN HYDE PARK

Opal Cushing – The Next Day
First Night of the Waxing Crescent Moon

"I just don't buy it," Frank Browning opined, looking down his aristocratic nose at the rest of the group as they walked down a dimly lit path in Hyde Park.

"Buy what—that a man can change into a monster by drinking a scientific potion?" Barry Ripper asked.

Frank scowled and shook his head. "Not any of it."

Four of his five companions laughed, amused by his discomfiture.

Opal did not laugh; she didn't even smile. She'd known it was a mistake to let her sister and their friends drag her out to a show tonight—though seeing a theatrical production under the summer stars at Hyde Park *had* seemed a charming idea. But if she'd known it was *this* show—a modern adaptation of *Dr. Jekyll and Mr. Hyde*—she'd never have agreed to come along. At the moment, for her, too many elements of that story struck too close to home.

Did Topaz know this was where we were coming? Opal wondered. She couldn't believe her sister had known.

Topaz had never said "I told you so," about the end of Opal's love affair with Paul Shaw, but it was easy enough to read that admonition in her twin's expressions, despite Topaz being very careful to shield her thoughts.

As Opal and her sister walked with their four suitors beneath the shadowed boughs of the park, Opal caught a flash of sympathy in Topaz's blue-green eyes. *"Sorry!"* the glance seemed to say.

Apparently, she *hadn't* known what the play would be.

Charlie Bates pushed a stray blond lock away from his round glasses. "Surely you s-see that the play is a metaphor, Frank," Charlie said.

"I heard it was based on a true story," put in Naveen Patil.

Frank rolled his eyes. Normally, Opal might have found this amusing, but tonight, it just made her want to grit her teeth. How could the rest of them yammer on like this? Couldn't they sense the vast, empty aching inside of her?

"Not, you, too, Patil!" Frank moaned. "You're still studying to be a chemist, aren't you? What would your father say if he heard you spouting this pseudoscientific claptrap?"

"He'd probably say we should consult an expert," Naveen replied. "So… What about it, girls?"

Frank seemed to suddenly realize that his skepticism of the paranormal might be treading dangerously close to how the twins' family made their living. "Right," he said. "Sorry about that Opal… Topaz. I didn't mean anything by it. I'm sure not *everything* that can't be explained rationally is rubbish. What do the two of you think? About the play, I mean."

"And about the idea of a m-man transforming into monster," put in Charlie.

"Is the Stevenson novella that Thomas Sullivan's play is

adapted from based on a *true* story?" Naveen pressed. "Do you know?"

Topaz glanced at her sister, but Opal's head was pounding now, so she didn't say anything.

The blonde twin shrugged. "I think I heard Father mention something about a Dr. Jekyll once," Topaz said. "But you'd really have to ask him. *He's* the expert on such things. Opal and I have picked up a lot of what we know by osmosis."

"Too bad your dad didn't stick around longer during his visit," Barry said. "I'd have liked to actually meet him."

"All of us would," agreed Naveen.

"Some people don't like to stay in one place very long," Opal muttered.

The rest probably thought she was talking about her father, but in her mind, she saw Paul. He'd drifted into her life seemingly at random—but it had really been part of some bizarre robbery plot. Now that his scheme had been foiled, why didn't he move on and find some other naive girl to deceive? Now that he'd broken her heart, why didn't he just *leave*?

Even thinking briefly about Paul made her soul ache.

"What did you say, Opal?" Frank asked, his tone kind and attentive.

She shook her head and it throbbed. "Nothing."

"Come out," her sister had said. *"It will be fun seeing a play under the stars. Besides, the opening of the combined exhibit went really well today; we both deserve a break—and some personable companionship. All the boys are coming, so it won't really be like a date..."*

Why had Opal listened? Why hadn't she just stayed home and wept, like she had for most of the past week?

"Not only is performing *Dr. Jekyll and Mr. Hyde* in Hyde Park clever on a word-play level," Charlie noted, "I think the proposition that Stevenson and the playwright pose is f-fascinating:

that each of us has a repressed b-beast inside, waiting to take control and run wild."

"I'm not sure I'd *want* to see your beastly side, Charlie," Frank joked. "I mean, you're so mild normally, if your inner beast came out, you'd probably tear us all to pieces."

"Like that maniac in the news lately," Barry added jovially—though Opal didn't find that series of grisly murders any laughing matter.

Charlie curled his fingers into claws and snarled. "Rahrrr!"

Everyone laughed. Except Opal. Her headache had become almost blinding.

Oh, Paul... Why did you deceive us? What inner beast drove you?

"There are plenty of examples in supernatural myth of people turning into other creatures, revealing their animal natures," Topaz elaborated, almost as if reading her sister's thoughts. "The werewolf of eastern Europe, the fox-women of Japan, the leopard-men of South America, the fish-wives of the Philippines, America's Indian skinwalkers… So, why not a good man changing into a bad one?"

"Or vise-versa," offered Charlie.

"Charlie, me boy," Frank said with a wink, "there may be some hope for you yet."

"I certainly think it's true that all of us have baser impulses as well as more altruistic ones," Barry noted.

"Most of us battle with such temptations every day," Charlie confessed.

Topaz pretended to be shocked. "Even you, my Bonnie Prince?"

"Bonnie Prince Charlie," as Opal had dubbed him, grinned. "Even m-me."

Topaz smiled, and the others all laughed, save Opal.

Did Paul struggle with his inner beast before he betrayed us—betrayed me? Opal wondered. He'd told their father that he was cursed, though he certainly seemed normal enough. More than normal... charming... handsome...

But... Why?

Opal vaguely remembered that he'd tried to explain, tried to talk to her through the door of her room. She hadn't listened that night, and he hadn't tried again since—not that Topaz or the Duprixes gave him the chance to be alone with Opal. Everyone seemed determined to not let Paul get close to her again.

Should she have listened? Could he have explained?

Barry pressed on with this thesis: "But could those baser instincts be set loose—or suppressed—by a drug?"

"With science, almost anything is possible," Naveen said. "Just a few years ago, actually *seeing* a broken bone inside someone's body was impossible..."

"And now they use fluoroscopes to fit your shoes!" Frank interjected.

Naveen looked abashed. "Well... yes. I'll admit, science isn't always put to the best uses."

"If you could take a pill," Charlie mused, "separate your good impulses from your evil ones... Would you do it?"

"If *Frank* did it, how would anyone tell?" Barry jibed.

"Can I help it if I live my inside life on the outside?" Frank replied genially. "If you could develop that pill, though, Naveen, the world would beat a path to your door. Maybe you should work on it."

"Maybe I will," Naveen agreed.

Opal couldn't tell whether they were joking or not. Bleak darkness had settled on her like a smothering cloak. In the depths of her soul, she felt a scream building...

"Please make sure you develop the *Jekyll* pill, not the Hyde one," added Charlie.

"I somehow doubt such a pill could ever work," Frank said,

growing serious once more. "People can't deny who they are inside. A man may conceal his baser instincts for a while, but when it comes right down to it, his true nature will come out. As in the play, the bad man inside a seemingly good man will *always* resurface."

"So, you don't believe in Dr. Freud, then?" Charlie asked. "You don't believe that people can put their p-pasts behind them and mend their ways?"

Frank shook his head. "People can't change. If you think they can, you're fooling yourself."

"I guess the trick then," Barry suggested, "is to find out who the *true* person is lurking beneath the civilized veneer, before committing oneself to anyone or anything. Find the truth *before* it's too late."

Naveen shook his head in mock sorrow. "If only Dr. Jekyll's fiancée had realized that."

"Stop it!" Opal screamed. "Can't you see that all this stuff about men and monsters is nonsense? Can't you see that it's just a silly play? It doesn't *matter*. None of it matters!"

As everyone, even her sister, stood in shocked silence, Opal broke into tears and ran away from her friends, hurrying off the well-groomed park path and into the comforting darkness beneath Hyde Park's sheltering trees.

Topaz Cushing

Opal's sudden outburst took Topaz almost completely by surprise. She'd sensed that her sister was growing more tense by the minute, but...

Barry, Frank, Naveen, and Charlie stood mutely alongside Topaz, gobsmacked, as Opal sprinted into the night-dark forest of Hyde Park.

With a glance to his fellows, Frank started to go after her, but Topaz put her hand on his elbow.

"No, Frank," Topaz said. "I don't think this is something you can help with. Let *me* go after her."

Opal's tall suitor pursed his lips and rubbed one long-fingered hand through his auburn hair. "Well, if you think that's best," Frank said. The other three boys exchanged puzzled glances.

Topaz nodded. "I'm sure of it. My sister hasn't been feeling… *well*, lately."

Naturally, neither she nor Opal had told their quartet of suitors about the Cushings' problem with Paul—nor about Opal's far-more-personal stake in the handyman's betrayal.

"Do you want an escort?" offered Barry, always the most gallant of the bunch. "I know this is a fairly civilized part of the city, but there have been those murders…"

The thought of the recent sensational killings sent a shiver down Topaz's spine, but she said: "No. We'll be all right. We can look after ourselves."

"We can help you search for her, though," said Charlie.

Topaz shook her head. "Sorry," she told the group. "In the mood she's in, I think I'd best approach my sister alone. I'll turn her up soon enough on my own. We have this… *twin* thing."

"Ah," Barry said. "One of those supernatural connections that our tall compatriot doesn't believe in."

"I didn't say *everything* could be explained rationally…" Frank began. "It's just that…"

Topaz cut him off. "You four can continue your debate on your way home," she said. "I'm going to find my sister." She hurried off into the darkness, following the direction Opal had taken.

"At least let us walk you home!" Naveen shouted after her.

"No need," she hollered back. "We'll be fine. I'll telephone you later."

"Nothing to worry about," Frank joked as Topaz disappeared

beneath the trees. "She's probably just having her monthlies." The other boys chuckled indulgently.

Topaz caught the words an instant before she ran out of earshot. She resisted the urge to turn around and lay into Frank. Dressing him down *wouldn't* help her sister, but the tall aristocrat could be such a *lunkhead* sometimes.

As predicted, without the boys tagging along, it didn't take Topaz long to find her twin.

Opal was sitting with her back against a tall willow by the bank of the Serpentine, weeping.

Topaz settled down next to her.

"Go away!" said Opal. The command came out muffled because her head was buried in her hands.

"Why?" asked Topaz. "So your anguish can torture me psychically from a distance?" Often, one sister felt what the other did, especially in times of distress. Though she couldn't precisely read her twin's mind at the moment, Opal's agony shone like a bright red light behind Topaz's eyes.

Besides, she didn't need to be a psychic to know what this little tirade was about. "At least you didn't sleep with him," Topaz said.

"Ha!" Opal barked. "That's cold comfort."

"At least it makes things a little less complicated."

"For *you* maybe."

"And for you, too—and for Father, certainly."

"Oh, God, Topaz... If you knew how *close* I'd come... If Father did..." Opal picked up her head and stared at her sister with fierce, tear-stained eyes. "Sometimes I wish that Father had gone ahead and shot Paul when he found him prowling around the chamber. Then at least..."

She buried her face in her hands once more. "Then at least I would never have found out why he was *really* making love to me."

Topaz shook her head and put a sympathetic arm around her sister's shoulders.

"I thought he loved me, but he betrayed me…" Opal sobbed, "…betrayed all of us."

"I know," Topaz said quietly. "It was a terrible thing he did—a terrible thing he *planned* to do. But…"

"But, what?"

"You know that I'm pretty good at reading people…"

Opal looked up at her. "Yeah…?"

"Paul's a tortured soul, no doubt about it," Topaz continued. "There are things in his past that hang like dark shadows over his present—I can sense that. But, even though he intended to steal from Father—from us—I don't think he really intended to hurt you."

Opal laughed bitterly. "And that's supposed to make it better?"

"I thought it *might* comfort you to know that he *does* feel something for you. It wasn't *all* a sham." Topaz drew a deep breath. "Of course, that doesn't mean you should *forgive* him."

Opal wiped her eyes with the back of her sleeve and shook her head. "And I *never* will."

"Good for you," Topaz said.

Opal put her arm around her sister, and the two of them sat silently for a while, embracing as they gazed at the stars reflecting in the glassy waters of the Serpentine. The murmur and thrum of the bustling city—London's living pulse—echoed to them across the serenity of the park.

Opal sighed. "Why can't we love things that are *good* for us?" she asked. "Why can't we love the Jekyll instead of the Hyde?"

Topaz shrugged. "Often, they come in the same package, I'm afraid. Everyone has their Hyde, I suppose—even you and me."

"I guess I let mine show a little too much tonight. Do you think the boys will ever forgive me?"

"Oh, sure," Topaz said. "They probably just think we're having our periods."

Opal chuckled, but it was a good clean laugh, not bitter or ironic.

"A fine pair we are," she mused. "Here we sit, you and I, with four handsome, well-to-do young men practically beating down the doors to court us... And I fall for a vagabond thief while you moon over a frozen giant."

Something inside Topaz prickled at the mention of the Ice Man. "I don't love him," she replied—perhaps a bit too quickly. "But I feel... sympathetic for his situation. Who knows how long he's been in that ice... alone."

"Topaz... He's *dead*."

"I know. But even though we've put him on display, that doesn't mean we can't treat him with dignity—like he is... I mean, *was* a real human being... once."

"He hardly looks human at *all*. He's some kind of freakish giant."

Again, something inside Topaz bristled. "All the more reason we should treat him like a person. If we don't... if we start treating him like all our other exhibits... how long will it be before we start treating other *people*—real, living people—like objects?"

"The way Victoria treats *us*," noted Opal.

"She treats *everyone* that way, even her husband."

"*Especially* her husband."

Opal buried her head in her hands again. "Why can't we be like other people? Why can't we just be... *normal*?"

Topaz hugged her. "Because we're not *like* other people. Most people don't have twins, for one thing. But we'll make do. We Cushings always have."

"Does that mean we can *never* be happy?" Opal asked miserably.

"I don't think so," Topaz said. "I think it only means we have to find our own way—like everybody else on God's green earth." And despite her sister's current sadness, Topaz felt confident that, like their father, they, too, would find their own oddball place in the world.

"I've been dreaming about him," Opal said. "Paul, I mean."

Worry prickled at Topaz again, washing away her confidence. "Oh?" Often, the twins' dreams seemed to predict the future.

"Last night, I dreamed our house was burning down, and it was Paul's fault," Opal confided. "We were trapped... calling to him for help, but... He left. He never came back. Everything burned to the ground."

Topaz let out a relieved sigh. "Well, even Charlie, *without* the help of Dr. Freud, could easily explain *that* dream. Paul's certainly made a shambles of our lives—especially yours. And even if he *wanted* to come back, *we* won't let him."

"So, you don't think it's a prophecy?"

"Nope," Topaz said. "I think it's a sign that you need to get some better sleep." She stood and offered her twin a hand up. "*Both* of us do. Come on. It's late. We need to go home—and get to bed."

Opal took her hand, and Topaz pulled her to her feet.

"I guess you're right," Opal said. "My head is splitting. I could use some rest. But I hope to God that I don't *dream*."

23

VINCENT'S GRAND SCHEMES

Vincent Duprix – 1951 Fisher St. – Several Days Later
A Night of the Waxing Crescent Moon

"Victoria, my dear, have you ever seen the days *following* an exhibit opening that are nearly as grand—and *profitable*—as the opening itself?" Vincent asked. He strode around their parlor like a lion patrolling his domain, his chest almost bursting with pride. The waxworks had just closed for the night after another day of impressive admissions. This was what it felt like to be successful once more! It had been ages since Vincent had felt this good.

"It was... adequate," his wife, perched on the settee and perusing a book, replied.

Leave it to Victoria to try to kill his mood.

Well, she'll get hers, soon enough.

"But have you ever seen displays so spectacular—outside of the British Museum, I mean? Your man Shaw really outdid himself—and with so little preparation time. He worked day and night, like a man obsessed. I'm starting to think that hiring him may *not* have been a mistake after all. Though I did note that he seemed to be trying to avoid the Cushing girls as he worked."

Victoria looked up from her book. "Oh?"

"Do you think that little crush Opal had on him was more serious than we thought? Even Topaz seems to be avoiding Mr. Shaw, though all three of them were very chummy before that fateful night Dr. Cushing returned."

"I hadn't really noticed," his wife said, returning to her reading.

Not surprising, Vincent thought. Victoria seldom paid attention to anything that didn't concern her directly—though she'd passed on the news about the girl's breakup with the handyman quickly enough…

"It's too bad Dr. Cushing couldn't stay longer," Vincent continued. "Seems like he's always running off to one exotic locale or another."

"Yes," Victoria agreed, not looking up. "It's a wonder that he can afford it."

"Oh, you're not going to delve into that old rent problem again, are you, Victoria? I thought you'd be pleased with the new revenues the joint exhibit is generating. We haven't had business like this in ages—and I doubt the Cushings have, either."

"I'll be more pleased when their share of this windfall finds its way into *our* bank accounts."

Vincent waved off her concerns. "Money…! Who cares about it? It's the *art* that's the thing."

"Our creditors care."

But Vincent wasn't going to let her drag the conversation in that direction. "And this is some of the best art that I've ever done—and, for once, the public seems to know and appreciate it. What do you think they like best? The accurate representation of Queen Bastiti's tomb? That was quite a job, wasn't it, all that plaster and papier mache... Or maybe they like the life-size recreations of scenes from the queen's life? Your friend Miss Carlson seemed to really enjoy those."

"Lily is easily impressed."

"The twins' friends seemed to appreciate them as well—Frank, and the other three. What are their names?"

"I'm sure I don't know."

"No. You wouldn't. You've never been much interested in young men."

If Victoria noticed the acid in his remark, she didn't show it. "I'm sure they're more interested in your half-naked sculptures—"

"Those are historically accurate!"

"—than they are in your actual artistry," she finished. "I'm certain the same goes for the rest of the public. Give them a pretty nude, and they're happy."

Despite himself, Vincent found his temper rising. His wife knew exactly the *wrong* things to say.

"There was a time when you weren't so opposed to nudes, Victoria," he reminded her. "A time when you were happy to shuck your clothing and display your body for the public. A time when… Say…. You *are* dyeing your hair, aren't you."

"Not a bit of it."

"Liar," he accused. "You expect me to believe that your hair has just *happened* to return to its former ebony glory? I *know* you haven't been plucking the grey hairs out; you'd be bald by now if you were. Unless you expect me to believe that you've found the Fountain of Youth, somehow…"

She looked up from her book and smiled ever so slightly. "Something like that." Then she returned to reading.

Vincent finally noticed the title of the volume in his wife's hands: *The Picture of Dorian Gray*.

"*Bah!*" he scoffed.

Why did he let her get to him like this? Vincent knew this

was what she wanted, to wheedle under his skin and annoy him. But he would thwart her

He would recapture his good mood, if only to foil her wicked plans. And the best way to do that was to kill her with kindness.

"Well, dye or no," he said, "I must say you are looking lovely in recent days, quite radiant."

"Why, thank you, Vincent," she said sincerely.

"It's almost as though you were thirty-three again—a lovely age, I think you'll agree, in the full blossom of womanhood."

"I prefer younger, I think," she mused. "And I thought *you* did, too, judging from your current sculpting."

"I must be true to life," Vincent replied.

"Indeed," his wife said with a puzzling inflection that he couldn't quite read.

"And Queen Bastiti died well *before* the age of thirty," he continued, the image of the queen—*his* queen—shining within his mind. She beckoned to him. *"Come to me!"* And he *wanted* to with all his soul. But he couldn't simply walk out in mid conversation, not even on his wife.

So he said: "You wouldn't want me to betray history, would you?"

"Only if it would bring more customers through the gates," Victoria replied, chuckling.

He chuckled as well, and found that he liked the feeling. For a moment, all thoughts of the bronze-skinned queen slipped from his mind. Was *this* what it had been like when he and Victoria were younger? Those feelings were so hard to remember now... But he clung to this brief jewel of youthful happiness.

How lovely to be with his wife and not feel bitter and jealous —at least for a moment.

"In any case," he said, "if we could bottle whatever you're

doing, we'd make even more money than we're making with the joint waxworks-chamber exhibit."

"Perhaps," she agreed. "Though I doubt my particular regimen would suit most people." She'd stopped reading now, and lounged on the settee, smiling like a Cheshire Cat.

What does she know that she's not telling me? Vincent wondered. Could it be her new *lover* who was putting the spring back into her step?

The thought shattered Vincent's transient happiness and made black envy boil up inside him once more.

Victoria, pleased at his flattery, didn't seem to notice her husband's sudden about-face in mood. "But you're right, Vincent. We *have* been doing well, since the new exhibit opened," she said. "That was a good idea that you and Dr. Cushing came up with."

"It was mostly mine, but yes."

"And I was thinking…"

"Oh?"

"Perhaps we should go out and celebrate our newfound fortune…" she said, "…leave this dreary old building and have a nice dinner somewhere, and then maybe take in a late show." She rose from the couch and straightened her burgundy dress. She did look lovely, despite her wickedness.

Again, the whisper in his mind. *"Come to me!"*

"Oh," Vincent said, torn between erotic desire for his wife and his queen.

Victoria frowned. "Is something wrong?"

"No, my dear, I'm suddenly tired, is all. The monumental work we've done must be catching up with me."

"Poor thing."

"But don't let me stop *you* celebrating," he said. "Go out and have a nice dinner, take Lily Carlson or one of your other friends with you. Take in that show you were talking about."

She arched one dark eyebrow at him. "And what will *you* do?"

"I'll just stay here and rest up. Perhaps read a little. Is that book you're reading any good?"

"It's a bit farfetched."

"Well, another book then. Or perhaps I'll take a nice, relaxing bath."

"You do that, Vincent," she said. The last remnants of youthful kindness had vanished, and her frosty demeanor returned. "I'll ring up Lily and see if she wants to go out."

She rang; Lily did.

So, less than a half hour later, Victoria bustled out the door of 1951 Fisher and hailed a cab—the usual London taxi kind; not the hansom with the strapping young man.

Good, Vincent thought, watching through the parlor window on the second floor as she left.

He'd seen the Cushing girls, dressed to the nines, go out with their stable of young men—again—after the exhibits closed. (The twins seemed to enjoy celebrating their newfound success.) The girls wouldn't be back anytime soon, either.

That fit in nicely with Vincent's plans, and it only left Mr. Shaw to contend with, although the handyman had looked exhausted after closing time. Victoria and the twins had worked him very hard during the remodeling, and since then as well; so, he might be sleeping by now in any case.

Vincent considered sneaking down the back stairs to check, but decided it wasn't worth the risk.

He won't be able to get into the new exhibits anyway... Not without a key.

Vincent strolled to his desk and fetched the key to the waxworks. Then he went to his studio and threw a few more things vital to tonight's mission into a burlap sack. Properly equipped, he trundled down the front steps—so as not to chance rousing Paul—and slipped into the exhibit, re-locking the door behind him.

Vincent didn't switch on the lights, but even in the semi-darkness, illumined only by light leaking in from the streetlamps, the new displays took his breath away. The glory of ancient Egypt—*Bastiti's* Egypt—stretched out before him.

And there his dream lover lay, Vincent's waxen image of her, anyway, reclining on her couch in diaphanous silks (an outfit the twins' suitors seemed to find very... *stimulating*)... And there she was again, nearby, designing her tomb with Sethotep... And over there, betraying and killing her husband, Sethmosis...

It all seemed so *tangible* to Vincent, more real than the mundane world of Jazz Age London, lately.

"*Duprix...!*" a voice whispered—not the sweet, seductive voice of his queen, but that of the architect, her lover and co-conspirator.

"Yes, yes... I'm coming," Vincent answered aloud.

He walked through the open portal now permanently joining the waxworks with the Chamber of Horrors, and down the short flight of steps into the Cushings' part of the mummy exhibit.

There, the three mummy cases stood upright, closed for the night: Sethotep on the right, the guard Nekure on the left, and in the middle Vincent's queen, Bastiti.

"*Duprix...!*" The voice came from the right-hand sarcophagus.

Vincent opened it and stared at the bandage-wrapped face of the architect's mummy. The thing's hollow eyes seemed to glow with greenish fire when it spoke, though its mouth never moved.

"*Did you bring the necessary items?*" the corpse asked.

"Yes," Vincent said, rummaging through his bag. "But I thought you said I would have to sacrifice a *life* in order to bring back my... I mean. *our* queen."

"Have you ever done anything of this nature previously?"

"No, but…"

"Then who would know better how to raise the dead: you or me?"

"You, I suppose."

"Correct. Tonight, we will not need a sacrifice, because tonight we will not be reviving the queen."

Vincent's heart sank. "We *won't*?"

"No. Do you think I would risk you reviving my queen when you've never even performed a simple spell before? It amazes me that people of your so-called modern age have forgotten so much. How do you survive without spells to ward off hostile gods and bind the universe to your will?"

"We have this thing called 'science…'"

"The old ways are better, as you will soon see. Tonight will be what you would call 'a trial run.'"

"Oh," said Vincent, deeply disappointed.

"I realize that you are impatient, my pupil. Yet, if you are successful, tonight's spell will bring results that I feel sure will please you."

"In what way?"

"In a way that will allow you to bring your enemies to heel—or destroy *them*."

Vincent's spirits buoyed once more. "That sounds delicious."

"Revenge is always *sweet*."

Vincent rubbed his hands together eagerly. "So… where do we start? What will we be doing tonight?"

"Tonight, we will re-animate the mummy of the guard Nekure."

"And then?"

"And then you will test the efficacy of our spell by having him slay one of your enemies—more than one, if you like."

A wicked glee filled Vincent, and he couldn't help but grin.

"I know exactly where to start…"

24

THE MUMMY WALKS

Vincent Duprix – The Chamber of Horrors
That Same Night

"Is that all there is to it?" Vincent asked. Somehow, he thought raising the dead should have been more complicated.

Sethotep merely chuckled telepathically in reply.

The reanimation spell had proven quite easy to execute.

Vincent simply followed Sethotep's instructions—as dictated from the *Book of Thoth*—saying the right incantations at the correct time, burning the incense, and brewing the proper noxious potions. Some of the ingredients had been tricky to procure—the *tana* leaves hardest of all—but Vincent had managed it over the past week via discreet visits to several out-of-the-way occult shops.

Thank goodness that Crowley nonsense is still popular in some circles.

The task of drawing the precise hieroglyphs on a papyrus scroll had been somewhat more difficult than the rest of the ritual. Formulating the period-appropriate pigments had required careful measurement and grinding of charcoal, oils, and iron oxides, and using the reed brush took some mastering as well. But eventually the inks were properly prepared, and the images of the necessary hieroglyphs came clear in Vincent's mind, projected directly, he assumed, from the genius brain of the mummified architect.

Vincent had never been as proficient at drawing or calligraphy as he was at sculpture, but he was a good artist and rose to the occasion.

Burning the resulting scroll to activate the spell had been the simplest of all; even a child could have done it.

As Vincent watched the last of the smoke drift up to the ceiling, he felt momentarily overwhelmed. *Is that all I am to Sethotep—a child? Merely a set of hands to carry out his plans?*

The notion worried Vincent, but then something astonishing happened:

The mummy moved.

It actually moved!

Nekure, the queen's bodyguard, still stood in the upright, painted sarcophagus that served as his display case, but his mold-encrusted fingers had twitched! Vincent had *not* imagined it.

As the sculptor watched, eyes wide, the ancient guardsman's arms unfolded from over its desiccated chest and slowly slipped down to hang limply by the thing's side.

Vincent expected the guard's first real movement after millennia to make a creaking sound, like a rusty door opening, but the reanimation caused barely a whisper—like leaves rustling across the grass in autumn. The air smelled of ancient spices and mildewed linen.

The expression on the cloth-wrapped skeletal face did not change, but a dim green light shone within the mummy's empty eye sockets.

"We've done it!" Vincent cried, momentarily forgetting all

caution.

"Did you doubt me, mortal?" The telepathic voice of Sethotep sounded annoyed.

"Of course not," Vincent replied, this time remembering to whisper, so as to not rouse the handyman (presumably) sleeping on the second floor. "It's just that this is so far beyond anything I've ever experienced—anything I ever dared to believe might be possible."

"With my power, all *things are possible.*"

Staring at the reanimated mummy, Vincent could almost believe it. Yes, the creature's bandages were moldering, and its skin had the appearance of shriveled leather, but it was tall— taller than the Queen or the architect by at least half a foot, taller even than Vincent—and, despite its mummification, its chest and shoulders remained broad, like the physique of a weight lifter or a wrestler. Before that ages-old finger twitched, Vincent had thought of the guard as just another dusty display, but now that he knew it could move, the creature looked… dangerous.

"What do we do next?" Vincent asked eagerly.

"Command him."

"Me?"

"It takes an actual voice to command, and until I, too, am reanimated, you must speak for me."

Again, a sliver of worry wheedled into Vincent's mind. *Am I Sethotep's puppet, as Nekure is to be mine?*

"I sense your doubts," the dead architect hissed, "but remember, this is merely the first step to revive my… our *queen.*"

The thought of Bastiti, in all her loveliness, alive and breathing once more, drove all qualms but one from Vincent's mind.

"But when we bring her back…" Vincent said, voicing his misgiving, "she won't be like *this*, will she? She won't be some crumbling husk."

"No," Sethotep replied. *"This is why you are practicing on this worthless one. You must learn your craft if you are to be worthy of Bastiti. When she revives, she will be as lovely as the day I first saw her along the banks of the Nile, lovely enough to stop the sun and moon in their paths, the most beautiful goddess to ever walk the sands of Egypt—or anywhere else. She will rule this new world as she rules my heart... and yours."*

Vincent nodded, his mouth suddenly dry; the love in the architect's telepathic voice came through so clearly that it was nearly overwhelming.

"Now command him. Command him by name."

"Nekure, rise from your sarcophagus," Vincent said, his voice low and grave.

Slowly, the mummy of Nekure put both hands on the rim of its upright mummy case and tottered forward. Small puffs of dust crumbled off the thing's ancient wrappings and fell to the floor. Its empty eye sockets burned brighter.

"What can it do?"

"Anything you command. It is strong as a hippopotamus and feels as little pain as a crocodile."

"Take that knife," Vincent commanded, pointing at a nearby small table. Atop it rested the iron blade he'd used to chop the *tana* leaves and other ingredients for his potion.

The mummy picked up the weapon.

"Stab yourself through the heart with it."

Without hesitation, the mummy plunged the dagger into the center of its chest.

Vincent winced at the impact, but Nekure didn't seem to feel the wound at all. More dust fell to the floor, and the air smelled of ancient embalming spices.

Eucalyptus and cloves? Vincent wondered. Then his mind returned to the task at hand.

"Now remove the knife and put it back on that table."

The mummy did as he commanded.

An irrepressible look of glee broke over Vincent's face, and his heart pounded with joy and anticipation.

Now came the exciting part:

Exacting his revenge!

The Streets of London – Later That Night

Victoria's coachman lover hadn't been too difficult to track down. Horse carriages had become largely extinct in London by 1920, having been replaced by the ubiquitous London Taxicab near the start of the petrol car era.

A decade later, a few of the antique modes of transportation still hung on, catering to hopeless romantics (like Vincent's wife) as well as to tourists, newlyweds, and certain members of the upper class who liked to show off their wealth by emulating the long-gone Victorian Era.

There was little wealth or romance evinced in the ramshackle Vauxhall neighborhood where Ralph Quarry, the coachman, lodged. He lived in a dingy flat above the weather-beaten stable that housed his horse and cab.

A few discreet inquiries and small bribes over the past week had led Vincent right to the door. Getting himself and the mummy there tonight had been only slightly trickier.

Luckily, Vincent had found a snoozing cabby neglecting his rounds while sheltered under the boughs on the edge of Olde Kennington Park. That hadn't been difficult, especially at this late hour. Vincent had observed the phenomenon before; some drivers just couldn't resist a little nap before the long-past-midnight crowd drifted out of the local bars.

Vincent had been proud of himself for not killing the fellow. He'd knocked out the driver personally, not trusting that the mummy Nekure could do so without crushing the unfortunate man's skull. He'd left his victim slumbering on a park bench, after pouring a bit of whiskey on him and tangling him in his own clothes—effectively tying him up without actually doing so. Vincent thought that improvisation quite clever.

If the driver was lucky, Vincent might even get the car back to the park before his dupe awoke.

After securing the taxi, Vincent had returned to the waxworks and loaded the mummy aboard, disguising the thing with an oversized coat and hat.

Dressed up that way, Nekure would still give a severe fright to anyone who got a good look at him, but in the dark, the big, lumbering figure might pass for a tottering drunk. Vincent had disguised himself similarly.

Now he and the mummy sat outside the coachman's stable-flat, Vincent in the front and Nekure in the back, as though the undead thing were an ordinary cab passenger.

Vincent's heart pounded with anticipation, and his knuckles went white as he gripped the wheel.

Dim lights burned in the flat above the tiny stable, and the sounds of music drifted out from inside. Occasionally, a shadow or two moved behind the curtained window.

He couldn't tell whether Victoria was inside or not; he checked his watch. Certainly, he'd given her enough opportunity to make her little rendezvous.

Part of him couldn't imagine his wife coming to this squalid hideaway to conduct her love affair, though perhaps the very shabbiness was part of the attraction. Lowering herself to the coachman's level might have given his wife an extra thrill, as would knowing the revulsion Vincent would feel if he were ever to find out.

Of course, she never thought he *would* find out—but he *had*.

Now the time had come to make her pay!

Vincent got out of the stolen cab and opened the rear door.

"Come, Nekure," he commanded in an urgent, low voice.

The disguised mummy shambled out of the taxi and followed Vincent toward the meager stable. The massive creature moved silently, save for the faint rustling of an ill-fitting coat and millennia-old linens.

The wooden steps leading up to the second-story apartment creaked under the furtive visitors' weight, but the music inside the flat easily drowned out the noise.

Vincent paused on the landing outside the apartment door. Sweat beaded on his forehead, and his breath came in excited gasps. He licked his lips; he could almost taste the sweet revenge already.

He took the mummy's hat and coat, so as to not get any blood on them. No sense making their escape any more difficult than it needed to be.

"Nekure," he said, pointing, "the door! On my command, kill everyone you find inside!"

The mummy lumbered past him, its arms outstretched. It reared back and struck the portal with both fists, shattering the frame and knocking the flimsy door back into the one-room flat beyond.

Vincent grinned with glee.

The handsome young man sitting on the worn couch sprang to his feet as the door burst in. He barely held onto the bottle of 100-proof vodka he'd been drinking. "What the—?!"

Even discounting the splintered door, the room wasn't very well appointed; it featured the couch, a sagging bed (more a cot, really) with stained sheets, a round table with a single candlestick in the center, a sink and a small gas stove, some cabinetry without doors, a set of stairs leading down (presumably to the stable), and two curtained portals, one obviously leading to a closet, and the other a loo. The room smelled like horses.

Victoria's really lowered her standards, Vincent thought. "Good evening, Mr. Quarry," he intoned from the doorway as the mummy towered just inside the portal.

Quarry stared at Nekure, his eyes filled with a mixture of fear and anger. "Who the bloody hell are you?" the coachman demanded. "What do you want?" He brandished the liquor bottle as if he might strike someone with it, though he couldn't seem to choose between the mummy and Vincent.

Vincent eyed the small table, set for one, with the remnants of beef gravy clinging to the dinner plate. The candle on the table was lit, though; apparently, Mr. Quarry was something of a romantic, even when dining alone.

"I'm Victoria's husband," Vincent announced almost proudly. "And this is my friend, Nekure, guard to Her Royal Highness Queen Bastiti."

Quarry had paled slightly at the sound of Victoria's name, but his anger quickly returned. "And what's this guard bloke? Some kind of circus freak? Or are ya plannin' to stop by a costume party after breaking up my place? Well, all right… You've had your fun… Get out now, and I *won't* call the police."

Vincent ignored the threat. "Is Victoria not with you tonight?" he asked. "How inconvenient, I thought she'd have dumped our friend Lily and made her way to you by now. Such a perfect night for a bit of adultery, wouldn't you say, Mr. Quarry? Oh, well. I'll just have to kill her later—along with her new lover, whomever he may be."

Quarry raised the bottle and charged toward Vincent. "Son of a—!"

But the mummy stepped between them.

The nearly full bottle shattered against Nekure's skull, drenching the monster's head and shoulders.

The mummy didn't even blink; with one enormous hand, he grabbed Quarry by the throat.

Vincent's eyes sparkled with glee; it was all he could do to resist applauding, as his creature picked the coachman up off the floor.

Quarry gasped for breath, kicking and flailing wildly as the mummy choked him.

"Kill him, Nekure!" Vincent commanded. "Kill him *now!*"

The mummy bore forward, and put his other bandaged mitt around the man's throat, strangling his victim with both hands now.

The coachman's kicks and blows had no effect on the monster, but Quarry's groping hands chanced upon the candlestick on the table behind him.

Quarry seized it and smashed the candlestick, butt first, into the mummy's face. Nekure's shriveled nose broke with a soft crunching sound.

The mummy didn't seem to care, but the candle in the holder broke and caught in the creature's chest wrappings. The still-burning wick set the vodka-drenched bandages alight.

With a resounding *CRACK!* the coachman's neck broke.

As flames licked up the mummy's torso, Nekure dropped Quarry; Victoria's lover slumped to the floor, lifeless.

"Excellent!" Vincent enthused. Then he noticed the mounting fire. The mummy didn't seem to mind the blaze any more than it did its broken nose, but the conflagration worried Vincent.

"Let's do something about those flames, shall we?" the sculptor said.

He grabbed the stained blanket from Quarry's shabby bed, and threw it over the mummy's head to smother the fire.

WHOOSH!

Whatever the blanket had been made of, it went up like a tinderbox.

The mummy, now blazing like a torch, began stumbling around the room. The flames quickly licked up to the flat's ceiling; everything the mummy touched caught fire.

"Put yourself out!" Vincent cried. "Extinguish the blaze!"

But if the mummy understood him, it couldn't seem to figure out how to follow the command. Instead, it kept shambling around the small apartment—and now, the flaming creature was blocking the door through which they'd entered.

"Get out of the way!" Vincent shouted.

But, again, Nekure either didn't hear him or couldn't fathom how to obey. Vincent couldn't get past the blazing monster to reach the exit.

Smoke filled the entire room now, and flames had engulfed the mummy from head to foot.

Fire threatened to surround Vincent, but through the conflagration he spotted the stairway leading down to the stables.

Coughing from the smoke, he stumbled down the stairs. "Follow me!" he told the mummy, but he couldn't tell if the creature either heard or understood.

The single horse in the livery neighed and whinnied with fear as smoke filled the stable.

Vincent tarried long enough to loose the animal from its stall, then he and the frightened horse both fled into the night.

Vincent leapt into his stolen cab and started the engine. Flames had begun licking out of the apartment's front window now, and he knew that he couldn't wait any longer for his undead compatriot.

Heart pounding, Vincent pulled the cab away from the stable and drove toward Olde Kennington Park and home.

Fortunately, the cab's owner remained asleep on the bench where Vincent had left him.

Heart still racing and drenched with sweat, the sculptor parked the taxicab nearby, dropped the keys on the floorboards, and crept back to 1951 Fisher, unseen.

Once inside the manse, he made his way downstairs into the mummy exhibit.

The blood was pounding so loudly in his ears that he could hardly think. A mixture of fear and elation filled him. He'd killed Victoria's lover! That was thrilling, but somehow, also, sickening.

It wasn't you that killed him, Vincent reminded himself. *It was the mummy.*

"Don't deceive yourself." The voice of Sethotep seemed to echo out of the darkest recesses in Vincent's mind. *"Yours was the command that did the deed. Revel in your enemy's death. Enjoy your victory."*

Vincent wanted to, but part of him remained repulsed. Perhaps it would have felt different if he'd caught Victoria in the act and killed her, too.

"Plenty of time for that," Sethotep assured him.

"But the mummy is destroyed," Vincent said aloud. At least, he felt pretty sure it had been. It would be *better* if it was, better if Nekure burned to dust so that the police would never find any trace. Quarry would just be another drunkard who'd had an accident with a burning cigarette, or some such. At least, that's what he *hoped* the police would think.

But what if they don't? What if the mummy survived, somehow, or they manage to trace its bones back to here? His eyes lit upon the guard's now-empty casket. And how would he implement his revenge on Victoria without Nekure to carry it out?

So many conflicting thoughts and emotions swirled through Vincent's head. For a moment, he thought he might swoon.

"Calm yourself, sculptor," Sethotep intoned. *"The second murder is always* much *easier than the first."*

"But how can there *be* a second?" Vincent whispered urgently. "Nekure is *gone*—perished in the flames. At least, I *hope* that's what happened. I hardly want him returning here and setting the whole manse ablaze."

"Bastiti's guard is destroyed; that I assure you. Nothing remains of him on this mortal plane save ashes. But he was never important anyway."

"Never important?! How am I going to explain a mummy

missing from our exhibit? The Cushings are bound to notice."

"No. They won't."

A chill ran down Vincent's spine. "You're not suggesting I kill the girls, too!"

"*Of course not,*" Sethotep's voice in Vincent's mind purred. "*Not right now, at any rate. Rather, I suggest that you use all the craft that your art possesses, and do it quickly. Make a replica of the worthless guard you've lost, before anyone can notice that the real Nekure is missing.*"

A light came on behind Vincent's blue eyes. "Yes, of course! I can sculpt a replacement!" Those pretty little waifs would never notice the difference. "But… What about my revenge?"

"*You'll have it, in due time.*"

Vincent's feverish worries had broken, now that he had a plan. Despite the near-disastrous outcome of his first foray into murder, perhaps things could be set to right after all. Although…

"I must say," he commented, turning away from the mummy cases and running one long-fingered hand over the sculpted form of Bastiti nearby, "I'm a bit disappointed in the results of your magic, Sethotep. Yes, the mummy was reanimated, and did my bidding well enough… but a simple flame set him ablaze like a petrol-soaked cloth. When you'd proposed resurrecting the guard, I'd imagined that the instrument of my revenge would be somewhat more… durable."

Vincent could almost feel the gaze of the dead architect burning into his back. He'd touched a nerve, it seemed. That pleased Vincent. Too often, Sethotep seemed to treat him as a minion, rather than an ally.

"*As I told you,*" the mummified advisor hissed, "*the reanimation of Nekure was merely a trial run. When I… When* we *revive our queen, it will take the fires of the gods themselves to destroy her. Now, you'd best get to work. There's much to be done, and the dawn will be upon us sooner than you think.*"

25

SEPARATED BY CIRCUMSTANCE

Opal Cushing – 1951 Fisher St.
The Next Morning

The early morning sun fell warm on Opal's face, chasing away the last vestiges of sleep, and any nightmares that might have lurked in the darkness.

She'd been doing better since the night of her outburst in Hyde Park. And the boys had been so pleasant and attentive in the days that followed. Each day, at least one of them would turn up with some small present for her—though actually Frank turned up *most* days.

The morning after the incident he'd arrived with flowers. Then Naveen had brought chocolates, Charlie her favorite tea (lemon blossom), and Barry a book on birdwatching. (She wasn't much of a birder—nor was he—but it was the thought that mattered.)

At least he didn't bring some sappy romance novel, Opal thought. *Or anything that might remind me of Paul.*

Paul…!

Annoyingly, he was still working at the waxworks.

Why?

Even more annoying, he *still* seemed to want to reconcile with her—but neither she nor her sister were giving him the slightest chance.

It still made Opal's heart ache (a little) to turn her back on him, but what else could she do? He'd proven beyond any doubt that—no matter how troubled his past or what curse he *believed* himself to be under—he couldn't be trusted.

And even if she'd *wanted* to make up with him now, even when Topaz didn't pop up to divert him, Victoria seemed to have developed some sixth sense concerning the handyman, too. Any time Paul seemed about to talk to Opal, Madame Duprix would swoop in between them like some great velvet-clad bat and spirit Paul away to do some task or errand.

Victoria isn't intercepting him for my sake. Opal felt sure of that. Did Vincent's wife have designs of her own on Paul?

The furtive way he glanced at the older woman seemed to indicate she did, and that he knew about it. He looked almost... *guilty* when Opal saw them together.

Opal knew she shouldn't care.

What did it matter to her, even if the pair were having a torrid affair? Opal squirmed at just the thought of it, but—even if that were real (and it *wasn't*)—that was really between the two of them and Victoria's husband. It wasn't any of Opal's business.

But...

She *did* care.

Despite everything that had happened, part of her still longed for Paul—for the feeling of his strong arms around her, for the taste of his kisses...

Why can't I just let him go? she wondered as the sunshine through the bedroom window turned the insides of her eyelids a rosy pink.

Opal opened her eyes and gazed out the window. Looking at

the blue summer sky, dappled with cottony white clouds, it was hard to believe there could be anything wrong with the world.

Today, I will let him go, Opal told herself. *Today, even if I see him, I will* not *think about him at all. He's merely another hired hand to me.*

Firm in her resolution, she sat up, and only then noticed that the bed beside her lay empty.

That's odd...

Topaz sometimes rose first, but usually, when she did, she made breakfast. Opal smelled no fresh aromas from the nearby kitchen, nor did she hear her twin bustling around the flat, nor could she sense Topaz nearby.

Where could she be?

Had one of the boys dropped by for an early morning walk? And, if so, why hadn't Topaz roused her?

The sisters had been out with their admiring foursome again last night. They'd stayed at a West End dance club until well past one, before Barry drove all them home. Now that Opal of it, she noticed that her legs still ached from cutting the rug all night long.

But it was a *healthy* ache. The dancing had done her good, gotten her mind off of... other things—things she remained determined not to think about on this new, glorious morning.

But where was Topaz?

Opal rose, threw on a dressing gown, and went to look.

She found neither her sister in the kitchen nor a note on the table, which indicated that Topaz had probably *not* gone out. (Her twin was very good about leaving messages if she ran an errand or something.) That meant Topaz was probably down in the Chamber of Horrors—though it was exceedingly early to be getting a start on the day.

Opal considered taking the servants' stairs down to the attraction, but that would have sent her past the handyman's room, and she didn't want that. Besides, that back entrance to the exhibits was always locked, now, and the Cushings' key was missing from its hook (further evidence of her sister's likely whereabouts). Not wanting to dig out the emergency key (or risk an unpleasant encounter on the back stairs), Opal took the front stairway down.

As she passed the second floor, a disquieting thought occurred to her. What if her sister was with *him*? What if the two of them were really carrying on in secret, the way Opal and he had been?

No! Don't think like that! Opal chided herself. There was no evidence that her twin was having an affair with anyone, never mind Opal's ex-lover.

Why do I think crazy jealous thoughts like that? I am over *him. I am! I will not think about him even a smidge.*

She was still telling herself that when she reached the front door to the Chamber of Horrors—unlocked, as she had expected.

"Topaz?" she called quietly as she opened the door and stepped inside.

Someone—not her sister—was moving around inside the chamber.

Opal froze.

Could Paul have snuck down here again to rob them? She and her twin had been very careful about locking all the entrances at night, including the newly cleared back stairway. She knew that the Duprixes had been just as vigilant.

Yet, a tall figure was moving around in the shadows to her left, near the mummy exhibit.

Taking a deep breath, Opal moved to the main panel and flicked on the light switch for that area.

"Oh!" the figure next to the mummy cases cried, and dropped something to the floor with a clatter.

"Vincent?" Opal said. She went down the short flight of stairs and across the exhibit floor to where the sculptor was standing, or rather, *stooping* to pick up what he'd dropped, which appeared to be some kind of paintbrush. "What are you doing here?"

"Me?" Vincent replied. "Just a bit of tidying up." He was standing in front of the mummy case of Bastiti's bodyguard, and looked very bedraggled—as though he might not have slept. And did he smell vaguely of smoke... or was that some ancient Egyptian embalming spice Opal was mistaking?

Vincent recovered his composure and grinned his wolfish grin at her. "You startled me, my dear."

"*I* startled *you?*" she said.

"Well, yes... I suppose we rather startled each other. You see, I came down here to derive some inspiration for my next sculpture of Bastiti. And, while doing so, I noticed things were a bit... untidy. So, I thought I'd spruce up a little before returning to my studio."

As Opal looked past him, she noticed that the mummy of Nekure *did* look quite a bit cleaner than she remembered it being. "You really shouldn't touch the exhibits, you know," she cautioned. "These mummies are very old."

"Oh, I realize that," Vincent said, "but that doesn't mean they shouldn't look their best—does it? We want them to be extra-presentable for the public, after all, don't we?"

"I suppose," Opal conceded. He didn't seem to have done any harm, but she couldn't help feeling that he wasn't telling her the whole story.

"Don't worry," he continued. "I was very careful—used a small painter's brush to dust with, as you may have noticed."

"I did," she said. But she sensed he was *still* withholding something from her. Opal frowned, not sure whether she wanted to know what was really on Vincent's mind, or if she was better off *not* knowing.

Not, she decided. So she asked: "Have you seen my sister?"

"Topaz? This morning? No. Why do you ask?"

"She's not in our flat," Opal replied. "I thought she might be in the exhibits somewhere."

"I suppose she could be," Vincent said. "I haven't been down here very long." He was sweating a bit now... But *why*? If Topaz had been here, she would have had a much clearer sense of his motives.

Vincent wiped his hands on his smock, having tucked his brush into one of the pockets. "Well, I'll leave you to it," he said. "Must get back to work. I'm sure your sister will turn up, but let me know if you need any help locating her."

"Thanks," said Opal. "I will."

With a courteous nod, he hopped up the stairs into the waxworks and disappeared from view.

Curiouser and curiouser.

What she'd said to Topaz the other night about them leading "odd" lives came back to Opal then, and that gave her an idea of where her sister might be.

Sure enough, she found Topaz sleeping in their father's old, overstuffed chair in the deepest recesses of the chamber, near the Ice Man exhibit.

Did she sleepwalk here, or...?

On the floor by Topaz's right hand lay an open book, *Paradise Lost*.

She came down deliberately. That's a relief. Topaz had gone through a bout of sleepwalking when the twins were younger—often associated with bad dreams—but her nocturnal wanderings had all but vanished after puberty.

Clearly, Topaz must have come to the chamber to read to her "friend," after the twins had returned home from dancing last night. Not surprising that Vincent hadn't noticed Topaz here, hidden in the shadows near the back of the exhibits.

The Ice Man stared at the sisters balefully from his frozen coffin. He looked like some dreadful ogre dressed in tattered Regency Era clothing.

Opal shook her head at her twin and sighed. "What a pair we make!" she declared softly.

She thought about rousing her sister, but decided not to. It was still early, and the chamber wouldn't open for a few more hours; better to let Topaz sleep.

As Opal gazed lovingly at her sibling, Topaz shuddered slightly.

She's cold, Opal realized. Located mostly below street level, the chamber often remained chilly, even in the summer, and being next to the refrigerated Ice Man exhibit wasn't helping this particular spot to warm up at all.

I'll get her a blanket, Opal thought, and headed back upstairs.

Once in their room, she quickly changed into a skirt and blouse—*In case I run into that lech Vincent again,* she told herself—and then pulled the top blanket off the bed she and Topaz shared.

As she did, something flew off the nightstand and hit the floor with a dull thud.

"Our tarot deck," Opal observed, frowning. She didn't remember leaving it out last night—though maybe Topaz had?

With a shrug, she retrieved the box of cards from the floor and was about to put it back in the nightstand drawer, where it belonged... But then she paused.

It had been a while since she'd turned the cards. In the past, during difficult times, she'd used the tarot to help focus her mind.

What could it hurt?

Opal stuffed the deck into the pocket of the peasant skirt she'd thrown on, gathered the blanket into her arms, and hurried back downstairs.

She practically ran into Paul on her way down, as he emerged onto the second-floor landing from the servants' door.

"I'm sorry," he said sheepishly, avoiding her gaze.

"Will you please get out of my way?" she demanded.

He stepped back against the wall. "I'm sorry," he said again, still not looking at her.

"You should be," she said, sticking her nose in the air and starting down once more.

But her foot tangled in the hem of her blanket, which had worked itself loose in the near-collision.

Opal tripped... pitched forward...

Just before she could fall headlong down the steep stairway, strong hands grabbed her from behind.

Without a single word, Paul pulled her back onto her feet.

"I..." Opal began, flustered. "Thank you."

He nodded earnestly. "You're welcome."

"But it wouldn't have happened if you weren't charging out onto the stairs like—" Only then did Opal notice the battered valise he'd set down on the landing.

"I don't think I was charging, exactly," Paul said. "More of a slow meander."

Despite her best intentions, she couldn't help but feel for him. He as so *likable*—even if he was a cad.

She gritted her teeth and narrowed her eyes, trying to remember her anger, despite his natural charm. "Are you *leaving?*"

He shrugged and picked up his suitcase. "I thought it would be for the best."

Part of her ached at the thought, but Opal managed to say, "Good!" She stepped back on the landing, out of his way. "Go!"

He looked at her, his eyes forlorn. For a moment, it seemed as though he might say something...

In her mind, Opal imagined the apologies he would pour out, and how she would reject them. Just *talking* to him was more than he deserved.

...But Paul merely clamped his mouth shut. He turned toward the front door and trundled down the stairs.

She straightened the blanket in her arms, so she wouldn't trip again, and followed.

"Is someone going somewhere?" asked an imperious voice from above.

Paul looked back to the second-floor landing, and Opal did, too.

There stood Victoria in a silken burgundy nightgown, gazing down on them, hands propped on her hips.

She looked ten years younger than she had when Opal had last seen her. *The morning light must agree with her,* Opal thought. Though Madame Duprix did look rather pale.

"I was just…" Paul began.

"Not planning on leaving, I hope," Victoria said. "We still have so much to do. And need I remind you, Mr. Shaw, you owe me—owe *us*, my husband and I. We've been very generous with you."

"Yes, ma'am."

Victoria's eyes narrowed. "And I expect to get my money's worth."

Paul merely nodded.

"I suspected something like this might happen, with you skulking about all the time," Victoria continued. "That's why I locked the servants' exit. We don't want you… sneaking off with anything that doesn't belong to you—or with your debts unpaid. Now put that bag back into your room, and let's get to work."

"Yes, ma'am."

Reluctantly, Paul turned and ascended the stairs once more.

Opal pressed herself against the wall to let him pass. Despite her best efforts, his strong body brushed up against hers. And despite her intentions, her feelings for him welled up inside once more.

He glanced at her, his eyes sad, almost pleading.

"It's no use," he whispered. "There's nothing I can do. I'm

sorry I hurt you. I never meant to." He kept climbing, and soon vanished into the doorway leading to the servants' quarters.

Victoria stared imperiously at Opal for a moment, and then, with a sweep of her skirts, turned and vanished back into the apartments she shared with her husband.

Opal sighed with relief, but her head spun with emotions.

What had just happened? Was Paul acting like a whipped dog because of what he'd done to *her*, or for some other reason? And was his subservience to Victoria part of that, or something else?

And why did Opal still feel *anything* for this man who'd betrayed her—betrayed her whole family?

She couldn't figure it out.

She wished she were Topaz, so she could read his emotions better, so she'd know what...

Topaz!

"Rats!"

She'd gotten so wrapped up in her own problems (again), that she'd completely forgotten about her twin—even though she was standing in the middle of a stairway with a blanket for her sister clutched in her arms.

Being careful not to trip again, she hurried downstairs to the Chamber of Horrors, where she found Topaz still dozing in their father's chair, next to the Ice Man exhibit.

Gently, so as not to wake her, Opal laid the blanket across her sister.

Then she crept back into a shadowy corner of the chamber and sat down to think.

A ray of early morning sunshine crept through the narrow street-level windows and made one of the exhibits to Opal's left glitter.

The scales of the *isda-asawa*—the Filipino fish-wife.

Even the exhibits reminded Opal of Paul now.

What was happening with her life? How could she make any

sense from these conflicting emotions welling up inside her? Why couldn't things be *simpler*?

She buried her head in her hands and leaned forward so that her elbows rested against her thighs, feeling she might go mad (despite the best efforts of her sister, Frank, and her other true friends).

Her right elbow touched on something hard in the pocket of her peasant skirt.

The cards...

Maybe the tarot could give her some focus, tell her how to move forward.

She retrieved the deck from her pocket, placed the box on the small table beside her, and held the cards in her hands. The pasteboard plaques felt unaccountably cold.

Should I do this? she wondered.

Topaz would warn against it. It was tricky, maybe even dangerous, to cast the tarot for yourself—even more so with just a short, five-card spread. But Opal didn't have time, or patience, for a longer reading.

She glanced across the chamber to where her sister lay sleeping, but could only see the corner of Topaz' blanket poking out between all the intervening exhibits.

Opal didn't want to wait for her sister to wake and help with the forecast.

She shuffled the deck while concentrating on her question and making a silent plea:

What does life hold in store for me? I wish I knew what to do next...!

She cut the cards in the prescribed manner and then laid out five in a row.

She took a deep breath and turned up the first card on the right—her past:

The Lovers, inverted.

Didn't that just figure. Her love life certainly felt upside-down right now, and the meaning of the card couldn't be clearer:

Get hold of your emotions or trouble may follow with family and friends. Make the wrong choices, and you will suffer.

Certainly, all of that seemed to apply to her relationship with Paul. She should have been more cautious. But now… It was like closing the barn door when the horse had already fled.

The second card, still her past, but more recent…

The Ace of Wands, inverted. Your aspirations don't work out. What should bring happiness, doesn't.

Again, the eerie reflection of her life and her hopes for her relationship with Paul. She'd fallen so hard for him that she thought he might be "the one." As Topaz had warned, there was more to him than it had first seemed—hidden secrets and darkness… The darkness that led to betrayal… Darkness that hung over him still.

The darkness of a thief and con man.

But all that was behind her now, or so Opal wanted to believe. The future still lay ahead, and that's what she was looking for—hints to tell her what was to come and guide her forward.

The next card, the middle one, would illuminate her present situation…

The Fool, inverted.

God! I certainly feel *like a fool!*

This upside-down illustration from the Major Arcana was clearly not just an admonition, but also a warning: You're being weak willed, and that will only lead you down the wrong path. By being selfish and self-centered, you will only add more anguish and suffering to what you're going through.

It was almost as if the cards were slapping her in the face, trying to wake her up.

Maybe that's what I need, another good, hard wakeup call.

But she also needed guidance going forward, so she turned

up the next card to the left, the first card that would indicate her future, the future close at hand.

The High Priestess, inverted.

Will any of the cards in this fortune be right-side up?

Yes, her entire life *did* seem upside-down right now, including her fortune.

Because this was the fourth inverted card, she also knew that the wish she'd made had little chance of becoming reality. She wasn't sure she really believed in that old saw about your wish coming true if more tarot cards were upright than inverted, but... (Certainly, Topaz, who believed in the power of the tarot generally, scoffed at the wish thing as "superstitious twaddle.")

Opal tamped town her irrational disappointment about her wish not coming true—*Did you really think the cards would tell you what to do next?*—and concentrated on the meaning of the newest card in the fortune before her.

The High Priestess was a card of hidden influences, of workings behind the scenes that you couldn't know about. Inverted, it, too, held a warning: Don't take things at face value.

That's exactly what she'd done with Paul, focusing on his charm and handsomeness, and missing the damaged man beneath the façade.

This was a reminder not to fall into the same trap twice.

The High Priestess also made Opal think of Victoria, and maybe her husband as well.

Schemers, both of them.

Only one more card in the reading to go—the final card of her future. Would it, too, be inverted?

Pulse racing, Opal flipped it.

The Tower... Disaster!

The only card right-side up, and it was the *worst* possible one to get—the same one that had come up months ago, when the twins had been forecasting for their father. Then, though, it had been a presage of things that needed to be guarded against, things that *might* come.

And while this contained a warning, too, it was a much stronger one:

If I continue down my current selfish path, I will lose everything I hold dear.

She *had* to give up on Paul, fully and completely, just as she'd decided when she'd woken this morning—before their brief encounter on the stairs. If she didn't…

"Good morning," Topaz said with a yawn.

Opal nearly jumped out of her skin. Her sudden movement overturned the small table and spilled the cards of her distressing fortune onto the floor.

"Oh! I'm sorry!" her sister said. "I didn't mean to startle you. What's up?"

"N-nothing," Opal replied. "I was just fooling around."

Topaz rubbed the sleep from her eyes. Even dozing in a chair all night, she still looked beautiful, her blonde locks falling carelessly around her shoulders. Opal felt a twinge of envy—not for the first time.

"What did the cards say?" Topaz asked. "Who were you casting for?"

"They didn't say anything," Opal lied. "I just started. I was… I was reading for myself."

Topaz hugged her and kissed her cheek. "Silly twin!" she admonished playfully. "You know that never works well."

"Yes," Opal agreed quietly. "Yes. I guess you're right."

26

LIFEBLOOD

*Victoria Duprix – 1951 Fisher St.
The Evening of the First Quarter Moon*

"Are you leaving already?" Victoria asked from her bed. She lay on her belly, enjoying the afterglow of lovemaking. She liked being taken from behind, sometimes, and this had been one of those times. She'd really thrown herself into the passion, and it felt better than it had since she'd been much younger, perhaps since her days at finishing school, decades past.

Can I really become that young again? she wondered. Certainly, she felt more youthful, and even her traitorous husband had remarked about the lack of grey in her hair. But she wasn't there yet, and that vexed her, as did the impending precipitous departure of her new lover.

"I have to get back to work," Paul said, pulling on his trousers. "There's a lot to do."

"But you work for *me*," she replied.

"Which makes what we're doing an even worse idea."

A cold fist formed in Victoria's chest, and she fought to keep from grinding her teeth. Shaw was temperamental, prone to mood swings and melancholy. Her becoming angry didn't work with him; she had to use "honey."

Victoria rolled onto her back, showing all her goods, and gazed wantonly at him.

"Are you saying you don't find me attractive, Paul?"

He stopped dressing, unable to keep from looking at her.

"I may not have the body of a teenager," she said, "but I like to think I more than make up for that with experience—and enthusiasm." She licked her lips—and then silently cursed her own stupidity.

Why had she mentioned *teenagers*?! That was sure to make him think of the Cushing girls, so near at hand. It was bad enough having to compete with the brats for Paul's favors without calling attention to them.

"You certainly are enthusiastic," he said, turning away once more. He rubbed the red mark on his shoulder where she'd nipped him during the preamble to their lovemaking. "And your body's just fine, too." He began buttoning his shirt.

She didn't believe him. If he was telling the truth, why had he turned away? Why was he dressing once more?

She needed to be younger, more attractive. Experience and zest in lovemaking wasn't enough to ensnare—and keep—a decent man these days. Not that this handsome drifter was so terribly *decent*.

Or *was* he?

Victoria suddenly realized that though he'd been working for her nearly a month, and sharing her bed (or rather, stolen moments wherever she could corner him) for more than a week, she didn't really know much of anything about the mysterious Mr. Shaw.

Certainly, he was handy enough around the museum, but his

hands were surprisingly soft (her body had quite a bit of experience with feeling them now), not callused like the paws of a common laborer.

Could he be harboring some kind of dark secret? Had he been born rich and squandered his money on gambling and women? Had he killed a man in a card game and been forced to flee from America? Certainly, Shaw sometimes harbored a fugitive look in his steely grey eyes.

How thrilling to think she might be bedding a criminal…

"Tell me about yourself, Paul," she cooed, still displaying all her feminine charms. "Where do you come from? What did you do before you became my… handyman, here?"

He spared her only a momentary glance, as he sat and donned his socks and shoes. (If not for what they'd just been doing, she might have thought he didn't *like* women.)

"We don't have time for that now," he insisted. "Your husband won't be gone long, you know."

"The supply shop he's visiting is eccentric—only open nights, or so he tells me—and it's clear across town." She almost purred the words. "My philandering spouse will be gone long enough for us to partake in one more round, I'm sure."

As he stood, she rose from the bed, put her arms around him, and pressed her naked body up against his chest. "There's plenty of time," she insisted, and then kissed him.

He barely kissed back and quickly disentangled himself from her arms.

"No," he said. "No, there's not. I have to leave soon. I've stayed too long as it is."

"Afraid the authorities will catch up with you?" she ventured.

For a moment, he froze. "No. That's not it. What made you say that?"

She shrugged her shoulders and turned away, sashaying back toward the bed. "Always in a hurry…" she said, giving him a perfect view of her rump. "...Always looking like you've been caught with your hand in the cookie jar."

"I don't *want* to get caught..." Paul began.

And a little thrill shot through Victoria. Was her lover truly a *murderer* as well? Could that be more than just fancy, on her part. If so, they were *destined* to be together.

"...by your husband," he finished, and her heart sank. "That's just one more reason I need to get the work done and get out of here. I've stayed longer than I meant to, anyway. In two more weeks..." He stopped midsentence.

"In two more weeks, what?" she asked, perching herself on the edge of the bed and trying to lure him back with her eyes.

Shaw squeezed his eyes shut and shook his head. "No... Not two weeks... One... At most. That's all I can possibly give you. I don't care what you or the Cushings think I might owe. I've done enough... *more* than enough. I need to get out of here—back on the road."

"Why? Why do you need to get out of here? What are you running from?"

"I'm not running from anything," he insisted, heading for the door. "This affair has been a mistake, and both of us know it. I won't compound it by staying longer than I have to."

She sprang to her feet, and if she could have cut him to ribbons with her glare, she would have.

"A mistake?! Why you ungrateful... miserable... *wretch*! I took you in! I've given you food, lodging... my *body*! You'll stay here as long as I want you to—until *I say* your work is finished!"

She walked toward him, seething, not sure if she wanted to strangle him, rip him to pieces, or throw him to the floor and take him again, forcibly this time.

"I'll stay until the work I promised to finish is done," he said, apparently not intimidated by the furious nude woman coming toward him. "That shouldn't take more than two or three days—four at the most."

"A moment ago, you said a week!"

"I did. Then I came to my senses."

Before she could pounce on him, he exited the door and closed it behind him.

Victoria stood alone in her room, naked, furious.

How dare *he...!*

"Victoria..."

Someone calling? ...Paul?

Was he coming back realizing he'd been a fool to leave?

"Victoria...!"

The voice sounded very far away...

Not Paul. *Erzsebet*, the woman in the mirror—Victoria's one *true* friend.

The sun must have set.

Victoria had noticed that Erzsebet seldom appeared during daylight hours, but since it was now twilight...

She locked the door, lest Paul *should* return, and then hurried to her mirror—that blessed mirror that would help her regain her youth.

Victoria gazed at her reflection, evaluating her figure, her breasts, the down of her womanhood, the sheen of her dark hair... still with a hint of grey in places.

She muttered a curse. "I'm not young enough yet." Even looking as good as she did now, how could she expect to compete with those delectable Cushing waifs for Paul's attention—or that of any other man?

She'd tricked Paul into bedding her, but to keep him as a plaything, he'd have to do better.

"Sssoon you will be younger."

The voice in her head sounded as though it were right next to her; it startled Victoria, almost made her jump.

Erzsebet emerged from the darkness that always seemed to cling to the edge of Bathory's mirror, and where the mysterious woman walked, the surface turned black, as if

Victoria were peering into the darkest pit of some distant dungeon.

"Sssoon you will reclaim all the lovelinesss that you posssesssed in your youth," Erzsebet whispered seductively.

"How soon?" Victoria asked. "You said I must bring the next victim to you, so you could show me—but that's impossible. I can't smuggle outsiders in here. My husband—or one of those dratted Cushings would notice. It's too great a risk."

"What you want requiresss sssacrificssse."

"Yes, sacrifice, but not foolhardiness! What good is it to have eternal life, eternal youth, if I must spend it behind bars?"

This notion seemed to take Erzsebet by surprised, as if the idea of getting caught committing murder had never occurred to her.

"Perhapsss more caussstion is needed," Erzsebet agreed.

"Good," said Victoria. "Then what more must I do before you fulfill your promise?"

A predatory smile crept over the face of the woman in the mirror:

"Practicssse!"

Just after Four A.M.

Victoria stood in front of Erzsebet Bathory's mirror and let her trench coat fall to the floor.

She smiled.

She looked as though she had been painted blood red from her collarbones right down to her garters. But it wasn't paint; it was real blood.

Instantly, Erzsebet swirled into existence out of the mirror's darkness. She looked more vivid, more lifelike, than Victoria had ever seen her before. In fact, it looked so much like she was in the third-floor bedroom that Victoria had to glance over her shoulder to make sure Bathory wasn't standing behind her.

But no. Erzsebet Bathory remained only in the mirror.

Victoria felt glad of that fact, too, because the mysterious woman licked her lips as she prowled around behind Victoria, seeming to look her protégé up and down, the way a hungry cat eyes a caged bird. And for just a moment, Victoria glimpsed the gleam of sharp, white teeth between Erzsebet's blood-red lips.

"How do you feel?" Erzsebet asked, dark brown eyes sparkling.

"I feel…"

How *did* Victoria feel?

When she'd stalked this victim—a slattern barmaid named Eve Leon—she'd been tense, even a bit fearful.

That had passed, though, as the drunken little tart had closed up the bar and retired to her small apartment above the pub, retired with one of the patrons, as it turned out (much to Victoria's chagrin). Would Victoria have to wait another night to take her revenge on this particular former paramour of her husband?

Victoria had waited impatiently in the alley below the apartment's back stairs, which debouched onto a deserted Soho backstreet. The alleyway afforded Victoria plenty of shadows to hide in. And, garbed in trench coat and hat, there had been little chance of her being seen, never mind recognized.

Fortunately, Eve's little tryst—though loud and enthusiastic—had lasted no more than fifteen minutes. Then the girl's patron/paramour trundled down the stairs and staggered back to wherever he'd come from (home and a wife, to judge by the wedding ring on his finger).

Slut! Victoria had thought, images of Eve dallying with Vincent running through her mind.

Swiftly and silently she'd moved up the stairs. The flat's door was unlocked, and she'd rushed inside, surprising the girl on her shoddy mattress.

Before the drunken, half-dressed barmaid could even

scream, Victoria's stiletto had found her left eye socket and the soft, greyish brain beyond.

Then came the fun part…

"…I feel, *exhilarated!*" Victoria told Erzsebet.

"Do you feel… younger?"

"Yes!" Victoria declared. And she did, young and full of life—the life of her husband's former lover.

She'd dragged the girl's still-twitching body to the flat's bathroom, cut her throat, filled the tub with her blood and then… bathed in it.

Immersing herself in the warm liquid had caused Victoria's skin to tingle as though it were on fire, and the sensation still remained, close to an hour later. The trip home via two cabs and on foot had been perilous, but having cleaned her arms and legs, the disguised Victoria made it home without incident.

Even through the crusty sheen of dried blood, Victoria thought she *looked* younger as well. She could hardly wait to wash off the gore to be sure.

"Is this *it*, now?" she asked. "Will I remain young forever?"

Erzsebet's low, amused laugh echoed in Victoria's mind.

"No, my dear," the woman in the mirror said. *"Thessse effectsss are transssitory."*

"How can I make them last longer, then? You said I could become young and stay that way."

"Yesss, my dear."

"Well? What must I do?"

"Jussst what you have *done. But the efectsss will lassst longer if you use the bathtub that I have ssspecsssially prepared."*

"The tub… *your* tub? The one that's downstairs in the Cushing exhibit?" Victoria asked.

"Jussst so. Bathe in the blood of your nexxxt victim in my tub on the night of the full moon, and your immortality isss asssured."

"Then that's what I'll do," Victoria said, licking her lips.

"*Choosssse your victim well,*" Erzsebet advised. "*Not jussst any will do.*"

"I already have some ideas in mind," Victoria said.

Should it be one of the twins… or *both*…?

Or perhaps… her husband…?

As the mirror image of Erzsebet Bathory licked the blood off her protégé's neck, Victoria Duprix smiled.

27

PAUL'S DILEMMA

Paul Shaw (Longmire) – 1951 Fisher St.
An Afternoon of the Waxing Gibbous Moon

I *can do this,* Paul thought as he sat in a dim recess of Dr. Cushing's Chamber of Horrors. The joint exhibit's morning crowds had cleared out, and the afternoon surge of visitors had not yet begun.

I can get out of here before I hurt anyone else.

He could spare everyone a lot of trouble if he left as soon as possible—everyone, that is, except himself. Paul couldn't run away from his curse, though he dearly wished he could.

I should leave today.

True, he hadn't finished *all* the tasks Victoria had assigned to him, but those that remained were simple enough that any handyman could do them. Hell, Victoria or Vincent could finish them themselves.

And the girls didn't really need Paul anymore, either. Between cold shoulders (which were their reception toward him most of the time nowadays), he'd managed to teach both twins how to service the machinery and maintain a constant temperature on the Ice Man exhibit. They'd have to do more cleaning and upkeep of the chamber without him, but...

Better a little hard work than risk being torn to shreds in a week!

Something bothered him about that thought, though—not the thought of the twins' possible doom, but another nagging sensation in the back of his skull.

Paul took the well-worn notebook calendar—the one he'd been using to keep track of the phases of the moon—out of his pants pocket, and checked it.

No! he realized frantically. *Not a week... Only* four *days!*

Could that be right? Yes, it *had* to be. He'd checked his calendar against the one on the wall near the entrance to the Chamber of Horrors this morning.

At least he felt *pretty sure* he'd checked today.

Why was it so hard for him to keep track of time?!

But he knew why:

The curse. The curse wants me to stay and kill the things I love—kill everyone here. But I won't! I'll beat it this time. I must!

He had to fight down the urge to walk to the exhibit entrance and check the calendar again, right that moment. But what good would checking again do?

There's still time, Paul thought, tamping down his panic. *And I still might learn something more before I leave... Where to go next... Where to find the* real *pelt of the Beast of Gevaudan.*

Paul fingered the spine of the weathered tome in his lap: *A True Historie of Werewolfery* by Glendon Hull. Dr. Cushing's library featured numerous books like this one—*The Werewolf and the Devil*; *Man-Wolfs of Transylvania*; *Werewolf, Vampire, and Ghoul: Satan's Plague Upon Mankind*, and others as well.

Paul had passed by this small occult library, hidden in a corner near Dr. Cushing's desk (and practically on top of the Ice Man exhibit), dozens of times and never taken note of it. He'd been too focused on the (fake) pelt to realize that the means of his salvation might be lingering so near at hand.

The key to beating this curse may lie somewhere in one of these books...

He'd discovered the precious collection after his dust-up with Victoria two days ago, and it had given him hope—and a reason to stay and work at 1951 Fisher a little longer. He'd even found a book on the Beast of Gevaudan, but it had only been a basic history; it stopped with the beast's death and completely dismissed any suggestion that the monster might have supernatural origins.

People don't believe in such things nowadays, he thought. *But they should!*

He'd been searching the other volumes in the library since then, but he'd yet to turn up any concrete information on what might have happened to the *real* pelt after the beast perished—if, indeed, it had died at all. Certainly, the killings in France had stopped, but in human form, a werewolf might move across Europe, and even the world, as Paul himself had been doing for more than a year.

Maybe that silver bullet in the stories didn't slay the beast. Maybe they only killed a regular *wolf, not a werewolf.*

That would explain why his curse continued. And somewhere out there lived an heir to Gevaudan… Perhaps that was where Count Zarkoff had gotten the werewolf blood he'd used to curse Paul, though the mad nobleman had claimed he'd obtained the sample in China.

I can't trust anything he told me, Paul mused.

But could he trust the gypsies, either? Certainly, Maria had no *reason* to lie to him, but the idea that his salvation could rest in destroying a magical pelt now seemed almost too simple.

I have to keep trying, though. What else can I do?

Paul's head ached, and he closed his eyes, knowing he'd have to put the tome away and return to work soon.

He needed to be cautious in his research, only reading during his breaks, and never daring to take any of the books back to his room. The Cushings were watching him carefully, and so was Victoria—who seemed determined to win him over once more. And he had to admit, Madame Duprix was hard to resist when she turned on the charm.

Unbidden, thoughts of their lovemaking rose up in his mind, and he absentmindedly rubbed the shoulder where she'd bitten him during their last session. You could still see the mark, and Paul was careful to keep his shirt on when working now, despite the summer heat. He didn't want anyone else to suspect what the two of them were up to.

But she was some woman!

Enthusiasm...! He thought with a careless smile.

"Not going to *steal* that, are you?"

Paul sat up with a start and found Opal standing before him, hands on her hips, her brow furrowed and her blue-green eyes flashing with disapproval. "None of these is very valuable, you know," she concluded.

"I wasn't going to steal it," Paul said, a bit more curtly than he intended. "Can't a guy do a little reading on his break?" He slid the book back onto the shelf, aware that her gaze followed his every move as he did so.

She doesn't trust me, he thought. *She never will.* He couldn't blame her.

He got up out of the antique chair and dusted himself off. "But don't worry. You won't have to keep an eye on me much longer. I'll be leaving soon—leaving for good."

That seemed to surprise her, and for a moment, the stern look faded from her eyes.

"How soon?" she asked.

"Soon. Maybe even today."

"B-but you still have work to do," she said, looking torn between anger and confusion. She brushed a stray lock of dark, wavy hair out of her eyes.

She looked very beautiful, despite her anger.

"It's nothing that you and Topaz can't handle," he said. "The place is pretty ship shape now."

"But what about Mr. Duprix? And Mrs. Duprix?"

Did she know something? Did she suspect? Or was there some other reason for her asking?

"You know, I don't have to go, if you don't want me to," he said—and then immediately wondered why he was teasing her. What if she did forgive him and asked him to stay?

You do *have to go, fool! The moon will be full in a week, and then you'll kill again!*

"Come or go as you like," she said haughtily. "I'm sure I don't care what you do."

So, she still cares for me, even after all I've done.

He resisted the urge to take her in his arms and kiss her.

"Just don't take any of Father's books—or anything else—with you when you go," she said.

He sighed and gazed directly into her blue-green eyes. "Look, Opal," he said, "I know you and your sister will never believe me, but I have—I *had*—good reasons for what I did… for what I *tried* to do."

"Most thieves think they have good reasons for stealing."

If only she knew!

"But I didn't steal anything," he countered.

"You *meant* to."

"But I didn't. I… I'm not even sure I could have gone through with it. If only you could realize how desperate I am…!"

"Desperate enough to break my heart!"

He felt like she'd kicked him in the chest. "I never meant to do that."

"No, you just meant to steal our father's artifact." She glared at him, her eyes narrow. "Tell me, Paul, if you'd actually managed to get the pelt out of its frame, if you'd stolen it… Would you have stayed, or would you have left for good?"

"Left, probably," he admitted.

"I *thought* so."

"But not because I don't care for you, or your sister. It's just that my… this curse is a death sentence to anyone I care for—"

"Ha! I guess that leaves *us* out."

He ignored the jab and kept going. "—anyone near me. And until I can cure myself, every person I'm close to is *doomed*."

Her eyes widened, as if she'd just thought of something.

"Oh my God, Paul… Did you kill you wife?"

"No, of course not! That was before I… Wait… How do you know about my wife?"

Opal crossed her arms over her generous bosom. "So, it's true. Topaz told me you were hiding something like that, but I didn't want to believe her."

This conversation was swirling out of control, and it was making Paul's aching head swim as well. "How did *she* know?"

"My sister is good at sensing connections like that," Opal said. "She's much better at reading people than I am. So, you *are* married."

"I *was*," he confessed. "But she died—a little more than three years ago."

Opal's whole body tensed now, and she spoke through gritted teeth. "And *you* murdered her."

"What? No! How could I…? I loved her. It was the villagers… the Filipino villagers, those superstitious fools! They set fire to the hut we lived in. I tried to save my wife and daughter, but they…" Paul sank to his knees and buried his head in his hands, unable to go on.

For a long moment, he wept silently.

…Until he felt a soft hand on his shoulder. "Paul…" Opal said softly. "I… I'm sorry. Is… Is *that* why you think you're cursed?"

He shook his head and tears dropped to the flagstone floor of the chamber. "No," he said ruefully, "that came *after*, when Count Zarkoff… Oh, what's the use… It doesn't matter. No one but the gypsies believes me, anyway!

"The important thing is that I'll be gone soon, and you and your sister—and everyone else here—will be safe... Safe from *me*, anyway."

"But... Maybe we could help," she offered warily.

He stood, anger rising up inside. "No one can help me. Don't you see that? No matter what I try, it goes wrong. I'm a danger to everyone around me. You and your sister should just stay out of my way. It's the only sensible... the only *safe* thing to do."

Paul *thought* she might have reached for him as he stormed toward the front door, thought there might have been tears in her pretty eyes, too, but he couldn't bear to look; he didn't want to know.

I don't need her pity. If she and her sister try to help, they'll just end up getting killed. I have to get out of here. I only need to throw a few things in my bag and leave.

He bounded up the short flight of stairs to the building's main entryway, and nearly bowled over a tall blonde woman exiting the waxworks.

"Oh!" the woman cried, startled, coming up short.

"I'm sorry," Paul said, recognizing her as Lily Carlson, one of the Duprixes' friends and a frequent visitor to the waxworks. "I should be more careful where I'm going."

"You should be, Mr. Shaw," Lily said. She straightened the fashionable sun bonnet on her head, and then tugged down the hem of her knee-length blue skirt, which had ridden up her silk stockings during the near collision.

"Visiting Madame Duprix?" Paul asked, not wanting to seem impolite, despite his hurry. He didn't need any complications with Victoria's friends slowing him down.

"I'd thought she might go for tea with me," Lily said, "but apparently she's busy."

"She's in the waxworks, then?" Paul asked. If Victoria was working, he'd have an easier time sneaking out.

"No," Lily replied. "I spoke with Vincent... Mr. Duprix. He informed me she's taking a nap."

Better still, Paul thought.

"Well, I won't keep you," he said, giving a little bow. "Enjoy your tea, Miss Carlson."

"I will," she replied, opening the front door. "And do be careful where you're going, Mr. Shaw."

"I will."

As soon as she closed the door, he shot up the stairs to the second floor and through the servants' hallway to his small room.

As he shut the door behind himself, he pulled the battered calendar out of his pocket and checked it against the one he'd pinned to the wall, the one with large, black "X"es marking off the nights until the next full moon.

Yes. Four more days left, as he'd thought. *Now is the perfect time to leave.*

With any luck, between now and that fourth day, he'd have time to find somewhere to lock himself up securely, a place where he couldn't hurt anyone.

I should travel with my own cage, he thought, remembering all the animals he'd captured for circuses and traveling exhibits during his years as a big game hunter.

How he regretted that now!

Now I know what it feels like to be hunted... to be trapped in a cage of my own making.

Maybe a cage was what he deserved though. If he turned himself in to the police...

But they'd never believe him. And, if they were even a little bit careless with him during the cycle of the full moon, he'd turn the precinct house into an abattoir, kill them all.

I can't risk it!

Far better to get out, away from everyone. To trust to his own devices.

He pulled out his valise, feeling the reassuring weight of the stainless-steel chains hidden in the bottom.

Opening the drawers of his rickety dresser, he began stuffing his clothes into the bag haphazardly.

"Where do you think you're going?" asked a sultry voice from the doorway.

Paul whirled as Victoria crossed the room, seized him in her arms, and kissed him.

For a moment, the whole world was her warm body, her hot lips, and her tongue dancing with his. Paul's skull ached, and everything spun dizzily.

Yes! thought one part of him.

No! cried another.

It took all his willpower to break the embrace.

"Victoria, no…" he muttered. "Your husband…"

"Has his head buried in his exhibits," she said. "No need for you to worry—never mind actually leave." Her hazel eyes gleamed at him, glowing almost red in the late-afternoon light leaking in through the room's small, high window.

Paul found it hard to look away from those eyes. Something about her stare made his head throb.

"I…" he began, "…I *can't*. I thought we agreed this had to end."

"You agreed," she purred. "I never did."

She kissed him again, pulling his shirt down around his shoulders as she did so, and then kissed across his neck to his right shoulder and bit him there.

"Hey!" he said, startled, drawing back. A glance at that shoulder showed a faint trickle of blood rolling down onto his deltoid. "That hurt!"

Victoria licked her lips. "I wanted your shoulders to match."

"How the hell am I supposed to explain these if anyone sees?" He mopped his shoulder with his handkerchief, and then pulled his shirt up again. Like the other wound, it was really no more than a pinprick, but…

"*I'm* the only one who will see," she said, her eyes still locked on him. She looked… *hungry*. "I'm the only one you're taking your shirt off for, aren't I?"

Her last words were more growl than purr, as if she was daring him to admit that he had another lover.

"Yes, of course," he said, frustrated. Wasn't it bad enough that he was sleeping with a married woman without her being jealous, too? "But it's hot working in the summer, even with the waxworks having air conditioning. It'd be nice to be able to take off my shirt sometimes without any embarrassing questions."

"I don't think the air is working quite right," she noted, still predatory. "I *thought* you were going to look into it before you packed off. You wouldn't want our exhibits to melt, would you?"

"Of course, not," Paul replied. "But I've done enough here—in every sense of the word. It's time I should go."

"But I don't *want* you to go."

Then her arms were around him, and she was kissing him again.

Without even wanting to, Paul found himself kissing back.

What was this hold she seemed to have on him? It couldn't just be the sex. Yes, that was nice after being lonely for so long… But it was hardly worth the risk, or the heartache, or the other complications it would cause if anyone found out.

She was kissing him harder now, as if she wanted to devour him.

As her pearly white teeth pulled on his bottom lip, he pushed her away.

"Stop!" he said.

"No," she replied, and came back at him very quickly.

She tried to seize him in a passionate embrace, but he grabbed her wrists.

She wriggled her right hand free and slapped him hard across the face.

"You'd deny me my fun, after all I've done for you?" The sunlight caught her eyes, and, for a moment, they looked like blazing coals. "Most men would risk their *lives* for what I've given you!"

Her open hand streaked toward his cheek again, but he caught her wrist, twisted her away from him, and pushed her toward the door.

The shove wasn't hard, but Victoria fell to her knees.

"I'm sorr—" he began. He hadn't meant to knock her to the floor.

She wheeled on him, eyes furious, crouching and ready to spring.

In that instant, she didn't look like Victoria any more, but rather like an enraged animal—a panther he'd cornered once in Africa. Part of Paul wished he had a rifle, as he'd had during that safari.

"How *dare* you?!" she growled.

Then Victoria seemed to master her anger. Slowly, she rose to her feet, transforming back into Madame Duprix as she did so.

"I could have you arrested for that, you know," she said through clenched teeth. "Men don't get to bully women that way in this day and age."

"I didn't mean to knock you down," he said. "It's just that this has to end—and both of us know it."

"All *I* know is that you have *secrets*… Secrets that you'd rather not reveal to the police, if I were to call them about this or any other little… incident."

A chill shot through him. What did she know? Surely, she couldn't have guessed…

"I don't have anything to hide," he said, hoping that a strong bluff would get him through this. "I never stole that pelt from the Cushings—or anything else from either them or you or your husband."

Victoria blinked at the mention of the word "husband," and some of the fire drained from her hazel eyes. "But you were going to run off just now, like a thief in the middle of the night."

"But it's *not* even night," he said, fighting to keep his composure. "It's Saturday afternoon. A man has the right to quit his job and find a new one, doesn't he?"

"Not when his... job remains unfinished," she said, cool and collected once more. "Not when there's still a temperamental air conditioner to repair. Not when he's shoved his employer's wife to the floor of his bedroom and would rather the police not find out about it."

Paul pursed his lips, trying not to let his frustration show; she'd only be pleased with herself if she saw how much control over him she had.

"I'll fix the air conditioner before I leave," he said.

Her eyes glimmered with satisfaction. She knew she'd won—for now. "And the other things you promised, too."

Paul glanced at the calendar, trying—despite the curse—to do the mental calculations necessary. He felt pretty certain that the full moon was Wednesday.

"I'm giving notice," he said. "I'll stay three more days, at most. I'll work on the air conditioner and whatever else I can get done in that time. But, come Tuesday, whatever happens, I'm leaving."

She cocked her head at him, like a cat regarding a tasty bird, and smiled. "Very well," she said. "You see? That wasn't so hard, was it?"

"No," he said, feeling relieved. "I guess not." Part of him felt like he'd fallen into a trap, but another part was happy that he now definitely had an agreed-upon date to leave. No more trying to sneak out. Now he could just finish his obligations and go.

"And you'll fix whatever I want... *do* whatever I want, between now and then?"

Reluctantly, he nodded. "Yes. So long as I leave three days from now, on Tuesday."

"Good," she said, triumphant. "Then take off your clothes and come here. I have a job for you."

28

DALLIANCES & DEADLY DECISIONS

*Vincent Duprix – 1951 Fisher St.
The Next Evening, Sunday*

Vincent peered out his studio window at the gathering darkness, his every nerve tingling.

Why couldn't the sun *set*, already? Why couldn't the night just get on with it?!

The length of the days, the endless waiting and anticipation, was becoming excruciating for him.

He paced from the window back to the piece he was working on, but even the clay breasts and buttocks of this latest sculpture held little allure for him now. The model was Bastiti again, of course, but…

What did cold clay or even sensually warm wax matter when his *real* queen would soon awaken?

How could touching such materials or even molding them to near perfection match the feeling of real skin against skin?

It couldn't. Not even the actual touch of his current lover could compare. He glanced at the nearby couch where they'd snuck in a brief dalliance earlier, when his wife had gone to make a night deposit at the bank.

Vincent smiled, thinking about the envious shade of green Victoria would turn if she knew the identity of his current mistress—green first… and then red with rage, undoubtedly. If he were lucky, his wife might even go from red to purple and die of heart failure right on the spot. Wouldn't *that* be something?

He chuckled with glee, and then frowned, realizing that he hadn't tidied up quite enough after his liaison. They'd had to hurry, after all, and apparently that had made them both careless. Vincent plucked a rag from the sink, cleaned a few spots and stray hairs from the burgundy velvet upholstery, and then a few more from the floor, and then rearranged the throw-pillows that had been tossed about during their passion.

Could it really be called "passion," though, when one participant was imagining holding someone else in his arms the whole time?

Of course, for all Vincent knew, his lover might be doing the same thing—imagining him as King Edward or Barrymore or Caruso or someone. The sculptor doubted it, though. No, Vincent himself was part of the allure of this ongoing tryst, the forbidden fruit, as it were, and that was part of the fun for *him* as well.

And making love while Victoria walked to the bank and back…? Well, that had been *very* thrilling, even if Vincent *had* been thinking of Bastiti the entire time.

His lover hadn't seemed to notice, and they'd snuck her out through the servant's exit with no one the wiser—though they'd had a tense moment sneaking past the handyman, who was bustling about noisily in his tiny second floor room. (If Vincent hadn't known the twins were working in the chamber, he might have thought Mr. Shaw had a *girl* in there.)

Tiptoeing past the servants' quarters to the manse's back exit had added to the thrill, too, and made the parting kiss that much sweeter.

But need they have hurried so? Had Victoria even returned from her bank errand yet?

If so, Vincent hadn't heard her come in. And probably that was good, as it gave him more time to clean up the "evidence."

He cast his artist's eye over the environs of the couch.

Everything looked normal—not spotlessly clean, no; that would have aroused suspicion—but carelessly casual with just a hint of clay, paint, and other art materials.

The same way the sculptor's studio *always* looked.

That was good.

Because despite his fantasies about causing his wife a heart attack, Vincent *didn't* really want Victoria to find out about this affair—not until *he* was ready.

And he hoped to be ready very soon.

Three more days... he reminded himself. *Three more days until the first night of the full moon, and then... Then Sethotep and I will resurrect our queen.*

After that, all need for pretense would vanish, and there would be no reason to keep Victoria around any longer.

Until that moment, though…

Well, the annoying nag might *still* prove useful.

After all, Vincent hadn't yet chosen the victim whose life force would reawaken Bastiti.

Part of him wanted to use Victoria (for obvious reasons).

But would her shrewish soul contaminate the process? Would something of Victoria seep over into his new love?

The thought of even a *shred* of his harpy wife living on in his queen made Vincent shudder.

Probably best not to chance using her for that reason, not unless no other viable alternative remained. (Which, indeed, was why he was keeping Victoria alive in the first place; just in case.)

Vincent's mistress *might* make a good choice. She certainly lacked the guile and bitterness that tainted his wife's personality…

But he *did* hate to do in the old girl after all the clandestine fun they'd had together.

So, Vincent supposed that his mistress would have to be his *second* to last choice.

The twins fell higher on his list. True, he was somewhat fond of the pair, and the thought of luring either (or both) into his bed still shot tingling sparks up his spine…

But wasn't excitement a *good* reason to use one of them, as well?

After all, he'd be giving the girl immorality, of a kind, and the idea of having both his queen and one of the sisters at the same time… Well, Vincent had to admit finding a little extra thrill in such a notion.

Which one should he use, though?

Opal would be the more obvious choice. Her young, curvy body practically reeked of animal sexuality.

More than once, Vincent had lay abed fantasizing about tumbling across the sheets with her, kissing and biting and clutching and…

Then there was Topaz: fair of hair and seemingly so virginal…

Was she a virgin, though? Vincent longed to plumb deeply enough to discover the molten heat buried beneath the blonde's somewhat-icy demeanor.

She'd probably be easier to bend to his will, too, whereas Opal might be more prone to fighting back.

That fire of resistance could be exciting, though.

It would be a waste to kill them *both*, however. And he certainly couldn't use one to revive Bastiti and then keep the other as his mistress. Three days hence, on Wednesday night, he would have only *one* queen—now and forever.

I must see her, Vincent thought.

Decisions on Wednesday's victim would have to wait; he couldn't bear to be without his queen any longer.

Checking his clothing in the studio mirror to make sure no trace of his dalliance remained, the adulterous sculptor gave himself one final brush up and then ambled to the studio door that led directly to the second-floor landing.

But as he turned the latch, he paused.

Was he imagining it, or did he hear someone outside? Someone talking not in a normal tone of voice, but a whisper?

Victoria?

Silently, he cracked the door and put his ear to the opening.

Yes. Definitely his wife, though he couldn't make out what she was saying. Her tones didn't seem harsh or urgent, which was unusual; rather, they seemed… *affectionate*.

Curious…

Vincent peeked through the crack, but, oddly, didn't see either his wife or anyone else on the landing. Was this some auditory trick—the kind of thing that made people think that Victorian manses such as this were haunted?

Perhaps. Because now he heard *another* voice as well—though, again, he couldn't make out what it was saying. This voice was deeper, more… masculine.

What…?

Peeking a bit further, Vincent saw that on the landing outside, the door to the servant's hallway suddenly cracked open, and the voices became clearer, though still not clear enough to actually understand.

The door opened wider and Victoria stepped out onto the landing, her right hand trailing off into the shadows of the hall, as if holding something.

Her arm lingered there a moment, and then, as if her hand had been released, that pale limb fell gently to her side.

She's been holding hands with someone… Her lover!

"...drop by again when I need you," she said.

Her lover, still hidden in shadow, said something Vincent still couldn't quite catch. His wife and her paramour were using the servant's entrance, just as Vincent and his mistress had done.

Victoria chuckled, a low, amused sound. "Don't worry," she whispered. "My husband is a fool. He doesn't suspect a thing."

A fool...? She was certainly *wrong* about that. Vincent *suspected* all right; he just hadn't been able to figure out who his wife was dallying with—who, exactly, he needed to kill... yet.

Part of him wanted to rush into the hall, catch them both, and cut them to pieces.

But, no... The nearest weapon was the knife by his sculpting table, and by the time he fetched that, one or both of the traitors might be gone...

"Go back to your room," Victoria commanded, turning away from her hidden beau. "You've got a lot of work to do tomorrow." The door to the servants' hallway closed, and Vincent's wife swept almost silently through the main door to the apartments she shared with Vincent. Her back remained to the partly open door to Vincent's studio.

"...your room..."?

The realization struck Vincent like a thunderbolt. He staggered back into the studio, pulling the door shut as he did.

How could have been so *blind*?

All this time he'd thought she was sleeping with that dead coachman, or some other charming fool, when the reality had lain *much* closer at hand.

Right under my nose...

In my own house...

Perhaps even in my own bed*!*

Vincent trembled with rage and frustration. Why hadn't he *seen* it before?

Shaw...!

It was *so* obvious!

Why would a man of Shaw's evident talent and good looks work for practically nothing in a place like this?

Vincent had thought that (perhaps) the hireling was a drunkard or on the run for some petty crime... But now it was obvious that the man was handy with more than *one* kind of tool.

Paul Shaw was a gigolo!

Had Victoria even *gone* to the bank tonight at all?

Vincent doubted it.

Well... Vincent thought, forcing his jangling nerves to calm down and suppressing his urge to rush out and murder them both.

...It looks like my list of potential victims has been narrowed down to just two...

Victoria... or her lover, Mr. Shaw...?

Would a *man* do just as well as a woman for the sacrifice? Vincent must ask Sethotep.

He'd do it tonight, if he could, because time was running short.

And now, more than ever, Vincent couldn't wait.

...Three more days...!

29

WAITING FOR THE MOON

Inspector Harry Dennis – Police Headquarters
Monday: A Day of the Waxing Gibbous Moon

Detective Inspector Dennis stared at the pile of papers arrayed across his desk and rubbed his head. He'd been looking through this stack of photos, witness statements, and other evidence for a long while—some of it for nearly a month—but he still couldn't make heads or tails of it.

Certainly, most of the facts seemed clear enough on the surface—a person or persons unknown had committed a series of grisly murders throughout London over the last month—but the police still had little idea who was committing the killings, or why.

And, much to the chagrin of the Superintendent Dexter (and those ranking above him), the Metropolitan Police Service had not, as yet, arrested one solid suspect.

Dennis and those working with him, both in the Detective Branch and the regular force, were starting to feel the heat.

Sergeant Hoey and the rest of the MPS had done the usual round-up of likely perpetrators, and they'd definitely removed quite a few undesirables from circulation, but they'd brought in no one they could pin any of the key murders to.

Unfortunately, since the slaughter at the docks, just a bit less than a month ago, other gruesome killings had sprung up, too. Some of these copycats the MPS quickly attributed to gangs seizing upon the opportunity to eliminate a few rivals (while hoping the murders would be attributed to the "Bloodbath Butcher," as the newspapers had dubbed the unknown fiend).

Fiend or fiends, Dennis reminded himself. He, Hoey, and many others still believed that the dockside murders and the throat-cutting ones might *not* be connected. Yet, how to explain the way this new wave of butchery followed on the heels of that slaughter?

It was as if that initial incident had been some sort of macabre signal to turn London into an abattoir

Gangs weren't the only perpetrators, either, more than a few disgruntled husbands, wives, and employees seemed to take the headlines as an opportunity settle old scores in the most grisly manner possible.

Luckily, most copycats were easily detected—lack of similarity of the crimes, etc.—and the true suspects were quickly rooted out from among the victim's family, friends, and known associates. (Victims tended to be murdered by people they knew, rather than complete strangers.)

Some slayings remained unsolved, though including the butchery of Mick and his bully boys and the slaying of at least three women by throat cutting: the whore Piper Miller, model Angela Court, and the most recent unsolved crime, Eve Leon, a simple barmaid.

Eve had been murdered four nights ago, her lifeblood drained into her small apartment's bathtub. But she'd been stabbed in the eye with something long and narrow (perhaps an ice pick?) before having her throat cut. *That* was a new twist.

Also, Dennis and Hoey had found indications that her killer

might have bathed in the poor girl's blood before leaving the scene of the crime.

What kind of monster does that? Dennis wondered. And might it be the same kind of monster who tore men limb from limb on a foggy night at the docks?

The inspector shook his head and rubbed his eyes, but it didn't do any good for the headache he'd been suffering with for nearly a month now. Maybe he should get his doctor to prescribe something. How long could this pain go on?

"Two more days..." Sergeant Hoey said.

"What's that?" Dennis asked, looking up from his desk. It was almost as though the sergeant had read his thoughts.

Hoey *wasn't* looking at his boss, though; he was staring at the image hanging on Dennis' wall. The picture was a lovely blue and gold piece of a young woman in a flowing gown standing on a windy hillside. The poster had been painted by the American artist Maxfield Parrish, and Dennis' sister, Ruth, had given it to him this past Christmas. She'd bought it while traveling to the states with her husband.

The print *was* a lovely thing, but at first Hoey's comment about it puzzled the inspector—until he realized that his sergeant wasn't looking at the subject of the painting, but rather at the small calendar affixed to the bottom.

"I said two more days, sir," Hoey repeated.

"Two more days until *what*, sergeant?"

"Until the full moon, sir," Hoey said. "If that Lady Kathryn is right, sir, the full moon should bring us another spate of killin's."

Dennis groaned quietly. "As if we don't have *enough* to worry about."

"Do you think we should do somethin' about it, sir?"

"About what? About a 'full-moon killer,' or about Lady Ashton patrolling the city looking to avenge her sister?"

"The former, I meant, sir," Hoey said. "Is it possible that her theory might be correct?"

Dennis shook his head. "No. It's nonsense. Superstitious twaddle. Lady Ashton may be a very clever girl, she may have a title and enough money to do anything she likes in Derbyshire..."

"It's *Lancashire* she's from," Hoey corrected. "It's me *dad* from Derbyshire."

"Yes, sorry sergeant, of course. The point is, wherever she's from, she's got a screw loose."

"Doris out front said Lady Ashton had dropped by several times, while we were off investigatin'. Said she intimated that we weren't solvin' the dockside case fast enough."

"Yes, well, Superintendent Dexter is of the same opinion." Dennis' headache throbbed again.

"Doris suggested that Lady Kathryn seemed determined to do somethin' about it *on her own*, if we didn't. Said that *she* said time was runnin' out."

"Time's running out for *all* of us, sergeant—whether we have an eccentric noblewoman looking over our shoulders or not. In any case, the dockside crimes still appear unrelated to the other three we've linked together—aside from the fact that original slaughter seemed to kick off all the rest of this madness."

"Madness is right, sir. Sheer lunacy."

"Yes. But none of it connected to the cycles of the moon. *That* is just coincidence."

"Or so we *hope*, sir."

"Yes..."

Hoey walked to Dennis' desk and leaned against the edge. "I know you're not goin' to want to hear this, sir," the sergeant confided, "but Doris said that—two days from now, on the night of the full moon—her ladyship *might* take things into her own hands."

"Well, she bloody well better *not*!" Dennis said, slamming his fist on the desktop. "If Lady Ashton wants to skulk about, patrolling Hyde Park—or wherever—on the night of the full moon armed with her rifle and any other weapons she thinks appropriate... Then heaven help her! We'll arrest her just as quick as we would any other scoundrel!"

"As should be, sir."

"And if she actually *does* anything stupid while walking around heavily armed... Then heaven help us all!"

Lady Kathryn Ashton – That Same Night

Kathryn Ashton crouched by the bed in her rented room at the Kensington Regent in central London and lovingly ran her hand over the stock and barrel of her Lee-Enfield Mark V rifle. It was a thing of beauty, power, and terror. But then, so was Lady Ashton herself, and she knew it.

Somehow, it seemed as if she'd been training for the upcoming confrontation all her life—though, of course, that was absurd, as her sister had only been murdered a few months ago.

Lady Kathryn had not lied to the police about her firearms prowess. She *had* first shot a rifle at age four, and brought down her first deer at six. That conquest had made her older sibling, George Thomas (often called "Tom" to avoid confusion with their father), more than a bit envious. The feat also left their younger brother, Henry, with competitive issues that Kathryn thought persisted to this day.

Of course, neither of them had wanted her to hunt at all—"A woman's place..." and similar rot. But, despite prodigious efforts on her brothers' parts, neither of them could match her outdoorsman skills, even to this day. Kathryn just seemed to possess the knack, and eventually, the rest of the family gave up as useless all efforts to dissuade her.

Only Nina, God rest her soul, had steadfastly admired her big sister's guts and determination. She'd listened to all of Kathryn's hunting tales with rapt attention and had even spoken of learning some of the fighting skills that Kathy (only her family called her that; and only Nina had actual permission to do so) had picked up during her hunting safaris and other adventurous trips abroad.

Kathryn could drink, swear, and bare-knuckle it with the best of them whenever she was of a mind to. If only she'd ignored their father and taken Nina with her on some of those expeditions…

If she'd learned to fight, she might still be alive today, Kathryn mused darkly.

But such flights of fancy were useless. Nina had always been a more delicate flower, a "real lady," the kind of girl the rest of the family, and society in general, expected a female to be. Kathryn suspected that *she* had been the only one to notice her sister's little rebellions. And unfortunately, one of those defiances—sneaking out at night—had gotten Nina killed.

The memory of it formed a knot in the pit of Kathryn's stomach.

She checked the sight of her gun. It looked good. And looks would have to do, as she had no place to test-fire it in the city. The sound of gunshots would surely make the police take notice, and Kathryn had done far too much to make the MPS take notice already.

I was a fool to go to them, to try to convince them. A fool to think they'd take me seriously.

And yet, she'd felt she *had* to make an effort—make it more than once. She'd been raised with enough respect for the British government and authorities that doing what she was about to do seemed almost unthinkable.

Almost.

As unthinkable as a werewolf killing my little sister…

Maybe I should drive the Rolls to the suburbs... Find a quiet place to take a few shots and calibrate my sights again...

Would Hampstead Heath be far enough? Would those big woodland hills be deserted enough that she could risk a shot or two without attracting attention?

Maybe if I went at night...

She wouldn't do it tonight, though. Perhaps tomorrow—the night before the full moon.

She had to be ready. And though she'd honed her sights before she left home in Lancashire, and checked them as often as possible on the road since, it had still been too long.

She laid down her Lee-Enfield and picked up the Remington. The 1894 repeating rifle had served her well over the years, and had a more rough-and-ready feel than the Lee. The Remington had taken down its share of deer and other game, but this werewolf wasn't a deer; it was a fiend from hell.

So, while she might keep the 1894 hidden in the Rolls as backup, what she needed for the night after next was a hellish weapon of war.

Of course, the Lee in and of itself wouldn't do the trick. If legends were to be believed (and Kathryn had good reason to think they were accurate), only a silver bullet could bring down a werewolf. Good thing she'd brought a pair of silvered five-round charger clips with her, as well as the usual ammo.

Those specially made bullets had cost her more than a few pounds, but they were well worth it. So were her other precautions: a silver-plated hunting knife big enough to gut a lion; twin silver throwing daggers for her boots; a two-shot derringer up her sleeve, and an eight-round Luger at her hip—both smaller guns with silver ammo, of course.

None of this traipsing about heavily armed was strictly legal, according to English law—and certainly not cricket in the crowded streets of London.

But Kathryn was willing to do whatever it took—even risk arrest—to accomplish her goal.

I hope it rains two nights from now.

In the rain, the hood and cloak she intended to wear to conceal her armaments wouldn't be as conspicuous; people seldom wore such accoutrements nowadays, save perhaps to the opera.

But she wasn't attending the opera. She was going to patrolling the city—Hyde Park probably—trying to look like an attractive victim to a werewolf.

Of course, she didn't know that the beast would be in Hyde Park come moonrise, but from what she knew, lycanthropes, like normal animals, preferred natural settings and greenery to crowded city streets.

It killed my sister in the woods...

How fitting if she could finish the damned thing in a similar environment.

Rain would knock down her scent, too—let her stalk it undetected. Unless, of course, it found her first...

Rain would be perfect.

Rain might keep the police at bay, as well. No flabby, underpaid bobby liked to go dashing about in a downpour.

Kathryn didn't mind the rain, though.

The damp and dark suited her mood. The drumbeat of the drops reminded her of the racing heart of her prey, trying in vain to escape.

She picked up the Lee-Enfield again, her weapon of choice for this hunt—this particular war.

She sighted down the barrel and slowly squeezed the trigger. *Click!*

Lady Kathryn Ashton grinned.

In just two more days, she would confront the fiend who killed her sister... and unleash Hell.

30

DRIVING, DREAMS, & DREADS

Topaz Cushing – 1951 Fisher St.
Tuesday: Final Evening of the Waxing Gibbous Moon

Topaz threw her chin back and enjoyed the rush of the wind through her blonde hair. The summer breeze was warm and heady, the air redolent with the smell of trees and green landscape. Driving around Hampstead Heath this way with the boys, it was almost like she and her twin were a million miles from London.

They weren't, of course. The park was barely five miles from the center of the city, as the crow flies. And, of course, it *wasn't* one of the boys who was driving, either; it was Opal behind the wheel of Frank's precious Bentley.

Topaz did her best to ignore that last fact. Neither she nor her twin had much driving experience, though their father had managed to see that they both obtained licenses using his long-defunct Model-T and vehicles borrowed from his friends (in between his expeditions, of course).

Most of the driving the sisters had done recently had been in Barry's Ford Phaeton. Barry was much more casual about letting other people drive, and seemed to take positive delight in giving over the wheel to one of the girls. But Barry wasn't with them this evening—he and Frank were having some sort of spat (over Jekyll and Hyde again?). Nor had Naveen been able to make the trip (a social occasion with his parents).

That left a very skittish Frank in the front with Opal, and Topaz enjoying the breeze in the back with Charlie. Frank's Blue Label Bentley 3 Litre was a convertible, like Barry's Ford, but it was probably worth three times as much. Thus, Frank's nerves.

"Woo! Look at us go!" Opal called from the front. Her mood had improved considerably since her encounter with Paul on Saturday, three days ago. Apparently, she no longer considered him Public Enemy Number One. "He really *does* think he's cursed," she'd explained to Topaz, and she now seemed to have a great deal of sympathy for the man who had so recently broken her heart.

Topaz remained cautious. Paul may indeed have believed that a curse drove him to do dastardly deeds, but he'd still treated the whole Cushing family, not just Opal, pretty shabbily.

He *did* seem to be working hard to make up for that, though, and Topaz had sensed no deception in him currently, other than the fact that he was carrying on with Victoria (which Topaz *still* hadn't told Opal about), plus the usual black cloud of his mysterious past and what this supposed curse really *was*.

Maybe I'm being too hard on him, Topaz thought.

Certainly, having one's wife and child murdered by crazed villagers, which is what he'd told Opal, would be enough to drive most anyone to desperate, even half-mad measures.

Her sister now wished that they could help him, and Topaz supposed that she did, too, but they could do nothing unless he opened up about what was *really* going on. Until then, they could only be patient. And wary.

We can't break a curse we know nothing about—if it even is *a curse.*

Oh, well. No use thinking about such mood-killers now. Not on this glorious evening, driving with the top down, and with handsome "Bonnie Prince" Charlie beside her.

"Yes, we certainly are going *fast*," Frank commented, glancing between Opal and the speedometer.

"B-better watch it," Charlie said jovially. "We wouldn't want to get pulled over."

"Oh, what does it *matter*?" Opal replied, shaking her head and letting her dark hair fly in the wind. "Suspend my driving license, constable! See what I care! It's not like I get to *use* it most of the time, anyway."

"I think that's *exactly* what Frank is worried about," Charlie confided to Topaz.

She laughed quietly.

"Well, it may be *your* license, but it's my *car*," Frank replied, trying to appear casual (though Topaz wasn't buying it, and she doubted Opal was, either). "And I'd hate to have it impounded."

"You bet," Charlie joked. "What would your *p-parents* say?"

Frank shot him a stern look that seemed to say: *"If I'd wanted clever banter at my expense, I would have invited Barry."*

Charlie shrank into the back seat just a little more. "Do you mind if I move c-closer to you?" he whispered to Topaz, a twinkle in his grey eyes. "Between your sister's driving and Frank's moods… I'm *terrified*."

Again, Topaz laughed, and she happily sidled closer to him. Charlie put his arm around her shoulders, affectionately, but casually.

Truth to confess, she liked *Barry* a bit more, but it was still nice to have a warm boy to snuggle up to in a breezy car.

They drove through the English countryside for the better part of two hours, though Frank (looking very relieved) took over again after the first half hour.

As they cruised and chatted, and Topaz enjoyed the warmth of the young man beside her, the stars twinkled to life and the moon poked its pale head above the eastern horizon.

"Full moon tonight," Frank observed.

"Not really," Opal corrected. "The full moon's not until *Thursday*, two days from now."

"Tomorrow will look full enough to the naked eye, though," Topaz added, "as will Friday. Tonight, it's only a 'waxing gibbous moon.'"

"Seriously?" Frank asked. "How do you know that? Did you twins take up astronomy recently?"

"It's our job," both girls replied simultaneously, and then broke into giggles.

"F-full moons bring out the wolves—even in young aristocrats," Charlie noted.

Frank shook his head. "The *supernatural*… I should have known. If it has to do with the Dark Arts, you two and your dad are bound to have your fingers into it—in a *good* way, I mean."

He laughed, too.

On the way back to the city, the four of them stopped at a little shop for ice cream, which proved excellent. (Frank was kind enough to *not* show off, and let Charlie pay.)

All too soon, though, the evening drew to a close.

"Should we come up for a night cap?" Frank asked as they pulled up outside 1951 Fisher. Then he backpedaled. "Or perhaps a spot of tea?"

He doesn't want us thinking he's trying to get us drunk, Topaz surmised, reading just the surface of his emotions.

"Not tonight, Frank, sorry," Opal said, giving him a chaste kiss on the cheek as she got out of the car.

"We have to work tomorrow, remember," Topaz added. She gave Charlie a peck on the cheek as well. Part of her longed for a bit more, but she didn't want to put her sister into a compromising situation. If Charlie *really* got kissed, Frank might expect that, too.

So, rather than linger, Topaz hopped up the front steps to where her sister was already opening the door.

"See you tomorrow?" Frank asked.

"Call us," Opal replied as she stepped inside.

"We want to make sure you haven't turned into a wolf," Topaz added playfully.

"*Wolves*, you mean," replied Charlie.

"Too late," added Frank.

Both girls laughed and shut the door behind them. The Bentley's powerful 3-liter engine rumbled off down the street.

"Well," Opal said with a sigh. "That was fun. I'm beat."

"I'm not surprised, with all the driving you did," Topaz replied.

"It was a bit nerve-wracking," her twin admitted. "Frank clutching tightly to the seat beside me didn't help. You'd think he expected me to wreck his precious Blue Label!"

"Even if he did, you didn't," Topaz noted.

"Nope. I'm a *good* driver, I am!" This in Opal's best Cockney accent.

Topaz laughed. It felt good to see her twin so buoyant.

But she still doesn't know about Paul and Victoria.

Should Topaz tell her?

No. Not tonight. Not after things have gone so well.

"Are you coming?" Opal asked, as they lingered at the entryway. She opened the door leading up to the apartments on the second and third floors.

"You go ahead," Topaz said. "I think I'll check the exhibits one last time."

"Wanting to say 'Goodnight' to your Ice Man?" Opal joked. "And here I thought you were falling for Bonnie Prince Charlie."

The jibe hurt—just a bit. "*No*," Topaz shot back, a little too quickly and a little too strongly.

"Seriously, sis," Opal said. "You look just as tired as I feel. It's been a long day. Why don't you come up to bed?"

"I will," Topaz replied evenly. (No sense giving her sister more ammunition.) "In a little while."

Opal rolled her blue-green eyes. "Okay," she said. "Be that way. You could have asked Charlie up for tea—or drinks—but instead you'd rather read a bedtime story to your frozen beau. Honestly, with you mooning over that thing constantly, I'm surprised you don't have nightmares."

Topaz's heart pounded in her chest as she ran for her life.

The unfamiliar woods became a blur around her. The full moon blazed down through the trees, but instead of illuminating her way, it made the forest a tangle of confusing shadows.

Danger lurked in those shadows; each one could be concealing the *thing*; the beast stalking her could be anywhere!

Through the twisting darkness, she spotted some light up ahead—a clearing, and could that be a fire?

Fire will keep me safe. It's afraid of fire.

She dashed out of the forest and into the open—not into a clearing, as she'd expected, but onto the frozen surface of a vast lake. In the middle of that lake, a bonfire burned, its bright orange and yellow flames licking toward the moonlit sky.

Topaz glanced behind.

Furtive red eyes lurked at the edge of the woods, peering at her.

She hurried toward the fire, going as fast as she could without losing her footing on the ice.

Why would anyone build a bonfire on a lake? she wondered.

But as she drew near the blaze, she stopped, and her blood ran cold.

It *wasn't* a bonfire… It was a *man*! A huge man standing amid the flames.

His arms were outstretched, as if begging for mercy, but no words escaped his blackened lips. The ice beneath him was melting into an ever-widening gray puddle.

Topaz wanted desperately to help the man, and for a moment, she forgot all thoughts of the animal stalking her.

She reached out, but the heat of the conflagration proved too great. She pulled her hand back, the fingers red and blistered.

And as she watched in horror, with a sound like crashing thunder, the ice beneath the man shattered, and he plunged into the inky waters below.

"No!" Topaz screamed, but it was far too late to do anything more.

Worse, the ice breaking *didn't* extinguish the blaze. Instead, as if the lake below were made of petrol, the fire began spreading across the cold white surface.

No!

Topaz turned back the way she'd come, but a dark shape now loped across the ice between her and the forest—a huge doglike figure with glowing red eyes and shaggy black fur that seemed to absorb the moonlight.

Topaz ran the other way, skirting around the growing blaze, heading for the far shore. Woods covered that shore as well, but she thought she'd spotted a building amid the leafless trees.

Yes! Now that she'd gotten clear of the fire, she could see it clearly: a tall Victorian house, sitting on the shore of the lake.

She ran, redoubling her efforts as the ice behind her moaned and snapped and the crackle of the conflagration grew behind her.

At least the fire will stop the beast, she thought.

But a glance back revealed that *not* to be true. Somehow, the dark, wolfish shape had passed through the inferno and remained patiently stalking her trail.

Fear surging through her veins, Topaz focused on the manse ahead.

Home... she realized. *It's home!*

1951 Fisher St. And in one of the topmost windows stood Opal, watching, waiting for her twin.

"I'm coming, Opal!" Topaz cried.

Sweat drenched her skin now, and soaked the light summer dress she'd foolishly worn out into the woods. Her heartbeat drummed in her ears, almost drowning out the roar of the fire behind her. Her skin prickled from the heat on her back.

"Opal, help!"

In the high window, Opal nodded and began to turn, to head for the door three stories below.

As she turned though, a dark shadow with blazing red eyes rose up behind her.

The wolf! Topaz thought.

But how could the beast be in the house? It was still behind her—at least, she *thought* it was, though she didn't dare look, lest she break her stride and fall.

Lungs aching, she sprinted the last few yards and crashed hard against the door of the Duprix mansion.

It was locked.

"Opal!" she cried, pounding on the weathered wood. "Opal!"

Topaz looked up, but she could no longer see her sister in the window high above; only darkness remained.

It got her! It GOT her!

And then, adding to the horror, flames sprang up on the roof.

The blaze quickly consumed the topmost floor, while Topaz pounded futilely on the door.

"Opal!"

The fire was all around her now. It howled and roared, cutting off her escape in every direction. Sweat drenched her body, but that proved no protection against the mounting heat.

And worse, even amid the wheezing crackle and hiss, she could still make out the guttural, rumbling growl of the approaching beast.

It was *still* coming for her!

With one last surge of strength, Opal threw all her weight against the door—and the aged portal finally gave way.

She found herself not standing in the foyer, though, but in the Chamber of Horrors. It, too, was burning.

"Opal!" Topaz screamed frantically. "Opal!"

But her twin didn't reply. Had the beast really gotten her before it came for Topaz? Was her sister already dead?

Topaz listened as hard as she could, trying to sort the roar of the fire from any human-made reply.

All she heard, though, was bells—fire bells, ringing.

The fire brigade was coming! But would they be in time?

Ringing…

The heat building around her…

Ringing…

The flames closing in…

Ringing…

A shaggy black hand reaching toward her through the flames…

They won't *arrive in time!*

And red eyes, burning even brighter than the fire…

Wednesday: Evening of the First Night of the Full Moon

The ringing of the telephone startled Topaz awake. It took every ounce of effort she could muster to stifle the scream building in her throat.

She looked around, heart pounding.

Where am I?

No forest. No lake. No burning house.

She was sitting in her father's favorite chair, by the Ice Man exhibit, drenched in sweat.

I must have dozed off.

Topaz took a deep breath and forced her heart to stop hammering.

Business at the chamber had been slow today, after a brief flurry just after opening. In fact, they hadn't had anyone stop in since lunchtime.

What time is it now? she wondered.

Rrrrrrinnng!

"Oh, shoot! The phone!"

Topaz jumped out of the chair and rushed up to the pay phone, near the entrance to the chamber.

Why hadn't Opal gotten the phone? The only people who ever called this number were…

"Hello?" she said, picking up the receiver.

"Oh, hi. It's Frank. Is that you, Topaz?"

"Yes. It's me." She knew that people often had trouble telling her from her sister on the phone. Frank seemed to have figured it out though—or made a lucky guess.

"Can I talk to Opal?"

"Sure." She put her hand over the receiver to muffle the sound and shouted: "Opal… Phone for you!"

When her twin didn't reply, she called again.

"Opal?"

But no answer came from the Chamber of Horrors.

"I'm sorry, Frank," she said into the phone. "I'm not sure where she is right now. Did you try our apartment?"

"Yeah. I called there first."

"Did you want to leave a message?"

"Nothing much," he said. "Just tell your sister that I was thinking of her. Hey, if she's free tonight, maybe we could take in a movie or something."

"Just the two of you? Or would the other boys be coming?"

"You could come and bring someone along, if you like."

"Not all four of you, then?"

Frank laughed. "Sometimes, four is *definitely* a crowd."

"Okay. I'll tell her. Bye, Frank. See you later, maybe."

"So long, Topaz."

Topaz returned the receiver to its cradle.

Where *was* Opal? It wasn't like her to duck out in the middle of the day.

Of course, it wasn't like Topaz to fall asleep on the job, either.

Opal was probably right, Topaz thought. *I shouldn't have stayed up so late reading to the Ice Man. It's not like he can really hear me. And she was right about me having nightmares, too.*

Not that Topaz actually blamed the Ice Man for her bad dream. She felt sure it was just life in general stressing her—and Opal—out. Their lives had been so jumbled lately.

Ever since Paul arrived...

Some of that drama was bound to work itself out through their unconscious, wasn't it?

And was Topaz actually avoiding the real world, as her sister had suggested? Was she spending time with the Ice Man rather than with *living* boys, like Charlie and Barry and the rest?

It had felt *so nice* with Charlie snuggled close to her in the car yesterday. And yet…

What am I afraid of?

Was she afraid of getting hurt, the way Paul had hurt her sister?

If she looked at the situation rationally, Topaz supposed that *must* be it.

That and the fact that having so many boys around all the time was still something new to both her and her sister. And unlike Opal, Topaz didn't want to hurt anyone's feelings by saying "yes" to one and "no" to all the others.

That very idea was irrational, though.
Life involved making choices.
And then paying the consequences.
Like her sister had.

But where *was* her sister? She tried to reach out with her mind, but whether it was because she'd just woken up, or because Opal was too far away, Topaz couldn't sense her twin.

Maybe she went to the bathroom upstairs. There wasn't a loo in either the chamber or the waxworks, but...

She's been gone an awfully long time.

Long enough to miss Frank calling both in their apartments and at the pay phone, anyway.

A cold chill ran up Topaz's spine, and she remembered the shadow looming over her sister in her dream. Had something *really* happened to her?

I better check, Topaz decided.

She closed and locked the door to the chamber, hanging the "Back in Fifteen Minutes" sign on the doorknob—not that any customers seemed likely at this point. The wall clock by the calendar near the entrance told her it was quarter to seven, nearly closing time on a Wednesday evening.

I slept the entire afternoon away.

Shaking her head at her own indolence, Topaz mounted the stairway and hurried up to their quarters.

She paused on the second-floor landing (where she *thought* she heard voices echoing from the servants' hallway), but only long enough to determine whether either voice belonged to Opal. Neither did, so she continued on to the Cushing residence on the third floor.

"Opal?" she called as she entered and closed the door behind her. But she spoke quietly, as she didn't hear anyone moving about.

Maybe she *fell asleep, too.*

She could hardly blame Opal if she had. Both of them had

been under quite a bit of stress, and though the sky had been clear and sunny today—a warm summer afternoon—with no customers coming through the turnstiles, it was the perfect time for a nap. (As Topaz had found out herself, despite her nightmare.)

Cautiously, so as not to wake her twin, she peeked into the bedroom they shared.

No Opal.

"Hmm…" she mused.

Not in the loo, either, and neither sister *ever* went into Father's bedroom, which left only the kitchen.

But she didn't find Opal there, either.

Topaz frowned, puzzled… Until she noticed that the doorway connecting to the back stairs—the servants' stairs—stood ajar.

Oh, no!

She could sense her sister now, on the other side of the door, near the top of the stairway. Topaz didn't like what she felt.

Carefully, quietly, Topaz opened the door and crept to the edge of the third-floor landing behind Opal.

Her twin was just standing there, trembling, clutching the railing and peering down toward the second floor.

Topaz didn't need to see what Opal was looking at; the image came to her as clearly as if she were seeing it herself:

Paul and Victoria, below, standing at the edge of the second-floor landing, engaged in a passionate embrace—kissing.

Opal's mind seethed with emotions so powerful—anger… sadness… heartache… betrayal…—that Topaz had to remind herself that the feelings were *not* her own.

Silently, she put her hand over Opal's mouth, so her sister wouldn't cry out, and gently said with her mind: *"Come away."*

Numbly, Opal obeyed, and the two of them backed from the landing into the Cushings' kitchen, where Topaz closed and locked the door to the servants' stairs.

Then Opal turned and ran, weeping, into their bedroom.

She almost slammed the door, but Topaz caught it in time, and slipped in behind her twin.

Opal threw herself on the bed, disconsolate.

Topaz put a comforting hand on her shoulder. "Darling," Topaz whispered softly, "we *knew* what kind of man Paul was. We knew we couldn't *trust* him. I know that you'd begun to think that maybe he could change, but…"

Suddenly, Opal sprang erect on the bed. Her tear-stained blue-green eyes peered furiously into the eyes of her twin.

"You knew?" Opal accused, her voice hoarse and low. "You *knew*!"

"I…" Topaz began, but it was no use. She realized that, in this moment, her sister could read her mind clearly. "I didn't *know*, precisely… I'd never *seen* them… together. I just…"

"Why didn't you *tell* me?"

"I didn't see the point…"

"The point?!"

"I didn't want to cause you any more pain…"

"So, you just thought you'd wait until I found out myself?"

"I thought maybe you *wouldn't* find out. I thought maybe he'd *leave*, and then it wouldn't matter anymore."

"And that would make everything *better*, then, would it?" Opal shot back bitterly.

"No, but…"

"Get out!" Opal said, pointing toward the door.

"What?"

"Get *out*! You're as bad as the rest of them. You're as bad as Paul, with your damn secrets and lies!"

"You don't mean that…"

"Get OUT!"

The shriek convinced Topaz there was nothing she could do right now. She'd have to wait until Opal settled down. "All right..." She backed toward the door, tears brimming in her eyes. "I'll give you some time."

"I don't care if I *never* see you again!" Opal wailed.

Topaz left. She had no other options.

She closed the door behind her as she went, heading downstairs to the chamber.

She paused at the second floor, in front of the servants' door. Should she go in and confront Paul? Lambaste him about what he'd done, how he'd broken her sister's heart—again?

No. What good would that do? He wouldn't change.

She only hoped that Opal *wouldn't* confront him either, that her sister would cry herself to sleep. Then maybe they could sort everything out in the morning.

Topaz descended the winding stairs once more.

Only when she reached the first-floor landing did she finally burst into tears.

Sobbing, she opened the door to Dr. Cushing's Chamber of Horrors and then flipped the sign on the door so that it read: *CLOSED. Come back tomorrow.*

Tomorrow... Would there even *be* a tomorrow for them? For the business? For their family?

Topaz felt as though her entire world had crashed down around her.

Normally, in a situation like this (though there never really had been anything as *bad* as this before), she would have turned to her sister, but...

Right now, that was entirely out of the question.

I can't really blame her, Topaz thought. *I should have told her what I suspected.*

But she hadn't, and—at least for the moment—that mistake had cost Topaz her oldest, dearest friend, the friend who was like the second part of her soul.

Weeping bitterly, she went to the deepest, darkest corner of the chamber and plopped down on the floor, next to the Ice Man exhibit.

Sniffling and wiping away the tears, she told the frozen giant: "You are my only friend in the world."

And in her mind, the word echoed…

Friend…!

31

THE BREAKS

Paul Shaw (Longmire) – 1951 Fisher St.
Wednesday: Evening of the First Night of the Full Moon

Paul broke away from Victoria's kiss and stalked down the servants' hallway toward his room. His mind swirled with conflicting emotions: lust... anger... fear... betrayal...

What was he *doing*?! Kissing Victoria in the hallway like that —kissing her *at all*—was madness. Even if they'd been in his room, it would be so easy for someone to catch them. This house was big, but it wasn't *that* big, and sound traveled in strange ways in the old place.

Laughing quietly to herself, Victoria followed Paul. She slipped in behind him as he tried to slam the door and close her out.

"You can't get away from me that easily," she purred.

"I'm leaving," he stated. He glanced at his wall calendar, at the days *X*-ed out leading up to the full moon. *Monday. It's only Monday.* He still had plenty of time. Better to leave a day early than an hour late, even though he'd promised Victoria one more day.

"You've said that before," she noted slyly.

"I know. But this time, I mean it." He began throwing clothes into his valise. The weight of the chains in its bottom reassured him, gave him confidence. He was doing the right thing.

She came up behind him and put her arms around his waist, trying to impede his progress. "You said you were leaving on Tuesday," she said. "Yet, here it is *Wednesday*, already, and you're still here."

Paul stopped dead, his body suddenly ice cold.

"What?" he gasped.

She held him tight and pressed herself up against him. "One might almost think there's *something* here that you like." She rubbed her body sensually against his back.

He spun on her, grabbing her by the shoulders, the fire of madness creeping into his mind.

"What did you say?!" he demanded.

She smiled seductively at him. "I said, maybe there's something here that you like." She unbuttoned the top of her dress, revealing the pale curves of her breasts.

"No, not *that*!" he said frantically. "The day! What *day* is it?"

Victoria looked slightly confused. "Why, Wednesday, of course. Wednesday *always* comes after Monday and Tuesday." She pulled open his shirt and kissed him on the chest.

Paul barely even felt it. Heart pounding, he looked at the wall calendar. *Monday*... By the marks he'd made, it should *only* be Monday!

"Though with all the fun we've been having," Victoria continued, "I can't blame you for losing track." She pulled his shirt wider and gave his left nipple a soft bite.

He pushed her away from him; she landed on her rump atop the bed.

The curse had gotten to him again. He'd lost track of the date! It was *Wednesday*—the first night of the full moon! How much time did he have left before moonrise? He couldn't even be sure of *that*.

He began wildly shoving his things into the suitcase once more. Where could he go tonight? Where would be safe? He could try to turn himself in, have the police lock him up…

But they would never believe him. And the curse hadn't even let him *confess*, the last time he'd tried it; he'd ended up walking in circles, never reaching the police station, until the full moon appeared, and then…!

Victoria rose from the bed, teeth gritted, hazel eyes ablaze. "Where do you think you're going?"

"I told you. I'm leaving."

She grabbed him by the shoulder. "Oh no you're not! I'm not *done* with you yet."

Paul shrugged off her hand, though her fingernails bit into the fabric of his shirt.

"Yes, you *are*," he snapped. "We're *finished*—like we should have been days ago. We never should have even started this crazy affair."

"I'll tell you when this 'crazy affair' is over!" she fumed. She grabbed his shirt and tried to pull him to her. "I could *still* have you arrested. I could call the police, tell them details—"

"I could tell them details, too," he countered, cutting her off, though his stomach clenched at the thought that she might carry through with her threat. "I could tell them all about this torrid little liaison—and while I'm at it, tell your husband, and the newspapers, too. I bet that would make fine reading for tomorrow's editions: 'Waxworks Lovers Carry On In Secret—Famous Artist Cuckolded!'"

The confabulated headlines seemed to hit Victoria like a slap, and she backed away, toward the doorway.

Paul seized the opportunity, sprang from his packing to the door, and opened it.

"You wouldn't dare!" she said, though the fear in her eyes told him that she thought maybe he *would*.

"Try me and see," he said, pushing her toward the open portal. "Goodbye, Victoria."

He stepped toward her menacingly, and, surprised, she staggered back over the threshold.

He slammed the door in her face.

"And don't come back!" he called. "Let me pack and get out of here, before it's too late."

"Oh, it's *too late*, all right," her seething voice replied from the hall.

Paul put his shoulder to the door. It had no lock, and he expected her to try and push her way back in, but she didn't. And after a moment, he heard Victoria stamping off toward the front stairway.

Good, he thought. *I don't have much time.*

In fact, the clock atop his meager nightstand had stopped. Clearly, when he'd forgotten to cross off the days, he'd forgotten to wind it as well.

The curse!

He returned to quickly shoving all his possessions into the valise.

He wasn't sure what he'd do or where he'd go once he packed, but he had to get out of this place.

He didn't have a lot of money, but maybe he could hire a cab, have himself driven out into the countryside, where he couldn't hurt anybody…

But he knew that would be futile. He'd isolated himself in Lancashire, and the beast had still found some poor girl to kill… and then that poacher in Derbyshire as well. Somehow, no matter what he did, the monster always found a way out, a way to carry on its reign of murder and destruction.

I should have let Victoria call the police, he thought.

Maybe it wasn't too late. Maybe if he *didn't* leave, and made enough of a ruckus…

No. He didn't have time to risk that kind of a ploy. Every moment he stayed put everyone in 1951 Fisher at risk—the Duprixes, the twins… and any other unlucky soul who might happen by. The sun hadn't set yet, not quite, but that only meant he still had enough time to get away.

The door behind him creaked open. Paul wished he'd thought to prop the room's sole chair against it.

He whirled, angry words bursting from his lips:

"Victoria… I told you—"

It wasn't Victoria.

"Opal!" Paul gasped.

She stood in the doorway, looking lovely even in the dim evening light. Shadows framed her curvy figure, and her dark hair fell carelessly across her pretty face. Her eyes were red and puffy, clearly from crying, but her face looked angry.

"I know you were expecting your adulterous lover," she snapped, "but it's only me."

He rose to his feet, hardly able to bear looking at her. Feelings of love welled up inside him, even though he knew it was no use.

"Opal, I—"

"Don't say it," she said, entering the room and closing the door behind her. "I don't think I can stand any more of your lies. I just came to tell you that I hope I *never* see you again, Paul Shaw."

Paul blinked away the moisture in his eyes and turned back to his packing. "Well, you won't have to. I've broken it off with Victoria. For keeps, this time. I'm leaving."

"Good," she said, though her voice cracked as she said it.

He turned to face her again, his heart breaking.

"I—" she continued. Then she burst into tears and rushed into his arms. "Oh, Paul!"

He held her tight, leaning his face against her head, tears streaming from his eyes into her silky hair. Her weeping stained his shirt, as she pressed her face into his chest.

"Why did you do it, Paul?" she sobbed. "Why did you lie to me? Why did you… sleep with… *her*?"

He shook his head. "I've made mistakes—awful mistakes. I-I can't explain them all. But it's like I'm caught in some horrible trap that I can't get out of. This *curse* … I … I have to leave tonight—right now, or you and everyone else I care for is in terrible danger."

"That *damned* curse," she said, softly pounding her fists into his chest. "It's just another lie. Another excuse to hurt people. Why don't you just admit you're making it up? Go away. See if I care. See if I *care*!"

"It's *not* a lie," he said, running his hand through her hair, holding her close. "The curse is *real*. I'm sorry. I'll try to write if… *when* I get someplace safe… if I ever find what I need to break free of it."

"Break free of *what*?" she asked, gazing up at him with her red-rimmed eyes. "What is it that's *wrong* with you?"

"I'm a werewolf."

The words tumbled out before he could even think to suppress them.

Opal's mouth hung open. She stopped sobbing and stared at him.

"I know you won't believe me," he said. "But every night the moon is full, I turn into a monster—I *kill* people."

"H-how…?"

Paul let her go and stepped back. "How did I become a werewolf? What does it matter? You don't believe me—nobody does."

"I need to know," she insisted.

He couldn't tell if Opal was still angry, but she no longer

seemed the blubbering teenager she'd been moments ago. Her blue-green eyes were steely now, determined.

But determined to do *what*? To punch him once he finished telling his fantastic story?

No matter. He'd come this far. Now he *had* to tell her.

"There was this madman," he began, "Count Zarkoff, a famous sportsman. He hired me as a guide to help him hunt wolves in Transylvania; that's what he said, anyway. But when I slept, he injected me with the blood of a lycanthrope—a werewolf. I guess he'd bought it during an expedition in China.

"You see, it was *me* he really wanted to hunt. Regular game was no longer good enough for him."

"Like that book I read in school," Opal mused softly.

"Yes," Paul replied. "Maybe he read it, too. Now he wanted to hunt the most dangerous quarry he could imagine—and since werewolves are hard to come by…" he said this last with bitter irony, "Zarkoff decided to make his own." A grim smile cracked his lips. "Let's just say the kill didn't work out like he'd planned."

"But, even if I believed all that…" Opal said. "Why *you*?"

"Because I am—or I *was*—a famous hunter, too. Zarkoff figured that a man like himself would make more challenging prey as a werewolf. My real name is Paul Longmire—Paul Shaw Longmire."

Opal blinked, astonished. "Wait… Of the *American* Longmires?"

"So, you've heard of us," he said bitterly.

"The Longmires are one of the richest families in the Western Hemisphere," she replied.

"Well, *I'm* not," Paul said. "My parents are dead, and my grandmother cut me off when… when I married my wife, Caliso, in the Philippines."

"Why?"

"She was the wrong color."

"But that's not *fair*!"

"Grandmother never much cared what was fair, only what was proper."

"But maybe now that... now that your wife is *dead*... Maybe your grandmother could help. Maybe with all that money, you..." Then her face hardened. "...Unless this is all another elaborate story."

Paul shook his head. "I only wish it were. Look, it doesn't matter whether you believe me or not. All that matters is that I have to get out of here tonight, before the moon rises. If I don't, I'll kill everyone in this whole damn building. You and your sister included." He resumed his packing.

"Paul..."

"What?" he snapped.

"Paul, look at me."

He turned, and she took his face in her hands and stared into his eyes.

"Opal, I... I have to go!"

"Shut up and let me concentrate."

Paul shut up.

For a long moment, her brilliant blue-green eyes remained locked on him.

When she finally let him go, she said:

"I believe you."

"You do?"

"Yes. I may not have my sister's gift for reading people, but I can tell you're not lying."

He laughed once. "So, either I'm a madman, or..."

"Or you're telling the truth."

Paul took Opal's small, soft hands in his own. He felt so large and brutish compared to her, but he also felt... grateful.

"Thank you," he said. "Only the gypsies ever believed me, before. So, now that you know, you must let me leave. Let me finish packing, and I promise I'll be on my way. I'll never darken your doorstep again. But I have to get out of here and find someplace safe to stay."

"Where?"

"Any place where there aren't many people. I have some chains in my suitcase. They've been strong enough to hold the beast so far, but…"

"Then you could stay *here*," she suggested. "We could lock you in the ice man's freezer—if you don't think the cold would kill you."

"It's harder than that to kill a werewolf," Paul said. "But even locked in a closet, the wolf almost destroyed the flophouse room where I was staying last month. Even chained up, I might tear your exhibits to shreds."

"Well, that won't do, then," Opal admitted. She pursed her lips, thinking hard for a few moments. "What about a crypt?"

"What crypt?" Paul asked.

"There are a number of abandoned crypts in Highgate Cemetery," she said. "They're not too far from Hampstead Heath. Topaz and I drove past the cemetery yesterday, when we were out with the boys, and our father took us there once on one of his little expeditions, when we were younger."

"But how would I get there?" Paul said. "I guess I could try the Tube or a cab, but if anything went wrong…"

"Someone innocent could get killed. I understand." Now that she believed him, Opal seemed filled with iron determination. She brushed away the last of her tears with her sleeve. "Well then, Topaz and I will just have to take you ourselves."

"What? No!"

"It's really the only way. We can't trust anyone else to do it."

"But how? You don't even have a car."

"We'll borrow one. Barry, or even Frank, is bound to agree if I ask… in the right way." Her pretty eyes sparkled mischievously, reminding Paul of why he'd fallen for her in the first place.

"All right. I guess it's worth a try. Find out when the moon rises, too, would you? I… The curse makes it almost impossible for me to keep track that kind of thing during this time of the month."

A smiled tugged at the corner of her pretty lips. "I have times of the month like that, too. Finish packing. I'll get Topaz and arrange for the car. Meet us on the first-floor landing, outside the door to the chamber."

"But will your sister believe you?" Paul asked.

Opal nodded. "She can read me a lot more easily than I could read you. She knew that you and Victoria were having an affair, and I only found out today, when I saw you kissing on the back landing."

A knot twisted in Paul's stomach. "About that, I'm sorry, I…"

She shook her head. "No time for explanations now. Get packed. We'll meet you downstairs."

And with that, she swept out of the room, gently closing the door behind her.

"What a girl!" Paul whispered to himself.

He'd been such an idiot to muck things up the way he did. If he'd only told the truth from the beginning…

She probably wouldn't have believed you.

But she was right. There was no time for recriminations or regrets now. They had to get to that crypt before moonrise, and heaven only knew when that might be. Already, the evening sun was casting lengthening shadows through the small, high window in his room.

He finished stuffing his meager belongings in the valise, pausing only a moment to cross out the correct number of days on his notebook calendar.

Maybe this time, I'll be able to keep track, he thought—but he doubted it.

Maybe if Opal and Topaz helped, though…

But that was crazy. He couldn't *stay* with the girls, whether here in the city or anywhere else. His being with anyone put them in constant danger.

"Time to go," he said aloud, as if doing so would force him to action.

He rose, picked up the valise, and stepped out of his room into the hall.

As he did, something struck him on the back of his head, and fireworks exploded in his brain.

And when the fireworks faded, Paul sank down into darkness.

32

VICTORIA'S FURY

*Victoria Duprix – 1951 Fisher St.
Wednesday: Evening of the First Night of the Full Moon*

Victoria paced angrily in her room on the second floor of the manse. "How *dare* he!" she fumed. "How dare he treat me like a common trollop? After I'll I've done for him… the *risks* I've taken…!"

From her dark mirror, Erzsebet Bathory chuckled. *"Do not conssscern yoursssself, my dear. He isss but a man, and all men are cattle."*

"Then I should slaughter him," Victoria hissed.

"If you wisssh."

Victoria's hazel eyes lit up as the flame of a wicked idea sparked in her brain. "Would he *do*? Would killing him tonight make me like *you*?"

Erzsebet frowned. *"Perhapsss. But girlsss are better."*

"Better how?"

"More… tasssty."

"But would it *work*? Could killing Paul—or my worthless husband—give me eternal youth? Would it make me immortal?"

The woman in the mirror shrugged and, turning her back to Victoria, paced further into the reflection's darkness. *"Who can sssay? I had little tassste for killing men."*

"It should be a woman, then," Victoria mused. She couldn't risk this *not* working. There was no guarantee she'd get another chance.

She cursed herself for not nailing down the details previously, but she'd been so obsessed with striking back at Vincent, who seemed the perfect victim (though Paul now fit that bill as well), that she hadn't arranged any alternatives.

Now she had little time to find anyone else.

So, perhaps one of the men would suffice. Certainly, it would be a pleasure to kill either of them.

For a moment, Victoria imagined plunging her slender knife into Paul's neck, feeling the warm spurt of his blood covering her naked body, reveling as his life energy flowed into her, restoring her youth.

Yes. One of the men would have to do. She didn't know where her husband was at the moment, but Paul remained close at hand.

Unless he leaves, she thought, and the notion leant urgency to her quest.

"Remember," Erzsebet said, as if reading her thoughts, *"you mussst drain the blood into my tub and bathe in it by the light of the full moon—and the blood mussst be fresssh."*

"I remember," Victoria said.

"And I mussst be there asss well. It requiresss my magic for you to become... one of usss."

"Yes," Victoria replied. She would have to move the mirror down into the Chamber of Horrors, as it would be too difficult to bring Bathory's tub up to the second floor. Fortunately, the girls' Bathory display was not too far from the servants' stairway.

But where were those two bubbleheads now? Had they

returned to their apartments after closing, or were they out with their young men? She hoped she wouldn't find either of them in the chamber. But if she did...

I can't let them get in my way, she thought—and then imagined bathing in *their* blood as well.

A smile crept across Victoria's wicked face. Wouldn't it be delicious to kill *all* her enemies in one night?

"And you ssshall, if you wisssh," Erzsebet said, again reading Victoria's thoughts. *"Onsssce you have joined usss, no power on earth can ssstop you. The whole world will be our...* your *prey."*

"Yes," Victoria replied.

She went to her wardrobe and fetched the bottle of chloroform that she'd secreted there. She couldn't kill her victim and then, afterward, take them to the tub, not tonight. This time, they needed to be *alive*, to be sacrificed at the proper time—time that was nearly upon them.

Victoria opened the hope chest at the foot of her bed and took out her stiletto. The blade was slender but strong, perfect for piercing necks. Part of her wanted to lick it, to see if she could still taste the blood of her previous victims.

But there would be enough time for such indulgences later. Now she had to secure *tonight's* victim.

Shaw will have to do... before he can escape.

"Yesss..." Erzsebet urged. *"Claim our prey! Tonight is oursss!"*

"Vincent?" Victoria said softly as she exited her chambers, wanting to make sure he wasn't around to interfere with her plans. (Or, if he was, to become the victim she needed.)

She saw no sign of her husband in the rest of their apartments, though the doors to his bedroom and the studio remained closed. Listening, she heard no indication that the old scoundrel was about, either.

Perhaps he's working downstairs, she thought. He seemed obsessed with the exhibits of late, especially the new Egyptian one. And if not there, perhaps he'd gone out to meet his current lover, whomever she might be.

I'll have time to find and kill her later, Victoria reminded herself. Once she had the power she craved, she'd enjoy torturing the name out of him. First, though, she had to become immortal.

Time to kill Mr. Shaw.

Moving stealthily, Victoria took the apartment's exit to the main stairs. Shaw would have to come this way to leave the building; the servants' stairs exit remained locked, and only the Duprixes and Cushings had keys.

But as she stepped onto the landing, a noise from above froze Victoria in her tracks.

"Topaz?" called an urgent feminine voice. "Topaz, are you up there?"

Victoria looked up and saw Opal above her, half way up the flight to the next floor, bellowing to her blonde sister as she went.

Victoria tried to step back inside her chambers—she didn't want to be seen—but before she could, the girl spotted her.

Opal stopped in the middle of the next flight, peered down at Victoria, and asked: "Have you seen my sister?"

Victoria shook her head, being careful to conceal the chloroform and rag behind her back. (The stiletto she'd secreted in her bodice.) There was no furtively escaping back into her rooms at this point. "Not today. No," Victoria replied.

The brunette descended the stairs to the second landing, a frown creasing her young brow.

"You're not going to see *Paul* again, are you?" the girl said, her blue-green eyes steely. She was standing only an arm's length away from Victoria now, and behaving as though the two were equals.

Victoria drew herself up haughtily. "No," she lied. "But I don't see that it's any business of yours, even if I were."

Opal didn't seem to believe her. "My sister and I know what you've been up to," she said, "and honestly, we don't care. However you carry on in private is your own business. But you have to let Paul *go*. He can't stay here any longer. He has to leave."

"I honestly don't know what you're talking about," Victoria said, but her eyes narrowed involuntarily. How dare this little slut pass judgement on her?!

"Fine," Opal said, though it was clear she didn't believe Victoria. "Good. Because if you *weren't* going to let him go, one of us might have to let your husband in on what's been happening in the servants' quarters."

"If I had any idea what you were talking about," Victoria said, "I might consider that a threat."

"Take it any way you want. Just, please, for his own sake—for everybody's—let Paul leave."

"I've told the handyman that he can quit at any time," Victoria said, wheels of fire and vengeance spinning in her mind. "If he goes today... so much the better."

"Good," said Opal. "Now, excuse me. I need to find my sister and make a phone call."

She turned to go upstairs.

Victoria covered the distance between them in two quick steps.

Before Opal could even cry out, the older woman had the chloroform-soaked rag over the girl's mouth and nose.

In only a few moments, Opal slumped into Victoria's arms, unconscious.

Victoria sneered. "Little tramp!" she whispered. "Thought you could blackmail me, did you? Thought you could protect your precious Paul? Well, you will—but not in the way you intended."

Swiftly, almost silently, she dragged the girl's limp body back into the Duprixes' apartments.

"Erzsebet said that girls were better for this," Victoria muttered to her new victim, "and now here you are, falling right into my arms—practically *begging* for it. And the best part is, Paul will never know that you sacrificed your life and saved his." Victoria chuckled, soft and low, as she heaved the girl toward her bedroom.

As she crossed the threshold, though, someone called:

"Vincent…? Is that you?"

The voice came from her husband's bedroom—a *woman's* voice.

For a moment, Victoria froze. Then she realized who it must be:

His lover!

Jealous rage welled up inside Victoria, overwhelming her lust for revenge on Paul and the Cushing girl.

Hastily, she dragged Opal's limp body into her closet and shut and locked the door.

"I'll finish things with you later," Victoria whispered, and in her mind, she imagined herself bathing in the pretty brunette's blood. Her body tingled at the thought. But that pleasure could wait.

Catlike, Victoria crept out of her bedroom.

"Vincent…?" came the soft, sweet call again.

Silently, Victoria crept down the hall and cracked open the door to her husband's bedroom.

A woman sat at his dressing table, alone in the room and half dressed, her fashionable clothes laid neatly over a nearby chair. The woman was brushing her long blonde hair.

Her back was to the door, but Victoria recognized her instantly.

Lily Carlson?!

In her wildest speculations, Victoria had never suspected Vincent's current lover was…

My own best friend!

The betrayal seared into Victoria's brain like a red-hot poker. Unwanted erotic images of her friend and her husband —*together*—sprang up in her mind and swirled into a cyclone of night-black hatred.

"Did you get rid of your wife, darling?" Lily asked, her back still turned to the doorway.

Victoria padded silently forward, her lips pulled back in a merciless grin.

"No," she replied. "No, he didn't."

33

PREPARED FOR SACRIFICE

Vincent Duprix – The Waxworks
Wednesday: First Night of the Full Moon

Vincent wiped the sweat from his brow and took a deep breath. Moving the mummies of Sethotep and Queen Bastiti from the Chamber of Horrors into the recreated tomb in the waxworks—and doing so without being noticed by anyone—had been harder work than he'd anticipated.

At first, he'd thought he might have to dispose of Topaz, who'd been lingering in the recesses of the chamber after hours. Fortunately, just before he might have been forced to strike, she'd left via the front stairway—off on some girlish errand, no doubt.

Perhaps to see one of those doltish boys who are always hanging around, Vincent thought.

No matter the reason, her exiting had cleared the way for Vincent to complete arranging the most vital part of tonight's ceremony—placing the mummies in their proper positions:

Bastiti, where she could be revivified, and Sethotep where he could direct Vincent in the needed spells and incantations.

Or maybe that was only the *second* most vital part. The first had been procuring a victim for the ritual.

That had proven easy enough, though. Fortunately, Vincent had the perfect subject right on the premises.

Paul Shaw lay strapped to Vincent's specially prepared altar —a perfect replica of the one from Bastiti's tomb. Victoria's lover remained insensate, thanks to a clever blow to the back of the head.

"Too bad, Mr. Shaw," Vincent gloated. "You *almost* got away with it—even packed your bag for a timely escape. I wonder, though… Was Victoria going with you? Oh, well. Time enough to find out—and deal with her—later." He turned to the mummified architect, standing in his sarcophagus nearby. "How soon, Sethotep? I can barely stand the waiting."

"Soon," came the unspoken reply. *"Very soon, the moon will rise, and my queen…* our *queen will live again."*

In his mind, Vincent imagined cutting Shaw's wrists and draining his blood, revenging himself on his wife's lover. Even the idea felt *glorious*. Better still, once the deed was done, his *new* paramour would arise… Queen Bastiti in all her youth and beauty. And then…

The thought of having a new lover triggered something else in Vincent's mind; a half-remembered notion flickered to light in the back of his head.

"Lily," he said aloud. "I was supposed to meet her tonight. She's probably upstairs in my room, even now."

For just a moment, thoughts of his Egyptian Queen were pushed aside in his fevered brain by memories of Lily Carlson's soft white body, her golden hair, her sensuous lips… Oh, what *fun* they'd had! And right behind Victoria's back…!

"That pale piece of meat is unimportant," Sethotep cautioned,

reading Vincent's thoughts. *"Tonight, the moon is full. Tonight my... our plans will at last come to fruition. Bastiti will live again!"*

Vincent turned from the altar and its trussed victim to the upright sarcophagus holding the mummy of his Queen.

Even wrapped in ancient linens and desiccated by the aeons, she retained a sensual, womanly shape. Vincent's imagination overlaid the lovely face from her sarcophagus lid onto the mummified form and, in his artist's mind, she came to life once more.

Bastiti stood before him, night-black oiled hair glistening in the light from the recreated chamber's torches, her naked body tanned and curved in all the right places, her skin smooth and soft, her lips warm and inviting...

He could almost *taste* her.

Bound to the altar by leather straps and still unconscious, Paul Shaw moaned and stirred slightly.

In Vincent's mind, Sethotep chuckled—a low, pitiless sound.

"Don't worry, Mr. Shaw," Vincent whispered to his prey. "You won't be in pain much longer. In just a few moments, your adulterous soul will have the honor of restoring my queen to life!"

34

ALONE IN THE DARKNESS

*Opal Cushing – 1951 Fisher St.
First Night of the Full Moon*

At first, everything was darkness, and Opal Cushing had no idea where she was.

What had happened to her? She'd been going upstairs to find Topaz, to tell her about Paul, and call the boys to borrow a car and… and…?

Suddenly, everything had gone black.

She blinked… and found that her eyes were already open. Had she gone blind?

She tried to stand, but couldn't.

She cried out, but something soft clogged her mouth, and barely a sound came out.

Oh my God, she thought, panic rising. *I'm tied up—tied up and gagged! And God only knows where I am!*

Suddenly, it became hard to breathe; the air seemed very hot and thin.

Don't panic, Opal told herself. *It's only fear clouding your judgement. You've got plenty of air.*

And though her rational mind knew that was true, the rest of her remained certain that she was about to smother here, alone in the dark, wherever *here* might be.

She squeezed her eyes shut. Concentrated. Tried to fight down the panic.

What's the last thing you remember...?

Going up toward their flat, calling for her sister…

But no, then she'd stopped and gone back down to talk to someone…

Victoria!

In an instant, it all came clear: someone grabbing her from behind… putting something soft over her mouth and nose… a sickly-sweet smell…

Victoria did this to me. She's out of her mind!

"Help!" Opal shouted. "Help!"

But what came out was more of a muffled *"Hmmph!"*

Again, fear rose within Opal's breast.

Why had Victoria done this? What did she intend to *do* with her?

Was she jealous? Was it because of Paul?

OhmyGod! Paul!

How long had she been out? Was Paul still waiting for her? Had the moon risen yet? Had he… changed?

Opal struggled with all her might, but her ankles were bound, and her hands tied behind her.

She felt soft things around her face, and near her kicking feet. Was someone else in here with her?

Her eyes had adjusted a bit now, and she saw a thin rectangle of light down near her shoes.

A closet! I'm tied in a clothes closet. That explained the soft objects all around, too. *I must be in Victoria's room.*

But for how long?

"Help!" she cried, thought the gag smothered her words again. "Help! Help!"

She kicked and wiggled, trying to work free of her bonds—but Madame Duprix had trussed her up well.

"Help!"

Where had Victoria gone? Would she be back soon?

If she was willing to go this far—to kidnap Opal—what *other* crimes might she be planning?

Victoria didn't know about Paul's curse. What else what might the madwoman do to keep Paul to herself?

She might even kill *me!*

"Help! Help me!"

The more Opal screamed, the more she kicked and struggled, the more futile it all seemed.

And where was her sister? Had Victoria gotten her, too? Was Topaz *already* dead?

NO! She can't *be dead. I'd feel it, if she were.*

"Help, Topaz! Help!"

She doubted anyone could hear her—certainly no one outside the Duprixes' apartments. Though that left another option…

"Vincent! Topaz! Anyone… HELP!"

They *had* to find her… *Someone* had to find her, before Victoria came back.

Opal felt certain, now, that she wouldn't survive the night if Madame Duprix returned before anyone rescued her.

There was no one, and nothing, that would prevent the older woman from carrying out some kind of twisted revenge on Opal.

"HELP!"

Suddenly, the door flew open, and blinding light streamed into the closet.

The figure of a woman loomed over her.

Opal screamed: "NOOOOOOOOO!"

Strong hands grabbed her, pulling at her clothes.

"NOOOOOOOO! HELP!" The gag all but smothered her

frantic cries. Fear set her brain on fire. She could hardly think at all.

"Opal, stop!"

She kept struggling. She wouldn't let Victoria kill her—not without a fight.

"Opal, stop!"

"Opal, stop! It's me!"

The projected thought cut through her mind like a knife.

"Topaz!" Opal wailed in relief, though all that came through the gag was a muffled sob.

Topaz quickly undid the gag and untied her sister. "You're all right, now," she said calmingly. "You're all right." She extended her hand, to help Opal up.

But as their fingers touched, something like lightning shot through the twins.

For a moment, the whole world was darkness, a rush of wind, and a roar like waves crashing against the beach, or a blazing bonfire.

Then images and sounds swirled up out of the cacophonous blackness:

Paul struggling and screaming...

Vincent laughing maniacally...

A wicked blade gleaming as it descended...

Victoria, naked, covered in blood...

The howl of a wolf...

Fire, blazing bright all around...

And then, the darkness of death.

Both sisters staggered and fell to their knees.

Topaz gasped. "Something *terrible* is happening."

"Paul's in trouble!" Opal added. She felt it with every fiber of her being.

Topaz clutched at her temples, as if she might drive away the terrifying visions. "This house... We're all in danger... *horrible* danger!"

Opal put a hand on her sister's arm. "Topaz," she said, "Paul's a werewolf."

"What?"

"I know it sounds crazy, but I'm *sure* it's true."

The twins looked into each other's blue-green eyes.

"I believe you," Topaz said. "But tonight's the first night of the full moon!"

"I know! How long was I locked in that closet? How soon will the moon rise?"

"I don't know," Topaz admitted, looking a little panicked herself now. "I was downstairs, after our… our fight. But I felt something… and I came up looking for you. When you weren't in our flat, I followed a hunch and found you here. It's almost dark, now, but I don't know what time it is. I wasn't paying attention."

"We have to find Paul," Opal said, "get him locked up before the moon rises."

"But where? How? That could be any minute?"

"We can put him in the freezer, behind the Ice Man display. He has some chains in his suitcase. Those combined with the freezer will hold him… I hope!"

"Okay. But where *is* he?"

Opal took a deep breath. The fear of confinement had left her now, replaced by a sense of purpose. They *had* to help their friend. "I don't know where he is," she confessed. "We'll have to look. I'll check his room and then the waxworks. You hurry to the front landing, he was supposed to meet me there, and then check the chamber."

Topaz nodded. "All right. And try to avoid the Duprixes if you can. Something's going on…"

"You're telling *me*!" Opal replied. "She knocked me out and tied me up!"

"No, I mean there's something very *wrong* with them. I can feel it. It's making my skin crawl. I wish I could *read* where they are, but the psychic energy has gone crazy in the whole house. If we didn't have to find Paul, I'd say we should get the hell out of here."

"We will," Opal assured her. "We'll get out as soon as we find Paul."

"And find a way to lock him up."

"Yes. And get him safely locked up." Opal took a deep breath and steadied her jangling nerves. "Let's go!"

35

RITUAL OF BLOOD

Victoria Duprix – The Chamber of Horrors
First Night of the Full Moon

Lily Carlson dangled from the ceiling of Dr. Cushing's Chamber of Horrors. She hung head downward, naked, over Countess Bathory's infamous tub, with her ankles bound tightly and her hands tied behind her back.

She looks quite lovely, Victoria thought, almost like the pale chrysalis of a caterpillar, all trussed up and ready to transform into something better.

Something better for me!

Lily swayed and twisted slightly as her eyelids fluttered open.

Countess Erzsebet Bathory stalked to the front of her mirror, which Victoria had stood next to the tub.

"The moon is risssing!" Erzsebet proclaimed. *"Do it, my aprentisssce! Do it NOW!"*

"Without taking a moment to luxuriate in my triumph?" Victoria scoffed. "Oh, no. I want to enjoy every glorious second of this."

"Where am I?" Lily asked, looking around, confused. "What's going on?"

"Do it!" Erzsebet urged. *"Join ussss!"*

Lily's blue eyes widened with fear. "Victoria? What are you doing?"

Victoria smiled sweetly. "I'm giving you what you *deserve*, Dear Lily."

The captive woman struggled against her bonds, which only made her sway and spin more. "No. Please. Let me go. This is some kind of mistake!"

"*Mistake?*" Victoria scoffed. "No, my dear, the mistake was you sleeping with *my* husband. The mistake was thinking that you could get away with it, that you *wouldn't* have to pay."

Lily looked around, like a rat caught in a trap, seeking assistance from anywhere. But no one else was in the room save the specter in the dark mirror.

"But… It wasn't anything *serious*," Lily explained. "The affair was just for *fun*. Just for a little while. You've had dalliances of your own, after all…"

"And you think my adulteries excuse your own—with my *husband*?! You… my 'best friend.'" Victoria said this last with all the venom she could muster.

Sweat dripped down Lily's naked body, now. "Victoria, we *are* friends. We *still* are. This is *nothing*—just a little mistake." Her eyes locked on the knife in Victoria's hand now, on the wicked gleam on its thin blade. "I-I realize you're *upset* but, please, let's not do anything drastic."

Victoria smiled at her. "No, no, Dear Lily… Let's *do* something 'drastic.' *Let's!*"

"Victoria, I swear… I'll scream." She took a deep breath.

With one swift move, Victoria drew the knife across the nude woman's throat.

Lily's scream came out as only a choked gurgle and bubbles of blood.

Victoria stuck the stiletto into her former friend's neck and twisted it, just for good measure.

Lily's blue eyes widened in horror and fear.

And then the light behind those eyes went out—for good—and her blood drained from the wound in her neck into Erzsebet Bathory's bathtub.

"Perfect," Erzsebet cooed. *"Now, get in. Get in!"*

Victoria quickly disrobed and climbed into the tub. The blood felt warm and wonderful on her bare skin.

The dead woman dangled above her, slowly spinning, the last of her lifeblood draining out into the tub below.

Victoria caught some of the remaining trickle in her hands and rubbed it over her face, and then her breasts.

She scooped up more from the tub and lathered the rest of her body with it. It felt good… *so good!*

I should have killed her ages ago, Victoria thought.

"Drink now," Erzsebet urged. *"Drink!"*

Victoria did, bringing a double handful of the gore to her lips and greedily slurping it. Then she tilted her head back and let the last of her late friend's blood drip down from the slaughtered corpse and spatter upon her face.

She opened her mouth, and the final drop fell directly onto her tongue.

She licked her lips.

"Mmmmm!"

Victoria's whole body was tingling now.

She rose, standing drenched in blood, feeling as though every part of her had been set ablaze—but it was a cold fire; it didn't hurt at all. In fact, it felt *wonderful!*

"Is this *it*?" she asked. "Is it happening?"

"Yesss, my aprentisssce. Now, we are becoming… one!"

Victoria looked at her nude, blood-stained body in the mirror. It was almost as though she were dressed in crimson silks. She moved slowly, touching herself all over, enjoying the electric thrill of her transformation.

She savored the taste of the blood in her mouth, and her delighted tongue felt her eye teeth grow long and sharp.

Why did I wait so long for this? Victoria thought, rejuvenated, slender figure trembling with pleasure. She felt younger, more vital, now than she had in ages. *All it took was a simple murder!*

Countess Erzsebet Bathory stood behind her in the glass, admiring, smile showing gleaming white fangs. She seemed to be embracing Victoria.

And then, as Victoria watched, her own gore-draped figure faded from view until she vanished entirely, and only Erzsebet remained in the dark mirror.

"W-what's happening?" Victoria asked. She looked down at her hands, suddenly smooth and white—youthful, with not a trace of blood on them—and at the daring red silks that now clad the rest of her body. She could see herself, and the diaphanous clothing, apparently woven out of her former friend's lifeblood… but not in the mirror.

In the mirror, not a trace of Victoria Duprix remained.

"Now you are one of usss," Erzsebet said proudly. *"Now, you are a* vampire!*"*

"A vampire…" Victoria echoed softly, her voice almost a purr. "Immortal!"

"Yesss! Now only God *isss your enemy! Only* He *hasss the power to dessstroy you!"*

"He's not my *only* enemy," Victoria replied. "There are a few more that I can think of—one or two, at least." She imagined plunging her new-grown fangs into the neck of her unfaithful husband, and the pleasure doing so would bring.

Too bad she hadn't been able to bite Lily as well. (But then, sacrifices had to be made.)

"So, you're telling me that nothing on this earth can hurt me?" She could imagine a thousand ways to kill Vincent—and

Paul and those simpering girls, too, now that she thought of it. Perhaps she would try them all!

"Not... pressscisssely," Erzsebet replied coyly. *"We can be ssslain by others of our own, or sssimilar kind... or harmed by the devisssces and cleveressst minionsss of the Mossst High—but sssuch beingsss remain few and far between."* The vampire Countess in the mirror smiled with satisfaction. *"Among ordinary men... You are invinssscible!"*

Victoria stretched out her arms to either side, feeling the power of the undead flow through her reborn body. Her crimson gown clung to her slender figure and fluttered around her arms like silken bat wings.

"Then it's time to settle accounts with my worthless husband."

36

WOLF TRAP

Paul Shaw (Longmire) – The Duprix Waxworks
First Night of the Full Moon

Paul awoke to a world of pain that seemed to emanate from the back of his skull.

Who hit me?

The answer to that question became apparent as soon as his eyes came back into focus:

Vincent?

Vincent Duprix stood nearby, garbed in some kind of weird robes, talking to someone that Paul couldn't see (or maybe talking to himself). What he was saying, didn't seem to make any sense. In fact, Paul wasn't even sure he was speaking English; he almost seemed to be... chanting.

"*Nebet... Nebet...*"

Where am I? Paul wondered.

It looked like the chamber... No... the *waxworks*... in one of the mummy display rooms. And were those two of the mummies nearby? Paul had to crane his head back to see them.

But they shouldn't be *here*; they should be downstairs in the Cushings' display. And, wait…

Am I on the altar?

Paul tried to get up, but he couldn't. He was lying, spread-eagled on his back, and his wrists and ankles seemed securely bound. He began to sweat.

"What the hell…?" he muttered.

Vincent, who had been looking at the mummies, turned to him. "Awake, now, are you, Mr. Shaw? Good. Good! I wouldn't want you to miss what comes next."

"What comes next? What are you talking about? Why am I tied up?"

"You're tied up because this seems a fitting punishment—to me, at least—for the man who's been sleeping with my wife."

A cold chill ran through Paul. "Look," he said, "I don't know what's been going on here, or what you *think* has been going on between me and Victoria—"

"'Think,' Mr. Shaw? Oh, no. We're far past *thinking* at this stage. I know what you've been up to. Did you think you'd get away with it? Well you *won't*—and neither will she."

Paul tried to look around the recreated crypt, but it was difficult to do, lying on his back. "What about Victoria? Is she here? Where is she?"

"No, Mr. Shaw. She's not here. To tell you the truth, I don't quite know *where* that shrewish little scamp is at the moment, but it hardly matters. I *might* have used her in this little ceremony, but you were far more handy." He grinned, a spark of madness flickered in his blue eyes, and he chuckled. "Do you like that, handyman? It's a little joke. Not very good, I'll admit, but very probably the last joke you'll ever hear."

"Now, wait a minute…" Paul said. Sweat was pouring off him now, and fear clenched his stomach—fear that the wolf could rear its bloodthirsty head at any moment, as well as fear at what Vincent might have planned. "What you're doing is dangerous," Paul insisted, "more dangerous than you can know. You have to let me out of here. I don't know how long I was out. The moon could be rising any time now—"

"Oh, yes, the moonrise. We're counting on that," Vincent said. "It'll be here in another few minutes."

Paul pulled at his bonds again, but they were stout leather; there was no chance he could break them. His heart drummed, loud and rapid, in his ears. "Then you *have* to let me go! I won't be responsible for the consequences, if you don't!"

"Let you go, Mr. Shaw? Oh, no. That's not part of the plan at all, is it?" With this last, Vincent seemed to be talking to someone else now—one of the mummies? "No. That's not part of the plan. What? Yes, I suppose we should be starting now."

"Starting?" Paul blurted. "Starting what?"

Vincent grinned insanely at him. "Starting the resurrection of Queen Bastiti, of course. The stars are right, the moon is right, and all it requires is a little blood… *Your* blood, Mr. Shaw."

With that, he withdrew a golden ceremonial dagger, set with red stones, from within his weird robes and slashed quickly across each of Paul's wrists.

"Aaaaaah!" Paul screamed. "What in hell do you think you're doing?!"

"Why, I'm *sacrificing* you, Mr. Shaw—sacrificing you so that my queen can live again. And now, if you'll excuse me, I must get back to chanting my incantations. It wouldn't do to have gone through all this trouble, only to fail now… *Nebet… Nebet…*"

"You're crazy!" Paul cried, but Vincent had turned back to the mummies and was no longer listening to him.

Paul glanced at his wrists, at his blood leaking down the altar. Fear tingled through every inch of him, and his heart pounded in his sweat-drenched chest. He could feel his life slowly slipping away, and he remembered a legend—God, he *hoped* it was a legend—the gypsies had told him:

"*A werewolf who is slain while a man becomes a werewolf forever!*"

If that were true, he'd come back and track down and kill everyone he ever loved in life. That was the Curse of the Werewolf!

God, please don't let it be true, he prayed. *Just let me die. Let me find peace, at last!*

Just a few yards from where Paul lay bleeding, Vincent seemed to have finished his chant.

He picked up a golden bowl from the base of the altar, where Paul's blood had been collecting, and held it high.

The bowl began to smoke.

"The time has come!" Vincent cried. "In the names of Seth and Nephthys, Rulers of Darkness, return to this mortal coil, my queen! Arise, Bastiti, Most Magnificent Ruler of all Egypt!"

There was a flash and a huge billow of white smoke, and Vincent dropped the bowl to the floor.

And then—impossibly—one of the two mummies standing in their sarcophagi beyond Vincent *moved*!

But it *wasn't* the sensual mummified form of the queen that took an awkward step from its resting place. Rather, it was the tall, wiry figure of the other mummy: the architect Sethotep.

"What?" Vincent gasped, staggering back, seemingly confused.

A deep voice, rumbling like the start of the landslide, emanated from the cracked lips of the reanimated mummy.

"I... *live!*"

"B-but it's not supposed to be *you*," Vincent stuttered. "It's supposed to be *her*—m-my queen!"

A smile creased the living mummy's ancient face. "Did you think I'd have you resurrect *her* and risk you not doing the same for *me*, mortal? Oh, no. I have not existed for millennia by being so foolish."

Vincent shuddered as the towering monster laid both crumbling hands upon his shoulders and gazed at him with its burning, green eyes.

"We *shall* resurrect my queen, you and I," the mummy of Sethotep said, "and we shall return her to her full glory. But first, we must mix the ingredients we need to make this ancient body of mine supple and whole once more. I may have the strength to topple this puny mansion from its foundations, but what good is strength if one does not have *vitality*?"

"Y-yes," Vincent stammered. "What good?"

"And, of course, we need more *blood*," Sethotep concluded.

"M-my blood?" Vincent asked nervously.

"No, fool! Nor that of your paltry victim. We need blood worthy of a queen!"

"Y-yes. Of course."

Paul's head swirled, and he felt ready to black out. He knew he must be imagining all this. Surely, none of it was possible: living mummies... raising people from the dead... Vincent as high-priest-cum-magician... It was a dying man's delusion, all in Paul's mind.

Already, his eyes were having trouble focusing; moment by moment, he could feel his life slipping away.

...Please let me die... in peace...!

Paul closed his eyes.

But then he felt it: his skin, tingling... cold fire running through him, from his toes to the top of his head.

The moon...!

The full moon was rising!

He couldn't escape the curse. Even death couldn't save him from it. It was too late!

"Paul...!" someone whispered from close to his head.

Paul's eyes sprang open. "Opal!" he whispered back.

She was crouching by his shoulder, hidden from the still-conversing Vincent and his mummy by the slab of the altar.

"I'm going to free you," she said.

"No!" he whispered urgently. "Leave me alone! Get out! Get out while you still can!"

And then he felt the hairs standing on the back of his neck… growing on his arms… his face… all over his body, as the terrible power of the moon surged through him, and everything that was Paul Shaw Longmire became subsumed into the beast.

37

THE VAMPIRE

Topaz Cushing – The Chamber of Horrors
Moonrise: First Night of the Full Moon

Topaz could *feel* that Paul was somewhere nearby, but the emotional chaos in the mansion was nearly deafening to her extra-sensory sensitivities—like a band blaring in her ear when she was trying to listen to someone across the room.

"*Paul?*" she wanted to call out, but she didn't dare. Within the mansion, the Duprixes also lurked, and Topaz had a *very* bad feeling about them. Even amid the psychic maelstrom, that much remained clear: something awful had happened to both husband and wife, something that made them *less* than human. Topaz couldn't tell whether they'd been overtaken by madness, or something even *worse*.

As she cautiously crept down the servants' stairs to the basement door, part of her wished she'd stopped on the second floor, checked there first. (It seemed so much safer.) But she had to trust that her sister would handle that job, just as she had to trust her twin on one startling fact that kept echoing through her mind:

Paul Shaw is a werewolf.

How could that be? Despite her history of psychic feelings, and accurate predictions with tarot cards, and prescient dreams, and all the rest, another part of Topaz had trouble believing in something so *purely* supernatural. This was the Twentieth Century, after all, an age where railroads spanned the continents, humans flew in airplanes, and radio travelled around the world instantly through thin air.

So, part of her suspected—even *expected*—that one day, each of the strange abilities that she and her twin shared would be explained by science. And the same would be true of all the eerie artifacts in their family exhibits.

A *werewolf*, though... A man who could change into an animal during nights of the full moon...? That was much stranger than the vision of a wolf—*Black Shuck*, or whatever it had been—that both sisters had experience last winter. Far stranger than her dream this afternoon. Omens and visions could all be in the mind, but a werewolf...!

Topaz wasn't sure whether she wanted to see such a thing, or *not* see such a thing. Certainly life, and the whole world, would seem a bit simpler if Paul was insane, rather than cursed.

We may find out, soon enough, Topaz thought as she neared the door at the bottom of the stairway, the back entrance to the Chamber of Horrors.

The door was supposed to be locked, with only the twins and the Duprixes having the key, but as Topaz approached, she saw that it stood slightly ajar.

Someone's down here.

Again, she almost called out *"Paul...?"*—but a prickling sensation at the back of her skull warned her not to. Instead, she cautiously pushed open the door, trying not to make any sound.

As she peered through the ever-widening gap, though, she almost gasped in terror.

Beyond the door, near the center of the exhibit space, lay a scene of utter horror:

A nude woman, dangling upside-down from a rope affixed to an overhead beam, twisted slowly above the bath of Elizabeth Bathory, the Bloody Countess. Gore covered the woman's chest and face; her throat had been slit, and her eyes gazed lifelessly into the darkness.

Topaz recognized the victim as Lily Carlson, a frequent visitor to the waxworks and, until this awful moment, a woman Topaz believed to be Victoria's best friend.

Yet, here Lily hung, slaughtered like an animal, and—as Topaz watched in shock and terror—Victoria, as naked as the day God made her, was *bathing* in her friend's blood!

It was all Topaz cold do to keep from screaming.

As she watched, transfixed with fright, Victoria rose from the tub, and the crimson fluid covering Madame Duprix's nude form transformed into a sheer, blood-red gown.

The wicked mistress of the house seemed to be admiring herself in a mirror near the tub—*Bathory's mirror*, which the twins had given her in lieu of rent, Topaz now realized.

Not only that, but Victoria seemed to be *talking* to someone, though the only other person Topaz could see in the room was the dead woman.

"So, you're telling me that nothing on this earth can hurt me?" Victoria said, stretching out her arms and admiring the fluttering red gossamer now covering her skin.

She paused, as if listening to an answer, though Topaz heard no reply.

Victoria smiled, showing gleaming white fangs. "Then it's time to settle accounts with my worthless husband!"

Get out of here! Topaz's mind cried. *Paul's not here. Get out!*

But the scene before her was so appalling that Topaz found

herself rooted to the spot, initially unable to even tear her eyes away from the gruesome sight.

Go! the more sensible part of her frantically urged.

Topaz backed away from the door, which now stood about half open.

As her heel bumped into the riser of the first step, though, Victoria spotted her; the two locked eyes.

Topaz's soul froze.

Run!

Victoria leapt out of the tub and hurtled toward the doorway.

Topaz turned and ran headlong up the stairs.

As she rounded the first turn in the stairway, Topaz heard Victoria say: "Come back, little rabbit!"

Ahead of Topaz lay the door to the waxworks, on the first floor. She grabbed the knob and twisted, but it was locked. She let go, and kept running up the stairs.

"No escape for you, little bunny," Victoria called, laughing, from somewhere behind her—but how close?

Don't look; just run! Topaz told herself.

She raced up another turn and threw open the door into the servants' hallway on the second floor and then slammed it shut behind her, cursing that the door had no lock.

She glanced into Paul's room—his door was open—as she raced past, but she saw no sign of him. Where could he have gone? Had Opal found him already? If only Topaz had time to think…

CRASH!

The door at the far side of the hallway burst from its hinges, revealing the red-draped form of Victoria Duprix. She stood atop the landing, both beautiful and terrible.

"Stop running, now, and I promise to kill you quickly," the madwoman said.

"Bugger off!" Topaz replied, reaching the far door, passing through, and quickly shutting it behind her.

Up or down? she wondered as she found herself on the second-floor landing. Perhaps Father had something to combat this creature in his room upstairs, but Opal (and Paul) more likely lay below, in the waxworks.

Topaz didn't stop long to think, but in those few instants, she heard the pad of bare feet, beyond the closed servants' door, approaching at a furious gate.

Down! Topaz decided, and practically flew down the long, twisting flight to the front entryway.

She slammed that door behind her, too, but as she did, she caught a glimpse of Victoria vaulting over the rail and plunging, heedless of any harm a drop from that height might cause her, toward the doorway.

Three closed doors faced Topaz. One led to the street, another down to the Chamber of Horrors, and the third to the Duprix Waxworks. Topaz knew behind which of the three her sister *must* be.

She slipped through the waxworks door and closed it just as Victoria shattered the door onto the landing.

"Come out, come out, wherever you are…" the thing that had once been Topaz's landlady called—because the younger twin had no doubt, after what she'd just seen, that the supernatural was *real*, and Victoria Duprix was no longer human.

As Topaz's mind reeled from that realization, the door she was leaning against smashed inward, sending her flying across the wax museum.

She landed with a bone-jarring *thud* near the entrance to the joint Duprix-Cushing mummy exhibit. Not daring to waste time getting to her feet, she scrambled inside.

"Come back, pretty bunny," Victoria called sweetly. "I only want a *little* taste."

Topaz crawled across the old oak floor as quickly as she

could. Ahead, she heard what sounded like people talking. The voices were coming from the tomb part of the display, right before the exhibit continued down the short flight of stairs into the Chamber of Horrors.

She stood up, keeping one of the largest of the Bastiti displays between her and Victoria.

"Opal! Paul!" Topaz cried. "Help!"

"Help! Help!" Victoria parroted mockingly.

Then, moving so quickly that Topaz barely even saw it, the madwoman was on the far side of the life-size diorama, reaching for Topaz.

"No!" Topaz screamed.

She heaved with all her might, and the display figures of Bastiti and King Sethmosis toppled onto Victoria.

With a startled squawk, Vincent's evil wife crashed to the floor, thrashing.

Topaz raced into the next room.

Then she stopped dead, the tableau before her even more mind-numbing than anything she'd experienced so far tonight.

The entire re-created mummy's tomb was lit by red-orange firelight from torches burning in sconces placed at intervals along the walls.

On the far side of the room, at the back of the crypt, rested an upright sarcophagus containing the mummy of Bastiti. In front of that, stood *another* mummy, at least, that's what Topaz *thought* the tall bandaged figure *must* be—but that mummy was *moving!* It stood, arms upraised, chanting as if praying or making an offering to the ancient gods.

"Mighty Seth," the mummy's gravelly voice said, "Ruler of Darkness, this humble servant thanks you for your beneficence. Oh, Nephthys, Mother of the Underworld, sister of Isis and keeper of the deepest secrets even your royal sibling does not know, thank you for granting the boon of rebirth to this unworthy one! Long will I serve you and your most faithful disciple, Bastiti…"

It's Sethotep! a voice inside Topaz declared. That was absurd, though; the Egyptian architect had been dead more than three thousand years. *He's come back to life!*

No! Impossible!

But was it? Was *anything* impossible on this reality-bending night?

Vincent, dressed in strange robes, stood near the tall mummy (whether actually Sethotep or some kind of weird, ceremonial masquerade). But the master of the waxworks seemed frightened, and was backing away from both mummies, toward the entryway where Topaz stood, gobsmacked.

Vincent sidled around the left-hand wall, avoiding not only the mummies, but the altar located in the middle of the room, which he seemed to be paying no attention to.

Opal sat crouched beside that altar, hidden from the sight of both Vincent and the mummies—though, from her vantage point near the entrance to the tomb, Topaz could see her sister clearly enough.

Worst of all, atop the altar lay Paul, tied down with leather straps and writhing horribly. His wrists had been cut, and his blood trailed down the sides of the slab.

Paul screamed in agony, and Topaz thought he must be dying from those terrible wounds and loss of blood.

But as she watched, still transfixed, Paul's body began to change: his chest expanded… his feet burst from his well-worn shoes… the nails on his hands and feet became longer and sharper… thick, coarse hair sprouted all over his body…

Opal watched all of this with as much shock and revulsion as Topaz, but then, as if by instinct, she turned and spotted her twin.

"Topaz!" Opal's voice came loud and clear in Topaz's mind.

"I'm here!" Topaz mentally replied. *"What do we do?!"*

Opal's eyes went wide with horror. "Topaz, look out!"

Topaz turned, but not quickly enough.

Before she realized what was happening, Victoria had grabbed her by the throat. The madwoman lifted Topaz off her feet as easily as a grown man picks up a kitten.

"Chase is over, little bunny!" Victoria sneered, baring her fangs.

"Let her go, you *bitch*!" Opal shouted, charging toward Topaz's attacker.

With a contemptuous laugh, Victoria tossed Topaz into her sister.

The twins crashed down, jumbled together, limbs flailing, and skidded across the floor. They came to rest against the wall near the exit from the fake tomb leading into the Chamber of Horrors.

The blow knocked the breath out of both girls, but Topaz and Opal struggled to untangle themselves as Victoria stalked closer, grinning a wicked grin.

"What *is* she?" Opal whispered, terrified.

"A vampire, I think," Topaz replied. "She was bathing in Bathory's tub. She murdered Lily Carlson."

"No," Victoria purred, stalking toward them. "I killed a traitorous slut who was sleeping with my hus—"

And then the monster who had been Victoria stopped.

Vincent! Topaz realized. *She's noticed Vincent!*

Victoria, now entirely focused on the sculptor, turned away from the scrambling, fearful girls. Silently, the vampire crept up behind her husband.

"Hello, my love," she whispered.

Vincent spun, taken completely by surprise. "Victoria!"

She grabbed him by the throat. "Yes… Victoria… Your loving wife."

"I… I…" Vincent stammered.

"At a loss for words, husband? Don't worry. Soon, you won't

have to speak at all. I've killed your lover, and now, it's *your* turn."

"Victoria, no! Stop!"

But she didn't stop.

Instead, she bared his throat and bit him.

38

ALL MONSTERS ATTACK!

Opal Cushing – The Tomb of Bastiti in the Waxworks
The First Night of the Full Moon

As Victoria's fangs sank into Vincent's neck, the sculptor's eyes rolled back in his head, and all life seemed to go out of him. She held him tight in her red-draped arms, clearly enjoying her power and her much-anticipated revenge.

Opal could hardly believe what she was seeing. In just minutes, the world had turned upside-down, and her life had become total insanity: Paul was a werewolf, Victoria had transformed into a vampire, and one of the mummies in their father's prized exhibit had come to life and was apparently looking to resurrect Queen Bastiti's mummy, as well.

A day ago—even an *hour* ago—Opal would have sworn *all* of this was impossible.

Keep it together, she told herself. *If you crack up now, none of us will get out of here alive.*

Maintaining her composure proved difficult, though, when the entire mansion had gone mad around her.

She and Topaz finished scrambling to their feet next to the faux-tomb wall, where Victoria had thrown them.

"Are you okay?" Topaz whispered urgently.

"Just a little bruised."

"What should we do?"

"We *can't* just leave Paul here," Opal replied. "We have to help him!"

"But…!" Topaz said, pointing.

As the twins watched in horror, the thing that had been Paul threw back his head and howled, his transformation complete. Fur covered his entire body, now, his hands and feet had become claws, and his face was a savage, snarling visage, half man and half wolf.

"H-he really *is* a werewolf!" Topaz gasped, seeming to have at least as much trouble believing it as Opal.

Opal nodded; her voice had deserted her, because, at this point, what could she say?

At least the wounds on Paul's wrists seem to have healed, Opal thought. That left the twins with an entirely different problem, though. Now her would-be boyfriend was a ravening beast, straining furiously at his bonds. Rescuing a man would have been difficult amid this madness, rescuing a *monster*…

"We *can't* let him loose," Topaz said, as if reading her thoughts. "He'd just kill us. He might kill *everyone* here!"

Everyone else here could use *killing,* Opal reflected darkly—but thoughts like that wouldn't help them, either.

"Leave my servant alone," rasped the mummy of Sethotep. During the confusion, he'd stopped his chanting, crossed to where Victoria was draining the life from Vincent, and seized her by the back of the neck.

She let go of her husband, and he slumped limply to the floor. Whether he was dead or merely unconscious, Opal couldn't tell.

Victoria hissed at the mummy like an enraged cat, spinning

in his grip and baring her blood-stained fangs. She slashed at Sethotep's chest with her fingernails, which now had grown into talons.

The claws raked across the mummy's chest and his wrist, sending up clouds of mildewed dust. He dropped her, but didn't seem much harmed. A smile cracked Sethotep's ancient lips.

"You cannot hurt me," he gloated. "The spell that resurrected me has made me impervious to all earthly harm. I am *immortal*."

"So am I!" Victoria hissed. Her face contorted with rage as she charged him, slamming her head and shoulders into his gut.

The force of the blow took the mummy off his feet, and he crashed hard into one of the fake tomb walls. The impact shook loose one of the torches lighting the exhibit.

The firebrand fell into the startled mummy's lap, and for a moment, Opal thought he'd go up like a tinderbox. He didn't though. Instead, he merely laughed, picked up the torch, and thrust it into Victoria's face as she came at him again.

The vampire screamed as the fire scorched her hair and burned her youthful countenance, sending up a cloud of misty smoke. She backed off, cursing and blinking cinders and ash from her eyes. But as she retreated, that greasy mist regathered around her. In just a few moments, her hair re-grew, and her skin mended itself until she looked inhumanly beautiful once more. Not even a scar or a trace of scorching remained.

The mummy laughed. "So…" Sethotep said, snuffing his torch by crushing its blazing head in his bandage-wrapped hand. "It seems that only the fires of the gods will harm *either* of us." Again, he smiled, almost seeming to relish the challenge of battling a foe as powerful as himself.

"There are *no* gods," Victoria said. "Only death!" She leapt at him again.

Snap!

Both Opal and Topaz jumped at the sound. The battle between mummy and vampire had held them mesmerized.

Snap! Snap! SNAP!

Just that quickly, the wolf-man who had been Paul Shaw Longmire broke the leather straps holding him to the sacrificial altar.

As Victoria and Sethotep battled behind him, the werewolf stood atop the altar and howled.

"We should go…" Topaz urged, pulling on her sister's sleeve.

"I…" Opal began, but she knew her twin was right. They couldn't help Paul now. Trying to do so before moonset would only get them killed.

Both sisters began backing around the wall of the faux tomb, toward the front exit, though Opal wasn't sure what they might do once they got there, aside from flee.

Maybe we can lock them all inside the mansion, she thought. But would that even *contain* these monsters?

Victoria and Sethotep were ripping at one another with their claw-like hands, tearing off strips of each other's undead flesh. But those chunks merely faded to mist or crumble to dust, only to re-form moments later, leaving the combatants as good as new. Whatever supernatural forces had created them apparently *had* made both monsters immortal, if not invulnerable.

The vampire charged again, snarling, slavering—a creature of claws, fangs, and fury.

But the mummy caught her and threw her across the room into one of the Bastiti displays. The collision with Victoria's body smashed the life-size diorama into shards of wax, metal wiring, and painted wood.

Opal gasped at the bone-shattering impact, but a moment later, Victoria rose again, apparently unharmed.

Hissing venomously, Victoria leapt at her foe once more.

"Oh, no," Opal muttered, a chill shooting through her; her initial gasp had drawn the attention of the werewolf.

Previously, the beast had merely been reveling in his

newfound freedom, but now he turned and gazed directly at Opal.

In the blazing-red eyes of the creature had been Paul Longmire, Opal saw no remainder of the man she loved, only feral bloodlust.

The werewolf stepped toward the twins, crouching to spring.

"Run!" Opal whispered, trying to keep Topaz behind her. She didn't want her sister to die because of her own foolish mistake.

"No!" Topaz replied. She snatched one of the burning torches from the wall and handed it to her sister. "Take this!"

Opal thrust the firebrand in front of her as the werewolf lunged.

The flaming head of the torch caught the monster full in the face. The beast growled as the hair and the flesh of its wolfish mien sizzled and burnt.

It quickly backed up, out of reach of the torch, hatred flaring in its blood-red eyes. But even as the wolf swayed warily, eyeing its enemies, its hair re-grew, and its damaged flesh knitted back together once more. It seemed that like the vampire and the mummy, the werewolf could not be permanently harmed by such an ordinary thing as fire.

Opal watched her foe, barely able to breathe, trying to remember what *did* harm a werewolf and also wondering if she would dare use such a weapon if she remembered.

She held the torch before her, hands trembling. At least it was *something*.

"Go, Topaz," she whispered, her throat dry and her voice hoarse. "Get out of here."

"Nope," her twin replied. "The fire may not hurt it, but it doesn't like the flames, either. We just need *more*." She looked around, but none of the other burning torches lay within easy reach.

The vampire and the mummy were heaving heavy display

pieces at each other now, as though the furniture weighed nothing. Sometimes, the intended target stepped aside, allowing the fixture to crash into splinters against another display or a wall, but other times the monster took the full brunt of the blow, only to laugh and rise unharmed once more.

Vampire… mummy… werewolf…! It was like something out of a nightmare.

Eyeing Opal's torch, the wolf-man crept closer.

"Here, light this!" Topaz said, thrusting something slender and golden toward Opal's torch.

As the tip of the object blazed bright white, Opal realized that her sister had retrieved the Torch of Sekhmet, the warrior goddess, from the entryway connecting the tomb exhibit with the Chamber of Horrors, below.

As this second torch flared, the werewolf stopped in its tracks.

Topaz had been right (though she'd always been better at sensing feelings than Opal); the werewolf *didn't* like fire, even if it could regenerate from any damaged caused.

"Get back!" Topaz commanded, stepping toward the beast. "Back!" The ancient torch shone brilliantly in her hands.

"Yeah," Opal reiterated, keeping side-by-side with her sister. "Back off! We don't want to hurt you, Paul, but…"

She couldn't tell if some part of the man inside the monster heard her, but the wolf turned and bounded away, putting the blood-stained altar between itself and the twins.

As the beast landed, though, a china doll cabinet—aimed at Sethotep—crashed full force into the wolf's hairy body. The mummy laughed wickedly at the mishap; the vampire merely snarled, angry at having missed her target.

The piece of furniture did no more harm to the werewolf than it would have to either of the other monsters. The beast rose from the wreckage, howling with rage, and leaped toward Victoria.

Surprised, the vampire backed up, and the wolf fell upon her, claws raking.

"Time to go," Opal whispered.

She and Topaz backed toward the main exit, keeping careful eyes on the creatures who had once been Paul Shaw Longmire and Victoria Duprix, as the two fiends rolled around on the debris-strewn floor of the faux tomb.

Suddenly, Topaz gasped, and her torch clattered to the floor.

Opal wheeled, and her blood ran cold.

The mummy of Sethotep stood behind Topaz, holding Opal's twin sister by the neck, lifting her off the floor.

A wicked smile cracked the undead architect's crumbling visage,

"I need more *blood*," the mummy said, "blood, to revive my queen!"

39

IN THE MUMMY'S HANDS

Topaz Cushing – The Tomb in the Waxworks
The First Night of the Full Moon

Topaz kicked and struggled in the mummy's grip, but it was no use. The hand holding her may have looked like withered leather and rotting linens, but it had a grip like iron. The pressure on her neck made her vision swim, and it was all she could do to keep from blacking out. The mummy held her aloft as though she were a rag doll.

"Let go of my sister!" Opal demanded, still clutching her burning torch.

The mummy laughed, a rasping sound like dry leaves rustling.

"You cannot harm me," Sethotep said. "Nothing in this fragile young world can." He glanced at the werewolf and vampire, still battling nearby. "These newer creatures may be able to tear each other limb from limb, but my power is eons older. The gods of my people reigned supreme when your gods had not even been imagined.

"Give up your useless struggles. I promise your deaths will

be quick. And your souls will live on in the reborn body of the glorious Bastiti, Queen of All Egypt! It is a fate that most mortals could only *dream* of."

"Dream of *this*!" Opal exclaimed. She lunged forward and thrust the blazing head of her torch into the mummy's left eye. A great *whoosh* of sparks and soot burst from the blackened eye socket.

Startled, the mummy dropped Topaz and then batted the torch away.

The force of the blow struck the firebrand from Opal's hand; it sailed across the room and landed against the wall of the recreated tomb. It lay against the hieroglyphic-inscribed plaster, smoldering.

"Whelp of a jackal!" the mummy rumbled, its damaged eye regenerating, and both orbs blazing bright green with fury. "For that, I shall make you *linger* before you die!"

Topaz groped aimlessly, trying to clear her head as the ancient monster advanced on her twin. Her hand found something warm and metallic.

Sekhmet's torch! she realized, picking it up and rising. Of course, the ancient torch was *still* burning; neither she nor Opal had been able to find any way, save for the golden snuffer attached to a chain on its bottom, to extinguish the artifact once it was lit.

Topaz wished she had a better weapon. But Opal's torch had blinded Sethotep for a moment; if Topaz could do the same, maybe she and her sister could *both* escape.

The mummy had backed Opal nearly into the altar now, while the werewolf and the vampire tussled on the far side of the room. Topaz had lost track of Vincent, but she thought he must still be over there somewhere, lying amid the rubble, too. A lot of the exhibits in this and the adjoining chambers now lay in ruins due to the battling monsters.

Fear knotted Topaz's stomach. If Sethotep forced her sister onto the altar, he might sacrifice her right then and there!

"Hey, you!" Topaz shouted at the mummy.

When the Sethotep turned, she thrust the Torch of Sekhmet toward the mummy's face.

But the undead architect must have anticipated her move, because as she stabbed, he batted the torch aside, and it was all Topaz could do to keep her grip on it.

"The two of you have spirit," the mummy said gleefully. "Good! That makes you all the more suitable to revive my… Eh?"

He gazed in surprise at the back of his left hand. Where he'd struck the torch, the bandages on his fingers were burning.

Annoyed, he tried to smother the small flame with his right palm, as he'd snuffed the blazing torch, earlier.

But the fire didn't go out. Instead, it spread from one hand to the other.

"*What?!*" the mummy said, puzzled.

Topaz seized the moment and thrust her torch into Sethotep's face.

The mummy tried to bat it aside, again, but too late. The blazing tip of the brand sunk into the creature's right eye socket. The eye popped, and the ancient flesh around it sizzled and charred.

Sethotep screamed with rage.

Topaz thrust the torch at him again, but half blinded, he managed to back away, and put the altar between himself and the blonde twin. Opal avoided the mummy's blind stumbling and quickly retreated to her sister's side.

The mummy's remaining eye glowed poisonous green with hatred, but the fires had spread from its hands up its arms now, and across its face.

"How?!" it raged.

Then its one blazing eye lit upon the makeshift weapon in Topaz's hand.

"The Torch of *Sekhmet*..." Sethotep muttered. "No...!"

Topaz remembered now that the torch had been discovered in the architect's tomb, along with his mummy. Apparently, though more modern powers—both natural and supernatural—could not harm this undead creature, the ancient magics from when he actually lived still held sway.

"Seth and Nephthys curse you!" Sethotep cried. "Do you know what you've *done*?!"

His whole head was burning now, and he was blundering around the devastated tomb, crashing into debris, smashing into the walls, and groping blindly with his powerful arms. Many of the places he touched caught fire.

"Let's get out of here!" Topaz urged. While the werewolf and the vampire lunged and leapt at each other near the exit leading to the Chamber of Horrors, she led Opal toward the waxwork's front door.

But before they could reach it, Opal cried: "Duck!"

She and Topaz hit the floor as the huge altarpiece from the exhibit sailed overhead—hurled at them by the enraged mummy.

The altar, made of wood and plaster (and burning, as well) smashed into one of the Egyptian-style support columns at the tomb entrance. Weakened by the ongoing monster battles, the pillars crumbled, bringing down a huge section of the ceiling with them. Some of that wreckage caught fire, too.

There was no way the twins could get out of that exit, now.

"I will slay you *instantly*!" the mummy bellowed. "Your infidel blood is not worthy to revive my queen!"

But the whole upper half of Sethotep was burning at this point, and the way he was blundering around, it became clear to Topaz that the mummy was now completely blind.

Opal must have noticed that shortcoming too, because she

didn't say anything, but pointed toward the only other obvious exit to the room—the short flight of stairs leading down into the Chamber of Horrors.

That escape, however, remained blocked by Victoria and the werewolf.

The two monsters clawed at each other, growling and hissing, both seemingly more beast than human. The werewolf's clothing had been torn to shreds, and the vampire's blood red gown hung in tatters. Each creature bled from numerous small claw wounds.

They can *hurt each other, even if* we *can't hurt them,* Topaz realized. Though, with Sekhmet's torch still clutched tight in her hand, perhaps the twins at least had *some* recourse if confronted.

As the mummy thrashed around near the destroyed main exit to the tomb, Topaz and Opal crept closer to the werewolf-vampire battle. The windows on the first floor of the museum, currently hidden by the plaster walls of the tomb, were barred against burglary. So even if they could have reached them, they couldn't escape that way.

"Girls…!" Victoria hissed, spotting the twins.

She prepared to leap at them, but before she could, the werewolf hurtled into her midsection, and both monsters crashed into the back wall of the tomb, near were the mummy of Bastiti still stood, patiently awaiting her resurrection.

"The girls?" the burning figure of Sethotep raged. "Where?!"

Opal stepped between the mummy and the other battling monsters. "Right here, you flaming arsehole!" she called.

With an incoherent roar, and speed much greater than Topaz would have anticipated, the mummy charged across the room.

Opal barely got out of the way in time, and the mummy blundered into the skirmishing werewolf and vampire.

This escalated the battle between the other two; they now began attacking the burning mummy as well as each other.

As quickly and quietly as they could, the twins stole across the room and down the steps into the relative peace and safety of Dr. Cushing's Chamber of Horrors.

Topaz spared only a brief glance back as they went, and saw all three monsters rampaging amid the building inferno.

She hoped that neither Sethotep nor Victoria would be able to deal Paul a fatal blow. But if they didn't… What next?

He really was *cursed!* she thought regretfully.

Even if they'd believed Paul, though, would she and her sister—or even their father—have been able to help him?

Topaz hoped that, somehow, they might still get that chance.

Then she lost sight of Paul and his undead foes amid the fire and smoke.

40

A BLAZE OF GLORY

Vincent Duprix – The Tomb in the Waxworks
The First Night of the Full Moon

Vincent's world was filled with *pain*—pain in nearly every part of his body, especially his neck and head—and *heat*, more heat than he'd ever felt before (aside from standing next to the bonfires at Guy Fawkes celebrations). In addition to that, everything seemed to be composed of dancing red and orange lights.

Where am I? he wondered blearily.

Then it all came rushing back to him...

He'd been about to bring Bastiti back to life, but Sethotep had betrayed them all, and arranged for his own resurrection instead.

That perfidy had shaken Vincent, left him unsure what to do next, and before he'd had a chance to recover his wits...

Victoria!

His bitch of a wife had appeared, seemingly out of nowhere, and *bitten* him—bitten him on the neck. The wounds on his throat still throbbed. He must have blacked out, then, but what in the name of heaven and earth did she think she was doing?

And where was this infernal *heat* coming from?

The realization hit Vincent like a thunderbolt.

It's burning! My waxworks *is burning!*

Vincent's blue eyes sprang open and, instantly, everything came into terrible focus.

Flames danced all around the mummy's tomb display, which now lay in shambles. The exit leading to the rest of the waxworks had collapsed, and the debris filling it was on fire, too. *Everything* seemed to be ablaze.

How did this happen?!

Then Vincent spotted the apparent cause of the disaster: the mummy of Sethotep, his bandages afire from head to foot, was stumbling blindly around the chamber, setting everything he touched alight.

The mummy was not the only source of the chaos, though...

Victoria, dressed in a tattered red gown, was leaping about the room fighting with something that, even with all the rest, Vincent couldn't quite believe he was seeing.

A werewolf...?!

How in the name of heaven could that be possible?

But then Vincent recognized the wolfman's tattered clothing, the same garments that had been worn by Paul Shaw, Vincent's would-be sacrifice. Somehow, like Victoria, the handyman had become a monster.

How...?

Vincent's head pounded as he tried to extricate himself from beneath the ruins of one of the room's displays. Certainly, being half buried under the rubble explained the source of many of his aches and pains, but as Vincent watched the terrible melee around him, he realized that the wreckage may have saved his life, as well.

As he pulled his bruised body out from under what had once been a cabinet displaying exquisite china dolls, he noticed the Cushing girls—rather sensibly—fleeing down the short flight of stairs into their Chamber of Horrors. Had the twins been involved with this calamity, too, somehow?

That hardly merited thinking about at this point. Of all that was going on around him right now, only two things mattered to Vincent…

My work! his mind wailed. *My art!*

Everything he'd done, all the carefully sculpted portraits of Bastiti and everything else, all the displays he'd built for the waxworks over the years, *all* of it was burning. Vincent's entire life was literally going up in smoke.

But part of him didn't care.

My queen! screamed that mad portion of his soul. *Bastiti, my love!*

As much as the destruction of his life's work pained him, the thought that the object of his desire might forever perish in the blaze was even worse.

Vincent coughed violently, his lungs filled with smoke, as he stood and tried to see his queen through the chaos and the conflagration.

Victoria and the werewolf had chased each other toward the blocked main exit, now, and were circling warily. Both were bleeding from numerous small cuts and slashes, and both kept looking at their wounds, as though surprised that they could be hurt at all.

Sethotep, still burning, had fallen to his knees nearby, where the recreated altarpiece had once stood. (Vincent had noticed the ruins of that altar lying next to the blocked exit.) And beyond the fiery mummy, at the back of the tomb…

Yes!

There Bastiti stood in her sarcophagus, still untouched by the ravening monsters and the chaos around her.

I'm coming, my love! Vincent thought.

All that stood between the sculptor and his queen were a few yards of rubble, a blazing mummy, and an unpredictable inferno. None of those things would stop him!

I must reach her before the fire does!

But before he could figure out a safe way to cross that hazardous distance, something hurtled toward him out of the fire and smoke.

Vincent ducked, falling to the floor once more, as a ball of fur and fury sailed past, barely missing the sculptor's head.

The werewolf, who'd apparently been thrown by Victoria, smashed hard into the tomb wall, crashing through the chicken wire and painted plaster. The crumbling set dressing revealed one of the barred first-story windows that Vincent had covered over to create a darker atmosphere for the tomb.

The wolf landed hard atop a pile of rubble, and howled in pain as a three-foot-long spike of wood stabbed into its back, near the shoulder blade. The barb pierced all the way through, coming out the wolf-man's righthand pectoral, near its shoulder. At the same time, a huge chunk of the ceiling fell on the monster's other arm, crushing that furry left limb completely.

The injuries almost assuredly would have killed a normal person, but the werewolf merely howled and writhed—like an insect stuck on a pin—trying to work its way free.

Before it could liberate itself, Victoria pounced.

She landed atop the struggling monster, straddling him, pushing him further down on the piercing wooden shard. Her claw-like hands found the wolf-man's hairy neck, and she began to squeeze.

The werewolf tried to slash at her, but its left arm was crushed, and the right couldn't move very far, because of the way the beast was impaled.

Victoria smiled in glee, showing her sharp fangs as the werewolf gasped for breath while she tried to crush its windpipe.

She's a... vampire...? Vincent though in confusion. *When did that happen?*

More importantly, what would the Victoria-vampire do once she finished off her former wolfish lover?

Vincent glanced from his wife and the werewolf to Bastiti, standing so near and yet separated from him by flame and rubble.

Once she's done with Shaw, she'll come for me! Vincent realized.

He couldn't allow that.

His wife leaned in close as she strangled her victim, her fangs nearly touching the werewolf's hairy neck. The beast gasped for air, and death rattled in its growling throat.

"Victoria!" Vincent shouted as he threw a fist-sized chunk of plaster at her.

The improvised missile flew wide of its target and shattered the glass of the barred window, just beyond the struggling combatants.

Victoria turned at the sound and spotted her husband. Her eyes burned red with hatred. "Vincent...!" she hissed. "You're nex—!"

The half-dead werewolf lunged forward and fastened its razor-sharp teeth around the vampire's neck.

Victoria shrieked in surprise.

The beast clamped down hard and then twisted and pulled. With a single jerk of its head, the werewolf ripped out Victoria's throat.

She screamed like a banshee and tore herself away, clutching futilely at her severed jugular as it sprayed black blood and misty ectoplasm into the hellish heat.

The vampire who had been Vincent's wife careened wildly around the devastated tomb, her eyes mad with hatred.

Vincent couldn't tell whether she was looking for him—for one last victim—or groping desperately to find help.

In just a few seconds, though, her wild gyrations slowed, and she crumpled—like a marionette with its strings cut—atop a pile of rubble near the blocked exit.

"But... I'm *immortal*...!" she gasped. Her head lolled to one side, revealing the extent of her terrible neck wound; the werewolf had nearly torn her head off.

How anyone could survive near decapitation for even an instant, Vincent couldn't imagine.

And still, Victoria wasn't quite done yet. Even as the last of her vampiric life blood seeped away, she muttered:

"I... *can't*... die...!"

Then the fire in her hazel eyes smoldered out, her claw-like hands twitched three times, and her unnaturally youthful body stiffened and moved no more.

Vincent smiled, enjoying his wife's gruesome demise.

"You never really did understand *irony*, my dear," he muttered, shaking his head scoldingly. "But you always were a blood sucker."

He chuckled at his own joke. Then his mind returned to the perils at hand.

"My queen!"

Burning rubble still separated them, but very little remained of Sethotep now, only a charred body, kneeling close to Bastiti's bandaged feet. The architect's mummy smoldered, the fires consuming it not yet burnt out, but it did not move.

The werewolf, on the other hand, was anything but dead. With its vampiric foe dispatched, it had resumed struggling to free itself. It had gotten its left arm—the crushed one—loose from the rubble, and already that limb looked almost as good as new.

How is that possible? Vincent wondered, stepping further away from the beast, and toward where his queen stood in her sarcophagus. The flames were licking ever closer to her now, but if the werewolf got free...

I'd stand even less chance than Victoria did.

"Vincennnnt...!" someone said, and the sculptor nearly jumped out of his scorched skin. "Vincent... help... me...!"

A shudder ran through Vincent as he realized it was the charred remains of Sethotep speaking.

The mummy looked small and fragile now, like a crude figure made of charcoal, with ashes for its skin. It smoldered slightly, and grey-white dust crumbled from its jaw as it spoke.

"Help ... me...!"

Vincent's gaze flashed between Sethotep's crumbling body and the werewolf, as, with one mighty heave, the beast tore loose from its impalement. Weirdly, while it was still slashed and cut in numerous places, the gaping hole in the monster's chest—like its crushed arm—seemed to be quickly mending.

"I think I have more pressing concerns right now," the sculptor told the remains of the undead architect.

Vincent locked eyes with the beast that had once been his wife's lover. In that moment, the sculptor couldn't remember whether one was supposed to stare down wolves or *shun* their gaze, to avoid being killed.

Too late to change tactics now, Vincent thought, wishing he had some type of weapon close at hand.

The werewolf glared at him... and then at the fire still building all around. It glanced at the barred window and made a choice.

In one bound, the wolf-man cleared the rubble and fastened its humanlike hands on the broken window's iron bars. Giving a mighty heave, it tore the bars from their moorings and cast the whole latticework aside, into the demolished tomb.

With a howl of victory, the beast sprang through the window and vanished into the night.

Vincent sighed with relief.

That's one less thing to worry about.

"Help... me...!" Sethotep's corpse repeated from near

Vincent's feet. "Help... me... and I... will reveal... my secretsss...!"

The sculptor circled around the blackened husk, moving closer to Bastiti. "Help you? Again?" Vincent scoffed. "The last time I helped you, you betrayed me!"

"I did it... for my... for *our* queen!"

"It's my queen I'm worried about, now," Vincent replied. He doffed his ceremonial robes and quickly wrapped the stained and torn silks around Bastiti's mummified form. Then he picked her up; she felt surprisingly light in his arms. "Don't worry, my darling," he told her. "I'll get you out of here."

The passage down to the Chamber of Horrors was blocked by flames now, too—nearly everywhere was—but Vincent had built a secret panel that led to the servants' stairway in the tomb wall. He'd used it earlier to drag Paul to the altar, and he could use it now to escape.

If only the fire hasn't reached it yet...

"*Take me... too!*" the psychic voice of Sethotep urged in the sculptor's head.

"Quiet, you!" Vincent barked, and he kicked the architect's charred corpse.

The body of Sethotep crumbled to dust, and his skull careened out of the ashes and rolled to rest against the tomb wall.

Vincent laughed. "Not so clever now, are you, old man?"

A low groaning echoed to the mad sculptor's ears. Vincent mistook the noise for Sethotep's plaintive reply.

"What's the matter? Bast got your tongue?"

The groaning grew louder.

With a shock, Vincent realized that the sound was *not* the mummy replying to him.

He looked up. Above him, the entire ceiling of the tomb burned like a Guy Fawkes day bonfire and groaned like a dying ox.

As the blazing wreckage gave way and crashed down on top of him, all Vincent could do was clutch the mummy of Bastiti to his breast and scream.

41

FIERY CHOICES

Opal Cushing – The Chamber of Horrors
Moments Earlier

Opal gazed back the way they'd come, into the burning tomb display in the waxworks, her heart breaking.

"What… What about Paul?" she asked. Her eyes were smarting, and not just from the smoke and heat; she could barely hold back the tears.

"We can't help him, now," Topaz replied, matter-of-factly.

"But the mummy… Victoria… They could *kill* him!"

In her mind's eye, she saw the vampire fastened onto Paul's neck while the mummy, still burning, held him down. Paul struggled against both monsters in vain as his life ebbed away.

"They want to kill *us*, too," Topaz reminded her. "There's nothing we can do for Paul. Going back would be suicide."

"But…"

"Opal, he's a *werewolf*. Lycanthropes are notoriously hard to kill."

The way her sister said it was almost as though she didn't

care about Paul at all. "Maybe hard to kill for *normal* people," Opal replied, "but we're talking about monsters—*real* monsters—not the kind of flummery and hocus pocus in our museum, and… *OhmyGod!* The museum!"

"I know," Topaz said calmly. "The fire is spreading. We can't stop it. I'm sorry about Paul, but our father's whole life's work is about to go up in flames. We have to choose."

For a moment, Opal stood torn. They'd come *so close* to helping Paul. If only they'd discovered his true problem earlier. If only he'd confided his secret to her or Topaz, maybe…

"We have to save the museum," Opal concluded. Her sister was right; even if they wanted to, even if the whole house wasn't burning down around them, there was nothing they could to do for Paul right now.

Topaz nodded, looking resolute despite the fear in her blue-green eyes; Opal felt that fear, too, and that same determination as well.

"Grab Father's books first," Topaz said. "We'll take them out the back bulkhead." She rushed to the small library and loaded up her arms.

Opal did the same, and the two hurried to the back of the museum, glad that the chamber had a loading area to escape through, grateful that exit wasn't blocked, and that the fire hadn't reached it.

Topaz unlocked the bulkhead, and the two of them dropped the books at what they deemed a safe distance away from the rear of the house, on the sidewalk by the edge of Olde Kennington Park. They'd managed to get the whole library out in one run. (Fortunately, that collection hadn't been very big.) Topaz snuffed the Torch of Sekhmet and left it beside the books.

"I hope nobody wanders by and steals any of this," she mused.

As they ran back inside, Opal wished they hadn't removed

the oak doors separating the chamber from the waxworks for the mummy exhibit. If they could have closed those doors, perhaps they could have slowed down the fire. As it was, flames had begun to flicker through the main display room of the chamber, and the whole place was rapidly filling up with smoke. Already, the heat felt almost unbearable.

"Should we save fewer bigger items, or more small ones?" Topaz asked. Her eyes darted meaningfully toward the ice man. The fire must have done something to the refrigeration system, because already a long puddle of water stretched out from under the freezer door.

"There's no way we can move that block of ice," Opal said. "I'm sorry." She tore a strip from her dress and wrapped it around her nose and mouth, to protect against the smoke.

Topaz nodded and imitated her sister's makeshift scarf. "I'm sorry, too. Let's rescue as many small items as we can, then we'll try for the bigger stuff."

The reddish pelt of the Beast of Gevaudan, hanging in its rustic frame on the wall, caught Opal's eye. "What about *that?*" Just looking at it brought thoughts of Paul, and the battle he was fighting upstairs.

"That old thing's a fake anyway," Topaz said, a note of bitterness in her voice. "Let it burn."

Working quickly, the twins gathered as many of the attractions as they could: the skull of the Marquis de Sade; the Tunguska fragment; the scales of the *isda-asawa*; the fossilized footprint of the *Mokele-mbembe*; Jack the Ripper's knife, and several other small exhibits.

Rescuing that much took them two trips, and both girls were hacking and coughing when they returned outside the second time. Unfortunately, by then, several of their prizes had already been consumed by the flames, including the Siamese Mermaid and the noose that hanged Burke, the body snatcher.

As they stood at the edge of the park, trying to catch their breath, a sudden *CRASH* sounded from the righthand side of the building, and a dark, vaguely human shape raced out of the 1951 Fisher and into the gloom beneath the trees of Olde Kennington Park.

"Paul!" Opal gasped, hoping she could believe what she was seeing. She began to wave, and took a deep breath to call to him.

"Don't!" Topaz warned, clamping a hand over Opal's mouth. "Let him go…"

Topaz might have said more, but just at that moment, she was overcome with a fit of coughing.

Opal gazed at her sister, not understanding at first. Then she realized that Topaz was right. The last thing they needed just now was a werewolf in their midst.

Slowly, she nodded, and Topaz removed her hand. "I'm sorry…" her sister finally gasped. "But…"

"I understand," Opal said, her tone making it clear no further explanation would be necessary.

"Okay. Let's try for a bigger artifact," Topaz suggested between coughs.

"Do you think we have time?" Opal asked, eyeing the smoke pouring out of the bulkhead door. Unfortunately, 1951 Fisher was isolated at the edge of the park. And while that made it easier for a werewolf to slip away from the calamity, having nearer neighbors might have ensured that *someone* would have called the fire brigade by now.

Opal heard no fire bells, or sirens, or other sounds of impending rescue.

Topaz nodded wearily. "We can save one. Maybe two," she said. And she dashed back inside.

"What should we try for?" Opal called as she followed.

"Baron Latos' iron maiden, maybe," Topaz replied. "Though I thought I saw Bathory's Mirror near the old exhibit, as well."

Opal frowned. "What's *that* doing downstairs?"

"I think Victoria may have brought it down to use in some ritual," Topaz said, and then blurted: "*Whoops!*"

She skidded on the puddle from the freezer, which had now spread all the way across the floor in front of the bulkhead landing.

Opal caught her twin before she could tumble onto her rump.

"Thanks," Topaz said.

"Don't mention it. Are you telling me Victoria used the Bathory artifacts to become a vampire?"

"I don't know. Maybe. I guess so." Topaz was practically yelling, now, so that Opal could hear her above the roar of the fire.

"Let's save the mirror, if we can," Opal shouted back. "Nobody knows who Baron Latos is, anyway."

"Okay. Besides, I doubt Victoria will be using mirrors in her present state," Topaz noted.

If the situation hadn't been so grave, Opal would have laughed.

The Bathory exhibit lay closer to the wax museum than the iron maiden, but the path to it seemed clear, so the twins hurried to rescue it. The bath and mirror of the Bloody Countess stood in their usual places, though there seemed to be some kind of reddish stains on the rim of the tub. Strangely, a burning strand of rope dangled over the display.

"*OhmyGod!*" Topaz said, backing away from the bath. "Don't look in the tub!"

"Why not? What's wrong?" Opal asked.

"With everything else... I... I'd forgotten about Lily. Her body is in the tub."

Opal swallowed hard and kept away from it. As she approached the standing mirror, though, a wicked laugh, audible even above the crackle of the blaze, permeated the chamber.

Despite the heat, Opal's blood ran cold.

She seized Topaz by the arm. "Screw the mirror," she said, and dragged her sister back toward the iron maiden.

"What? Why?" Topaz asked. Pieces of the ceiling were falling around them now, and they were both coughing between breaths.

"I *saw* someone in the mirror," Opal explained. "Some woman. She was *laughing*."

"I-I thought I imagined hearing that," Topaz confessed.

"I think it must have been *her*—the countess. Bathory."

Topaz shuddered. "Yeah," she agreed. "Screw the mirror." She put her arms around the iron maiden. "Ow! Watch it! It's hot."

Opal wrapped her arms around the big, human-shaped sarcophagus as well. "Are you sure we should do this?" she asked, coughing. "Maybe we should just… leave."

Topaz kept coughing as she gazed into her twin's eyes. "Maybe you're right," Topaz agreed.

CRASH!

A huge, flaming beam fell between the sisters and the bulkhead stairs. One end of it struck the floor first, and the other careened into the ice-man exhibit, shattering the viewing glass and the ice remaining behind it into a million pieces.

A deluge poured out of the broken display, but the surge of water didn't put out the fire on the timber, which now blocked the twin's best escape route.

Dammit! I hate *being right,* Opal thought frantically.

"We're trapped!" Topaz cried.

"Look out," Opal shouted, and pushed her sister out of the way, just as another burning beam fell.

Opal tried to dodge the falling timber, too, but it smashed into her forehead, and all the world went black.

42

DOOMED

Topaz Cushing – The Chamber of Horrors
The First Night of the Full Moon

"Opal!" Topaz screamed as her sister fell to the floor. The burning beam crashed down next to her, and it was only by the Grace of God that Opal wasn't crushed.

Topaz knelt and pulled her sister away from the blazing timber. A four-inch gash creased Opal's forehead. The wound had soot around the edges, but it didn't look too deep, and Opal appeared to be breathing—though the smoke in the air couldn't have been doing her any good.

"I'm sorry," Topaz gasped between the tears. "We shouldn't have come back in. I'm sorry!"

But she knew her sister couldn't hear her.

CRASH!

Another beam came down, taking with it the framed "Pelt of the Beast of Gevaudan." The display's wooden frame was burning, and the class enclosing the pelt had smashed to slivers, but —ironically—the fake fur piece itself appeared unharmed.

Some lies are hard to get rid of, Topaz thought ruefully as another coughing fit seized her.

She seized her sister under the arms and, despite the coughing, managed to haul Opal to her feet.

She tried to head for the back exit, but fire seemed to be everywhere now. Topaz knew the Chamber of Horrors as well as she knew her sister's face, but with all the smoke and flames and confusion, she wasn't even sure where the exit lay anymore.

Peering through the scorching gloom, she spotted the corner of the Ice Man exhibit.

The bulkhead's that way...

Half dragging, half carrying Opal, she staggered around the burning beams toward it.

WHOOM!

A burst of fire rushed past, sucking all the oxygen out of the air.

Topaz gasped... staggered... and fell, taking Opal down with her.

"I'm sorry..." Topaz muttered, weeping. "I'm sorry!"

She attempted to stand, but her legs felt like rubber.

She tried to take a deep breath, to gain some strength, but despite her makeshift scarf, only heat and ash filled her lungs.

Flames crackled all around her, and the world spun out of focus.

Topaz closed her eyes.

I'm sorry!

Blackness swirled in.

Then...

Suddenly, she was flying...

No, *not* flying...

Someone had picked her up.

She felt strong arms supporting her, and soft, warm fur over her face. She could even breathe a little.

I'm not *dead.*

"My sister…" she managed to gasp. "Save…!" but then coughing took her breath away.

"She's safe," a deep voice rumbled. "I've got her. I've got you both."

Topaz had the sensation of motion, as if the person carrying her and her sister were running—though she couldn't imagine how that was possible.

CRASH!

Something smashed down around them, and a rush of clean, cool air hit her fur-shrouded face.

She pulled the fur away from her mouth and nose and gulped down great lung-filling breaths.

The person carrying Topaz laid her down on the grass by the edge of Olde Kennington Park, next to her father's possessions. To her great relief, she saw Opal lying beside her as well; her sister coughed and moaned softly. But what was this furry blanket covering them…?

Topaz felt the coarse, red-black fur between her fingers.

The Pelt of the Beast…?

The fur wasn't scorched; it wasn't even warm.

"Are you all right?" the deep voice asked.

Topaz peered up at the huge figure looming over her. The burning building behind the huge man cast his face into shadow, but his greenish eyes seemed to glow in the darkness.

Was it a fireman, or…?

Topaz reached up and touched his face. The man felt cold… *very* cold.

A chill ran through her, and not from that touch.

"It's *you*, isn't it?" she asked.

"Yes," he said. "It's me."

"But…" she began, "but how…?"

The man shook his shaggy head. "I can't explain. Not now. But I'm glad you're all right. I'm sure your sister will recover, too."

He stood and gazed at the burning mansion. In the distance, fire alarms sounded.

Topaz tried to stand, as well, but her legs still felt like rubber.

"I have to go," the man said, still gazing at the blazing ruins.

She managed to grab hold of his hand, a giant hand almost twice as large as her own.

"Wait," she said.

He gazed down at her, and now his eyes looked golden in the firelight.

"Before you go… at least tell me your name."

"Ash," he said softly. "All I've ever been is Ash. But for you, it can be… Ash Milton."

Then he slipped his hands out of hers, and in three big strides, the Ice Man vanished into the darkness of Olde Kennington Park.

43

FINAL HORRORS

Dr. Leigh Cushing – Olde Kennington Park
The First Night of the Full Moon

Dr. Lee Cushing was practically bursting with pride as he drove his canvas-back truck beneath the shadowed boughs of Olde Kennington Park, heading for home.

This expedition had turned out brilliantly. The fabled Organ of Bones rested safely in the back of his ramshackle lorry (the best he could afford, under the circumstances), and the whole venture hadn't even taken a month—scarcely more than two weeks, in fact.

"Possibly the best I've ever done," he said, chuckling happily to himself. "Just wait until the girls see!"

He would rouse them if they were sleeping, and then the whole family would haul *el Organo de los Huesos* down into the Chamber of Horrors. It wouldn't do to leave such a valuable artifact sitting in the truck overnight. Yes, the neighborhood of 1951 Fisher was very safe (with remarkably little hooliganism), but one never knew, these days.

In his mind, Cushing could already imagine the artifact's resting place, right between the Bathory exhibit and the Bastiti mummies.

Thought of the ancient queen and her small court made Cushing wonder how the twins and Duprixes were doing with their joint exhibit. He probably should have written to them and asked, but since he was chasing down leads about the organ all over Spain and Portugal... Well, where would his daughters have written back to?

Too late for regrets about that, anyway. There would be plenty of time to catch up on things now that he was home.

Until the next expedition, of course.

Dr. Cushing stroked his chin, fuzzy with three days' stubble. Now what should his next quest be...?

"Hmm..."

The trees ahead of the lorry parted, and Dr. Cushing glimpsed something strange ahead, something he'd never seen before in the neighborhood of 1951 Fisher. Was it one of those new, moving neon signs?

If so, it was an uncommonly large one. And he didn't remember any establishments in the vicinity that might benefit from such a gaudy display.

Whatever it was, it was yellow and orange, very bright, and flickering like fire...

Fire!

"God in Heaven!" Cushing blurted.

The Duprix mansion was *burning* from basement to rafters. Huge gouts of flame licked from the top of the now-skeletal roof into the early morning sky.

Cushing's heart pounded, and he broke out in a cold sweat.

The girls! My girls!

He stomped on the accelerator. The old lorry coughed and picked up speed. Cushing fought hard to keep it on the narrow, twisting road through the park. Several times, the awkward truck nearly overbalanced, but Cushing hardly even noticed.

His blue-grey eyes remained focused on the roaring conflagration ahead. He could see now that numerous fire brigade trucks were arrayed around the blazing edifice, but the spray from their hoses seemed insignificant next to the howling power of the inferno.

Please, Dear God, he prayed. *Please...!*

He'd nearly reached the edge of the park, now, and he could see figures running back and forth in front of the burning building, silhouetted against the fire. Most of them appeared to be firemen.

Please, God... Please!

Now he spotted another group of firemen standing at the edge of the park, huddled around something on the ground, perhaps bodies, or…

"Oh, thank Heaven!"

Cushing screeched the lorry to a halt, leapt out, and dashed across the short distance to the circle of people.

"Girls!" he shouted. "Girls! Are you all right?!"

From the middle of the huddle, two slender figures, one blonde the other brunette, rose. They were wrapped in furs, despite the heat of the blaze, and soot had blackened their faces. Their blue-green eyes, however, remained bright and alert.

"Father!" they both cried when they saw him.

And then they doffed the fur and ran into Dr. Cushing's arms.

The three Cushings embraced and kissed each other, tears running down all their happy faces.

"I'm so glad you're safe," Dr. Cushing said. "When I saw the fire, I feared the worst."

"Father," Topaz said, pressing her blonde head to his chest, "we tried to save everything we could, but…"

"Never mind about that now," he replied. "Never mind."

"You wouldn't believe the things that have happened tonight…" Opal said, hugging him so tight that Cushing feared she might break his ribs. "…What we've been through since you've been gone…!"

"Plenty of time to discuss that later," he assured her with gentle pats on her back. "Tell me about the others, though—the Duprixes and that man, Paul… Did they make it out as well?"

The twins exchanged a glance that Cushing couldn't quite read, as if sharing some secret information. Cushing was used to that with his daughters, though, and knew they'd tell him everything they needed to—in due time.

"We're pretty sure Paul is okay," Opal finally said.

"He… he wasn't working when the fire broke out," Topaz elaborated. "We're not even sure he was in the house."

"No," Opal confirmed. "No, we're pretty sure he wasn't."

"And Vincent and Victoria…"

Both girls shook their heads.

"They're dead," Topaz said.

"Pretty sure," Opal added. "Pretty sure they are." And the twins exchanged another mysterious glance.

Dr. Cushing took a deep breath and smeared the tears from his cheeks with the back of his sleeve. "What a pity," he said. "Of course, I never cared for *her* much, but *he* was an artist of great talent. Ahead of his time in some ways, I think."

Another twin glance.

"And behind it, in others," Opal commented.

"We're pretty sure he was working in the waxworks, on the mummy exhibit, when the fire broke out," Topaz said.

"We think his wife was home, too," Opal added. "Maybe they were… working together."

Dr. Cushing shook his head. "Such a great loss of artwork… And the artist, too, of course. What a pity!"

As the three of them spoke together, a fireman with a white

helmet (clearly some kind of officer) broke away from the crews working the blaze and approached them.

He came directly to Dr. Cushing, but did not extend his hand, as it was covered with soot and grime.

"You live here, sir? With the girls?" the fireman asked.

"Yes. When I'm not traveling," Cushing replied. "In the apartments on the third floor. I've just returned from a trip abroad."

The fireman nodded. "Lucky you weren't home at the time. Mighty lucky that your girls got out."

"Yes, very lucky indeed." Cushing hugged the twins close. "I gather that the Duprixes were not so fortunate."

"We don't hold out much hope for them, sir," the fireman said gravely. "If they were inside of *that*... Well, something that hot, we'll be lucky if we even find any bones. I'm afraid the rest will be a complete loss."

"No, not a *complete* loss," Cushing, glancing at his daughters, said. "Nothing near. Nothing near that, at all."

"I take your meaning, sir. Like I said, lucky your girls got out. Even luckier that they saved some of the objects from your... exhibits."

"Yes, I take that as a stroke of immense good fortune," Cushing replied. "Though far more providential, though, that my children have escaped such a catastrophe unscathed."

"Indeed, sir. Well, I better get back to it. Someone will drop by soon, make sure you have someplace to stay while we search the wreckage for anything that might be salvaged—after the whole thing cools down a bit, of course."

"Indeed. And how long do you think that might take?" Cushing didn't dare hope that any of their other possessions might have survived. Still, one could never tell…

The iron maiden, perhaps, unless the fire got hot enough to melt it.

"End of the day at earliest," the fireman said. "Maybe longer. Depends on how much in there is left to burn against how much water we can put on it." He tipped his hat. "Well, like I said: Back to it." With a bob of his head and a smile, he returned to fighting the fire with the rest of his crew.

Cushing took the twins on either arm, and they all walked back to where he'd first spotted the girls, an area which he could now see held numerous items from his collection.

The fact that anything at all had survived warmed his heart.

"We saved *all* your books," Topaz said proudly.

"We knew they'd be hard to replace," Opal added.

"Not as hard to replace as you, my dears," Cushing said, giving the pair another hug. Then his eyes lit upon something peculiar amid the collection. "I see you even saved my old 'rug.'" He indicated the reddish-black pelt slumped on the ground nearby.

Again, the twins exchanged their "secret" glance.

"Actually, it saved *us*," Topaz said, "you might say."

"It sheltered us as we… escaped," Opal told him. "We don't know why, but it didn't catch fire. Not even a bit."

Dr. Cushing smiled. "I'm not surprised at all. I'm sure I mentioned that the pelt of a Transylvanian dire wolf could not be harmed by blades, arrows, or possibly even fire. Now we have actual *proof* of that legend. Remember, I told you it wasn't the *real* Beast of Gevaudan, but I never said it wasn't *extraordinary*."

Both girls hugged him again.

"Lucky that old fake was good for *something*," Opal noted.

"I guess we should have listened to your explanation more carefully," concluded Topaz.

"Speaking of listening…" Dr. Cushing said, sitting down on the warm grass next to their artifacts. "I imagine you have quite a story to tell me."

Once more, that mysterious twin glance.

"You can say *that* again, Father," Opal replied.

Topaz took a deep breath. "And parts of it… even *you* might not believe…"

44

MORNING

Paul Shaw Longmire – Olde Kennington Park
Thursday: The Following Morning

Paul awoke lying face down on a patch of dew-covered lawn. A silvery pre-dawn glow surrounded him, and the air and grass felt cool on his bare skin—which, now that he thought of it, seemed to be *most* of him.

Where am I? he wondered.

Memories of the night before remained dim and confused in his brain. He seemed to remember someone leering down at him... someone else screaming... fighting... And was there a fire...?

I was the wolf!

As always, the realization that it was the morning after a full moon provoked a queasy sensation in his stomach.

He sat up, wiped his hand across his mouth, and looked at his fingers.

Blood!

Again, the blood! Again, the gut-wrenching knowledge that he might have—*probably had*—killed someone last night.

But who? Why was it always so hard to remember?

The curse! The God-damned curse!

Only tatters remained of his shirt and almost as little of his pants, and of course he was barefoot. He always awoke barefoot the morning after a transformation; if the beast didn't like clothes, it liked shoes even less.

Blood stained what was left of his shirt, too. So, he yanked it off and used the rags to wipe the blood from his face and body.

Curiously, when he had finished, he discovered that some of the blood may have belonged to *him*. His wrists had healed where Vincent had cut them (obviously, a "gift" from the curse), but numerous scratches, like claw marks, covered Paul's torso, arms, and legs. None seemed too severe, but several proved quite painful. He winced as he mopped them up.

That's never happened before...

Did that mean the beast had actually been *hurt* during the fighting he vaguely remembered? What could hurt a werewolf? Had he faced a foe with silver weapons, or...

Victoria!

He remembered more of it now. His would-be lover had turned into some kind of monster... And had there been a mummy? And...

No. That's absurd!

But was it any more absurd than turning into a wolf when the moon was full?

Paul shook his head, trying to clear away the last of the early morning cobwebs.

A fine mist permeated the air, smelling vaguely of smoke.

Smoke... The fire!

Images of the blaze came rushing back to him, along with earlier memories: being tied to an altar, and someone trying to help him... two people, actually:

Opal and Topaz!

But what had happened to them? Had the beast hurt them? Had they been trapped in the fire? He needed to know.

Almost before he'd even decided to do so, he rose to his feet and began running, following the smell of smoke.

As always during the cycle of the full moon, his human senses remained sharper than normal (though nowhere near as keen as those of the wolf). Trailing the scent of smoke through Olde Kennington Park—for that's where he now realized he'd awoken—was as easy as following the lines painted down the middle of a street.

He dashed through the woods and across the manicured lawns of the park, knowing that anyone who saw his shirtless visage would think him mad—but he didn't care.

Opal... I'm sorry...!

As he ran, his mind played gruesome scenarios of the twins' demise: Opal with her throat torn out, trying to talk through bubbles of blood; Topaz disemboweled, pleading for her life; the monster inside him feasting on the girls' steaming corpses while the Duprix mansion burned down around them.

Please, God, if ever I was a good man... if ever you existed... Please spare them. Do what you want with me, but let the girls be all right!

The burnt-out husk of the mansion rose before him now, great white clouds of steam and smoke filling the morning sky. Fire trucks, perhaps a half-dozen of them, were parked around the building, their crews still spraying the crumbling hulk with water.

It looked like a scene from which no one—no one save a *werewolf*—could have escaped alive.

Oh, God... Oh, God... Please...!

And then he spotted them—three figures huddled under blankets at the edge of the park, surrounded by piles of books and strange artifacts: Dr. Cushing and his daughters... *both* of them.

They're alive! Oh, thank God, they're alive!

Paul slowed and took cover behind a large oak tree, where he could watch what was going on but not be easily seen by the fireman working the scene. His wolf-keen ears allowed him to hear the conversations as well.

Both girls seemed to be weeping softly.

"There, there, now," Dr. Cushing said, sitting between the twins and patting both of them on their shoulders. "Everything will be all right. It's not the end of the world, you know."

"But Father," Topaz said, "all the exhibits... All the work we put in..."

"Never mind that, now," Dr. Cushing replied. "Exhibits can be rebuilt, you know. And the items that were lost... Well, we can do just as well without them."

"Can we do without clothing, food, and shelter?" Opal asked bitterly. "Because all of that just went up in smoke, too. We only had a little bit of money in the flat, but we didn't save even a shilling of it. We were too busy trying to rescue the artifacts."

Cushing hugged her. "And you made the right choice. Money comes, and money goes, but some of these pieces—like you two, as well—are irreplaceable. Besides, I've got a few pounds laid aside for future expeditions and such. We can use that to get what we need."

"But, where will we *stay*?" Topaz asked miserably.

"I had an idea about that," her father replied. "Perhaps we could take our exhibit on the road, travel to where the customers are, as it were. We could fix up this old truck of mine and trek through the countryside—across to Europe, even. I've heard that traveling shows can be quite profitable."

The twins looked skeptical, though Paul could see the light of hope beginning to return to their lovely blue-green eyes.

"What about Paul, though," Opal said. "He can't have gone far. We need to find him. We have to *help* him."

Maybe she had a premonition or something, because as she

spoke, she began to look around, as if sensing that Paul lurked nearby.

He pressed himself behind the tree, so neither she nor anyone else could spot him.

I can't stay here, he realized. The moon would still be full for two more nights, and when it rose, he would be a danger to everyone he knew and loved, especially Opal and her family.

"If what you've told me is true," Dr. Cushing said, "that young man does indeed need help. But I'm afraid that it is beyond our power to do so."

"We could research his curse," Topaz suggested, "find out how to cure it…"

"Indeed, we could, and we shall," her father replied. "However, right now, there's nothing we can do—especially if Mr. Shaw, or Longmire, or whatever he calls himself, chooses to remain hidden from us."

That's what I have to do, Paul thought. *Remain hidden... Hide until I can find the cure.*

Just then, as if to punctuate his decision, a police car pulled up to the Cushings, and several grim-looking detectives climbed out.

Cautiously, not making even a sound, Paul crept away from the scene of the fire.

Maybe someday I'll be able to go back, he told himself. *Maybe someday I'll be able to see them—to see Opal—again.*

Tonight, though, the moon would be full once more.

And first, Paul thought desperately, *I must find a cure...!*

45

AFTERMATH

Inspector Harry Dennis, 1951 Fisher St.
Thursday: Second Day of the Full Moon

Inspector Harry Dennis rubbed his head and sighed; he noticed that Sergeant Hoey was doing the same.

"This is a right big mess, isn't it, Inspector," Hoey opined.

"Yes," Dennis agreed. "We'll have a devil of a time finding any more bodies in that wreck." They'd uncovered two corpses to this point, both women, the coroner (who'd been none too pleased to be woken this early) had ventured, though it was difficult to be certain from such charred remains without further examination.

"Fireman First Class Sangster told me that anyone buried deeper in the ruins might have been entirely cremated by the heat," Hoey offered.

"So he informed me, as well," Dennis said. The presence of bodies was what had brought the detectives to the scene—that and the fact that the coroner said one of the bodies had her throat cut and the other was nearly decapitated. Gruesome business all around.

"Maybe the killer got caught in the fire," Hoey suggested, mirroring Dennis' thoughts. "Maybe this makes an end of it."

"Perhaps," Dennis replied. "We can hope so, anyway."

But he remained unsure.

The Cushing girls had told him that the fire started in the waxworks—so far as they knew—and then spread to the rest of the building. They said that they'd been working after hours in their father's so-called Chamber of Horrors when it happened, and that they'd had no chance to call for assistance after realizing the mansion was burning.

They *thought* (though they couldn't be sure) that Mr. Duprix and his wife had been working in the waxworks at the time, and they assumed that the couple had perished in the blaze. The twins (though the girls looked nothing alike to Dennis) said they couldn't know for sure, as the heat had been too intense to brave, and that's when they started evacuating their exhibits from the basement.

One of the girls, the dark haired one, Opal, had even intimated that the Duprixes didn't get along very well, that perhaps they'd had some kind of spat that led to the disaster.

"We'll look into that, miss," Dennis had assured her.

The only other person known to live in the establishment was a handyman by the name of Paul Shaw, but both girls seemed certain that he had been out last night.

"Odd that he hasn't returned yet," Dennis had noted.

"Yes, it is," Opal and Topaz, the blonde daughter, had said simultaneously. Eerie that; must have been some kind of twin thing, psychic connection, and all that nonsense.

"I think he might have quit yesterday morning," Opal said.

"So, he could be anywhere by now," Topaz added.

"Don't you worry about it," Hoey had assured them. "We'll find that handyman soon enough."

But Dennis remained unsure whether the girls *wanted* the Duprixes' employee to be found. In fact, he had a very strong feeling that the two of them—and perhaps their father as well, who claimed to have just returned from a trip to the continent—had omitted more than a few facts from their stories.

Oh, well. Time enough to question them again later. The police had arranged a hotel for the family to stay at today, so it would be easy enough to track them down.

"What do you think, sir?" Hoey asked, indicating the nearby smoldering heap. Several fire crews remained behind, still spraying it down with water, lest the blaze spring up again.

Dennis rubbed his weary eyes. "I think I could have used another cup of coffee this morning," he replied.

"I could use one m'self, sir," Hoey admitted. "I probably won't, though. Volunteered for a second shift today, I did. I've a fancy to catch a bit of a nap in between, and coffee would keep me up, I'm afraid."

"Well, we don't want you napping on the job, do we?" Dennis said. And then: "Oh, God. Please tell me I am *not* seeing what I think I'm seeing."

Hoey followed Dennis' gaze to where a white Rolls-Royce Phantom had pulled up and parked nearby. A woman in a khaki shirt and jodhpurs hopped out, looking angry. She made straight for the detectives.

"I'm afraid your eyes remain undeluded, sir," Hoey replied.

Dennis decided to go on the offensive. "Lady Ashton," he said with the biggest smile he could manage, "nice to see you. What brings you out on such a fine morning?"

"Fine morning, indeed," the blonde heiress huffed. "And I'm lucky to be *out* at all. Did you know that your *fine* constabulary had me locked up for most of the night?"

"I'd heard a rumor to that extent," Dennis replied. (Secretly, he'd been pleased by the news.) "Something about illegal carrying of weapons in Hyde Park, I believe?"

"Illegal my eye!" she barked. "You know what I was doing there."

"I know what you *intended* to do there, and, as you well know, I did not endorse nor in any way approve of such vigilantism."

"But I was trying to catch the werewolf!"

"And did you, m'lady?" Hoey asked.

"Yes..." pressed Dennis. "...*Did* you catch said werewolf, or, indeed, *anything* at all during your unauthorized night patrol?"

Lady Ashton's tanned face reddened. "You know that I did not."

"And were there, in fact, any reports of 'werewolf slayings' anywhere in greater London last night, milady?" Dennis asked politely.

"That's what I'm here to find out," Lady Ashton said. "I've had reports that there was a wolf sighted in Olde Kennington Park early this morning."

"Oh?" said Dennis, wondering what her sources might be, as *he* certainly hadn't heard anything of the kind. "Sounds like pure fantasy to me."

"Additionally," she continued, "my sources say that not one, but *two* bodies were found in the wreckage of this smoldering heap that you and your compatriot seem to be guarding, and that at least one of those bodies had its throat torn out."

Now how the devil did she get hold of that information? Dennis wondered. He tried not to let his consternation show on his face.

Hoey didn't do as good a job of hiding his surprise, though.

Lady Aston's blue eyes narrowed. "So, it's true!"

Dennis stiffened his upper lip. "While it may be true that two bodies were discovered in the wreckage here," he said, "we are as yet unable to confirm what caused their deaths. Though you only have to look at the scene to realize that *fire* seems the likely suspect." He would be damned if he gave her even an ounce of confirmation to spin further conspiracies on.

"I might have been here—I might have *seen* what happened—if your foolish force hadn't locked me up!" she fumed.

"I doubt that, milady," Dennis said. "It seems to me that you'd have been 'patrolling' Hyde Park until the first rays of dawn—or until you'd mistakenly shot some poor vagrant for a werewolf—*if* the loyal officers of the London constabulary hadn't caught up with you. And I, for one, am glad they did, as all law-abiding citizens should be."

Lady Ashton's face reddened further; clearly, he'd gotten her goat this time, rather than the other way around.

"This isn't over," she said through clenched teeth. "You *can't* stop me looking for him. The moon is only full for two more nights this month, but I'll *never* give up hunting for the lunatic who killed my sister, not until I've caught him and put a silver bullet through his heart!"

"I'd have to advise against that, milady," Dennis said, "as murder remains a capital crime of the highest order."

Apoplectic, she spun on her heel and stomped back to her Rolls.

Sergeant Hoey leaned close to Inspector Dennis and whispered:

"If you ask me, she's a bit of a lunatic herself."

EPILOGUE

Sergeant Hoey, 1951 Fisher St.
Thursday: Second Night of the Full Moon

Sergeant Hoey yawned and took a long drag on his Thermos full of coffee. He knew his wife would scold him for not using a cup (one came attached to the bottle, after all), but it had been a long day, and he just wasn't interested in such niceties at the moment.

He had, indeed, caught a nap in between shifts, but "nap" might have been too generous a word for it, more of a "doze" or a momentary "closing of the eyes," really. Now, as the hour pushed closer to midnight, he was beginning to regret volunteering for this extra shift.

Still, bills must be paid, and his wife—bless her—did enjoy her shopping. So, bucking up for a second stint in the force this evening wasn't much of a price to pay for domestic bliss.

He took another drink of coffee.

The boredom was the thing getting to him, just standing around hour after hour, watching the charred heap that only last night had been the Duprix home and waxworks as well as housing that weird Chamber of Horrors.

Now the Duprixes were almost certainly dead, though no other bodies had been found in the ruins, yet, and the Cushings were lucky just to be alive—though they remained, for the moment, homeless.

Wonder where they'll go and what they'll do now, Hoey thought. The two girls—twins, they said, though they looked almost nothing alike—had managed to save most of the old man's collection of weird art objects. Maybe they could start again in some other place. They'd be lucky to find a new spot in London, though. Despite the depression, the price of flats and storefronts near the inner city remained prohibitive.

Had he heard them say something about taking the objects on the road and doing some kind of tour?

Hoey fondly remembered the traveling circuses and gypsy caravans that had rumbled through Longford when he was younger—though his policeman father didn't much care for the gypsies. "Thieves and scoundrels, the lot of them," he remembered his old dad saying.

Still, everyone's got a right to make a living, I suppose.

Nearby, a few workmen were poking through the blackened ruins, looking for more bodies and rescuing whatever valuables they might find. One of Hoey's jobs tonight was to make sure that any costly discoveries weren't "rescued" into the workmen's pockets.

So far, the small contingent of laborers had been quite good about staying honest.

And they'd only had a minor scare or two when one of the men had poked into a charred heap only to get a small puff of smoke and flame.

The sole fire truck remaining on the scene had quickly seen to those incidents. "Nothing to worry about," the chief of the watch assured Hoey. "Just a couple of bad pockets here and there."

Hoey could put up with that. And, happily, at least so far, there had been no sign at all of Lady Ashton's supposed "werewolf."

Off her nut, that one, Hoey though. *All that supernatural rubbish!*

"Oy!" one of the workmen called. "Lookee here!"

Hoey meandered over to the men. "Found somethin', have you?" he asked.

"Found somethin', all right," said the man. He and his companion were holding a large—almost man-sized—object between them, but in the dim light, Hoey couldn't quite make out what it might be.

"Bloody miracle it is," said the second man, "thing like this, coming out of all that fire and ruination. Shoulda been smashed to pieces."

Hoey scrunched up his nose. "Is that a *mirror?*"

"Appears to be, gov," the first man replied. "Like out of a lady's boudoir."

"Beautiful looking glass," the second workman opined. He ran his hands over the edges, which were covered in golden scrollwork. "Right valuable, too, if you ask me, big stand-up mirror like this."

"Well…" said the first, "it *would* be, if it weren't *broken.*"

"Broken?" exclaimed the second. "What you going on about?" He ran his hand over the smooth, dark glass of the mirror's face. "Not a scratch on it!"

"But it don't show no *reflection,*" the first man pointed out, waving his hand in front of it. And, indeed, he was right. "Musta been damaged in the fire."

"Well, damaged or not, set it safely aside," Hoey said. "We'll take it back to the station, along with anythin' else you find." If it didn't belong to the Cushings, perhaps the heirs to the Duprixes—whomever that might be—would want it.

"Right you are, governor," said the first man. He and his companion took the mirror to the edge of the park and set it down where a few other not-quite-destroyed objects lay. Broken or no, the mirror was clearly the prize of the lot.

Hoey wandered back to his post, grateful for the momentary distraction.

When a distant clocktower rang, he checked his pocket watch.

Midnight, all right.

Time seemed to be just creeping by.

Then another noise caught his attention: the sound of hoofbeats.

Odd. It was late for any kind of horse-drawn tour of the park, even a romantic one.

Yet, as Hoey watched, a long black carriage with the top down, pulled by four inky horses, emerged from Olde Kennington Park and came to a stop by the far side of the ruins.

Curious, thought Hoey, and he meandered in that direction. Perhaps the carriage held a pair of young thrill-seekers inquisitive about the fire.

Better tell them to clear off.

As he walked toward the carriage, though, a top-hatted driver dressed all in black debarked his seat and opened the carriage door. Out of the back emerged a tall, slender woman, dressed all in white. Her skin was pale and smooth, and her golden hair fell in gentle ripples across her bare shoulders.

Before Hoey could reach the woman, she was talking with the workers that Hoey had just spoken to. The men were smiling and bobbing their heads deferentially. Hoey couldn't make out what anyone was saying, except for the workmen's occasional, "Yes, milady," "No, milady," and "Of course, milady."

In two shakes of a lamb's tail, the pair fetched the mirror and carried it over to her carriage.

"Hear, hear!" Hoey called. "What's all this? Put that back, immediately!"

"Oh, that won't be necessary, captain," the woman in white said.

"It's just sergeant, miss," Hoey replied, trotting up to the woman. "But I'm very much afraid it *is* necessary. Everythin' found in these ruins belongs to the former tenants or—in cases of their being deceased—to their heirs."

The woman extended one white-gloved hand in greeting.

Without even thinking, Hoey took the hand and kissed it.

"Very nice to meet you, sergeant," the woman said. "Though, in this case, I'm afraid you're mistaken. You see, my company *insures* these premises, and anything recovered from this fire belongs to us—to cover our losses in the incident. As you can see."

From somewhere (Hoey didn't see where) she produced a piece of parchment with a lot of legalistic writing upon it.

"This all *seems* to be in order," Hoey noted, examining the paper.

"Though I assure you," the woman continued, "that my company will deal fairly with both the former tenants and any heirs in question."

Something about the woman's face, her clear blue eyes maybe, made Hoey believe her. "I'm sure you will, miss."

"Thank you. But I am a Lady, sergeant."

Hoey bobbed his head in a slight bow and corrected himself, "Milady."

She smiled, showing rows of straight, white teeth.

"Thank you, sergeant," she said. "And now, I must be on my way. It was only a bit of chance that brought my nightly carriage ride past this particular property."

"Lucky nip of fortune that you arrived when you did, milady.

Take good care of that mirror, now. Bit of a miracle that it survived as well as it did."

The woman turned and walked languidly back toward her carriage. "I don't believe in miracles, sergeant," she called over her shoulder. "But I *will* take good care of it. That I promise."

Hoey suddenly realized something. "Excuse me, milady, but I don't believe I caught your name."

As she stepped aboard her carriage, the woman in white turned back to him and smiled once more.

"Lady Godalming," she called. "But you can call me 'Lucy.'"

Then she settled into the back seat, next to her newly reclaimed mirror.

"Goodnight to you, sergeant."

Hoey bowed again. "And a very good night to you, milady."

She signaled her driver and the coach pulled away, heading toward the heart of London.

Hoey let out a long sigh as they went.

Quite a lady, indeed! A real stunner.

Something nagged at him, though…

Just as she'd left, as the coach had turned toward the city, Hoey would have *sworn* that he saw a reflection in the dark glass of the "broken" mirror.

Funny thing, though: the woman in the reflection didn't look much like Lucy—like *Lady Godalming*—at all.

It must have been a trick of the light, because the woman in the mirror had *black* hair, not blonde, and her eyes were *dark*, not a bright, compelling blue.

And though Lady Godalming's heart-warming smile lingered as she rode out of sight, it appeared to Hoey that the woman in the mirror was *laughing.*

The End…?

ABOUT THE STORY

Dr. Cushing's Chamber of Horrors is the longest stand-alone piece of fiction that I've ever written. Sure, I've done trilogies for other series that might be longer put together (*Legend of the Five Rings* and *Dragonlance*, at least), but this is the first time I've ever written a single book that's well over 100,000 words long.

It was *not* my intention to make this story epic length.

My goal was just to write a ripping-good Monster Rally yarn. (For those of you not in the know, a Monster Rally is a story where you have a lot of monsters and they either team up or battle each other or, most often, both.) I hope I've succeeded in creating just such a tale. But how the story got so *long*... I'm not entirely sure.

I think maybe it's because, right at the start, I tried a method of plotting that I've never done before. Usually in a book, I write up some character background/bios and an outline of the key plot points I want to hit, and then I dive into the writing.

This time, though, because I was dealing with so many characters, backgrounds, and motives, I wrote out a separate plotline for each character—focusing on who they were and what

ABOUT THE STORY

they wanted—and then wove all of those separate storylines into the master plot.

Those initial notes got so complex that I don't remember if I actually ever *finished* writing them all. I certainly finished *most* of the individual stories, but I think at some point, when I knew the plots were intersecting, I ended up just going with what I'd written for one point-of-view—likely the twins or Paul—and then blended that into the rest.

Plotting the book that way was fun. And it was *exhausting*.

I'm not sure I'll ever go that way again. And since I've recently been revising my *Frost Harrow* series, I've re-discovered the joy of writing "short and punchy" chapters for *much* shorter books.

So, there's some chance that *Dr. Cushing's Chamber of Horrors* may *remain* the longest thing I've ever written. We'll see what the future brings.

It's probably obvious to most readers that this book is heavily inspired by the Universal and Hammer monster movies (as well as by *Dark Shadows*, which has fingerprints on pretty much every book I've ever written).

That being the case, there are *tons* of little tips of the hat and Easter Eggs for Monster Kids who read carefully. For instance, sculptor and wax museum owner Vincent Duprix is obviously a tip of the hat to horror great, Vincent Price, and his classic role in *House of Wax*—but there's more to that tribute as well. His family surname, *Duprix*, is a pseudonym once used by two friends I worked with at TSR, Inc. (the original makers of *Dungeons & Dragons*), brothers Michael and Patrick Price—because *du prix* is French for… Price. So, that Vincent tribute is probably even more direct than you thought.

Vincent's wife is named Victoria in honor of the dead wife of Dr. Phibes (in those great Price horror films) who was played by Caroline Munro—a heartthrob of mine. See how easy finding some of my hidden "secrets" is?

ABOUT THE STORY

Clever readers will also find references to the Hammer podcast *1951 Down Place*, to various writers, directors, and movies, as well as the obvious references to monsters, both public domain and otherwise. Some of the former actually *appear* in this story. Plus, of course, you can hunt for my traditional use of the words "dark shadows" somewhere in the book. (If I haven't done that in *all* my novels, it's probably just because I forgot.) My search function says you should find it here three times.

What's my favorite TV show of all time? I'll give you a hint… The initials are "DS."

One more tribute to send you off on your Easter Egg hunt is our werewolf, *Paul Shaw Longmire*. His first name is a tribute to both filmmaker Paul Naschy (King of the European Werewolves —whose most famous creation is featured in an upcoming book by me) and to my friend, author and filmmaker Paul McComas. The werewolf's middle name is taken from a character who searches for the Loch Ness Monster in one of Paul M's films. Paul even gave me a Shaw family coat-of-arms banner that hangs in my studio. However, the character's *last* name is *not*, as you might by now expect, a tribute to any movie or TV characters. Rather, it's a simple combination of the words *long* and *mire*, an indication that my beloved werewolf has a tough row to hoe ahead of him.

Despite all those hidden goodies, I also thought it *supremely important* that this story be accessible to novice monster-readers, too. As my late friend Stan Lee famously said: "Every comic is someone's first comic," meaning that your work should always be enjoyable for people who just happened to pick it up, as well as for longtime fans.

I think my "no prior knowledge required" approach worked, but—as with all books—you readers will be the judge.

Now, here's my Classic Monsters epic, all in one place, for your reading enjoyment!

ABOUT THE STORY

Two "raw" chapters (lacking final edits) of *Dr. Cushing's Chamber of Horrors* ran on my site—www.stephendsullivan.com—every month for more than two years. Those chapters are still there, if you care to read it in serialized form.

Why did I take up writing a crazy-long monster story?

The book was inspired by the initial rumors about Universal's attempt at a Dark Universe monster continuity. What news my friends and I could piece together at the time seemed to indicate that Universal's efforts were *not* going to be what we Monster Kids were hoping for.

So, I decided to do my own.

As it turns out, Universal's DU didn't do so well in its first iteration; so they've retooled it at least twice since. The most recent attempt seems much more promising to me, more in the tradition of the original "outlaw" Universal Monsters approach from the 1930s and '40s.

But I still think that *my* monster rally out-rocks their flicks so far. Again, though, you can be the judge.

And if Universal—or anyone else—wants to make *Dr. Cushing's Chamber of Horrors* into a movie…? Well, I'm *not* hard to find, and I'm *definitely* open to the idea.

The original werewolf header for the series on my site was a heavily manipulated selfie of me in a werewolf mask. I think we'll all agree that Mark Maddox's awesome cover is a HUGE improvement.

Thanks, Mark! (I guess there's a reason you've won all those Rondo Awards!)

I want to thank all my fans and Patreon patrons for their encouragement on this project, as well as my Monster Kid buddies, including Derek M. Koch (of *Monster Kid Radio*), Rod Barnett (of *The Naschy Cast*), and many more supporters including friends from my college days who stepped up for some proofreading. And no "Thank you!" would be complete without mentioning the Kenosha Writers' Group, who have put up with me reading chapters at our dinner meetings for months… well, years, actually—especially Steve Rouse, Vicki, Doris, and Christine.

Will there be more Cushing Horrors books?

It somewhat depends on what kind of support this one gets.

If I sell a lot of copies—or if my patrons demand it—I certainly have more material.

In fact, I have titles and rough plots for at least four more novels in the series. If and when the story continues, the next book will be: *Dr. Cushing's Caravan of Horrors*.

I'll leave you to speculate about what the others might be.

But, please, let me know…

What would *you* like to see next?

Next, that is, *after* at least a couple of *Frost Harrow* novels and my next book, *The Curse of the Werewolf*—featuring the return of Europe's favorite werewolf, Waldemar Daninsky. (I'm sure you'll enjoy that!)

Anyway, after that…?

Let me know.

Until then… Keep watching monster movies!

And keep *reading*!

Thanks!

—Steve Sullivan
June–July 2020

ABOUT THE STORY

MUSIC TO READ BY

The following soundtracks often played in my studio while I was writing this book. Feel free to have them on in the background while you're reading.

The Words & Music of Frankenstein – presented by Rob Zombie
Bride of Frankenstein – Franz Waxman
House of Frankenstein – Hans J. Salter & Paul Dessau
The Monster Music of Hans J. Salter & Frank Skinner – Salter & Skinner
Classic Scores of Mystery & Horror (Sherlock Holmes & the Voice of Terror, Ghost of Frankenstein, and more) – Salter & Skinner
Cliffhangers: Music from the Classic Republic Serials – Various Artists
Hammer Legacy: Science Fiction & Horror – (2 albums) Various Artists
Hammer the Studio that Dripped Blood – (2 CD) Various Artists
The Best of Hammer Horror – Various Artists
Hammer Horror Classics – Various Artists
Dracula: Classic Scores from Hammer Horror – James Bernard, Christopher Gunning, David Whitaker
Nosferatu – James Bernard
The Shadow – Jerry Goldsmith
Vertigo – Bernard Herrmann
Dracula – John Williams

ABOUT THE AUTHOR

Stephen D. Sullivan is the award-winning author of more than fifty books, including the *Tournament of Death* series and trilogies for *Legend of the Five Rings*, *Spider Riders*, and *Dragonlance*. Other cool stuff he's worked on includes *Dungeons & Dragons* and *Star Wars* (games), *Teenage Mutant Ninja Turtles* and *The Simpsons* (comics), *Iron Man* and *Thunderbirds* (junior novels), and the 2017 film, *Theseus and the Minotaur*.

His latest projects include *Dr. Cushing's Chamber of Horrors* (a monster rally novel), *Frost Harrow* (modern Gothic horror), and a Classic Monster RPG (MonsterRPG.com). Be sure to check out Steve's *Scribe*-winning novelization of the "Worst Film Ever Made"—*Manos: The Hands of Fate*. He is a regular guest on Monster Kid Radio and is a founding member of the Monster Conservancy, a group dedicated to preserving and expanding classic monster traditions in films, books, and other media. You can support Steve through his Patreon at www.PaySteve.com and by buying his books online and at better stores everywhere.

www.StephenDSullivan.com – www.SaveMonsters.com

WALKABOUT PUBLISHING
Great stories by great authors.

Manos: The Hands of Fate • Unforgettable • Canoe Cops vs. the Mummy • Fit for a Frankenstein • The Crimson Collection • Manos: Talons of Fate • White Zombie Uncanny Encounters — LIVE! • The Twilight Empire • Stories from Desert Bob's Reptile Ranch • This and That and Tales About Cats • Luck o' the Irish • Martian Knights & Other Tales • Carnage & Consequences • Fables from Elsewhere • Zombies, Werewolves, & Unicorns • Daikaiju Attack • Under the Protection of the Cow Demon • Uncanny Encounters: Roswell • Tournament of Death 1—4 • Pirates of the Blue Kingdoms • *And More!*

Walkabout Publishing
P.O. Box 151
Kansasville, WI 53139
www.walkaboutpublishing.com
Official Home of the Blue Kingdoms.

Printed in Poland
by Amazon Fulfillment
Poland Sp. z o.o., Wrocław